Additional Acclaim for *Mr Mee*

"This book is fabulous stuff: erudite but not patronizing, elegantly and simply written, jumping ambitiously across centuries but with a good dash of down-to-earth lust for entertainment. More than once, Crumey makes his reader pause, rest the book in his lap, and acknowledge that life is really quite extraordinary."
　　　　　　　　　　　　　　　　　　　—*The Times* (London)

"An intellectual romp . . . Andrew Crumey has spun a delightful brain-tickler of a novel that undermines its own pretensions."
　　　　　　　　　　　　　　　　　　　—*Time Out* (New York)

"Erudite entertainment . . . A book about books and about the threat to reading posed by electronic technology, Crumey's novel, like those of Umberto Eco and Milan Kundera, reaffirms the vitality of the printed page."
　　　　　　　　　　　　　　　　　　　—*Salem Press*

"*Mr Mee* is an archly amusing cerebral delight. . . . Crumey moves his chess pieces with consummate skill: a playful master at work."
　　　　　　　　　　　　　　　　　　　—*The Scotsman*

"Crumey has written another novel of ideas in the grand tradition of Calvino, Borges, and Kundera . . . tantalizing . . . Crumey's light treatment of hefty material should win the minds, if not the hearts, of his readers."
　　　　　　　　　　　　　　　　—*Publishers Weekly* (starred review)

"[A] richly amusing novel . . . [with] wonderfully obsessive characters . . . Rattling back and forth between two centuries, this agreeably serpentine tale speaks volumes about the folly of scholarly preoccupation and the unreliability of its received wisdom, while never neglecting to entertain the bedazzled reader."
　　　　　　　　　　　　　　　　　　　—*Kirkus Reviews*

ALSO BY ANDREW CRUMEY

Music, In a Foreign Language

Pfitz

D'Alembert's Principle

MR MEE

A Novel

Andrew Crumey

PICADOR USA
NEW YORK

www.picadorusa.com

For information on Picador USA Reading Group Guides, as well as ordering, please contact the Trade Marketing department at St. Martin's Press.
Phone: 1-800-221-7945 extension 763
Fax: 212-677-7456
E-mail: trademarketing@stmartins.com

Library of Congress Cataloging-in-Publication Data

Crumey, Andrew, 1961–
    Mr Mee : a novel / Andrew Crumey.—1st Picador USA pbk. ed.
        p. cm.
    ISBN 0-312-26803-3 (hc)
    ISBN 0-312-28235-4 (pbk)
    1. Encyclopedias and dictionaries—Authorship—Fiction. 2. College teach-
ers—Fiction. 3. Book collectors—Fiction. 4. Cosmology—Fiction.
5. Internet—Fiction. 6. Aged men—Fiction. I. Title.

PR6053.R76 M7 2002
823'.914—dc21   2001051011

First published in Great Britain by Picador, an imprint of
Macmillan Publishers Ltd

First Picador USA Paperback Edition: March 2002

10 9 8 7 6 5 4 3 2 1

For Lionel Gossman

Thanks to Alain Gnaedig for help with a number of points; to Northern Arts for a Writer's Award; and to Princeton Eighteenth Century Society for inviting me to give the first public reading from *Mr Mee* at their conference at Princeton University on 8 May 1999. Above all, thanks to Mary, Peter and Katia for everything.

CHAPTER 1

It's said of the Xanthic sect that they believed fire to be a form of life, since it has the ability to reproduce itself. They regarded the sun as being the original life-centre of the universe, and the colour yellow was held to be the primary hue from which all others could be derived by a process of 'heating' or 'cooling'. I expect you're wondering how I know all this, and why I'm telling you. Certainly, when I mentioned it to Mrs B some time ago, while she was dusting, that was her immediate reaction; and you know I take Mrs B's opinions on all matters to be a good indicator of public attitudes in general.

As I explained, while warning her to keep the duster away from a manuscript page I suspected still to be wet, I owe my discovery of the Xanthics (and hence of Rosier's Encyclopaedia) to the coincidence of a flat tyre and a shower of rain, both of which occurred within an hour of each other, just south of a small town whose name you'll probably know (Mrs B did), though it can only be of significance to the people who live there, or to the lorry drivers who have to pass through the place on their way to and from the huge potato crisp factory nearby. In an earlier letter I already mentioned to you the reasons for my journey; I shall now tell you the strange consequences which followed from its brief interruption.

Mrs B said to me, 'Did ye no have a spare tyre in the boot?', and I said: Would you be careful with that one, Mrs B, it's a first edition.

'I don't know why you have to live with so many books on top of your head,' said Mrs B. As you are aware, this is one of her customary phrases, and I expect that you will ignore it just as I did.

'Aye,' said Mrs B, 'there's some men's the kind who always have a spare wheel with an inflated tyre in the boot o' their cars, and there's others'll have left the flat one from the last time the wheel was changed because they were too busy thinking on other things, and you know which kind is you, Mr Mee.'

While Mrs B was giving me this lecture I saw that she was in danger of knocking over a particularly important stack which I had placed on the edge of the desk, so I thought it best to nod in agreement, in order that she'd return to her work before my library became too disrupted. I'm sure that you remember as well as I the damage once sustained by several precious volumes of Hogg, because of Mrs B's unfortunate generosity with regard to furniture polish.

No, I shall not even pause to invent some reasonable excuse for my not having a spare tyre in the boot, nor any means of carrying out the repair myself. Instead, I walked the two miles back into town (a long way for a man of eighty-six, I'm sure you'll agree) where I found a garage and was told that the boss would help me in an hour or so, after his lunch.

'That's chust typical,' said Mrs B.

I, on the other hand, was more sanguine, and decided to savour the local sights in the meantime. That was when the rain started.

'And I can guess where you went to dry out,' said Mrs B, still waving her duster like a regimental banner. 'There's some men'll find shelter in the nearest pub, and there's others'll go and find a wee second-hand bookshop full of horrible dirty dusty rubbish that good people canna tolerate in their houses any longer, and they'll come out when the rain stops with a heap o' trash they'll never read in ten lifetimes.'

Yes, this was how I found the Xanthics. Not in Rosier's Encyclopaedia (a work which still eludes my every enquiry), but rather in a book called *Epistemology and Unreason* which I lifted from the shelf thinking it to be a biography of J.F. Ferrier, an author whose unsolved disappearance from my collection some years ago was the result of one of Mrs B's notorious periods of rationalization.

I quickly judged the volume to be irrelevant, poorly bound and somewhat overpriced. But then I chanced upon the Xanthics; and their notion that fire is a form of life was one that seemed sufficiently memorable to make the book worth buying, in order that I might maintain some reference to a quotation I felt bound at some time to repeat.

'I tellt ye,' said Mrs B.

I shall not describe the mundane continuation of a story which involved the purchasing of the book and an altercation with a dishonest car mechanic. Instead I shall reproduce for you the rest of the passage which I was able to read later in the comfort of my home:

If life is defined by the property of self-reproduction, then fire lives in much the same way as a virus, contaminating some medium, igniting it, producing more flames; and the behaviour of fire, its motion and power, has meant that from the very earliest times people have easily regarded it as being infused with some divine spirit.

'I don't know why you waste your time on such stuff and nonsense,' said Mrs B, lifting an early edition of Carlyle, displacing the bookmark I had carefully left within it, then returning the cleaned but useless volume to a new position where I'd be bound to forget both it, and the page number which interested me. All this, while I read aloud to her:

It may be objected that fire is not a substance but a process; yet all animals live by virtue of a similar process of oxidation, of combustion, for which their bodies serve merely as vehicle and furnace.

'Aye, that's canny.'

And to those who protest that fire, unlike living creatures, can arise without a parent (the striking of a match being something which the Xanthics would have found bewildering and miraculous), one might reply that the very first organism to have appeared on our own planet must likewise have been of a kind requiring no animate precursor.

'It was a clever man who wrote this book, and a fool that bought it. Have ye no got enough volumes already to be going on with?'

At what point did certain chemical processes of the primitive Earth become worthy of the term 'life', a word which some would still hold back from fire? This is like a riddle known to Aristotle; a child passes through the years into old age, but when exactly does he become 'old'; or if no such moment exists, then does the word have any meaning? Similarly, a single grain of sand cannot form a heap (*soros* in Greek), therefore no amount of sand can do so; hence the name 'sorites' given to a class of problem which must, we see, include the emergence of life itself among its number.

'Aye, I like Aristotle well enough,' said Mrs B, who, as you know, has in the course of our many conversations developed a system of taste with respect to the various authors I have told her about, their works and personalities, which is, like all tastes and preferences, purely arbitrary. If she so much as sees a copy of *The Wealth of Nations* on my desk she'll start berating it like a foul dog, while Hume almost brings out the romantic in her.

Sorites, Mrs B, I reminded her; when did a reptile become the first bird, when did grunts and squawks become the first language, when were words like ours first coined, and how were they ever understood?

'If ye don't mind, I'll chust pass the hoover across this carpet and be done.'

And finally, what of fire: is it alive or not? The choice is ours; the Xanthics chose a definition upon which an entire philosophy was constructed, a system of thought which held sway among its clandestine followers for centuries until a final purge whose last victim met his death with the words: 'May my thoughts ignite yours; may my soul burn forever in your hearts.' In a certain sense, perhaps, there was no last Xanthic.

On re-reading this passage after Mrs B had left me in peace, I was struck by its vagueness. When exactly did the Xanthics flourish; and where? The only reference given was to a work I had never heard of: *L'Encyclopédie de Jean-Bernard Rosier*.

My curiosity lay dormant during the lunch which Mrs B prepared for us; one of her finest broths, from which I was moreover distracted by an account of her sister's recent health problems. But then it was time for Mrs B to leave, and for the puzzle to return to my attention, like those mushy balls of potato mixed with meat fibre which I'd found at the bottom of my bowl when all the liquid was removed, while Mrs B was talking about gallstones.

A close study of several other books in my possession shed no further light on the Xanthics; and since the author of *Epistemology and Unreason* calls himself merely 'Ian Muir', omitting any further details which might enable him to be singled out from the countless other good souls who share his versatile name, the problem of tracing him in order to question him about his sources seemed insurmountable. Such elusiveness, moreover, took on a distinctly suspicious character when I observed that the book lacked an ISBN; a momentary perusal of *Harp's Guide* easily satisfied me that 'Torus Academic', the alleged publisher, was merely an impressive badge behind which to conceal an act of vanity publishing. I therefore had every reason to suppose the whole thing to be a hoax; a dusty academic joke, or the opportunity to expound a pet theory. Only if I were to locate Rosier's Encyclopaedia would I be able to contradict my suspicions; and this, as I have mentioned, is something I have still been unable to do, despite much careful research in recent weeks, which has even prevented me from writing to you. What I have managed to unearth, on the other hand, is a mystery far more engrossing than the story of an obscure and vanished sect.

At first, however, I forgot all about Rosier and the Xanthics. My search of available reference books having yielded nothing, I got on with my work (this happened some four months ago, at a time when, as you know, I was writing an important account of certain local memorials for *The Scots Magazine*). Perhaps it was simply due to the embarrassment of failure that I did not consider the incident worthy of discussion in our correspondence at the time.

But then, three weeks ago, I happened to be glancing through the index of a new book I saw on sale, dealing with the publishing industry in eighteenth-century France, when I noticed the name Jean-Bernard Rosier. I bought the book at once.

'Dyod, no anither o' thon tamn things!' said Mrs B, angrily resorting to the most extreme form of her singular dialect when she saw what I'd brought home, then went to attend to some laundry. As you know, I have always been in agreement with Boswell's opinion on the harshness of our more northerly accents, which I cannot transcribe without the aid of a dictionary, and then only imperfectly.

The book, by a Professor Donald Macintyre, informed me that in 1759 Rosier was seeking to publish a philosophical treatise outlining a 'new theory of physics'. Unpublished documents and 'private communication' were cited in support of this fleeting and infinitely suggestive comment.

Then Mrs B came back and said, rather more coherently but only a little less crossly, 'You'll be wanting your dinner now, I suppose?'

Yes, already it was lunchtime again, when I would be treated to another of Mrs B's fine soups. Today it was the version which my studies suggest should properly be called a kail brose; and over which I said to her, after hurriedly sipping some water to soothe a lip scalded by salty and delicious fluid: Do you remember the Xanthics, Mrs B?

She'd calmed down by now. 'Oh aye, I ken them well. They thought fire to be a form of life, did they not?'

Indeed they did, I said; and I told her about the happy coincidence which had brought the name of Rosier once more to my attention.

'A bit like that tyre you never carried in the boot o' your car. Aye, there's some men'll forget all about a name as soon as they've heard it, and there's others'll let it cling to their mind like a dried-up knapdarloch on a sheep's behind until the day it turns up in some book they pay a ridiculous amount for, when they've already got enough dirty dusty rubbish to be going on with.'

I was, I admit, not wholly attentive to Mrs B's wise and kindly observations, since I was wondering what could possibly be meant by Rosier's 'new theory of physics'. Soon it was time for Mrs B to leave again, but she hesitated at the front door, after putting on her coat.

'Is something wrong, Mrs B?'

'I was chust wondering if four days is enough for you now.'

'What on earth do you mean? It's been four days for the last twenty-eight years; why ever should we change?'

Mrs B's eyes were inspecting a patch of carpet inside the

door for some reason I couldn't understand. 'I chust think you might not be looking after yourself so well on the other three. Four isn't really enough for you now, is it?'

I told her I'd give the matter my urgent attention and said goodbye. Then as soon as she'd gone I rechecked the scant details in Macintyre's book and resolved to renew my attempts to track down Rosier's Encyclopaedia.

A visit to the library later in the afternoon proved to be in vain, producing only another shower of that drizzly kind which doesn't merit an umbrella, but left me soaking wet by time I arrived at the enquiries desk where Margaret greeted me with her usual warmth. A thorough search of all available catalogues yielded no further information, and Margaret suggested I go and buy myself some Vicks before heading for home; but my skull by now was so full of class numbers that I quite forgot about my sinuses, and on my return I contented myself with a cure you know well, namely a 'wee nip'. I then wrote a letter to Professor Macintyre asking him for help, addressed it care of his publisher, and sealed the envelope with a glowing sense of optimism to which the whisky may partly have contributed.

Well, you see, it was all becoming a very intricate story, and you shall understand the dreadful point of it eventually; but Mrs B was getting impatient.

'So you're writing to professors now?' she quizzed me next morning, when I gave her the letter to post. It was as if my correspondence with him (unlike my letters to you, whose stamps she's happily licked for many a long year) were somehow a challenge to her domestic position; to the extent that I reassured her I was not inviting the professor to come and 'do' for me on those remaining three days which Mrs B was so concerned about. 'Well I think you need one more day at least,' she said, 'Or two mornings.' Then Mrs B entered into some kind of negotiation to which I wasn't a wholly comprehending party, since I was too busy wondering where Professor Macintyre might lead me next, in my search for Rosier, Xanthism, and goodness knows what else.

A week later, Mrs B was settling into her new regime, having annexed a day and a half from me by means of a stratagem almost Napoleonic in its swiftness and ingenuity. 'It's frae that professor of yours,' she said, sternly handing me an envelope, before leaving the room with an inexplicable air of displeasure.

Professor Macintyre had kindly sent me a photocopied article which began with a translated extract of a letter, dated 3 June 1759, from Jean-Bernard Rosier to the distinguished mathematician Jean le Rond D'Alembert:

Sir, you may know that many years ago one of our countrymen was taken prisoner in a remote and barren region of Asia noted only for the savagery of its inhabitants. The man's captors, uncertain what to do with him, chose to settle the issue by means of a ring hidden beneath one of three wooden cups. If the prisoner could correctly guess which cup hid the gold band, he would be thrown out to face the dubious tenderness of the wolves; otherwise he was to be killed on the spot. By placing bets on the outcome, his cruel hosts could enjoy some brief diversion from the harsh austerity of their nomadic and brutal existence.

The leader of the tribe, having hidden his own ring, commanded that the unfortunate prisoner be brought forward to make his awful choice. After considerable hesitation, and perhaps a silent prayer, the wretch placed his trembling hand upon the middle cup. Bets were placed; then the leader, still wishing to prolong the painful moment of uncertainty which so delighted his audience, lifted the rightmost cup, beneath which no ring was found. The captive gave a gasp of hope, and amidst rising laughter from the crowd, the leader now reached for the left, saying that before turning it over he would allow his prisoner a final opportunity to change his choice. Imagine yourself to be in that poor man's position, Monsieur D'Alembert, and tell me, what would you now do?

I was still trying to understand the question when I was interrupted by the sudden, unheralded commencement of Mrs B's latest onslaught on my study. She came in pushing a roaring vacuum cleaner and evicted me from my chair like one whose simple shelter has been requisitioned by an invading army.

'Mrs B!' I shouted.

'I'll no be a minute,' she shouted back. The din could hardly have been worse if she'd brought an aeroplane into the room.

'Mrs B, will you please turn that thing off!'

'I'm nearly done already.'

'Mrs B!' I went out of the study, towards the wall socket on the landing where the vacuum cleaner was connected, but Mrs B, ever a shrewd tactician, pre-empted me, dashing quicker than I could possibly manage at my age, and blocked my access to the socket. The vacuum, meanwhile, was left unattended in the study, where it bellowed redundantly upon a single patch, by now very clean, of my carpet.

'Ah'm no budging,' proclaimed the doughty Mrs B, who

was standing against the wall in such a way as to make it impossible for me to pull out the plug. Instead I closed the study door, to the extent that the vacuum cable allowed, and this gave the two of us a degree of peace.

'Mrs B, I apologize,' I said, 'but I was in the middle of trying to understand a very subtle problem.' Then I explained the story of the cups to her. Should our unfortunate captive change his choice?

Mrs B, no doubt moved by the man's plight, decided to give the matter some thought, though she wasn't shifting from the wall where she was pinned like a beetle. 'It canna make a difference now which ane he chooses; the odds are equal.'

I agreed, and we went back into the study to read the rest of the letter once Mrs B had agreed to switch off the vacuum cleaner, at least temporarily.

If the leader, when he turned over the rightmost cup, made his choice at random, then the prisoner now has an even chance of holding the ring beneath his hand.

'I tellt ye.'

But the leader must have known where the ring was placed, and he may have decided to turn the rightmost cup precisely because he knew the ring was not beneath it. In that case the prisoner's chances, originally one in three, have not been improved by the leader's gesture; instead, it now becomes twice as likely that the remaining cup conceals the ring, so that the prisoner, if he loves life, would be well advised to change his choice!

'I canna agree wi' that,' said Mrs B. 'The man's as big a fool as you, Mr Mee.' And yet, undeterred, I continued to read out Rosier's letter:

What the story illustrates, is that the cups can somehow tell whether the leader acts randomly, or out of choice. The probability that the prisoner holds the ring is either one half or one third, depending on whether the leader knows in advance which cup the ring lies beneath; an observation which startled me greatly when I arrived at it, and kept me awake for an entire night as I followed its many implications; for I was led to conclude that the acts of observation, of thought, of consciousness, are inextricably linked to the reality of the world. Nature, I realized, cannot be regarded as consisting simply of cold inanimate matter, proceeding according to laws which you, Monsieur D'Alembert, and your esteemed colleagues, would have us believe you can discover. To understand the world, we must comprehend the human mind and its interaction with all that it perceives and to which it thereby gives existence.

'Can I chust switch on the hoover again now?'

And just as the cup experiment, through many repetitions, provides a means of discovering the leader's strategy, so might we contemplate the possibility of constructing a greater kind of trial, a game against Nature in which would be demonstrated the presence or otherwise of some omniscient consciousness, some cosmic dealer of Fate's cards. Then the laws of physics would truly reveal the mind of God.

'I really have tae finish hoovering here.'

What of our prisoner? He accepted the leader's offer, placed his feeble hand upon the leftmost cup, and when it was turned and nothing was found beneath it, his throat was opened without further ceremony. The leader retrieved his bauble from beneath the middle cup, and all that remained of this sad event was a ballad which became popular in the region, and an account of the tragedy which I found in Théodore's *Excursions*. We could imagine a multitude of worlds, in a third of which the outcome was happier, and neither that book nor this letter might ever have been written.

Yes, Mrs B, I then said to her, you may now finish hoovering. And I left the heavy whirring behind me, above me, as I went downstairs, thinking of the prisoner's death, Rosier's theory; mysteries multiplying beyond my grasp.

I hadn't yet finished reading the photocopied article, however, which remained in my hand while I stood exiled in the kitchen, the vacuum cleaner trundling back and forth above me like an overweight insect slowly recovering from a newspaper's inadequate blow, its hellish racket soaring and throbbing as it probed the corners of the room.

D'Alembert's reply to Rosier has not been preserved; but we do have a subsequent letter in which Rosier claims to have begun constructing a new philosophy of the Universe based entirely on the laws of chance, which, once completed, would render archaic and redundant the contents of the celebrated *Encyclopédie* of which D'Alembert, together with Denis Diderot, had been editor. It is said that during the following years Rosier perfected his theory to such an extent, and felt so indignant at the indifference shown to him by the scientific establishment, that he personally undertook a complete rewriting of the *Encyclopédie* in the light of his doctrines, which seem to have been heavily tinged with Berkeleyan Idealism, and to have anticipated in some respects modern quantum theory. Of Rosier's Encyclopaedia, however, no known trace survives.

And yet, not only was I aware that the Encyclopaedia might indeed exist, but I also knew it to be the source of my elusive Xanthics; revealed now as the obsession, perhaps the invention, of an eighteenth-century mystic or charlatan. I put the photocopied article to one side – noticing that the 'work surface', as such items of kitchen furniture seem to be called nowadays, still exhibited a clinging film of clean dampness, and the smell of synthetic pine – and read the remainder of Professor Macintyre's letter (the continuing explorations of the vacuum cleaner making it necessary for me to study some of the paragraphs more than once), in which he explained that unfortunately he didn't know the article's original source; for he himself possessed no more than an identical photocopy, lacking any title or author name, which he believed may have been passed on to him by a fellow delegate at one of the many academic conferences which the professor regularly attends.

The cleaning offensive eventually ceased upstairs, and I decided to return to my work. My article on local memorials having long been completed, to the satisfaction both of myself and of the august editors of *The Scots Magazine*, I was now engaged in a study of certain affinities between Stevenson and Hume, which are subtle but not inconsequential. I met Mrs B at the top of the stairs and found her to be lugging the now-placid vacuum cleaner. Aware of the reply I would be sure to receive, I have long desisted from offering help to her on such occasions.

The true meaning of Rosier's letter was still not apparent to me, nor could I understand why an impenetrably obscure riddle concerning a ring and three cups should have caused its author such excitement; but I was able to appreciate that his Encyclopaedia, if I could locate it, might amount to an entirely novel view of nature, based no doubt on wholly fallacious premises. I therefore decided to give the matter my most serious attention; but the following days yielded little progress in anything except my comparative analysis of Stevenson and Hume. Then Mrs B (we are now a mere week before the day on which I write, and therefore nearly at the terrible end of this letter, and hence at the beginning of whatever events must succeed it) had an idea. She said to me, 'These dirty dusty things are only good for a museum. What you need is a computer.'

Mrs B informed me that her neighbour's children spend seven or eight hours of each day gazing at the flickering screen of one of these gadgets; and since I can happily spend a similar length of time allowing my eyes to be caressed by the lines of a book, some analogy suggested itself to her; and the obvious conclusion, according to her unique logic, was that I should trade one for the other, and pack away my library in favour of a machine which need not, she assured me, be too expensive, and would moreover be much easier to clean.

There the matter might have ended, were it not for the fact that later that day I made another visit to the library and mentioned my unprovable theories to Margaret, who showed little interest in the analogies between the *Treatise of Human Nature* and *Dr Jekyll*, but shared my excitement for the idea that there could exist somewhere, thanks to Jean-Bernard Rosier, the authentic encyclopaedia of what would amount to an alternative universe.

'We must do a web search!' she said, almost breathless in anticipation of its possible results, and her enthusiasm made me eager to discover what on earth such a procedure might amount to. She then invited me to sit down before the screen of a 'PC', several of which seem gradually to have intruded themselves upon the library during recent years, and none of which I had ever before concerned myself with, believing them to be some kind of advertising medium sponsored by the local tourist office. Margaret told me to enter a 'keyword' into the 'search engine', and so, using one finger, and with a degree of hesitation attributable not merely to age and a recent recurrence of my angina, I typed the word 'Rosier'. She then did something which I couldn't quite follow, but which involves moving what I now know to be called a 'mouse'.

The results, I admit, were impressive. My weeks had been filled with chance encounters, indices searched in vain, letters more optimistic than fruitful. The 'search engine' (whose workings I shall not even guess at) was able to study, as far as I can make out, just about everything that's ever been written, in a matter of seconds, and then reported to Margaret and myself that it knew of 28,242 documents haunted by Rosier's hitherto elusive presence. I need only 'click' on various parts of the screen, in order to 'access' any one of these.

The very abundance was almost disappointing; a rare flower had been transformed, instantaneously, into a weed.

How was I to make my way through so many items? I asked Margaret if it would be all right to try a few other names, just to get the feel of things, and she said I could play with the machine as long as I liked, then went back to her desk.

I resorted to the comfort of old acquaintances. The entry 'David Hume' delivered 19,384 items (less, strangely, than Rosier), but the very first of these (a 'website' to which I was directed) showed that the whole of the *Enquiry Concerning Human Understanding* and a significant portion of the *History of England* were stored, miraculously, some- where within this ungainly machine which I'd always thought to be simply a device for finding out about local events and 'heritage' walks. I recalled the not inconsiderable space which Hume and his commentators occupied in my own modest library, whose every item was an affront to Mrs B, and I began to wonder if she might not have had a point after all, when she suggested that 'new technology' could save me a considerable amount of space and time; dimensions, the abolition of which is the primary occupation of modern civilization. When Margaret came back after half an hour I had already decided that I must purchase one of these contraptions for myself. Are they for sale, I asked her.

Margaret sent me off with directions to 'Dixons', a high- street retailer of machines which by now I was already calling 'PCs', as if I'd known them all my life. There I encountered as my assistant, a tall thin lad called Ali, who guided me towards a thing with loudspeakers on each side and a television display showing various swimming fish. None of these adornments seemed particularly relevant to my intended perusal of Hume's *Enquiry*, or any other beloved works which it might please the computer to shelve within its inscrutable workings, and Ali seemed strangely perplexed when I explained what I was after.

He said, 'Is it word processing you want to do?'

I gather this is a term used now to denote what was known in our day as 'writing', and I told him that this would account for ten per cent at most of my proposed activity, since I would use the machine primarily for reading, an archaic habit the correct name of which I didn't know, unfortunately, in the jargon of 'new technology'; and so Ali had to call for some higher assistance. A young lady whose badge named her as Mrs J. Campbell, and whose outfit and demeanour marked her as Ali's superior, was able to act as a kind of interpreter. Eventually, after I gave her an account of my fruitful and tantalizing session in the library, she agreed with Ali that 'web browsing' was my chosen aim. Yes, I said, that's the term I was looking for. Indeed, I must remind myself in future that you no longer 'read' my letters, but 'browse' them, like a sheep. Then they showed me a device which, for less than two and a half thousand pounds, would, they assured me, deliver every book I could ever want to study. As long as it has Hume and Stevenson in it, I said, patting the machine, and some volumes of Hogg which Mrs B once spoiled with the furniture polish, then I'll be quite happy. They then accepted both my cheque and my handshake, and we parted on very pleasant terms. Let me tell you, if ever you want to buy yourself a 'PC', then be sure to go to Dixons. The service is excellent!

Delivery was fixed for the following day, and I decided not to say anything to Mrs B. Such small surprises are the way in which I can compensate her, every now and then, for all the trouble I cause to her domestic routine. But when the doorbell rang downstairs and Mrs B went to answer, it sounded as if she might even send the delivery man away.

'What's in that box you're heaving?' she challenged him. 'I hope it's no a pile o' books, for we have enough of them already.'

I'd reached the door by now, and the delivery man was placing the first carton on the floor. 'That's the monitor,' he said.

The small surprise I'd planned for Mrs B hadn't yet passed from its apprehensive phase to the pleasurable. She said to me, 'What monitor is this, then? Are you collecting school books now?'

I told her to be patient, and when the last of the three boxes had arrived and the door was closed, I informed Mrs B that her advice to me had been heeded, and from this day hence there need no longer be strewn across my desk a dozen books left open at a time.

'Well, there's some men'll think o' buying a computer, and they'll read every magazine and ask every friend for advice and visit ten shops for the best price; and there's others'll chust walk blithely into the very first place they find and take whatever they're offered, at a ridiculous price, and you know exactly which kind is you, Mr Mee.'

Despite these instinctive reservations I nevertheless could see that she was delighted.

'And when will we be boxing up all those dirty dusty books o' yours, if you won't be needing them?'

Clearly, Mrs B was getting carried away somewhat. I said we could think about that another time, and then she helped me take the computer's bits and pieces to my study.

Our correspondence, my dear friend, has never fought shy of digression, never felt the need to hurtle towards some conclusion, as if the ending alone were important, and what comes before merely an inconvenient delay. So many people nowadays, don't you think, are obsessed with arriving; yet we know that the true and final destination of us all is one which needs no hurrying. Even so, there are times when I feel I must summarize a little, sparing you certain details which can only detain you from some more profitable activity; and this is how I feel in relation to the day and a half I now spent trying to make my computer work. I shall not labour you with my frustrations, as I read and re-read the instructions, written in seven languages including a form of English which might as well have been Dutch. In fact, at one stage I realized that it really was the Dutch section I'd chanced to begin reading, and it was making a certain amount of sense to me, but this was only because I'd recited the relevant English passage so many times (concerning the insertion of keyboard connector C into serial port B, being careful not to force or bend the connecting pins) that it had become as drained of meaning as those poems we used to memorize at school. The foreign version I'd stumbled into at least gave me new words to accompany the pictures, and a fresh angle on things. But even when all the bits were finally hooked together, this was only the start of the true anguish.

'There's some men'll struggle for days on end and get themselves in a fankle wi' things they canna understand, and there's others'll chust phone the customer support number it's got written here on the guarantee.'

You can see why it's best for me to summarize. Where had my thoughts on Stevenson all flown away to? What about Rosier? All I could think about was my 'boot drive', and something called 'system configuration' which seemed to exist in a realm devoid of colour, shape, or even extension; a place, somewhere inside my stubborn computer, which Kant would surely have found worthy of analysis. The voice at customer support was called Dave, and showed little interest in the possibility that I'd been sold a machine which did not, after all, contain a copy of the *Enquiry Concerning Human Understanding* within its suspiciously lightweight components. He offered to send an engineer at a cost which he described as being very reasonable, considering; and which, in any case, I was in no position to refuse. I won't tell you what Mrs B thought about the engineer's rate when he left me the bill, having completed the job in less than fifteen minutes.

But at least my computer was working now, and I have managed to transport us a day and a half nearer to the present, when this letter, arriving at the sorrowful moment in which I began to write it, must surely end.

I started to 'get the hang of things', and soon felt like an expert 'net surfer'. You see how quickly the new language can be assimilated, even by so stubborn a mind as mine! A pleasant afternoon spent reading an amusing story called *The Counterfeiters* (an 'on-line' discovery which had distracted me from the *Virginibus Puerisque* I was seeking), made me quite forget all about the Rosier mystery. The session also left me with a strange tiredness of the eyes, and I noticed that for several hours afterwards, white pages or walls had a curiously pinkish hue. Mrs B came in the evening, quite unexpectedly, in order to drop off some groceries. She gave one of her little screams when she saw me, and said I should consult an oculist, as my eyes were in a state which, she declared, was 'no fit fae seein' oot frae'. I thanked her for her solicitousness, and returned to my computer after she'd left.

Since you are unfamiliar with the 'World Wide Web', I should explain, parenthetically, that it resembles a library to the extent that it contains a colossal number of 'pages', any one of which can be displayed on the computer screen; however, these are filed without any order whatsoever, unsorted and uncatalogued, and their content is rather different from the sort of thing which Margaret would be acquainted with. A great many consist of pictures, and a great many of these, I have discovered, show young women wearing little or no clothing, and indulging in various activities which can be of no possible interest to you or me. In fact, I first chanced on such material during my renewed 'Rosier' search, when I 'clicked' on an item and found it to be a 'live video link' from someone's bedroom. How such things are possible I have no idea; certainly, if I'd known that the machine they sold me in Dixons contained, in addition to the books I was looking for, the contents of numerous strangers' houses, then I might have asked them whether something cheaper wouldn't suffice, for my machine clearly holds far more than I can have any need for, especially at my age.

But let me return to the 'site' I mentioned, which purports to be 'live video'. This at least was the title I saw at the top of the 'page' on my screen, which showed a still photograph of an empty bed with the covers turned back. I was greatly perplexed by this. You see, I've always understood 'video' to mean those large cassettes which young people hire from disagreeable outlets such as 'Vista Rental', which several years ago came to supplant the fruit shop in

Victoria Road; and I've furthermore assumed that these cassettes contain only the vapid adventures which it pleases the public to gawp at, in the comfortable seclusion of their homes. Clearly, the word 'video' was being re-defined by computer usage, just like everything else. A moment's reflection reassured me that there was no abuse of language, as long as the word remained anchored to the sense of the Latin *videre*, which governs seeing, regardless of whether the object in view is a feature film of exploding motor cars, or an unoccupied bed with its covers turned back.

The fascination of the 'site' I had found would be unfathomable to you, were it not for what happened next; for while the picture remained on my screen, it suddenly began to 'refresh' itself, another new word I've picked up; and here I do suspect some improper usage, since I take the origin to be French, and concerned with the restoration of health or vigour through renewed sustenance, a word having only an extended metaphorical connection with the spontaneous recreation of the picture on my screen, rolling down before me like the view revealed on an unfolding banner, and showing a woman lying wholly naked. One moment there was an empty bed, the next I saw the motionless image of a young woman, unclothed, but reading a book as she lay there, propping her head with one hand while the other held the volume open to her view, and I was deeply intrigued that such a phenomenon could be called a 'live video link'. By live, I understood that the event I was witnessing was happening at that very moment; and as for 'link', this can't possibly be Latin, French or Greek. I assume there must be a Norse connection here, which we might pursue further at some other time.

You see, there were so many intriguing aspects to this

phenomenon, that I abandoned the young lady on her bed, even before the picture could 'refresh' itself once again, and I resorted to my friendly 'search engine' in order to seek more examples of 'live video'. In this way I was led to discover a truly fascinating site which displays the current activity of a street in Aberdeen, viewed from a security camera positioned outside a bank. Who would have guessed that such a world of detail could be bought in a little box (well, three boxes), for less than two and a half thousand pounds?

And so once more I had been led along a new path; what began as a search for the Xanthic sect had by now become a tour (which lasted for most of the night) of every 'video link' I could discover.

Might it be that I myself was the subject of such a 'site'? Were unknown people watching my own room on their computers; was my machine the means by which such images could be relayed, portraying to their curious audience nothing except an elderly gentleman who has forsaken his books in their locked cases, in favour of the glowing screen which now compels his attention? I doubted it, but I have no real idea how these 'links' are produced, and shall have to pay another visit to the good people at Dixons some time, since I am sure they will be able to enlighten me.

Let me only state that after an extended perusal of the nocturnal activities of that street in Aberdeen (three people eating chips provided the highlight of a fascinating half hour), I returned to the place I'd started from. There was, after all, some connection, as yet to be discovered, between the unclothed woman and the mysterious Rosier, the search for whose name had led me into her bedroom.

I found the woman now lying on her back, the book still

raised to view. Her pose upon the bed was rather unladylike, resembling that of childbirth, I believe. I might also mention that my serendipitous discovery of so many unclothed women inhabiting the 'Internet' has been an educating experience; as well as being quite comfortable 'scrolling' or 'zooming' the image before me, I was also confident that the somewhat hirsute condition of the amply exposed *pubes* of this unknown woman is a common feature, if not a universal one; a fact whose discovery had at last clarified for me an anecdote which long puzzled me, concerning Ruskin's wedding night in Perth.

Of chief interest to me, naturally, was the book which the young lady was reading. I had to wait several times while the image 'refreshed' itself (regretting on each occasion the inappropriate use of this word), until at last the reflections posed by the room's lighting moved themselves sufficiently for me to be able to read, on the glossy cover of the book, the words 'Ferrand and Minard'; which of course meant nothing to me. It seemed, in the unnatural state of superfluous enthusiasm which, I have learned, is the typical condition produced by interaction with computers, that it might be interesting for me to try and locate this book. Thus was I led even further from my original intentions (my essay on Stevenson, you'll have noticed, has gone right out of the window in the meantime), and since the reader's image, perhaps due to some random clicking on my part, apparently intended now to refresh itself no further, I decided I could try and decipher the book's author later, once my eyes had returned themselves to their normal size. I went to lie down.

When I awoke, I found myself in the morning of the day on which I write, for at last I am reaching the terrible point and purpose of this letter to you. I had been woken by a sound in my study; the hour was late, and I saw that for the first time in more than twenty years I had overslept. The new world which the computer had brought to me, I realized, was one of late nights, strained eyes, and a curious headache whose strongly localized nature made me wonder whether there might not after all have been some truth in phrenology, and whether I had overstimulated the portion of the cerebrum, hitherto unused by me, which is reserved solely for the enjoyment of 'live video links'.

What had woken me was a disturbance in my study; a noise which, in the confusion of half-sleep, I took to be an animal let loose and crying out. I put on my dressing gown and hastened to the scene. Mrs B was there. She was staring at the screen of the computer, which still showed the young lady reading a book in an attitude which, as I mentioned, was not particularly ladylike, and hence, I quickly deduced, somewhat offensive to Mrs B, who would no doubt have preferred the anonymous woman to have crossed her legs.

I'm hoping to locate this book, I began to say, pointing towards the part of the image that showed *Ferrand and Minard* held aloft before the reader's face, and finding that my finger was instead resting on a few 'pixels' (as Ali had called them in Dixons) representing a nipple. Mrs B said nothing. She looked at the screen, then at me, then at the screen again, but all this to-ing and fro-ing must have hurt her eyes, for she now closed them. A certain degree of visual strain is a hazard to beware of, I began to explain, not wishing Mrs B to end up with a headache like mine, but the good woman merely gave her head a shake, her eyes still clenched like little fists upon her face, as if she neither wished to see nor hear anything, particularly if it issued from my direction. This precaution against a mild fatigue of vision seemed somewhat excessive. At last she managed to release her face from the unnatural rictus which had seized it (they told me nothing about such side-effects at Dixons), and began to say, 'There's some men'll keep their secret habits to themselves for twenty-eight years, and there's others . . .' But it was too much for her, and the screen had irritated her eyes to such an extent that they were by now watering quite profusely. She left the room, I began to follow, but before I could even begin to descend the stairs in pursuit, hoping to suggest a remedy for the ocular strain she'd suffered, she'd reached the front door and was putting on her coat. She left without a word.

That's what happened this morning. As you can imagine, the hours which have passed since then have been very painful, and not only to my head which continues to ache in the region I overstimulated last night. The time for lunch has passed, and there still has been no sign of Mrs B. How I long for one of her delicious broths! There is no sign of her, no indication of whether she intends to come and clean – she who declared four days of such attention to be inadequate for a man of my advanced years!

This, then, is the misery which has been brought upon me by a computer bought to please my housekeeper, and a mysterious encyclopaedia which seems more untraceable than ever. When you read this, who knows what other disasters might already have occurred, in a life thrown suddenly from its tranquil course? And are you any good with a hoover?

CHAPTER 2

They met by chance, as such people always do. One was sitting on a bench reading a book, while the other, walking past and seeing this to be the kind of place where a man might enjoy a brief rest and perhaps some conversation, decided to sit down next to him. It was the spring of 1761, and Paris was a warm and pleasant place.

It would have been impolite for the two gentlemen not to have acknowledged one another, but after they had performed this nodding courtesy, the reader, who was short and stout and looked like a perpetual law student preparing to retake his examination for the fifteenth time, continued to peruse his book; while his companion, tall and thin in complementary form, watched a few birds on the eaves of a building some way off; until at last, impatient at being ignored, he said:

'I do believe there are certain birds which hatch from fire.'

The reader, still without lifting his eyes from the pages of his small book, said, 'And I believe, sir, that you refer to the legendary phoenix.'

'Ah yes, of course.'

Once more they fell into a silence which, if it had

continued a moment longer than it did, might have prevented their friendship from ever forming. But then the taller man said: 'Or do I perhaps mean the salamander?'

This made the reader give a mildly impatient grunt. 'The salamander, sir, is an amphibian; and the story of its generation has been shown to be as mythical as that of the phoenix.'

'Of course, of course,' the tall man, bookless and hungry for conversation, quickly conceded. 'But I believe it is asserted in some scientific quarters that fire itself may be considered a species of living organism.'

Now the reader lowered his book. He turned to look at his companion, who, holding out his hand, said, 'Monsieur Ferrand, sir, at your service'; to which the shorter man, reaching out to accept the greeting, replied, 'Monsieur Minard, your honoured friend.'

They were equivalent in every sense except appearance. Minard had indeed failed his law examinations, and a great many others besides; while Ferrand's hopes of becoming a cleric had been dashed by a scandal which was as groundless as it was fatal to his prospects. He had found employment as a clerk in a church college; Minard performed an equally lowly role in an office of the Académie des Sciences. Both were copyists; both had furthermore lost their jobs recently, and were surviving on irregular commissions while seeking new posts. This coincidence was enough to convince them that they should become the best of friends, having wasted every hour of their lives which had already passed in ignorance of one another.

Their first conversation revealed a common enthusiasm for questions of philosophy, roast duck, and the game of chess, and confirmed the agreement of their tastes in all matters of importance. Since neither had yet found a wife (though each was past forty), they would be free to arrange as many meetings and matches as they liked, in as many cafés as they cared to frequent; and this was quickly to become the major occupation of their lives. The Magris established itself as their favourite rendezvous, Ferrand expressing some distaste for the crowded Régence, where Philidor's exhibition tournaments drew a crowd which could, at times, be unsavoury.

'Indeed it can, sir,' Minard agreed one afternoon, contemplating an awkward knight fork.

Their chess games, like the meeting on a bench which, in a sense, defined the entire pattern of their friendship, would usually consist of Minard doing most of the concentrating, since he spent longer over his moves, while Ferrand, sitting tall and straight like a church steeple, would play according to whichever whim took his fancy, interrupting the game with any comment that happened to pass through his mind; a habit which Minard would acknowledge with a grunt calibrated according to the seriousness of his position. Ferrand won exactly half their games, but when he lost it was through foolish mistakes, and Minard suspected his friend merely allowed him to win as a misplaced gesture of comradeship.

Within three or four weeks of first meeting one another, each knew no more or less about his companion's life than was already apparent after that first conversation on a bench. They knew their similarities to be so profound that any attempt at exploration would simply be a form of introspection, a habit with whose dangers they were well acquainted.

'Monsieur Minard,' the tall man ventured on another occasion, as his opponent shifted his queen from a dangerous square.

'Yes, Monsieur Ferrand?'

Ferrand was inspecting the position now before him, as if Minard's forced move had been entirely unanticipated. 'I am in an unfortunate situation.'

Minard gave one of his typical grunts. 'It is surely I who am the unfortunate one, since I am doomed to lose my rook.'

'No, sir; I mean that I am in a dilemma of a domestic kind. I am shortly to be compelled to leave my lodgings, where my landlady refuses every generous offer I make of deferred overpayment. I therefore find myself temporarily in need of alternative accommodation. From, let us say, tonight.' He lifted Minard's rook from the board and replaced it with his bishop.

Minard said: 'It would be my pleasure, as well as my duty as your loyal friend, to invite you to reside at my own humble lodgings.'

And so they began to live together. Minard's lodgings were even more humble than he claimed; and a curtain, hung across the single room they were now to share, provided the only means of privacy. And yet, for two men so devoted to one another, this intimacy was wholly natural, and their chess games would often continue late into the night, by the light of a candle which Ferrand would at last blow out when they went gently to their respective beds.

Their happiness would have been complete, were it not for the difficulty they were each finding in obtaining a steady source of work. Tall, thin Monsieur Ferrand and short, stout Monsieur Minard sought consolation in chess; but their visits to the Magris became less frequent, replaced by games played out in their shared room, during which their taste for philosophy provided a distraction from hunger, rather than a substitute for the roast duck which they silently conjectured.

'I believe it is the case,' said Ferrand on one occasion, 'that if the circumference of a circle is divided by its diameter, then the same answer will always be arrived at, no matter how large the circle.'

Minard triumphantly lifted the pawn he had captured, heard what Ferrand was saying, and told him, 'Of course; the number is called *pi*.' He was cross that Ferrand barely acknowledged his sudden advantage; he therefore continued: 'I also know that Monsieur Buffon has found this number in another place. I once transcribed a report on it. Apparently, if you mark a series of straight lines on a piece of paper, then drop a great many pins of the same length, you will find that the proportion of pins which cross a line is equal to *pi*. Or something like that.'

'How extraordinary,' said Ferrand, who now stood up. 'Perhaps we should try.'

The game was abandoned, much to Minard's annoyance. Writing materials were in plentiful supply; but for pins, Minard had to go two floors downstairs, to the flat of a seamstress who showed some reluctance in lending what he asked, until Minard pulled a loose button from his jacket and left it as guarantee. Then the two men performed the experiment which Minard wished he had studied more closely when he had been copying it all out.

He couldn't quite remember if he'd got the arrangement of parallel lines correct; had he drawn them too close together, or too far apart? And all the pins weren't quite the same length, though M. Ferrand didn't see how a detail such as this could make any difference. If they were good enough for the seamstress then surely they would suffice for the experiment. And so the two men spent five minutes dropping the pins, and the best part of an hour studying how they lay, until they made their final totals and came up with a figure for *pi* of somewhere around twenty-four.

Minard shook his head. 'If only I'd read the report more closely while I was writing it out.'

Ferrand gathered up the pins, then went to fetch the chessboard so that they could resume their game. 'My friend, some of the greatest scientific discoveries of the age have passed through your hands, yet you've learned nothing from them. And while I've copied out many pious sermons and elevating tracts in flawless handwriting, my own life has not always been exemplary. Do you think there might be some kind of moral here?'

But if there was, it was lost on the two friends, who carried on playing.

Some days later, Ferrand came home in great excitement. 'Tonight we shall dine at the finest restaurant we can find!' he proclaimed. He was carrying a large bag crammed with papers. 'There's enough copying here to last us a month, and we're to be paid very handsomely for it!'

Then Ferrand explained how, contrary to habit, he had chosen during one of his solitary excursions to visit the Régence, simply in the hope of attaching himself to a patron who might be in need of a secretary or assistant. No man of quality was to be seen dining there however, nor were there even any chess players; but in the café, quiet at that time of day, Ferrand had found himself in conversation with the provider of all the documents he had brought home for reproduction.

'I was alone at a table in the corner when I saw him,' said Ferrand. 'He walked past, paused when he noticed me, and said, "You look like a literary man." I nodded and explained my profession, then he laughed and said, "A copyist? Even better. You're just the sort of person I'm looking for." He took a seat beside me, and I noticed the satchel he'd been carrying, which he placed on the table.

' "I am the possessor of a collection of documents whose publication will be guaranteed to bring fame and admiration."

' "How very nice," I said.

' "If you would be willing to make them ready for the press, I would pay you handsomely."

'Even nicer, I thought. "But what exactly are these documents of which you speak?"

'He opened the satchel, and drew out a number of items in different hands. One appeared to be a treatise on probability, and I immediately thought about you, Minard. Anyway, no matter what sort of literature this was, I was bound to accept his generous offer. "May we arrange terms?" I asked.

' "How does ten per cent sound?"

'I'd never been made an offer in this currency, but I was sure it amounted to a great deal, and so we shook hands. "Give me everything," I said, "and in four weeks I will have it ready." '

'You mean he didn't even ask you to give a demonstration of your copying?' Minard interjected, with a tone of incredulity.

'He could see that I was an honourable man; and besides, I wrote my address for him.'

'Why on earth did you do that?' asked Minard, who regarded the attic room in which he had enjoyed prior occupancy as being *their* address, rather than just Ferrand's.

Ferrand continued, 'He told me that he was temporarily unable to give a permanent address of his own where he could be found by me; and he was unwilling to suggest a public meeting place, such as the café where we sat, in which our subsequent business could be transacted.'

'Why ever should he object to so conventional an arrangement?' asked Minard.

'He said the nature of the documents was such that they must remain absolutely secret; I was to tell no one about them, and I didn't even admit to him that I would be working with you in copying them. He warned me that if they were to fall into the wrong hands, there could be consequences . . .' Ferrand paused, as if he'd only just realized the potential hazard of the undertaking.

Minard was staring at the satchel. He spoke slowly. 'Have you got us into some kind of plot?'

'Of course not.' But it was not without trepidation that Ferrand opened the satchel, having failed to inspect the contents closely before striking the deal he'd felt so proud of.

Minard was leafing through the manuscript pages now in his hands. 'Where did he go then, this strange benefactor of yours? And what's his name?'

'I don't know.' Ferrand was reading as anxiously as his friend. 'We shook hands again, I took the satchel, and that was that, until the month is up.'

'But he knows where we live. And if he's some kind of subversive, if he's interviewed by the police . . .' By now Minard had found an essay which appeared to be on mechanics, but which on closer inspection proved to be concerned with poetry. Ferrand unearthed an article outlining a new theory of sun dials.

Both men felt relieved. These papers were learned works of some very obscure and esoteric kind, and could be of no harm to anyone. Ferrand's mysterious friend had merely shown the obsessive secrecy characteristic of inferior artists, who believe their ideas might be worth stealing.

'We'll need a lot more than a month for all this,' said Minard, putting his hands through his thick wiry black hair. 'More like a year.'

'It was agreed that we could have extra time if necessary.'

'Then we needn't begin work until tomorrow. You said we'd go to a restaurant tonight; how much did he give you?'

'Who?'

'Our new employer, of course.'

'He didn't give me anything. We arranged that he'd come here in a month's time, that's all.'

Minard looked again at the pile of papers which burdened their flimsy table. 'You propose that we spend four weeks copying all this,' he cried, 'when our nameless ghost might not even return to collect it, never mind pay us!' He was genuinely angry. 'Ferrand, I can't believe your stupidity.'

'You're simply jealous because I've been able to bring in so much work.'

Minard's retort was quick and sharp: 'If that's what you think, then why don't you go and find your sleeping quarters at your friend the ghost's, instead of here at mine!' Minard walked out.

It was the first time they'd argued, but when Minard slammed the door of their apartment behind him, Ferrand didn't follow him to apologize. Minard waited at the door, hoping that he'd see the handle turn, if only so he could run downstairs before Ferrand could catch him; but from within the room there was not a sound, unless it was of the stifled sobs which Minard believed he could detect. He waited only long enough, his ear to the door, to establish that the moaning was in fact the dragging of a chair, followed by the rustle of papers being cleared from the little table as Ferrand prepared to do the work unaided. Very well; let him! Minard walked downstairs, the bannister swaying loosely in his grip as he descended the dusty steps.

Disturbed by the noise of the argument, several fellow lodgers had opened their doors. All watched him in silence, their curiosity briefer than the irritation displayed on their hostile faces, until, two floors below, he encountered the young seamstress again. The other doors closed when he stopped to acknowledge her, and he excused himself for having disturbed her from her work.

'Never mind,' she said simply. 'But you still owe me some pins.'

He'd told Ferrand to return them; the idiot had proved incapable even of this. Minard explained, and humbly apologized to her again.

She smiled. 'You can give me them another time. I've still got your button; I could sew it back on to your jacket if you like.' She was staring at the loose threads remaining from where he'd pulled the button free during their earlier encounter. She stood aside to let him in.

There appeared to be two rooms leading off from the one in which he found himself, this one bearing, other than the evidence of the girl's occupation, little in the way of furnishing; though it was more pleasant than his own room, more homely. He took off his jacket and sat down on one of the two chairs. 'How old are you?' he said.

'Nineteen.' She quickly made ready to mend his coat.

'Where are you from?' Since she was alone here, he guessed she must have come from the country in order to earn enough to marry.

'My family live north of here, near the forest of Mont-morency,' she said, and broke a length of thread with her teeth. Her name was Jacqueline, and as her hand began to move back and forth, drawing the silver needle through Minard's black coat, slowing with the pressure of the cloth, then following swiftly, drawing the thread tight before repeating the movement, she told him about her parents and their cottage, about her two brothers and her sister, and about the little hill where, as a child, she loved to play with a doll which her father once made for her.

'I don't know what happened to that doll,' she said, 'though I loved it so.' And Minard thought he could see a bright tear glistening in the corner of her eye, as she resumed her sewing.

Soon it was finished. Jacqueline stood up and gave his coat a shake, and in her skilful hands it suddenly looked to him like a smart and brand new garment. He went to take it from her, but she held on to it a moment longer than was necessary, so that for a second or two they both gripped the coat between them. She withdrew.

'You have beautiful hands,' Minard told her, and she blushed, then moved towards the door, which had remained open throughout Minard's visit. It was time for him to leave.

'I owe you a twofold debt,' he said. 'Not only shall I return the pins, but I must repay you for mending my

ANDREW CRUMEY

button.' He took her hand lightly in his, momentarily felt its warmth and softness, then wished her good day. He glimpsed, as he rounded the flight of stairs he now descended, her face retreating behind the narrowing crack of her closing door.

He felt ready now to enjoy a bout of justifiable anger against Ferrand. Strengthened by his flirtation, he could savour his companion's ineptitude, and he could forgive it. He realized moreover, as he began to walk in the street outside, that Ferrand's commission was the nearest they'd come in weeks to any real work, and they were in no position to turn it down. Ferrand had been right to accept, and if they were at the mercy of their employer then there was little they could do about it.

Every flower-seller he passed, every lace-maker's shop or fine leather-worker's, made him think of Jacqueline, and of the little present he'd love to buy her. It would have to wait until the month was up and they were paid; though when their mysterious patron chose to call at their apartment, what a scene that gentleman would discover! Seeing the squalor in which they lived, he might decide he had nothing to fear by leaving them without a sou. But Minard knew the law. He'd studied it at least five times.

Minard's stroll took him much further than he expected. Like a sleepwalker, he found himself half an hour later at a market on the very edge of the city, where he made his way between fruit stalls, each laden with produce he couldn't afford, then strolled into the adjoining meadows. Birds were singing, he watched butterflies and lizards, and he tried to imagine the forest of Montmorency, which he had never visited and where perhaps he should go in search of a natural world known to him only through the scientific reports he had copied at the Académie, without really reading any of them.

Minard made his way home with a bunch of wild flowers in his hand. He'd been away for some hours; when he ascended the stairs he knocked on Jacqueline's door, but received no reply. Then he went up further, until he came to his own room, and found Ferrand working inside.

Ferrand looked up from the pages he was copying, saw the flowers in Minard's hand, but made no mention of them, saying only, 'Don't worry, Minard, I shall do all the copying myself. And if I'm paid, you shall receive what you're due.'

'Dear friend,' said Minard, offering him the flowers, 'let us work together. Even if we receive no payment, we might at least derive some entertainment and instruction from it. Let us regard our labours together as being like a game of chess, a shared pleasure costing nothing; or like these flowers, which grow beneath our noses, though we only have eyes for the ones to which men attach a price.'

This pretty speech ended with a fond embrace, and the two friends agreed that even a lifelong friendship will sometimes be tested by disagreement. Then Minard took off his coat and sat down next to Ferrand, who had had time to examine in more detail the thick bundle of papers they had been given.

Ferrand was working on an article translated from the work of a Scottish philosopher named Magnus Ferguson. 'An adherent to the Jacobite cause, it would appear,' Ferrand explained.

'In that case, a man of safe political affiliations,' Minard noted with relief, as he still harboured some suspicions about an enterprise he was nevertheless powerless to resist. Minard perused the essay, which was called 'Cosmography', appeared to be about a voyage among the planets, and made no sense whatsoever.

'We're to spend a month copying the likes of this?' said Minard, scratching his head. 'If we take good note of what we write, we shall become wise men indeed.' And he rolled up his sleeves, ready to share in his friend's labour.

An hour and a half later, they were both very tired and very hungry.

'At this precise moment,' said Minard, 'I would be willing to march naked into the front line of the fiercest battle, be suspended in a bath of frozen water, have burning matches applied to the ends of my fingers, and would then publicly declare every sin of deed or thought which I have ever committed; if only I were sure to be rewarded at the end of it all by a fat and juicy roast duck.'

'I would endure even greater torture,' said Monsieur Ferrand, though lack of food never seemed to trouble him quite as much as it did his shorter, more spherical friend. 'However, such an option is not available to us. On the other hand, it's late now, and if you go to the Saint-Jean market you should be able to buy enough spoiled food for us both to survive another day.'

'Yes, I shall do that, Monsieur Ferrand; though I expect I shall have to wait a while, with all the other wretches who can afford no better. I shall take something to read, so that I'm not mistaken for a beggar.' Minard lifted a handful of uncopied papers from the pile on the table.

'Do you not have a book to hand?'

'Of course; but I have resolved that from now on I shall take note of whatever I transcribe, and I can save myself a good deal of time by reading in advance.'

Ferrand eyed with some disapproval the bundle in his friend's hands. 'Be very careful with those,' he said. 'Remember that their owner sets great store by them.'

'Huh!' Minard grunted. 'The importance literary people invest in their scribblings is as ridiculous as that attached by a common serving girl to her own virginity.' And on this needlessly coarse note, he left.

While one or two readers (and doubtless most writers) may dispute his latter point, Minard was correct in his previous assertion; for he had indeed to wait a considerable time at the market in the Place Baudoyer before being able to take his pick of bashed fruit, unwholesome vegetables and meaty shreds of undefined provenance. So much for the restaurant which Ferrand had promised! While he'd been waiting, Minard had read an article proving the non-existence of the universe, which in his famished state had hardly been consoling; but now he was ready to bring home his harvest, and he was careful to put aside a perfect-looking apple, destined for the sweet lips of his young friend.

Minard knocked on her door again, on his way upstairs, and this time she was in. 'I came to repay you,' he said, when she opened the door, narrowly at first, but then fully as she recognized her caller. He brought out the apple. 'This is hardly sufficient recompense.'

Somewhat nervously she took it, thanked him, and remained standing in her doorway as she studied it, her face illuminated by gratitude.

'There are still the pins, of course,' he said. 'How silly of me to forget them yet again.'

'Are you always so forgetful?' Jacqueline asked, reading every mark and feature of the apple as if it were a breviary.

'On the contrary, my memory, in certain respects at least, is indelible.' He lowered his voice. 'There are some things which, once seen, are never forgotten.'

'Then you are a most unusual man,' she replied, 'since most have short memories.'

Minard said, 'Perhaps you might like me to return the pins a little later, once I've found them upstairs.'

Jacqueline pursed her lips thoughtfully, as if some great negotiation were taking place, instead of a conversation over a few pins. Then she shook her head. 'I'm not in urgent need of them. But if you'd like to join me, I'm about to make a tisane.'

This time she closed the door behind him. Minard took his seat, while Jacqueline got some water ready to boil on the stove. He put his parcel of food and his papers on the table, and watched her slim waist as she moved. For the first time in his life, he was in love.

The tisane made her strangely busy, too preoccupied for words, and Minard also remained silent. It was like the preparation for a religious ceremony. Then when it was ready she offered him a warm glass, and they drank together.

'Each debt repaid begets another,' he said. 'One apple is hardly enough.' Then he pulled open the parcel so that she could see the food inside.

'I need none of it,' she told him.

'Please,' he implored, 'take as much as you like.'

And so they dined together. She fried the meat, whose juices bubbled and wafted their flavour up as far, no doubt, as the nose of poor Ferrand, who would have nothing more on which to sup; she boiled the carrots and made of the other ingredients a meal which pleased Minard more than any restaurant could. Ferrand's promise of good food tonight was thus fulfilled; and Minard, aware that his thin friend would be in need of some sustenance, kept aside a few pears and a piece of bread.

'The woman who can cook such a meal,' said Minard, wiping his lips, 'would surely make a wife whom any man would be proud of, if he were lucky enough to find her.'

Now her blushes, which had temporarily left her while hunger had prevailed over decorum, returned even more deeply. 'You must go to your friend,' she said. 'Tomorrow, you may bring me those pins.'

'I shall bring them, and whatever else my heart can offer,' Minard gushed as he was ushered to the door, where Jacqueline handed him his coat and the last of the food. It was only when the door closed and her face was out of sight that the spell was suddenly broken, and he realized what a wretch he was.

Minard ascended the stairs with a weary heart, planning in ever greater detail the story he was to tell. As soon as he entered his room and saw Ferrand still working as if no time had passed and food were merely an inconvenience to him, Minard began his performance.

'Friend, I was attacked,' he said.

Ferrand stood up. 'What happened?'

'There were two of them; one I could have handled, but a pair, and with knives – forget it. They were clever all right; followed me as far as Rue Plâtrière, then jumped me when I turned into a side street. But don't worry, I'm not injured. And I even managed to save some food which I'd put in my pockets – look here.' He brought out the pears, and the bread. 'You can have it all; I feel so ashamed . . .'

'Never mind that,' said Ferrand. 'What about the papers?'

Papers? Minard had forgotten all about them. 'Oh, those. Gone too, I'm afraid.'

'You lost them? You let them be taken by thieves?'

Minard remembered that they sat on Jacqueline's table. He could get them tomorrow, if they really mattered. 'Calm yourself, friend; I'm sure I can retrieve them.'

'How on earth do you propose to do that? Did these thieves leave you their card?'

'No, no; but they would have no use for a scientific article about the non-existence of the universe; they'd throw it to the ground as soon as they realized it wasn't a contract or promissory note. I'll go out tomorrow and find it lying in the street not far from where it was stolen – you'll see.'

Ferrand was shaking his head. 'This is simply not good enough, not good enough.' He was becoming more and more anxious by the minute. 'What did these thieves want from you?'

'My money, of course.'

'And seeing that you had none, what did they take? A few pieces of spoiled food? Why did they not slit your throat, or kick you for sport? Why should thieves care for a bag of poor scraps?'

Minard, who felt that his perfomance, excellent and ingenious as it was, was being less than wholly appreciated, shook his head slowly. 'I don't know. Perhaps they were just practising.'

'Practising?' Ferrand shook his companion by the shoulders. 'It was the papers they wanted, you fool! Why else would skilful crooks go to the trouble of accosting a man who evidently has less of value on him than anyone with a decent blade up his sleeve?'

Minard pushed the other man away. 'Please Ferrand, calm yourself.' Minard was nearly believing it himself, almost worried by Ferrand's scenario. 'I'll find the papers tomorrow, somehow or other.'

'You'll never find them.'

'In any case, it doesn't matter. A few missing pages out of that great heap; do you suppose that your patron will count every sheet before paying us? He'll never notice.'

Ferrand was pacing up and down the room; Minard was wondering whether to help himself to a pear for dessert. 'Who took them, that's what I want to know,' said Ferrand, talking to himself. 'And why? How many people are trying to get their hands on this collection which is so dangerous that their owner wouldn't even give me an address?' By now Ferrand was getting himself into a state of panic, and Minard tried to comfort him.

'I can go and look now, if you like.' But it was already dark, and Minard knew in any case that he shouldn't trouble Jacqueline over a few pages he could retrieve at the appropriate time. 'It'll all seem easier in the morning,' he assured his friend, who was gnawing, with a mildly obsessive air, at his knuckles.

Eventually Minard was able to persuade him to eat the bread, and one of the pears (Minard helpfully consumed the other, by way of encouragement), and the two men went to their beds. 'Sleep well,' said Minard; but throughout the night he was woken repeatedly by the sound of Ferrand turning on his bunk, behind the curtain which hung across the middle of the moonlit room.

ANDREW CRUMEY

Next day Minard woke early, but Ferrand was already up. 'We should go straight away,' the tall man said through the curtain, as soon as Minard began to move. 'If those papers really are to be found in the street then we can't afford to waste a minute.'

Minard yawned, rubbed his chin, and knew that it was still far too early to trouble Jacqueline. He would see her this afternoon at the very soonest; until then, all he could do was to try and stop Ferrand making himself ill with worry. 'Very well,' said Minard, rising from his bed to dress himself. 'Let's go together. We shall cover every inch of Paris if need be, but I swear, Ferrand, that we shall find your damned papers before sunset.'

And so they walked. With nothing more than the last of the bread to line their stomachs, and some milk they bought along the way, they marched to the Place Baudoyer; circled and bisected it, then began to eliminate one by one the adjoining streets; Minard still yawning frequently, quietly waiting for the time to pass, while Ferrand turned with his foot every rag and scrap that soiled their path. Over a discarded yellow page, revoltingly stained, he spent some minutes – Minard meanwhile looking up and down the street in some embarrassment – before Ferrand confirmed the item to be a veterinarian's bill for the treatment of a horse.

They walked all morning. Their search had begun with the market place as its focus, but gradually blurred itself out to encompass ever greater circles of possibility and ultimate failure as each of the neighbouring streets was fruitlessly subjected to scrutiny. Eventually Minard, deciding that it was now late enough for him to be able to visit Jacqueline in decency, said it would be best for them to split up. 'Why search together? We could finish the job twice as quickly if we work apart.'

'But how will I know which streets you've visited?' asked Ferrand.

They considered splitting Paris in two, across some arbitrary line passing, like a meridian, through the Place Baudoyer. But without a map, such a scheme seemed unfeasible.

'I know,' said Minard. 'If the street name begins with a letter from the first half of the alphabet then it's mine; otherwise you take it.'

The sheer arbitrariness of this proposal reinforced its apparent fairness and practicality. 'Done,' said Ferrand. Then he paused. 'There may however be an excess of names in the second half. Just think for example of all those called after saints, which I presume we count under S.'

'All right, we'll do it the other way; you take everything up to M, Ferrand.'

'I can hardly allow you to devote yourself to such a vast labour.'

Minard was going to go straight home, of course; he was merely trying to find a way of minimizing Ferrand's futile exertions, while also hoping to keep his friend occupied for another hour or two, while he was seeing Jacqueline. 'I insist. All the streets from N onwards are mine.'

Ferrand shook his head. 'I feel we ought to come to some more equitable arrangement, in the name of comradeship, if not in the interests of successfully completing our task. Should we not make the division at J, say; or even G, to be on the safe side?'

Minard, tired and exasperated, and impatient to see his Jacqueline, said, 'All right, forget the alphabetic split. You do the Saints, and I'll do everything else.'

'I couldn't allow that.'

'Please, just do it.'

'No, friend. You do the Saints; it is I who should take the rest.'

'Agreed,' Minard declared, beginning to walk away.

But Ferrand still wished to speak. Rubbing his chin as he contemplated the latest proposal, the tall man said, 'Minard, I am unhappy with this.'

'What do you mean?'

'It's just that the Saints might be apt to come in clusters with a great expanse of waste between . . .'

'For God's sake Ferrand, take whichever streets you choose, but let us not stand here and waste another minute!'

And Minard marched off, hearing Ferrand's voice call after him: 'What have we decided? Who's to do the Saints?' But Minard made no response, continuing at a swift pace until he rounded the corner, unpursued by Ferrand.

Minard hurried home; he arrived and quickly ascended the stairs, then knocked on Jacqueline's door. There was no answer. He knocked again, but still there was no response. Behind him, at the other side of the landing, old Blanchot emerged from his apartment.

'Banging does no good if a person's not at home.'

Minard turned, and asked him: 'Have you seen her this morning?'

'The young lady? I expect she's out. Perhaps decided to move to a better kind of neighbourhood.'

'What do you mean by that?' Blanchot seemed to be

hinting at something by his unpleasant remark; Minard went and stood close to the bent old man, who was even shorter than Minard himself.

'I mean that you ought to be careful what sort of people you consortimatize yourself with, Monsieur Minard.'

'Are you suggesting that the mademoiselle . . . ?'

'Heavens no, monsieur. The young lady is a creature of spotless reputation, as I told the officer.'

Minard gave a start. 'Officer? What's been going on here?'

Blanchot, clearly enjoying himself, was in no hurry to explain. 'Came first thing this morning; I was just putting out the night-soil when I saw him arrive.'

'An officer? A soldier in uniform?'

Blanchot laughed. 'That would be a fine sight! No, he was a police agent, that's what I mean. Very respectable looking. I thought he might be wanting to have a word about those pigeons they keep feeding upstairs, but no; he sees me and says, "Do you know where I can find Monsieur Ferrand?"'

Minard suddenly knew what it means to feel as if one's blood has turned to ice. 'And what did you tell him?'

'I said, "Ferrand? Certainly; he lives on the top floor with Monsieur Minard. You'll easily extinguish them, officer; Monsieur Ferrand is tall and thin, while Minard is short and fat." Pardon me for putting it so bluntly, monsieur, but it does no good to be erasive with the police, and if you take my advice you'll keep yourself out of trouble.'

'What did he want with Ferrand?'

'Actually, he seemed more interested in you.'

'But he asked for Ferrand, didn't he?' Minard could hear

a note of desperation intruding into his own voice, as all Ferrand's fantasies suddenly began to take on an aspect of dreadful plausibility.

'That's right,' said Blanchot, his knowing smile still undimmed. 'Asked for Ferrand, but when I mentioned your name, he said, "You mean there's two people living in the apartment? We only know about Ferrand." He wanted me to tell him how long you'd been staying at the address.'

'But I was living here before Ferrand!' Minard protested, somewhat indignantly.

'I know, monsieur, that's what I told the policeman; and he said, "Do you mean that Ferrand is only here temporaneously?" and I said, "That's right, officer, and by the looks of him, I wouldn't be at all surprised if he turned out to be the type what moves on without a moment's notice, and without paying his dues." We had one like that downstairs last year, you know.'

Minard would need a drink of water before long. 'You mean you denounced poor Monsieur Ferrand, a loyal subject and an innocent man, to the police?'

'I had to tell the truth, monsieur; it does no good being elusive and uncommensurative with authority.'

'You stupid old man!'

'And I did add that you'd been spending rather a lot of time in the apartment of the young seamstress, a girl of unvarnished reputation, as I assured the officer.'

'So you've denounced Monsieur Ferrand, myself, and a poor innocent girl to the authorities?'

'I believe in being a good neighbour, monsieur.'

'And I've a good mind to kick you down the stairs.'

'I wouldn't do that if I were you, monsieur; after all, they know everything about you now.' And with that,

Blanchot calmly retreated to his apartment, while Minard felt his life fragmenting around him, falling like the loose green flakes of paint surrounding Blanchot's closed door.

Minard went up to his room, his pace heavy but his mind whirring. What if the police agent had searched the place; what was there to find? And then when he opened the door, Minard gasped at what he saw. The table on which he and Ferrand worked was completely cleared; the documents, and their satchel, all were gone.

He wasn't sure which was more shocking; the thought that his room had been invaded and that he was therefore an object of official suspicion, or that the papers, in search of two or three pages from which Ferrand was still combing the streets, had now evaporated in their entirety. In a way he was glad they were gone; but what incriminating material, what coded messages, might the police have discovered? Minard sat down on Ferrand's bed and put his head in his hands.

He had hardly altered his position when Ferrand returned half an hour later. Minard gave a start as the door opened, not expecting his friend to return so quickly, and for a moment he suspected that Ferrand had likewise decided to leave the work of searching to the other. But before Minard could say anything, Ferrand, his voice still raised in pitch by anxiety, had already begun to explain. 'I've decided the best way is to retrace every possible route you could have taken from the Place Baudoyer...' He noticed the empty table. 'Where have you put them, the papers I was copying?'

'Sit down, Ferrand,' said Minard. 'This is not a good day for us.' And less than a minute later, Minard was watching the pitiful sight of his friend crying like an infant, once he knew what had happened. 'Please, Ferrand, cheer up.'

'Why ever should I want to do a thing like that?' Ferrand uttered between sobs.

'Well, the pages I lost yesterday might still turn up.' But even Minard himself wasn't consoled by the knowledge that those fragments, to be retrieved from Jacqueline, would be all that their patron would find if ever he returned; or that those worthless sheets alone had avoided the scrutiny of the police.

'The lost pages hardly matter now,' said Ferrand, wiping fresh tears from his eyes. Then he made Minard stand up, while he began to rummage in his bed.

'What are you looking for?' Minard asked him, and he saw Ferrand begin to draw out, through a hole in the mattress, manuscript sheets by the handful.

'The papers on the table were only the ones on which I intended to work first. I put the rest here for safety.'

Minard congratulated his friend on what, if he'd known about it earlier, would have seemed an act of ridiculous secrecy.

'But this merely leaves us with yet another problem,' said Ferrand, once all the pages (most, in fact, of the original consignment) lay tumbled and scattered on the bed. 'For what are we to do with these? If the police suspect we're involved in some plot then this can only incriminate us further; but when my patron and his lackeys come back on the appointed day, what are we to say if we have nothing to give them? Can we dare to keep these documents and continue our work?'

Ferrand and Minard, though they had a mutual interest in questions of philosophy and games of strategy, found this logical conundrum not to their taste.

Ferrand proposed that he should move to other lodgings;

it was he who had brought this predicament upon Minard, and it was he who must deal with it alone. Minard protested; their friendship, sealed upon the bench where they first met, must surely be able to withstand an ordeal even such as this. These sentiments, warmly expressed, reinforced their sense of common loyalty, but did little to advance their cause.

'You've done nothing wrong,' Minard told his friend, 'and I do not condemn you for accepting this ill-fated commission. No, it is I who must seek forgiveness.' And then he confessed his deception of the previous day, when he had been with Jacqueline; and seeing Ferrand's face trembling with the threat of renewed tears, Minard followed up by saying it was a blessing in disguise; for it had ensured their absence during the police officer's visit, and meant that they would also be able to retrieve a few more papers which otherwise would have been among those confiscated.

Ferrand showed no emotion. His tears were kept in check as he listened to his friend's account of betrayal; and then, like a wife who forgives but will never forget, he seemed to draw the moral strength he needed to come to some decision. 'We shall visit the seamstress,' he said, 'and take back the papers. Then, with all that we have, we shall leave this place and seek refuge elsewhere. In a month's time, I shall return to face whatever is to be my destiny.'

Minard would later assert that this was indeed Ferrand's finest hour.

The two men gathered up their belongings, all of which they then wrapped in a canvas sheet so as to make a large bundle, heavy yet portable. Now they were packed and ready to leave. 'I'll go and see if Jacqueline is in,' Minard suggested.

'No,' Ferrand declared grandly. 'We shall visit her together.' Perhaps he merely wanted to see who the girl was, who had led his friend so sadly astray.

They went quietly downstairs to her landing, checking to see whether Blanchot or anyone else might be about, and Minard knocked very gently on her door. Still there was no answer; Minard tried a little louder, looking over his shoulder all the while. Ferrand reached for the door handle. 'You can't!' Minard hissed, but Ferrand had already turned it, and the door opened. They paused only long enough to be sure there could be no soul within, and then Minard pushed the door wide so that they could enter.

She was sitting on the floor at the far side of the room, her back propped against the wall. She made no movement, no response, and looked as though she had slid into her present position in a kind of reverie, unwilling or unable to support herself. Her eyes were open, and her lips were dark blue.

Minard was still standing in the doorway while Ferrand hurried to try and assist her, somehow doubting that she was dead. He was slapping her face, and this was helping to confirm for him what must be obvious to anyone. She had been strangled.

Minard came in and closed the door, went and knelt beside Jacqueline's body as if at a shrine, held her cold hand, and could think only of the way it had glided back and forth while mending the button on his coat; so young, and so full of life.

'Where did you leave the papers?' Ferrand was searching the room.

'They're on the table,' Minard heard himself say; though when he nodded in that direction he saw with some indifference that they too, like the other pages, were gone. He turned to look at Jacqueline again, then felt Ferrand's hand on his shoulder.

'Go, Minard; I shall bring our belongings. Meet me at the Temple. All Paris is not safe enough for us now. Whoever visited this place today was not an agent of the law, and would easily do to us what he did to this poor girl, for the sake of a few pieces of paper. And when her body is found, you know who'll be the suspect; it'll be you, Minard, though we'd no doubt hang together for it.'

Minard stood up. 'I know where we must go. The forest of Montmorency will hide us. There are people there who'll want to know the truth of what has happened.'

Then they both crept from the room; Minard to go downstairs and into the anonymous streets, Ferrand to fetch the parcel of belongings from their room. If only he'd kept his nose firmly in his book when he was reading on a bench one day, Minard might have reflected ruefully, then none of this need ever have been written.

CHAPTER 3

I wish to explain how it was that this strange book ever came into being.

I was writing a story set in eighteenth-century France, but for some time I had been feeling unwell with what had started, not long after my forty-ninth birthday, as nothing more than a vague irritation in my abdomen. It wasn't until I began discharging blood that I bothered to seek medical advice, and this was only at my wife's insistence after she noticed a crimson residue in the toilet bowl and discovered my predicament; but already by then my condition had come to seem like a terrible secret, as if it were somehow connected with my greater problem, about which Ellen still knew nothing.

The doctor had a look and a poke, said it was probably nothing to worry about – told me, with a wipe of his grey and bristly nose, that he was retiring in a few weeks, which hardly reassured me – and made an out-patient referral to the local hospital. I was to undergo a procedure involving the insertion of a small camera, its lens mounted on the end of a long and mercifully thin tube, into the colon. 'It's all perfectly routine,' the doctor assured me, with undoubted sincerity. During the next ten weeks I got on with my work, thinking of little else except my invisible malady, but still had neither recovered nor died when at last a letter of appointment dropped on to the doormat, as welcome as a coveted Christmas present, as ominous as a tax reminder.

My bowels void as instructed, I went, and I waited. The measurement of clinical time, like the calculation of a dog's effective age, proceeds according to a scale quite different from that of life elsewhere; thus a simple ten minute procedure can take the best part of a day. Eventually my turn came.

'Good morning,' said the surgeon/cameraman (I never found out his name), with a fresh, nonchalant air, when I was shown into the 'endoscopy suite'. He looked the sort of person who could be a plumber or a school headmaster; chubby, bald and friendly in that completely impersonal way perfected by those who deal extensively with the general public. Probably an authority on malt whisky and golf. 'Well, what do you do for a living?' he said breezily, scribbling something on a form as I handed my trousers to the nurse and found my hand to be trembling. He directed me to climb on to the steel-framed surgical bed. 'That's right, just roll up your sleeve.'

'I'm a writer,' I decided to tell him; then, securely prostrate, felt a prick in my arm.

'Writer?' He muttered something technical to the nurse, quickly explained to me whatever he thought I ought to know about the adventure we were shortly to undertake. No, there was nothing I wanted to ask. 'And what sort of books do you write?' Now he moved round to the other side of the bed, out of my view.

What sort of answer did he expect to receive? Imagine for instance another author, asked to sum up his work in a sentence, who says he writes only a single novel, of a kind which 'concerns a person called "I", who is not always myself'. Would this seem like a satisfactory account, a good advertisement? But we'll never get to meet that author, since Proust died a long time ago. When I was younger, my infatuations more abstract and serene, meeting Proust seemed the most wonderful dream imaginable; one to make heaven itself an attractive proposition. I no longer feel quite the same way, now that I can better appreciate the point Proust was making; but this 'person called "I" who is not always myself', a character to be found, at times, in every one of us, and of far wider significance than the narrator of *À la recherche du temps perdu* (the single unfinished novel to which Proust's comment referred), is one who would preoccupy me quite considerably in the coming weeks.

'What sort of books do you write?' the endoscopist asked. If he is reading these words now, I can at least say: 'this sort'. I felt something cold and wet on my buttocks; then, 'I'm just going to insert the tube,' he said helpfully. I'm sure I'm not the only man who's always wondered what it must feel like to be buggered (though Proust, of course, knew). 'Detective? Thriller?' It was no wider than a finger, however, and slid into me with dreadful ease until I could feel its prod deep inside me. 'That's it, just relax.'

The nurse was bearing down with her hand, very gently, on my bare upper arm, probably only so as to restrain me; but this physical contact became strangely important to me, wonderfully comforting. It was as if all my fear and anxiety were gathered, like the rays of a distant star, upon that small patch of skin she now depressed with such skilful tenderness. I realized how disconnected I had become of late, from the simple beauty of touch.

Something was pinging or bleeping in the machinery behind me, the surgeon was uttering cryptic messages to the nurse; but he still wanted to know about my writing, as if concentration had made him forget he no longer need do his preliminary 'put the patient at ease' routine. Yet if my life's work held any significance at all for him now, well advanced in his tour of my colon, it was only as a way of keeping my muscles relaxed while he delved and wandered through the suburbs of my body, revealed to him on a video screen I neither could see, nor wished to, with all the banality of an estate agent's advertisement in the local newspaper.

I could have told him about my academic publications, my research, or the conferences I attend such as one in Prague recently where I discussed Rousseau with my old friend Donald Macintyre. But none of this had made me describe myself as a 'writer'. It was my novel, though only a hobby with which I hoped to escape from more serious concerns, that had prompted the description I gave of myself to the dextrous cartographer of my bowels. 'Historical fiction,' I said.

He murmured polite interest, and the fibre-optic python inside me gave another exploratory kick and twist. 'Ever thought of writing something modern?'

I didn't really want to get into a conversation about this if it meant the surgeon might give anything less than his full attention to what he was doing. 'Yes, I've thought about it,' I said, concentrating all the love and dread in my body onto the small solemn spot where the nurse's hand still rested like a benediction.

'Well, I expect you'll want to put this little episode into one of your books some day,' he said.

'Yes, I expect I will,' I replied. And indeed I have.

'There we are Dr Petrie,' he said not long afterwards, though it seemed long at the time. 'All finished.' The final part was no worse than shitting a few yards of garden hose.

'Could you see anything?' I asked once it was over, breathless and exhausted for some reason. I think he probably began to explain why I might need to have an X-ray, maybe several; a few tests. I gradually realized he was professing a subtle form of ignorance, and I was about to undergo another progression in my career as medical experiment. Like a lucky contestant in a game show, I was being given an opportunity to participate in the next round. And yet I already knew the real, hidden cause of my ailment. Or rather, I was aware of the origin of my depression, and hence of the illness with which my body had sought to distract me.

Rousseau postpones, until the end of the second book of his *Confessions*, the incident (the stealing of a blue ribbon, for which he passed the blame onto an unfortunate servant) which, having irritated him like a swollen kidney for many years, had at last precipitated itself in the writing of his extraordinary work. I haven't waited quite so long. The truth, the banal fact which had long been tearing at me, peeling as if at a stubborn label, worrying and fraying itself upon some hidden membrane in my bowels, was that for more than a year I had been painfully and hopelessly in love with one of my students.

I would see her ever Thursday; at first there were others in the group, but if any failed to attend I did nothing to encourage their return; and while the original pretext was the discussion of a short course of lectures I gave, it soon became a time simply for talking, to which everyone was

invited, officially; but only Louisa would come, faithful as a
lamb.

Already, simply by naming her, I find myself rushing
ahead. If the endoscopist reads this then he can smile and
know the reason why his camera showed him nothing. And
if Ellen reads it? Then my wife will know far more than was
revealed to her by some blood pooled heavily in the toilet
bowl's incongruously scented water. Yet it is because of
Louisa, and her unwitting effect on me, that my ailment and
this book have come into being; and by now, if indeed this
is a book (in the surgeon's hands, in yours, in God knows
who else's), then all must have been revealed, and whatever
is to follow from this moment must already have followed.

Rousseau also says, incidentally, in connection with his
first lover, a woman thirteen years his senior whom he called
his *maman*, that once, while dining together, he told her he
noticed a hair in the food on her plate; whereupon she spat
out the piece she was chewing, Rousseau picked it up, and
put it into his own mouth. This was Rousseau's formula for
love; similarly, he would kiss the bed she had vacated, the
floor she had walked upon. It was a condition he was never
to feel for his mistress Thérèse, during all the thirty-three
years they were together, and during which Rousseau says
he had their five children sent, one by one as soon as they
were born, to the Foundling Hospital to be adopted. Love,
for Rousseau, was proved and demonstrated, indeed, consisted solely, in the urge to kiss dirt, to put a woman's
chewed food into his own mouth.

And I know this urge; I think of Rousseau's monstrous
anecdote in connection with one concerning Louisa. Our
tutorials having become private meetings between the two

of us in my office, I noticed one day, as soon as she entered the room, that she was having her period; the tang was heavy, cloying, unmistakable. This smell, as obvious as a new hat, amounted, for me, almost to a sense of physical contact between us; for I had never yet so much as brushed my foot against hers, and this after months of infatuation. I later arranged to see Louisa several times in succession, during the fourth week following this incident, and was able to establish that her cycle lasted twenty-nine days. I could then plan our subsequent meetings – citing fictitious lectures or engagements when re-scheduling our usual Thursdays – so as to repeat the pleasure indefinitely.

But still I rush ahead of myself. The surgeon who so happily assumed I would want to include his work on me in my own future book – even though my only published volume to date is an academic study concerning Rousseau's years in Montmorency, and his subsequent madness – can in any case draw some satisfaction or amusement from the fact that my passing of blood may have amounted to a kind of hysterical menstruation; though perhaps one should more accurately call the phenomenon 'testistical'. As for those other readers who might now exist to judge me, I can only assume they will find me just as loathsome in my frankness as Jean-Jacques in his.

'Can I go?' I asked, having put my trousers back on. While I had been submitting myself to the surgeon's intrusions, I admit, it was Louisa I had been thinking of. The nurse's hand on my arm had become my student's, and in this way I had achieved some kind of calmness during the procedure, while also being reminded of the despair, the unresolvable loneliness, which had brought me here. The friendly surgeon – who now knew my colon better than I can recognize my own back garden – had been telling me why further tests might be needed, whose subsequent failure to clarify the problem was obvious to me even then. Eventually surgery would be the only thing they still hadn't tried on me.

When I went home, Ellen hugged me and said I shouldn't worry so much about it. But I would do little else, and I was to find myself thinking a great deal about that character called 'I' who is not always oneself. My entire life, it seemed, was being focused narrowly through a lens fashioned out of sickness, morbidity, infatuation. Even my most beloved authors revealed themselves to me only by way of their ailments. Montaigne: gallstones; Rousseau: urinary disorders; Flaubert: epilepsy; Proust: asthma. And of course Pascal, dead from cancer at thirty-nine; his end, in those days before effective analgesics, a torture we can barely contemplate.

Physicians are well acquainted with the self-consciousness of their patient's confessions, in which the first words may have been rehearsed carefully beforehand. A pain in the lower abdomen, perhaps, or a difficulty in breathing, neatly formulated after a swift 'good morning'. Physicians are used to this, just as experienced readers are used to the self-consciousness which marks the beginning of a book, when first words are brought out from the storehouse where they have been treasured and perfected by their anxious author. But then the patient forgets himself; truth begins to reveal itself, and everything comes out in a great tumble of relief.

All right then, says the physician; a new one now, the previous fellow having retired to the bowling lawn and Rotary Club. He's got all my records on his computer, but still wants to hear my version of events, if only to save him the bother of checking. All right, he says, but perhaps we'd better go right back to the beginning. When exactly did the problem originally appear? And if this physician were to be my reader, and if I were to be completely honest about it, I would of course have to start by recalling the circumstances under which I first saw Louisa.

I was to give some lectures on Proust as part of the first year twentieth century module. I didn't usually cover this, and I did it more or less as a favour to Jill Brandon, who was going on sabbatical. Jill is one of that breed whose practice it is to take a single, rather modish contemporary writer whom they then use as a kind of road map to the whole of human understanding; though Jill, having proved herself not to be a terribly good navigator, had in this way ended up on more than one occasion doing the intellectual equivalent of a three-point turn in a cul-de-sac in Kirkcaldy. For Jill, Proust must be seen principally as a gay writer; everything else is secondary, though his half-Jewishness and ill health do come high on the list. Proust's financial interest in a male brothel, to which he donated a large amount of the furniture he inherited from his mother, was then of more relevance to her form of literary analysis than, say, his similarities with Montaigne, the influence of Chateaubriand, or his use of the *passé simple*. I couldn't promise to follow Jill's exemplary method, but told her I'd do the lectures.

In fact Proust, though he was my first love in literature, is a writer who, for a very long time, I had neglected. What I mean is that I knew him to the extent that I believed I need no longer think about him. Whatever thoughts I still had were like timbers of a ship, rotted with the passing of years, which had been replaced one by one with remarks and formulas bearing only a superficial resemblance to the genuine ideas they once expressed. Proust, in other words, had been superseded in my mind by that dulled imitation which represents the true state of our memories with regard to most things, and forms, incidentally, the basis of our whole educational system, which can be likened to a photocopier in which one merely makes copies of earlier copies, having left the originals on the bus a long time previously (this happened to me once, you know).

I set aside a couple of weeks in order to remind myself of the novel which represented the great passion of my adolescence, though chance had subsequently wedded me to an earlier age. It was good to have a legitimate excuse to renew an affair which Ellen easily noticed in the dreamlike expression she saw many times on my face, when I'd lose the thread of her conversation among drifting thoughts of Bergotte or Elstir still clinging to me, like marine filaments, an hour after closing the book.

Then the first lecture came, and I tried to persuade a horde of deceptively fresh-faced students why it was, that the work of a reclusive, insomniac, asthmatic Frenchman should rank among the dozen or so most significant literary creations in the whole of human history.

Proust's novel concerns a person called 'I', who, Proust wrote in an explanatory newspaper article, 'is not always myself'. This narrator describes his childhood in Combray (a non-existent town), his affair in Paris and elsewhere with Albertine (a non-existent woman), and his growing determination to become a writer. The novel ends, after a brief soirée in which various sounds and impressions have evoked involuntary memories of the past, with the narrator's resolution to begin writing a book which, probably but not certainly, is the one we have by now finished reading (like another great comic novel, *Don Quixote*, the *Recherche* is a book which is 'not always itself'). Only once in the novel is the narrator named, and then almost grudgingly, or rather despairingly, since it comes at a very low time, when he is most tortured by Albertine. Proust (if it is he who speaks at this point) momentarily decides to call 'I' by his own first name, Marcel.

The non-existent town of Combray owes much to the existing town of Illiers, now officially renamed Illiers-Combray and the madeleine-producing centre of the universe. The non-existent woman Albertine owes an almost equal amount to Alfred Agostinelli, Proust's driver and then lover, with whom Proust became obsessed to such an extent that he eventually held the poor man prisoner in his cork-lined apartment on the Boulevard Hausmann in Paris. Agostinelli, who unfortunately couldn't swim, met an untimely end not long afterwards, during a flying lesson, when he ran out of fuel over the sea, and sank with his biplane while a boat was being rowed out to him from the shore. Photographs show him to have been plump, moderately handsome, and quite unlike Albertine, whose death was caused by falling from a horse.

None of this, of course, has any bearing on the reason why Proust's novel should be among the dozen or so most significant literary creations in the whole of human history; but students enjoy copying down stuff like this.

Proust's pleasure, I told them by way of conclusion (such facts are the very genome of literary biography), was for him to go to his favoured brothel armed with a photograph of his dead *maman*, where he would invite young men to insult her image. He also enjoyed a trick with rats.

This seemed like a good parting shot. I gave them the page reference for the scene in Jupien's brothel, told them to read the death of Bergotte and the essay on Flaubert, and went to have some coffee.

Later that day, there was a knock on my office door.

Three girls had come. 'We wanted to ask you some questions,' said the boldest, and I invited them inside, asking them to make themselves as comfortable as they could. I have never been fond of overly keen students.

This boldest, who will be of such little further relevance that I won't even invent a name for her, needed clarification on some spellings and book titles; an enquiry so tedious as to be infuriating. The second boldest, equally irrelevant to what will follow, was particularly concerned to know whether a detailed knowledge of Proust's life would be required in the end-of-term exam, as she hadn't had time to copy down all my comments about Agostinelli. I told her not to worry. And this left Louisa, who for a long time said nothing, so that I wondered if she was an idiot.

When she spoke, at my prompting (I only wanted to get rid of them all), it was with apparent effort, silence being more abundant in what emerged from her than speech. Each word seemed weighted, deliberately chosen and individually considered, like those of a headline put together for an old-fashioned press, slowly, out of metal plates, while the compositor's mind is somewhere else entirely.

'What are the Categories of Kant?' she said eventually, with an embarrassed smile.

She was wearing a summer frock, white, with a pattern of blue flowers, and met my eyes only as she reached the last word of her question. This moment of the onset of my illness is as clear to me now, as much a dividing point of my life into 'before' and 'after', as a victim's recollection of a road accident.

'The Categories of Kant?' I answered, not very helpfully. Earlier, I had quoted Proust's memorable comment that Flaubert, in his use of the present participle and certain pronouns, had renewed our vision of the world almost as much as Kant with his Categories. I had brought out a remark which had lain untouched in my mind for years, like those cigars which are only for passing around but are never smoked by anyone; and yet the fact was that I didn't know very much at all about Kant, or his Categories. Not my field. So I winged it, waffled a bit about the *Critique of Pure Reason* (a title I knew from my own undergraduate days), mentioned David Hume (safer ground for me, thanks to his unfortunate connection with Rousseau), told Louisa where to look if she needed more information, and to my relief the girl seemed satisfied. Next time I mention Kant and his bloody Categories, I decided, I'll check first.

Even so, I quite liked being found out by her. I liked the fact that she'd dared to say what everyone else must have been thinking, but was afraid to ask.

Now the bold one took the lead again. 'If we have any other problems, is it all right if we come and see you?' They had their own tutors, for God's sake, and I had my own students; but what else could I say?

Each Thursday, after my lecture, and always at the same time, they would come. The bold one had all the pushiness and charm of a door-to-door Jehovah's Witness, but Louisa was welcome, and I knew that it was because of her that I began actively to encourage these visits. I thought of them as my own 'little band'.

And of course, during the lectures, I would notice this

band. The bold ones sat right at the front, nodding wisely, absently, like government ministers thinking only about their prospects of promotion. Louisa would be somewhere in the middle, to the left, and it would often take me a moment or two to find her, her head usually bowed over sheets of A4 whose inscriptions, in green ink, would come to be as precious to me as if they were illuminated by the patient embellishers of the *Très Riches Heures*. Yet whenever I glanced in her direction she would be looking elsewhere, and to catch her eye seemed an impossibility. Why I should have wanted to do this, I still didn't know, other than that her face was as compelling as the obscenity I once heard myself think, while speaking to the class about Baudelaire.

I'd never really noticed her before. She was like an early evening star whose light, though it must already have long been present, has waited patiently for an appropriate moment in which to introduce itself to the consciouness of an observer gazing in search of the flicker which suddenly disturbs the tranquillity of his thoughts. She was older than the others; I guessed this from the start. The fact was further supported by one or two comments she made during the light conversations which would bring our meetings to an end (these conversations were to become a little longer each time), and was confirmed when I checked her date of birth in the records. She was twenty-four, a mature student, and single.

Our diseases have ways of developing and perfecting their secret vocation while remaining quite independent of their unwitting hosts. As one week passed, and then another (each punctuated by the visits which became their highlight), my life continued in apparent good health, though Ellen said on several occasions that she found me even more quiet than usual. The accountancy firm for which she works was having some difficulties at this time; her job seemed sufficiently in danger for her to be checking the classifieds with more than usual interest. If the worst came to the worst, Ellen said, she might have to take something a long way off, perhaps see me only at weekends. My immediate thought, instinctive yet surprising to me, was that this might prove very convenient. I even felt a lump of excitement in my throat, which was, I suppose, the first forewarning of later complications.

That night Ellen wanted to make love, and to say that I thought of Louisa would hardly be a confession in Rousseau's sense, since there can't be a married man in all the world who has never thought of another woman while making love with his wife.

'Something's wrong,' she said. I told her I was reluctantly thinking about a lecture on Proust which I had to prepare. 'Makes a change from Ferrand and Minard,' she said, referring to my more usual scholarly obsession. 'Still. As long as there's nothing else the matter with you.'

My wife, however, a woman and an accountant, is no fool.

Already, after just three weeks of exposure, I had become manifestly afflicted by a condition as old as man, as ubiquitous as the flu, as tedious as a dose of piles, as embarrassing, and as easily treated. I would merely have to sleep with Louisa in order to cure myself. I had never been unfaithful to Ellen, certainly had never considered doing anything unethical with any of my students. But Louisa, like a new flavour of a drink you previously thought not to your taste, was different.

The following Thursday was to be the fourth and last of

my lectures; and with it, the indebtedness to me of Jill Brandon (now deconstructing discourses somewhere in Canada) would reach its completion, my favour to her would be discharged. It would also mark the end of my *entente* with Louisa. I felt like a man about to smoke his last cigarette, having finally resolved after all (while Ellen slept peacefully beside me) to lead henceforth a life of health, happiness, and total abstinence. I waited for Thursday to come, delivered my lecture without once looking at any of my 'little band', then afterwards longed for the time to arrive when they would come to my office to pay me their last visit, after which I could forget the whole episode.

The protocol of those meetings was, by now, a familiar one. Usually the session would begin with the boldest one asking me to confirm certain obscure words in her notes, which she seemed unable to believe I had actually said. 'So that was really what you meant?' she'd say incredulously. Then the second boldest would ask if she was expected to buy the Maurois or Beckett books I'd mentioned, and point out that since I hadn't put them on reserve at the library they were permanently checked out to a guy who'd last been seen three weeks ago, driving away with a dismantled hang-glider strapped to the roof of his Polo. After formalities such as these had been dealt with, I would then await Louisa's contribution, sometimes having to prompt her before the bold ones could think of another fatuous objection with which to bewilder me. Perhaps, as occasionally happened, I might have caught Louisa's eye while the other girls troubled my peace with their inane comments, and I might have seen in Louisa's look a wise and quiet agreement with my irritation, almost a smile of complicity at the corner of her lips. And then at last, her time having come, she'd lower her face in final preparation, summon up the words, and say, for instance:

'If Proust knew barely enough English to be able to order a steak in a restaurant, then how did he translate Ruskin?'

To which I'd reply that Marie Nordlinger translated *The Stones of Venice* into French, and then Proust translated it into literature; and in any case, Proust's French amounted to what he himself regarded as a translation, word by word, from some secret language written upon his own heart.

Then the second boldest one, who'd be copying this down, would say: 'Is Ruskin on reserve?', and my eyes, which would never leave Louisa's lowered brow while I brusquely nodded or shook my head in reply, would see her face gradually raising itself, her lips tensing and pursing around another question swelling inside her, about to pop forth like the jettisoning of a fertile seed-pod, and at last (if the boldest one refrained, on this occasion, from putting her oar in as well), Louisa, indicating as though it were a solemn contract the notes she'd made from my lecture, might then say:

'What exactly did you mean, when you said: "The *moi* of Proust and the *moi* of Rousseau are fundamentally similar?'

And I might begin to outline the theory, explained by me in a book to which I referred her with boyish pride, that while naive readers take Proust's novel to be his memoirs, equally naive readers take Rousseau's *Confessions* to be true in every detail. But then once more, the second boldest might disturb these waters which would, by now, be forming a spreading pool around Louisa and myself, silent and reflective, as if we were floating away side by side on a boat, bidding farewell to the girls we were leaving behind on the shore. 'Do we need to know about Rousseau?' calls out second boldest; 'He's not twentieth century, so he can't be in the exam, can he?' She regarded everything I or any other lecturer ever said to be nothing but a coded premonition of the end-of-term paper, a Delphic message whose interpretation she could leave to others, before merely copying down the results of their wise analysis.

Then it would be just Louisa and me; I would be watching her face, her pale skin, her hair which rippled from a parting slightly to the right of her scalp, created a kind of bouquet around her clear, hopeful eyes and her cheekbones, smooth and cool like the egg of a swan. I would be waiting for another question from her, one which could keep us held aloft a little longer on this liquid surface of beauty, abstraction, literature. But there would only be silence, and then the taking in of breath from bolder or boldest, loudly, in that manner of social punctuation which says it's time to go, after another polite pause has been endured. We would therefore have arrived at the meeting's landing point, and I would begin whatever I was to say with: 'Well, then'; perhaps I'd lightly slap my thighs, in that gesture of mild embarrassment which Ellen diagnosed a week or two after we first met, when she began reducing me to the sort of man she could confidently marry. I'd say, to bolder or boldest, that it looked like good weather for hockey, that a trip home to the parents in Ayr this weekend would be a very nice idea; for already I knew their leisure interests, their backgrounds, the limits of their aspirations, with a degree of detail which surprised and depressed me. But to Louisa I could say nothing, except that I hoped to see her again next week; to see them all in fact, I would quickly add. Then they would leave, and I would forget about Louisa while I went back to my work. I would go home, would be having dinner with Ellen, seeing my wife's lips form a comment about the troubles of her accountancy firm, and I would recall the little boat in which I had briefly imagined myself to be rocking with Louisa beside me; and if anyone asked me, I would say that I was merely thinking of a certain book I loved passionately in my youth.

This was the state of play after the third week. It was one of those mild, fanciful obsessions which help fertilize a life and marriage gone slightly cool, adding a little seasoning to thoughts and fantasies which amount to no more than a side salad, while you concern yourself with the more significant ingredients of your existence; the electricity bill, a floor that needs cleaning.

But then the fourth week arrived and I gave my final lecture (Proust's theory of art; Sainte-Beuve, etc.). I was waiting in my office for the last visit from the little band – a session which would break the spell and allow me to go back to Rousseau – when there was a knock on my door, I opened it, and I saw Louisa, alone.

'Oh,' I said.

'Is it a bad time?'

'No,' I said. 'In fact, you're exactly on time.'

She came in and sat down; I closed the door, noticed at the corner of her pink V-neck the black strap of her bra, and abruptly, like a lost traveller who suddenly catches distant sight of his destination, felt myself to be on the outskirts of sexual arousal. The life of abstinence still lay ahead, I assured myself, but a single touristic adventure beforehand seemed worthy at least of contemplation.

My sickness had firmly, deeply established itself; all that remained was for me to find a way of extending these meetings, so that this would not be the last. We shall see how this was achieved; and if any of these lines really are to be read by anyone – by my retired doctor between rounds of golf, by the endoscopist between other trembling bottoms, by my wife or even by Louisa, wherever she now is – then my own story must be finished, and perhaps those stern, disinterested readers of my tenderest parts, before condemning me, will also have been able to read whatever punishment it is that I am fated to receive, beyond the uncertainties of the hospital bed where I now lie writing these words, wondering whether my suffering is to prove fatal, or whether greater torments lie yet in store.

But I must remember to ask Ellen to bring more paper next time.

CHAPTER 4

I know exactly what you're thinking. You're saying to yourself: 'How on earth has that old rogue been managing without the help of Mrs B? And why has he taken so long to write back and tell me about it?' I shall explain myself fully.

The first few days were the hardest. I had no idea that dust could so rapidly deposit itself on surfaces I'd not even been aware Mrs B was wiping each time she visited! My new computer seems particularly prone to this form of pollution, and I would dearly like to consult Mrs B on the best way to keep it clean. I quickly dismissed soap and water, after an experiment which had unfortunate consequences (including another visit to my friends at Dixons, and one from my well-paid adviser at 'customer support'); however the machine is now working properly again, and continues to divert my mind from the various tragedies and misfortunes which have chosen to befall me.

The picture that provoked Mrs B's strange collapse and flight from my house remained untroubled upon my screen for two whole days, until a new friend of mine (whom I shall introduce to you shortly) showed me how to 'save' the image. But when I revisited the 'site' I discovered a new unclothed woman, doing something strenuous with a large pink object. How far I have wandered, I said to myself, in my search for Rosier's Encyclopaedia! Every day or two, I have learned, the latest in a succession of young ladies is to be found in that bedroom; all very fascinating, but not really what I had in mind when I began my search for an ancient philosophical sect.

So let me tell you how I learned to make soup. It was the second day of my solitude, and as lunch hour approached I was aware of a churning in my stomach which was part hunger (I'd been living on bread and jam), part nostalgic sorrow. Oh for one of Mrs B's finest broths! I resolved that if a man of my age could master the use of a computer, he could surely manage a pot of soup. I put on my coat, and went to the supermarket.

It took me a while to find what I was looking for. In fact I must have walked past the relevant part of the shop several times, but my attention was fixed upon the unhelpful notice-boards hanging from the ceiling which nowhere mentioned soup. Although the supermarket is the size of an average library, its indexing system has about as much logic to it as the chaotic 'World Wide Web', and the only 'search' facility was a plooky boy stacking boxes, whose shoulder I tapped.

'I'm trying to locate the soup section,' I told him.

He stared blankly at me, as if my query were particularly difficult (perhaps he was new), then asked if I was looking for 'packet soups'. I thought hard, trying to remember whether any empty containers had ever accompanied the preparation of one of Mrs B's renowned creations, but all I could recall was the evidence of some chopping and peeling. I told the lad that I was looking for the ingredients in their most raw state, perhaps bound up in one of those red string bags which I had occasionally found in the swing bin, when I was discarding some unsolicited mail which Mrs B had left for my perusal on the kitchen table. The plooky lad seemed to have a great deal of difficulty with all this; he was no better than that other boy in Dixons, and really I don't know what they teach young people in schools these days. He said I should go to Fruit and Veg, and when I asked him where that was, he said it was on the right, before Tins. Your directions, I told him, sound clear and accurate, if only I knew where Tins might be.

'Och all right, come on,' said the plooky lad. He led me to a pile of potatoes, carrots and the like, which I must have passed six or seven times.

'And will I find the meat here as well?' I asked, explaining those singular lumps of soft and fatty flesh with which Mrs B would enrich her offerings. But by now the sullen lad had already gone back to his stacks of cardboard boxes; a pastime, I reasoned, wholly commensurate with his manners and abilities.

It was all guesswork, of course; I decided to take a little bit of everything, and just hope for the best. Some of the vegetables were very strange; there was even ginger, whose gnarled roots, I now realize, provide an appropriate metaphor for Mrs B's toes, which I would see sometimes when she sat down in the armchair and eased off her slippers with a groan. Whether ginger ever featured in her 'broses' or 'skinks', I have no way of knowing (*Noctes Ambrosianae*, my main guide to the correct naming of her dishes, leaves the plant unmentioned); but it seemed appropriate that my proposed homage to Mrs B's skills should include some reminiscence of her appearance.

A kind lady, seeing that I was having some difficulty

clutching and balancing the growing number and assortment of items on my arm, went and fetched me a basket. Another, equally kind, equally unknown, asked what exactly I wanted to do with all these vegetables, and offered invaluable advice. She even took me to the section where split-peas and lentils were shelved; ingredients of whose profound significance I had hitherto been wholly unaware.

But eventually my mission was complete; now I had paid for everything, and was walking home with the great burden hanging from the ends of my arms, in several plastic bags. It occurred to me that such a weight would surely equal an awful lot of soup, even before the water was added.

As I walked back along the road, I saw a figure running towards me. It was a girl of nineteen or twenty, wearing a light blue top moistened with perspiration. Her blond ponytail swung gaily as she ran, and I also noticed that her breasts moved quite considerably as a result of her rapid motion. As she approached, I raised an arm (not easy, such was the weight suspended at its end), and stopped her. She looked slightly surprised, and couldn't in any case hear my voice at first, as she was wearing small earpieces of a sort which the young appear to find entertaining, though the only sound I could hear from them was a tinny and repetitive rhythm resembling that of a dental grinding device.

'You shouldn't run like that, my dear,' I said. 'The unnaturally exaggerated forces on your body will cause parts to sag and droop, and before you're thirty you'll already look like my good friend Mrs B.' I confess that I was thinking principally about the young girl's breasts, and my concern for these was motivated by my study of the naked lady reading a book, which had rashly made me feel as much of an expert in female anatomy as I was in the use of computers. You see how my new hobby was educating and improving me! While I chatted amiably to this young girl, I could easily imagine her lying similarly unclothed, and so it was as if she too were part of my quest for Rosier's Encyclopaedia.

By now she'd removed her earpieces. I told her that Mrs B had left me suddenly (she looked concerned), and that I was taking these vegetables home in order to try and make a broth which, I knew already, could not possibly be delicious. In fact, if it even approximated one of Mrs B's very worst, rather than her finest, then I would consider the experiment a triumph.

'Can I help you with those bags?' said the girl, who is called Catriona, and I accepted her offer with gratitude. As we walked slowly together, I learned from her that she's a student of life sciences.

'A scientist of life!' I exclaimed. 'Now that must be a fine way to pass the time.' She was carrying more bags than I, and had switched off her 'Walkman', I'm glad to say. I noticed that her breasts moved a good deal less now that she was proceeding at a sensible pace, and I was relieved about this. 'I've always wanted to meet a scientist,' I said. 'There's a question I'd like the answer to.'

'Go ahead,' she said. We were nearly home by now.

'Why aren't there any green cats or dogs?'

She seemed puzzled. 'What do you mean?'

'Well, you get green birds and insects and snakes; and you get cats that are orange and red, and even a sort of blue. But never green. I'm sure it would be a very useful colour to be, so that you could hide yourself more easily.'

Catriona stopped walking, and was looking at me with a

smile. 'I don't know,' she said. 'I really don't know the answer to that one.'

'My house is just round this corner. I can manage on my own now if you want to continue running, though I don't think it's advisable.'

But Catriona said she'd help me all the way, and when we reached my door I said that she could come inside for a cup of tea and a piece of bread and jam if she liked (I proposed to give her some money as a wee treat for helping me), and she said, 'All right then.'

Well, this is all very strange, I said to myself, as I tried to work out where the tea was, and wondered how many spoonfuls to put in the pot. Catriona was in the living room. Who would have thought, I reflected, that a flat tyre and a shower of rain, the chance discovery of a book, a curious photograph on a computer screen and a trip to the super-market should have led me to meet this interesting new friend? And however was I supposed to make the tea? She must have heard my noises of searching, fumbling and general confusion, because she came into the kitchen and said, 'Do you want some help?' I told her that I wanted not merely 'some', but rather 'all', and then I let her take over. But at least I can now report that among the many things I have learned since I became interested in computers, and was abandoned by Mrs B, is how to make tea. I'll bet that even you didn't know the bit about warming the pot first.

Catriona found the whole thing rather strange, though. 'You honestly don't know how to make a pot of tea?' she said.

'No. But then, you're a scientist, and you don't know why there aren't any green cats or dogs.'

'That's different,' she said, as she carried everything on a tray to the living room.

'Is it?' I asked, following behind.

'Yes. Making tea's a lot more important than a cat being green.'

'Not if you're a cat,' I said, and we both sat down. She poured, and asked me more about Mrs B, my life, et cetera. Since you already know absolutely everything there is to know about me, I need not even summarize my responses. Yet every so often, Catriona would interrupt with a comment such as, 'You mean you've never been on an aeroplane?'; 'You mean you've never owned a television?'; 'You mean you don't know how to make soup?' We'd already established that she was going to show me how to do this, and I confess I found her incredulity almost a little tiresome. I went to look for some biscuits, she came and found them for me (a few digestives in a tin I'd never seen before), and I said, 'Do you drive?'

'I'm taking lessons,' she said.

'Oh, I've been driving for years,' I told her triumphantly. 'But I'm apt to forget to have the tyre repaired if ever a wheel is changed.' Then I told her about how I discovered Rosier's Encyclopaedia, or rather, the book which referred to it. I even went and fetched my copy of *Epistemology and Unreason*, in order to show her the passage concerning the Xanthics. I imagined that a student of the life sciences might be intrigued by a doctrine which regarded fire as a living organism. 'Isn't it marvellous?' I said. 'To think that a book might exist somewhere which constitutes an alternative philosophy of the universe. Would you like another digestive?' And she said yes.

We were back in the living room again when I asked if

she had a boyfriend, for even I can tell she's very pretty, and she said she's recently split up with someone called Ewan or Gary or something. What a shame, I said; a little like myself parting company with Mrs B, and she nodded and smiled. She clearly had nothing better to do of an afternoon than to go running on her own, or else to sit with an old bore like me, poor thing.

'Were you ever married?' she asked, though I should have thought the answer was already obvious to her. 'Or . . . been in love?'

'Heavens no,' I said, gathering some crumbs from the bottom of the biscuit tin. I was more than ready for some soup.

'That's sad,' she said, and I found the comment very strange. There didn't seem to me to be anything at all 'sad' about my existence, which in all its many years has been disturbed only by the flight of the good Mrs B. But the same thing can look totally different to different people, and if all the events of my life were scooped up and funnelled into hers (I assume this was what was going on in her head), then they'd make her 'sad'. As for me, I was just rather hungry.

'Have you ever read Hume?' I asked.

'No,' she said.

'Well, I'm sure that being in love, no matter how wonderful and extraordinary the experience, can hardly compare with the inexhaustible pleasure of savouring and recalling that author's exemplary prose. Were you in love with Ewan?' (Or Gary, or whatever she'd just called him.) She had to think about it before shaking her head, and this imprecision made me wonder whether she'd ever really been in love either. I can say with complete certainty that I've read a particular book, and found it admirable or otherwise; I regard such experiences as being more authentic, durable and significant than something you've got to think hard about while chewing on a biscuit, before finally deciding in the negative.

She said, 'Don't you get lonely?', and I told her that Mrs B's absence was an inconvenience, but that my imagination and my library had always been ample companionship. She seemed to find this slightly less 'sad', and I suggested we make the soup.

In the kitchen, Catriona quickly dismissed the ginger; the sweet potatoes and avocado likewise were put aside for future use. She chopped everything with her nimble hands, threw the bits into hot water ('Is that all there is to it?' I asked in wonderment), but still showed no great urge to leave, even when the mixture was simmering peacefully on the stove, and there was nothing left for her to teach. She admitted she was hungry, and asked if she might stay to eat with me; and this turned out to be a good suggestion on her part, because I might otherwise have spent the whole afternoon looking for where the cutlery was kept.

It was while we were eagerly consuming our meal together that I mentioned my continuing bewilderment that Mrs B should have fled in tears after such brief exposure to my computer.

'Why did it upset her so much?' Catriona asked with her mouth half full.

I said, 'I've no idea; I suspect it might simply have been the strain to her eyes. Perhaps you can explain it, since you seem to know about a great many things that are quite beyond me.' I was thinking about tea-making, soup, personal stereos, et cetera.

Once our bowls were empty, she followed me upstairs.

'I must apologize for the slight disarray. Mrs B would have sorted it all out this morning, if only . . .'

Catriona was staring at the computer monitor, the study door having been opened for her by me, and she having entered, then momentarily glanced at the locked and redundant bookcases, next at the glowing screen. She looked at me, at the screen, at me. Just like Mrs B, in fact.

Now, you are aware that I have always taken Mrs B to be a model or exemplar of humanity in general. If ever I want to know 'what people think', I always ask Mrs B, and whatever she thinks (or says she thinks, and perhaps even thinks she thinks) is what I confidently assume to be the opinion of any other 'ordinary person' to whom I might address the same enquiry. Thus it was Mrs B's reaction to the bright and cheerfully coloured photograph, still flickering on my computer, of a book entitled *Ferrand and Minard* being read by an unclothed woman (or rather girl, for the anonymous reader was hardly older than Catriona herself, who was still staring at the image with a fish-like expression; and the nude woman's choice of reading matter, incidentally, is one which Catriona and I would subsequently share, for we would locate the volume in one of those gaudy high street 'bookshops' which have become so popular recently, as I shall explain), it was Mrs B's response, to continue, that must, I assumed, constitute the reaction which any 'right-thinking person' would display; and certainly Catriona's eyes, already a little fatigued by the apparition, were indeed twitching and flitting between the screen and my face, just as Mrs B's had. But the experience had made Mrs B's eyes water quite uncontrollably; Catriona's on the contrary remained dry, resolute, enquiring. She declared, 'This is sick.'

As I have said already, it is a matter of infinite curiosity to me, the way in which we can all see the world – the same mute, immovable world – in entirely different ways. During all the long hours I had stared at my naked woman, wondering if there was any more information I could glean from her concerning the elusive Rosier (might the colour of the wallpaper be significant? Was it the pattern on the bedspread, or the title of the book, which had caused the 'search engine' to associate this 'site' with the lost Encyclopaedia?), I had never once imagined that my anonymous unclothed companion – peaceful, thoughtful, and engrossed by the pages held before her – might in any way be unwell.

'Why do you think she's sick?' I asked, moving towards the screen, while Catriona backed correspondingly away from it.

'Not her. This. The whole thing. I'm sorry, maybe I should leave.'

'All right,' I said. 'Thank you so much for the soup.'

Catriona, her behaviour as inexplicable as Mrs B's in similar circumstances, though of a different form, remained motionless where she stood, even though she'd just announced her intention to leave. I wondered if she wanted me to go and fetch her coat, but I recalled – after giving the matter some thought during a tense second or two – that she hadn't been wearing one.

'Before you go,' I said, 'could you explain to me why Mrs B might have behaved as she did? Do you think the screen may have damaged her eyesight in some way? Perhaps I should advise her to seek medical attention; I know she had trouble with cataracts two years ago . . .'

Catriona sat down; a bold gesture, as the only chair in the room was the one of which even Mrs B would never dare to deprive me, being the seat from which I do all my work (including the writing of this very letter, while Catriona sleeps in another room; but of that I shall tell you more when the time comes). She said, 'You really don't get off on any of this, do you?' I transcribe from memory; I had no idea what her ungrammatical sentence may have meant, but the abrupt conjunction of 'off' with 'on' has imprinted her cryptic comment quite clearly on my recollection.

'I suppose not,' I said. 'But do you mind if I sit down?' – you know that standing for long periods is bad for me – and she yielded the chair to its tired owner. I said, 'If you can't explain Mrs B's reaction, then do you have any idea what connection might exist between this photograph and Rosier's Encyclopaedia?'

Catriona looked as if I'd just reminded her of something. 'Oh yes, Rosier. That's all genuine then?'

'Rosier? Of course?'

'It wasn't just a way of making me look at this?'

I had no idea what she meant.

'And you . . . you really aren't some kind of pervert?'

I considered the many ways in which *pervertere*, the 'wrong turning' of the Latin which was our mother's milk, might now be applied to my delinquent pursuit of Jean-Bernard Rosier; but I chose only to shake my head.

'All right then,' she said. 'But do you think we can get this picture off the screen?'

That was when she showed me how to 'save' it, after I explained the importance of preserving the image. The procedure is no more complicated than making soup, and a 'file' containing the mysterious reader and her bedroom was quickly deposited in some easily relocatable corner of what Catriona called my 'hard disk', leaning across the desk while she swished and clicked the mouse until the procedure was completed with a beep.

'I'm greatly indebted to you,' I said; for I was now able to resume my search for Rosier, which I would do as soon as Catriona left me. But despite all her earlier comments, she still showed no sign of going.

'Why don't we have some more tea?' she said.

The proposal wearied me, since you know that an excessive amount of fluid at my age merely implies a corresponding need to get up and exert myself in unwanted visits to the toilet. 'Why don't you just make some for yourself,' I suggested. 'I'm going to get back to my web search.' You see how casually I had assimilated the wonderful new language of Ali and Mrs Campbell, and my friend the support engineer!

Consistently illogical in her responses, Catriona, having expressed a desire for tea, now said she ought to go. 'But look,' she said (Where? I wondered, detaching my gaze from the screen). 'If your cleaner doesn't come back. If you need some help . . .'

Of course! I'd forgotten to give her that wee treat, to thank her for carrying the messages, making the soup, saving the 'file' . . . I got up, and reached into my pocket for change, bringing out the handful I'd collected in the supermarket, and plucking the pound coin which lay among a heap of coppery shingle. 'You can get yourself something with that,' I suggested, but she seemed to find the notion amusing, and pushed my hand back. I insisted; she continued to decline politely; you know how people always think they have to act when you're only giving them their due.

'Look,' she said (I was still confused whenever she said this, though I managed not to turn to face the window this time), 'if you need a cleaner or a help, I'm willing to take over. I don't know what the going rate is, but I'll settle for whatever Mrs B charged you, and I'll probably do a better job. How does that sound?'

It seemed ridiculous to accept Catriona's offer, kind though it was. Of course Mrs B would return, my life would continue as normal ... But what if Mrs B were not to return? Suddenly, the terrible thought became a possibility.

'Just until Mrs B comes back?' I said.

'Of course. Do you need me tomorrow?'

I nodded, Catriona smiled and shook my hand, and was already out the front door while I was still trying to make sense of this strange turn of events, in which I'd no sooner learned about things like 'web searches' and 'files', and how to make soup, and what women look like without any clothes, when suddenly I'd acquired a new housekeeper! Young people move so swiftly; too fast for the likes of us, eh? Catriona had reached the street by now (I saw her from the window of my study; she looked back up and waved, then began to run, though I'd advised her firmly against it); and all this had started from nothing more than an encyclopaedia of an alternative universe, which I was still no nearer to locating! I gladly relieved myself in the toilet of all that tea, then came back here and set to work, entering 'Rosier' once more in the search engine.

Now let me reproduce for you the article which, from among the thousands proposed to me, was my next discovery.

Nicolas Clairy's investigations began conventionally enough, with a study of classical verse metre. It was his contention, in common with a number of theorists, that the most perfect rhetorical utterance should be one pivoted about a central balancing point, though this 'poetic fulcrum' need not be located in the actual mid-point of the phrase. The standard example, commented upon by Boileau, is Reuillon's 'Pour Nostre-Dame', where, it is agreed, the axis is to be found in the word *coeur* in the fourth line. Clairy however, some time in the 1750s, took these familiar perceptions much further, to create his theory of 'mechanical poetry'.

Clairy himself describes the moment of insight. Listening to some lines of Clément Marot read aloud to him, Clairy realized that not only could a rhetorical fulcrum be perceived (it happened to be at the word *mon*; or more precisely at the comma which preceded it, Clairy noted in his *Journal*), but, moreover, the harmonious effect of the verse in question was completely ensured by the distribution of every word on either side of this pivotal point; for Clairy, he tells us, saw these words, suddenly, as weights arrayed on the arms of a floating balance, whose arrangement perfectly implied the equilibrium of the whole. Clairy's subsequent theorizing would confirm that one can indeed mathematically discover, within certain particularly pure forms of verse, those points of suspension about which all else is made to sway, held with the certainty of a goldsmith's scales.

He therefore set about analysing the 'distribution of weights' in the metrical patterns of verse and drama. By ascribing notional masses to syllables, adjusting for punctuation and stress, he was able to calculate the centre of gravity of any line, or more generally of a stanza, a poem, an entire tragedy. This theoretical fulcrum would provide the focus for a subsequent interpretation or understanding of the work in question; Bérénice becomes equal, for Clairy, to the second syllable of *enfance*; Britannicus is epitomized in *bois*, while Phèdre has at her heart a full stop. The proposed interpretations were never carried out, however, for they became indefinitely delayed by the unchecked ramifications of Clairy's theory.

His 'catalogue of poetic equilibria' was merely the start. Clairy believed he could easily extend his reasoning to prose, and even to ordinary speech; he soon found, however, that the simple leverages of verse could no longer be observed in general. Instead, when Clairy attached his 'rhetorical weights', for example, to a passage of Mademoiselle de Scudéry, he found that in order for the words to find a static and coherent centre of gravity, they must be construed as a device consisting of seven rods, on each of which three masses are placed (these rods being supported on a light frame to which connecting threads adhere). Clairy attempted to build this device, but its equivalence to the passage in question (the opening of the eighth volume of *Le Grand Cyrus*) was something for which his exasperated landlord was unable to show enthusiasm, and it is reported that the machine landed in the street outside, from where it was soon taken as firewood.

Nevertheless Clairy had demonstrated, in his own words, that 'every speech which may be made by the voice of man is equal to a device which can be fashioned by his hands.' Clairy thus set about discovering what 'devices' might lie hidden within anything from Corneille to the street cries of a fish-seller; though, following his unpleasant experience with his landlord, Clairy thought it best to restrict himself merely to making elaborate drawings of these machines, and their illustrations remain the greatest pleasure of his treatise, *De la poésie mécanique*.

For Clairy, any text amounted to an overall balance of forces; the internal structure of a work was a complicated system of action and reaction, load and tension. His detailed analysis of Montaigne's *De l'expérience* is the most celebrated example, in which Clairy showed its equivalence to a mechanical system having two thousand nine hundred and fifty-three components, realized as a large, six-legged table upon a smooth floor, a ladder leaning against an adjoining wall, various objects distributed with delicate precision (some books, a skull), and a somewhat idealized rug partially draped across the table's neglected surface.

Other constructions were equally revealing. An obscure legal document concerned with the transfer of land to the illegitimate son of the Marquis de Ronand becomes, in Clairy's mechanical translation, an apparatus on which a ball, launched on to a curved ramp, is free to drop through various apertures (each of these constituting a legalistic sub-clause), before eventually coming to rest in a rectangular tray, specified as being of 'elm or similar wood' on the diagram, where it is examined by an elegantly drawn lady whose expression, while betraying perplexed admiration, indicates no awareness that what she beholds is really a contract between aristocrats, its contents amounting to a few acres of poor soil, a derelict barn.

Clairy could begin with any text – of prose, verse or even ordinary conversation – and by analysing its constituent forces according to his scheme, could then provide a corresponding mechanical representation. The apparent arbitrariness of his theory was quickly condemned by those to whom Clairy hopefully showed his growing manuscript, though Clairy was able to rebut the objections raised by some, that differing enunciation, the lengthening or shortening of vowels or syllables, would amount to a redistribution of notional mass, a complete alteration of the corresponding mechanics. Clairy, of course, dealt only with ideal pronunciation, in just the same way that his mechanical systems made free use of frictionless pulleys, or light, inextensible threads.

Nevertheless, he remained unable to find a publisher willing to take on the task of producing such a complicated volume, enriched with those meticulous, precious illustrations which Clairy would carefully construct, during long nights of solitary labour recorded, somewhat painfully, in his anguished, disturbed, but intriguing *Journal*. Most of those whom he approached were simply content to take the word of Clairy's landlord, that the man was an utter lunatic.

And yet he continued, undeterred. A concerned letter from his mother is reproduced as a jumble of fishing rods in a cupboard; a children's song is a number of pins inserted along the hem of a dress. Meanwhile, Clairy continued to develop the details of his theory; though even his supporters (there were by now some three or four; how he encountered them is not clear) were doubtful that the complete text of a novel should give rise to any form of mechanical balance, for the novel was a trivial medium fit only for women, and on which, they told him, Clairy ought not even to waste his time. Nevertheless, in his most ambitious project to date, Clairy set about analysing the mechanics of the *Princesse de Clèves*. To each word and symbol he ascribed a mass, according to his system; then he set about resolving the countless forces these produced, hoping to find the means by which individual passages, and then entire chapters, could be brought into equilibrium. Yet after weeks of frustration and failure, Clairy realized that the difficulty, the impossibility of achieving his aim arose precisely because the text was a fiction, a lie. Truth, Clairy decided, is what gives balance to whatever we say; a natural harmony imposed by us as effortlessly as the elaborate grammatical rules which we follow, even when we murmur in our sleep. By constructing the mechanical apparatus of our own utterances, he conjectured, we might achieve the means of judging the testimony of accused wrongdoers; we might even discover the validity of those unvoiced comments with which we silently reassure ourselves, but which may amount only to self-deceit.

Therefore, having written a proposal for a 'universal judicial indicator of mendacity' (an unfeasible contraption whose settings would correspond to the words of the defendant or witness, the 'indication' being made by a pointer upon a circular face having *oui* inscribed at the top, *non* at the bottom), Clairy returned with renewed vigour to questions of literature, and realized that although the truth of a novel cannot be judged without reference to the reality which creates it, the work itself ought to maintain some autonomous – possibly unstable – equilibrium. Clairy's inability to solve the novel of Madame de Lafayette could now be rectified, he triumphantly reported in his *Journal*, using the concept of the 'intricate lie', a falsehood introduced as a mere pseudo-force, apparently dispensable, yet ensuring the overall resolution of the whole. In his theory, the application of this idea amounted to no more than a reversal of sign in a single term of his calculations, concerning an episode in Chapter 14. The trick worked, however; Clairy's joy, expressed in the *Journal*, is evident.

Every work of fiction, Clairy conjectured (once he'd calmed down), must contain at least a single falsehood which maintains the work's consistency. This would form Proposition 28 of the *Poésie mécanique*.

Clairy now generalized his work by introducing motion; he believed that literary works are subject to 'centrifugal' forces (the tendency to introduce new characters, sub-plots, and other information which is apt to make the whole swirling contraption fly to pieces), and counterbalancing 'centripetal' effects, whereby details converge and unite on a common centre, realized as the hub of a wheel in a number of beautiful if imponderable illustrations. Soon, his diagrams were starting to look more like manifestos for conjectural planetary systems, or pulsing networks of living arteries corresponding, for instance, to certain fashionable works by Montesquieu or Rousseau. But by now, even his three or four followers had abandoned him, and those who knew of him at this time later reported that Clairy, if he was to be seen at all outside his lodgings, would generally be accompanied only by a black dog of medium size and sorrowful temperament, which had formerly frequented the shop of a nearby butcher. This is believed to be the animal which destroyed the latter portion of Clairy's manuscript, whose contents are known only from the tantalizing comments in his *Journal*.

Clairy could turn any text into a mechanical device; but what if he were to reverse the process? Pondering a broom left leaning against a wall, he wondered what coded message such a system might imply. A swift calculation was enough to satisfy him that it represented a poorly phrased sentence describing the speaker's gift of a ring to his beloved; however there was considerable arbitrariness in the masses which Clairy had estimated, a large possibility of error. He therefore analysed the broom more carefully, counted and weighed its every bristle, leaned it against the wall once more and measured its exact angle of inclination. With the more refined data he acquired, Clairy was able to establish that the ring was an inheritance, the beloved somewhat cold, the poor phrasing due to anguish. Everything, it seemed, might hold a communication such as this; and the search for these messages, the attempt to retranslate the world back into the text of which it constituted no more than a beautiful yet fundamentally misleading illustration, was to be Clairy's final obsession, witnessed only by the dog whose tooth-marks punctuate even the *Journal*; and recorded in entries of increasing frenzy, as the writer's surroundings – the dwelling, street and city which had formerly been no more than an unconsidered backdrop to his researches – suddenly took on the form of an expanding, infinitely unfolding script, addressed to its only reader:

'*He repeats the request. The sun intercepts drifting memories.* (Stairwell).'

Or, somewhat later:

'*I shall be arriving a little after twelve o'clock and hope the cheese is ripe.* (Upturned cart).'

And then at last:

'*Planets – stars – divine unending motion. Fire, fire! Word of God.* (Water pump).'

The end of his life is as obscure as the conclusion of his *Journal* (though there is no evidence that the dog was involved in the former as well as the latter), and the posthumous publication of Clairy's treatise was delayed by years of indifference. Parts appeared in the periodical, *Observations sur la physique, sur l'histoire naturelle et sur les arts*, but the complete text (including the diagrams, now magnificently engraved) did not come out until 1779, with an explanatory introduction by Jean-Bernard Rosier which gives us the only information we now have on the man he calls 'the Newton of Poetry', concluding his account by noting that resistance to the international acceptance of Clairy's theory arises only from the objections of those who, on seeing the orbits of the planets decoded as the poetry they must truly constitute, would have to concede that God does after all speak the language of Racine.

So you see, I had found Jean-Bernard again, still active some twenty years after his first appearance, and I was very pleased about it, I can tell you. But now I was ready for a rest. The following day's events, and everything else until the very moment in which I now write these words while Catriona sleeps peacefully downstairs, I shall 'save' for another letter. When she wakes up, I'll get her to post this one, and you'll just have to wait a wee while before I start the next.

CHAPTER 5

Ferrand and Minard had walked for hours, and this in itself would have been hard enough, especially for the shorter, plumper Minard, without the additional handicap of the heavy canvas bundle containing everything they now owned, including the strange documents which had already brought about a young girl's murder and the friends' flight from Paris. It was twilight now, the birds sang peacefully in the trees and the smoke and dirt of the city was far behind them, but Minard still kept repeating to himself every few minutes the sad invocation, 'My poor Jacqueline!', often accompanied by tears, which he'd been saying ever since they started, and which had been as much of an irritation to Ferrand as the flies, a sore toe, and the heavy burden of their luggage.

'I told you we should have packed it in two pieces,' said Ferrand, looking over his shoulder towards his melancholy companion, who was dragging the bundle behind him. They had tried carrying it between them, but their differing heights meant that Ferrand's paces were longer, so that unless he walked unnaturally slowly, and Minard accelerated accordingly, they were apt to go round in circles. They therefore alternated the load, and this had been the cause of some disagreement between them; for how was each man to judge the duration of his turn? Minard had suggested using songs in order to measure the time, Ferrand had agreed this might lift their spirits, but a strange phenomenon quickly revealed itself; namely, that one is apt to sing quicker while carrying a heavy weight. And Minard kept bursting into tears anyway, so that he repeatedly had to try and gauge how many lines and verses he was losing to sobs of complaint about his poor Jacqueline, whose lifeless form, white face and blue lips, haunted his every step.

Ferrand preferred not to think about it. 'You must forget her,' he said. 'You must forget everything.' Since Minard had managed to fail so many exams in his life, forgetting ought to be the one thing in which he was a true expert. 'This is a new beginning for us. We shall even have to change our names.'

'That may be, but I'd rather just deal with one problem at a time if you don't mind,' said Minard, who now had the bundle held in front of him, and was waddling like a duck. Ferrand relieved him of the load, and they continued for a while in silence.

Darkness would soon be falling, and they had long been among just the kind of forested country they sought. Minard believed they must be near Montmorency, where Jacqueline's parents lived, but Ferrand wanted to remain in the thickest, loneliest piece of woodland, where the two of them would be safely beyond human reach.

'I'm not sure that I really want to be beyond human reach,' observed Minard. 'Not if it puts us within non-human reach.' Insects were chirping, and occasionally an unidentifiable howl or screech would remind Minard how little time he'd given to the study of natural history. 'Don't you think there might be bandits living in these parts?'

'Nonsense,' said Ferrand. The two of them decided to take a rest, and Ferrand sat on the bundle while Minard tried to inspect, by the fading light, a small hillock which he thought it safe to sit on, as long as it didn't contain ants, rats or snakes. He perched nervously on it, periodically alternating his ample weight between left and right buttock, with the idea that if one side were bitten then at least the other would be spared, and he could escape the ant, rat or snake which attacked him by hopping furiously away. 'I don't think we'd better walk any further. Why don't we find a place to camp?'

He meant they should decide which piece of bare ground to lie down upon, and there was plenty of choice. Ferrand got up and paced around, as if it made any difference where exactly they were to spend their night of discomfort.

'Might there be wolves here?' asked Minard, looking into the blackness that was already taking hold of the densest parts of the surrounding forest.

'I don't think so,' said Ferrand, kicking a stone.

'You mean you aren't sure?' Minard's concerns shifted from his buttocks to his throat, which he imagined forming a light snack for a passing monster.

Ferrand said, 'Perhaps a wolf hasn't been seen in these parts for two hundred years, but that doesn't mean there are none at all. You can never prove a negative.'

'Whereas our chewed bodies would provide evidence of a positive kind . . .'

'Don't worry, Minard, they rarely eat people, as you should know.'

'What about the little girl in the story?'

'Which story?'

'You know, the one about the child who is told to take

bread and milk to her grandmother, and as she's walking through the forest a wolf asks her where she's going, and she says, "To Grandmother's house," and the wolf says, "Which path do you take; the path of the pins, or the path of the needles?"'

'Ah yes,' said Ferrand, 'my mother used to tell me that one. And she says she's taking the path of the pins.'

'No, the needles surely.'

'I'm sure it's the pins.'

'Sir, I'm sure you're mistaken.'

Ferrand didn't want to get into an argument here in the middle of the woods, and since they had already agreed that you can never really be certain of anything, he was happy to concede the point. 'I believe I may have been told a variant of the story.' But now Minard was sobbing. 'What's wrong? Don't cry, man, you can have your tale exactly as you want it.'

'My poor Jacqueline,' Minard moaned, wiping his tears. 'And all for the sake of a few pins we never should have borrowed.'

Ferrand sat down next to Minard, took him in his arms and spoke to him in the softest, gentlest voice he could manage. 'Yes, Minard, I remember it now. The girl said she was taking the path of . . . said she was taking one of the paths, and so the wolf took the other.'

'That's right,' Minard sighed, burying his face in Ferrand's breast.

'And when the wolf arrived at Grandmother's house he killed her, poured her blood into a bottle, sliced her flesh on to a plate, put on her nightdress and got into bed.'

Minard suddenly stood up.

'What's wrong?'

'I heard something.'

'Probably a mouse,' said Ferrand.

'Or a wolf?'

The two listened, and from some way off among the trees came a crackling sound of movement.

'It's a deer,' Ferrand said calmly. 'Now, the little girl arrived at the house, where the wolf told her to take off her clothes . . .'

'Quiet,' Minard hissed. 'It's coming this way!'

The two men crouched down in silence, trying to see the origin of the heavy crunching which became louder as it slowly approached.

'By God, it's a bear!' said Minard, putting his hand over his own mouth to try and stop himself crying out.

'No, it's a man.' Ferrand could see him walking, not far from them now. He whispered to his friend, 'Minard, remember that if he finds us, we are to say nothing of who we are or why we're here. We should decide now what our story is to be.'

Minard was too frightened to give the matter much thought. 'What do you mean, our story? Is this not our story?'

'Think of a name to use.' The moving figure stopped. He must have heard them.

'I don't know,' Minard murmured, 'Louis . . . Mazarin.'

Ferrand looked towards the standing stranger, who was turning his head as if in search, and Ferrand spoke urgently into Minard's ear. 'Think of anything you can call yourself, and think quickly!'

'How about Molière?' The poor fellow's mind was a blank, just like in all those exams he'd failed.

'Use your mother's maiden name,' Ferrand suggested, then they heard the dark figure cry out:

'Hello!'

And Minard, who had never been far from tears today, bubbled, 'I don't know it.'

'You don't know your own mother's maiden name?' Ferrand couldn't believe his ears.

The stranger began walking again. 'Hello!' he called, looking left and right. 'Anybody there?'

Ferrand was about to ask Minard how he could possibly be so ignorant of his own family history, when the figure took an unexpected veer in precisely their direction and the moment of meeting was marked by a loud scream coming simultaneously from all three men. Ferrand and Minard stood up to acknowledge the frightened peasant who stood before them.

'Thought you was that wolf that's been seen round here,' the peasant said, taking off his hat.

Now everything was all right; their pursuer was simply a rustic idiot, and Minard felt relieved to have been rescued from the forest's dangers before night could fall. 'You see, Ferrand,' he said, 'I told you there must be wolves here; though all you could say was, "Don't worry, Minard, they don't eat people." Ha!' But Ferrand's stony expression made him realize his mistake. 'Ah yes,' he said sheepishly. 'Our names.' He therefore said to the peasant, 'You notice I called my companion Ferrand, but that isn't his real name of course.'

Both Ferrand and the peasant regarded Minard in silence.

'Nor am I called Minard. I mean, it's the name by which I am called, and in that sense it's my current name, but I assure you it's not my real one.'

'Of course, sir,' said the peasant, puzzled but not in any position to disagree.

'Actually,' Minard continued, 'the names were those of our mothers, before they married.' Ferrand was shaking his head despairingly. 'Though they weren't their real names either. In fact they only truly belonged to our grandmothers, and we borrow them from time to time . . .'

'Shut up,' said Ferrand, and the peasant suggested he maybe ought to leave them to work out who exactly they were meant to be, but Minard wasn't going to be abandoned now.

'With wolves and bears around? By dawn there'll be nothing left of us!'

Ferrand was all for staying, but the peasant agreed these woods were no place for two gentlemen such as themselves, and if they followed him he'd be happy to give them a bed for the night. And so they followed him, Ferrand and Minard walking side by side behind their guide, who even took the bundle from them and seemed to have little difficulty with it, and Minard made conversation by telling him, 'Just forget what I said about our names. Our mission requires us to use false ones, but we hadn't quite worked them out when you met us, and I chose Ferrand and Minard only because I read them once in a book.'

Ferrand prodded him painfully in the side, and the peasant said, 'That's very fine, sirs, getting to appear in missions and books. Very fine.'

Eventually, with night now taking hold, they emerged on to a sloping meadow, and arrived at a small, low building, lit within. Opening the door, they were greeted by the sight of the peasant's wife and four children sitting silently in a single room which contained a table, a bed, and a fire with a pot boiling on it. This latter was of particular interest to Minard, who detected a promisingly pigeon-like odour.

'The king sent these two gentlemen on account of their grandmothers,' the peasant explained to his wife.

'That's nice,' she conceded, and went to stir the pot.

Ferrand's complete survey of the room having been accomplished almost before the door was closed behind him, he now asked, 'Where will we be sleeping?'

'Why, here, sir,' said the peasant, indicating the large bed.

'And where do you and your family sleep?'

'Why, here, sir,' the peasant said, indicating same.

Ferrand and Minard looked at one another, at the peasant, at the peasant's wife, and at the four children.

'Is there really a wolf out there?' asked Ferrand.

'A mighty one,' the largest child – a boy – now offered with some enthusiasm. 'He ate a horse and half a tree last week.'

'Well, I think I could eat a horse too, though I'll do without the tree,' Minard quipped, going to the fire and looking down into the great iron pot; though the bubbling sludge it contained represented a small fraction of its full capacity. The peasant's wife gazed up at him while she stirred. 'Looks delicious,' Minard consoled. 'But perhaps you shouldn't let it boil much longer, otherwise we'll have breathed the whole lot in before any can reach our tongues.'

The pot was carried to the long table where the diners took their places, the host at one end, his wife at the other, and all four children squeezed on to a bench at one side while Ferrand and Minard were offered a similar bench on the other. The children had arranged themselves in order of height, and the reason became clear when the guests realized that after their own plates were filled there wouldn't be enough food to go round. The wolf-boy had stationed himself nearest the pot, then each of the others had formed a queue in accordance with his or her physical strength, so that the second child, another boy, got a decent helping, while the two small girls at the end were left to share a dish between them.

Ferrand, moved by their plight, leaned across the table and donated part of his own portion to them, his gesture being greeted by a silence broken only when the assembled company began to sup and slurp. The meal might have passed without a single word being spoken, were it not for the fact that Minard suddenly began to weep uncontrollably.

'Forgive us,' Ferrand apologized. 'You see, my friend has suffered a recent bereavement.'

The peasant nodded sympathetically. 'Was his grandmother old?'

'Eighty-one,' Ferrand told him immediately, deciding that their only hope now was to go along with whatever story their host chose to invent.

The peasant lowered his plate after sipping from it, wiped his lip and said, 'I don't believe I know of her.' Then to his wife, 'There's been no deaths, has there?'

'She didn't reside here.' Ferrand explained, patting Minard's back as he slumped sobbing over the rough table, beneath the children's puzzled gaze.

'Ah,' said the peasant. 'But the king sent you with the news?'

Ferrand nodded wearily. 'Not quite the king, but you're on the right track.'

Then Minard, raising his face and brushing away his tears with the back of his hand, announced to the peasant, 'I wish to find the family of a nineteen-year-old seamstress from Montmorency named Jacqueline,' and he interrupted his own words with a sound far stranger than any he had made while crying, because Ferrand had kicked him very hard in the shin.

'Jacqueline?' The peasant pondered the name before licking another scrap of nourishment from his plate. 'You might mean the daughter of Cornet the woodturner, lives on the edge of the estate.'

'Yes, I believe that's the one.' Minard received another kick, and glowered at Ferrand.

'Was she a friend of your grandmother's?' the peasant asked.

'No,' Ferrand interrupted, 'just another name he read in a book.' This left the peasant sufficiently baffled for silence to return. Minard concentrated on his food, which soon became an object of concentration for everyone else, since he had begun with the largest helping and was the last to finish.

'The pigeon here is unusually mild in flavour,' he suggested, when he eventually emptied his plate.

'It wasn't pigeon,' said the wife.

Now the four children got off their bench and went outside, where a moment later giggles could be heard as they relieved themselves. Their father went next, then his wife, and when the whole family were back inside Ferrand and Minard decided it must be their turn. 'Come on,' said Ferrand, taking his friend by the arm, and they went out into a darkness made total as soon as the door was closed.

'Where are we supposed to piss?' Minard wondered. Then, 'Ferrand, stop it! You're wetting me!'

'You deserve worse,' said his friend, redirecting a flow which neither could see.

'Why do you say that?'

'You told these people who we are, and that's the very last thing on earth we wanted to reveal!'

'Calm yourself,' Minard told him, now sprinkling his own water on to unknown leaves before his feet. 'I've been thinking about it, and I've come to realize that if you want to hide your identity then using your real name is actually the very best plan.'

'Your explanation had better be good,' warned Ferrand, 'because I've got half a bladder left for you otherwise.'

'You see, whatever name you give, people will get suspicious. If I'd called you Mazarin or Molière, I'm sure the peasant would immediately have doubted it to be genuine.'

'Thus far, I believe I can agree with you.'

'So, by using our real names, we only play into people's natural mistrust; it's a double bluff, which leaves everyone convinced that whoever we are, we certainly can't be called Ferrand and Minard . . . No! Stop it!'

Ferrand relented (or simply ran out), and said crossly, 'In future, just let me do all the talking. Now let's get some sleep.'

They went back inside where the family had already retreated to bed, lying squashed together in their nightshirts so that a space was left for the two guests. The fire had been put out, and the glow of its embers revealed the bed's occupants to have taken up a pattern in which they lay in alternating directions, the head of one poor wretch confronting the feet of the next. How many bodies were packed in this way could only be deduced by a process of arithmetic; the two smallest girls were curled on blankets on the floor, and this left another four souls beside whom Ferrand and Minard were supposed to pass the night.

They stripped to their shirts, Minard giving his trousers a shake and hanging them to dry, and then climbed on to a bed which, in everything except size, proved to have the physical properties of a horse's nosebag. It was huge, but still not huge enough, and Ferrand hoped, for the sake of the peasant who lay crushed somewhere in the tangle, that his family would grow no bigger. Pondering the matter further, Ferrand also hoped that no attempt at such an increase would be made at any time during the night, since in a bed containing so many bodies, and in such unusual attitudes, it would be easy to take the wrong one by mistake.

Minard, squeezed between Ferrand and an unidentified individual who either had foul feet, or else a very strange head and even fouler breath, was lying on his right side in order to face his friend, but he was unused to resting this way, and was sure that all the blood would rush out of his heart during the night and leave him dead in the morning, since he'd heard that this can happen if you don't change position frequently enough. So he made an effort to rotate himself slightly, but found it impossible, for he was set like a fruit in jelly. Already the family appeared to be asleep; snores, an occasional belch, and the intermittent scratching of a lousy head were the only sounds, and Minard dared not say anything to his companion which might be answered with another jab, or worse. So he tried, with each breath he took, to make himself slightly larger, in the hope that he would eventually be able to create enough space to allow himself to adjust his posture and let the blood return to his heart.

The dawn found him still alive, and Ferrand lying on the floor with his head resting upon their bundle. 'Let's go,' Ferrand whispered.

Sunlight was filtering through the shutters of the small window, and through the cracks in the door, but Minard knew, with the instinct of one who never likes to get out of bed unless he absolutely has to, that the hour was far too early. Ferrand stood up, stretched himself, and repeated that they should be out of here; but Minard closed his eyes, and so Ferrand began pulling at him.

'Stop that, Ferrand!'

'Sssh!'

'What's that you say, sir?' The peasant had been woken by the noise; his voice came from the bottom of the bed, his head emerged from a grubby cluster of toes.

'We thank you for your hospitality,' Ferrand said quietly to him, 'but now we must be leaving.'

The peasant conveyed with his eyebrows the shrug which his trapped shoulders were unable to express. 'Is it the funeral today?'

'What funeral?' said Minard, and now the whole bed was coming to life, with heads and feet twisting into view all over the place. The older boy emerged gasping from beneath the blanket (Minard wondered what he'd been getting up to in there), the wife was crossing herself out of respect, and Ferrand at last pulled his friend on to the floor.

'Is your granny with the angels?' asked one of the tiny girls from under the bed, while Ferrand and Minard began to dress themselves before their sleepy but attentive audience. At least Minard's trousers were dry.

'Take a piece of bread, some milk, a few eggs,' the peasant offered, and Minard readily complied, cracking a shell into his mouth and washing it down with sour milk from the jug, and then Ferrand picked up the bundle, took Minard by the arm and led him to the door, amidst farewells and prayers for the departed.

As soon as they were outside, Minard burst into tears. 'My poor Jacqueline!'

'Not another day of this, please,' said Ferrand.

The woods provided a stream in which they could wash and shave, and a place for them to rest until they felt strong enough to search for better shelter than the peasant had provided. Then, after an hour of wandering, they caught sight of a village with a group of fine buildings at its edge.

'We shall make enquiries there,' said Ferrand. 'And promise me, Minard, that you'll keep your mouth shut this time.'

Minard nodded, his lips pursed, and managed the bundle as best he could, until they reached an imposing gateway and saw before them an edifice at once too grand and too sombre to be a house. They walked up the long curving path, with not a soul in sight until, emerging from the door of a walled garden to their right, they saw a priest, who nodded in response to their courteous bows. He approached them. 'You are most welcome to our Oratorian School of Montmorency,' he said. 'Do you seek anyone in particular, or have you come to inspect the college?'

Ferrand began to speak. 'We, er . . .'

'Inspection,' said Minard, and Ferrand scowled at him, while the priest's eyes probed the heavy canvas bundle at his feet.

'Then let us go to the chapel,' the priest suggested.

'That would be a good place to begin,' Ferrand responded, with a devoutly solemn bearing which Minard imitated to the best of his ability, as the two friends, suddenly cast in the role of inspectors, followed the priest to the end of the path, through an arched entrance and into the main courtyard, from where the small chapel was plainly visible.

'We thank you, Father,' said Ferrand, who then sharply pulled Minard, with bundle, towards the chapel door.

'Do you wish to make confession?' the priest asked, and Ferrand and Minard stared at each other before answering in unison: No.

They went inside and found the place empty. Minard gratefully deposited his luggage at the door, then went to join Ferrand who had knelt before the altar. Ferrand prayed that his life and that of his friend would be spared, and that they would work out what to do with the secret papers they carried; Minard prayed for roast duck, then for the soul of his poor Jacqueline, then for his own, and he wept bitterly.

The priest had left them, but soon afterwards they were joined by someone else. Ferrand heard coughing as this person approached and entered the chapel, but didn't turn to look, preferring instead to continue his prayers, or the appearance of prayer, while the stranger's footsteps came up behind him, drawing nearer on the smooth flagstones of the aisle. The footsteps ceased; the stranger had come to a halt, and Ferrand made himself ready to see who it was who had joined them.

He crossed himself, rose and turned, Minard did likewise, and they saw a second priest, tall and stout, and rather more distinguished in appearance than the first; a man whose mouth smiled broadly in response to his new and unknown visitors, while his eyes, cold and calculating, carefully recorded their features for subsequent analysis. Ferrand immediately felt suspicious of him.

'I am Father Bertier,' he announced smoothly, after Ferrand and Minard had bowed to him. 'I should be delighted to show you our beautiful Oratory, which is a place of scholarship, reflection, and prayer, and welcomes any who share our devotion to God's infinite wisdom.'

At this moment, Ferrand could hear the sound of running feet in the courtyard outside; many children by the sound of it, and then a voice barking: 'Single file, boys!'

Ferrand thought Bertier's name familiar, but couldn't place it. 'We are honoured, Father,' he said, glancing at Minard, who was beaming as broadly as their esteemed companion. The boys were coming into the chapel now; Father Bertier patted one or two heads as they came past to take their places, and he directed Ferrand and Minard to follow him outside, so that their tour could commence. Returning to the bright courtyard, now ringing with the sound of marching feet as more pupils made their way to the chapel, the visitors were escorted towards a doorway which brought them on to a long corridor, well lit by large, evenly spaced windows on either side.

'Might I ask,' Father Bertier enquired, as he indicated the entrance to the library which lay ahead of them, 'what form of business it is, that brings you to Montmorency?'

Before Minard could speak, Ferrand pushed himself ahead of his friend and said, 'We are here for the summer.'

'Of course,' Father Bertier nodded, continuing to walk. 'The area is a delightful and popular one. Under the benevolent care of Monseigneur le Duc de Luxembourg, the estate has been able to relive some of the splendour and glory it enjoyed in former centuries.' He paused at one of the windows, open because of the fine weather.

'Behold,' said Bertier grandly, gesturing towards a far-off building obscured by trees. 'There is part of the château of Enghien, where Monseigneur le Duc resides during his twice-yearly visits. He is there at the moment; a fine man, with a most accomplished wife.' The Father gave a little cough; he clearly enjoyed associating himself with such noble figures.

'Only last week,' he continued nonchalantly, 'I had lunch there with Jean-Jacques Rousseau.'

Minard gave a start. 'Rousseau? The author of *Julie*?'

Father Bertier began casually examining one of his finger-nails. 'Jean-Jacques is a dear friend of mine. In fact, I might say that I am one of his principal companions here in Montmorency.'

'How truly fascinating,' said Minard. Rousseau's novel *Julie, or The New Héloise* had been published some months earlier to sensational effect. The first editions had sold out so quickly that booksellers had resorted to lending out the individual volumes by the hour; Minard had been quoted twenty-four sous for sixty minutes, but reckoned that a complete reading would leave him starving for a week, and so he had yet to see the most fashionable novel of the day. 'And you, Father, are personally acquainted with this man of genius?' Minard turned to Ferrand. 'Well, aren't you impressed?'

Ferrand could see that if Minard allowed his awed emotions to get the better of him then he risked compromising them both again. 'Shall we go now to the library?' Ferrand suggested, and Father Bertier complied, leading the way with a broad sweep of his arm, though Ferrand couldn't help feeling that the priest resented being cut short just as he was about to speak of his famous friend.

'Our Oratory provides the very best education,' Father Bertier said as they walked. 'The boys are instructed in everything necessary to prepare them for the life ahead. As you are aware, the Confraternity of Oratorians is renowned for the breadth and liberality of its curriculum; physical education and dancing are particular strengths here.'

'What subject do you teach, Father?' Ferrand asked, as the heavy door of the library was opened for them.

'Physics,' said Father Bertier. 'The boys receive a thorough grounding in Aristotle; the modern theories of Bacon and Descartes are not left untouched.' He paused to allow his companions to appreciate the splendour of the library, whose several bookcases laboured beneath volumes of impressive size, age, and deterioration.

'This is most marvellous,' said Minard, whispering, since one or two priests were either working or else asleep at their desks. Father Bertier felt no need, however, to modulate the confident resonance of his voice. He led them towards one of the bookcases. 'See, for instance,' he boomed: 'here is Bacon.' The priest drew out the book he wanted, opened it at a page he appeared to know well, and indicated to his guests the classification of knowledge which Bacon proposed. 'Look; the three faculties: Memory, Reason, and Imagination. Each then branches into a whole tree of knowledge; and does it perhaps strike you as being familiar?' Minard nodded swiftly, politely, and entirely ignorantly; Ferrand rubbed his chin. 'It's the "tree" of Diderot and D'Alembert's Encyclopaedia,' said Bertier. 'They simply plagiarized Bacon. We told them as much in the *Mémoires de Trévoux*.'

Now Ferrand remembered Bertier's name; it had come up in one or two ecclesiastical tracts he had copied. The journal Bertier mentioned was devoted to the Jesuit cause; yet here was this priest of literary ambition now employed by an institution which could hardly be considered sympathetic to the educational methods of the Society of Jesus. It seemed that the cunning Father Bertier belonged to a breed which enjoys success in every walk of life; he was a person who knew how to be all things to all men.

'Oh yes,' Bertier continued proudly, 'We had little

difficulty showing how much the editors of the *Encyclopédie* merely copied from earlier sources. Their volumes of plates remain to be published, but I can already tell you that these will be as second-hand as the rest.' The priest appeared to be well informed about the activities of authors with whom he could not be on particularly friendly terms.

Minard, meanwhile, was still pondering Bertier's connection with Montmorency's famous guest. 'Is it not the case,' he said, 'that Rousseau has also contributed to the *Encyclopédie*?'

'Certainly,' Father Bertier replied, leading them now towards a second and more modest door at the far end of the room. 'His genius as an opera composer entitled him to furnish every article pertaining to music. But Jean-Jacques has suffered grievously at the hands of those he loved and called his friends. Both Diderot and D'Alembert wounded him deeply; he has endured many hardships since settling here in Montmorency.'

'You clearly know Monsieur Rousseau intimately,' said Minard, following at the priest's heels like a puppy. 'I should dearly love to learn more about him.'

'And I should be delighted to tell you everything you wish to hear,' Father Bertier replied, renewing the smile which never occupied more than the lower half of his face, and could be controlled, it seemed, with the swiftness and ease of a writing desk's secret drawer. 'I do hope you will be able to dine with me.'

Minard had already responded heartily in the affirmative before Ferrand could have time to consider whether this was a good idea; and the shorter man followed his nod with, 'Monsieur Ferrand and I are indeed honoured to make your acquaintance.'

'You are too kind,' said Bertier, while Ferrand, his mouth going dry as his identity was once more revealed, quietly saw their hopes sink even lower. 'And your name, monsieur?'

Minard, now that he had to supply it, seemed to realize what he'd done, yet again. 'Er . . . Minard. But it's not my real name, you understand.'

'I see,' Father Bertier responded, his expression remaining quite unperturbed, while Ferrand hoped the Lord would strike them dead now and get the whole thing over with. 'Why don't we go to my own rooms, where we may put ourselves more at ease?'

They followed him out, along a corridor rather less impressive than the last, then upstairs, arriving eventually at the Father's suite. The three sat down together, and Father Bertier, directing his words to Minard, though he allowed his eyes to seek out every direction while he spoke, said, 'Is there any part of our Oratory which it would particularly please you to inspect?'

Minard shrugged, and looked at Ferrand. 'A general tour will suffice,' the latter suggested.

'I see.' Father Bertier flicked a speck of dust from his lap, then closed his hands together, almost as if in prayer. 'You act, I take it, on behalf of someone who considers sending his son here for education?'

'Oh no,' said Minard, immediately closing off an option which Ferrand had regarded as possibly their last hope.

Father Bertier nodded silently. 'Interest in our institution comes from a number of quarters. The Jesuit schools, it is widely rumoured, may not be around for much longer.' He paused, as if waiting for the others to speak, though they hadn't a clue what he was on about. Bertier stood up, began to pace slowly, and raised his fingertips to his lips while he considered his next attempt to understand the possibly sinister reason for the presence of these mysterious visitors, who had been announced to him by Father Roche, the priest who had summoned him to the chapel, as 'two inspectors with a big bag'. 'Naturally,' he continued, 'we welcome Jesuits here.' He paused again. 'I may indeed claim to be one myself.' Then another pause, as Bertier found himself standing over Minard, looking down at him. Minard was glancing towards Ferrand. 'I take it, then,' said the priest, 'that we are all brothers in the Society of Jesus?'

Minard saw Ferrand give a swift shake of the head. 'No, Father,' Minard told him. 'No, not Jesuits. We're Jansenists, as a matter of fact,' and Ferrand's heart, if such a thing were still possible, sank even deeper.

'Jansenists?' said Father Bertier contemplatively, resuming his slow pacing while he pondered the implications of this latest piece of information. 'How very, very interesting. We do of course embrace the Jansenist cause here, just as fully as any other which is just and proper. And we appreciate the fine work which members of your congregation contribute to the Parlement . . .' Bertier aimed a smile at each of his companions, but Ferrand saw that it was humbler now, uncertain of its authority. Bertier, so sensitive to the respective ranks of men, had by now persuaded himself that his visitors were men of power, deserving of cautious respect. And if these visitors were representatives of the Parlement, Bertier could only conclude that their purpose was to gather information of some kind, and that they were people with whom it would be wise to curry favour.

'Do tell us about Jean-Jacques,' said Ferrand.

'Jean-Jacques?' Bertier's face became illuminated with an

expression almost of relief, and he sat down again. 'I should be delighted to tell you whatever you want to know about him. He is an author not untouched by controversy.'

Minard intervened, 'And a sublime genius.' Ferrand was not grateful for any comment with which his friend might choose to divert the conversation once again.

'A genius, yes,' said Bertier, who was trying to decide whether his influential visitors were Rousseau's persecutors, or else his supporters.

'Just tell us about him,' said Ferrand. 'I promise you,' he momentarily cast his eye on Minard, 'that we will not interrupt.'

'Very well,' Bertier said. 'Monsieur Rousseau first came to Montmorency some five or six years ago . . . '56, it must have been.' Bertier had by now become rather nervous, but his anxiety dissipated as the words streamed ever more quickly from him. 'Initially he was the guest of Madame d'Épinay, and resided at the cottage she owns not far from here, called the Hermitage.' Bertier looked first at Ferrand, then at Minard. 'However, after a year or two, Rousseau's friendship with Madame d'Épinay came under some strain, and so Rousseau then moved to a house on the Montlouis estate, and it is here that he presently lives; indeed it was here,' he continued, glancing again at Minard, 'that he completed *Julie*, the novel of which you spoke so warmly.'

Minard took this bait. 'To think that a masterpiece of literature was created among the very woods and meadows through which Monsieur Ferrand and I walked this morning!'

'Jean-Jacques receives many admiring visitors, you know,' Bertier went on, immediately responding to Minard's enthusiasm. 'Also letters from all over Europe.' Then he stopped speaking, and looked again at Ferrand, as if aware that he was digressing. 'I can show you the house if you like,' he said. 'I can even introduce you to Jean-Jacques, if that is your wish.'

'Perhaps,' said Ferrand. 'But do continue.'

'Very well. I . . . I can tell you what sort of house it is. Quite plain and simple, as befits a man who has shunned society. When Rousseau and his housekeeper Mademoiselle Thérèse first went there they both suffered terribly from the cold. And then he had to endure the further anguish of being spurned by Diderot and D'Alembert . . .' Bertier checked himself. 'Honourable men, of course. Why, I saw Monsieur D'Alembert only last night, in Paris, and he has not forgotten my generous comment in the *Mémoires de Trévoux*, that the *Encyclopédie* would be an unparalleled achievement once its initial imperfections were remedied. But the house, yes; it has been much improved. When Monseigneur le Duc first visited Rousseau there, it was feared the entire party might actually fall through the rotten floorboards! Rousseau had to receive his guests in the little garden pavilion where he had made it his habit to write, exposed to the cruelty of the elements. Seeing his plight, Monseigneur le Duc immediately and most benevolently ordered that extensive repairs and alterations be carried out, and he invited Rousseau to come and stay at his own Little Château in the grounds of Enghien until the work was finished.'

'Do tell us about this Little Château!' Minard interjected. 'It sounds quite charming.'

'Yes,' Ferrand said calmly, 'Do tell us,' aware that by gaining control of Bertier through the priest's own fears, and through Bertier's desire always to be on the same side as whoever he was with, they might win a valuable protector.

Bertier nodded. 'It is indeed a pretty and a very comfortable dwelling. I have not personally visited it,' he coughed, 'but have heard it described in great detail, and can almost see it with my own eyes, such are the reports I have heard.'

'Your power of imagination is much to be admired,' said Ferrand.

'Yes. Well, work at Rousseau's house was finished long ago, but he remains free to use the Little Château as he pleases. Whenever his grace is in residence, Jean-Jacques divides his time between Enghien and Montlouis; luncheon with the duke and duchess, supper with Thérèse. And at night, he has a choice of beds.' Bertier paused again, hoping to have won his listeners' interest.

'Do you really think we might be introduced to Jean-Jacques?' asked Minard, almost wriggling with excitement, and seeing this, Bertier grew warmer.

'I'm sure I can arrange it. I can see that you are both very interested in the man and his work.'

'Of course,' Minard agreed.

Father Bertier went on, 'I can tell, in fact, that it is Jean-Jacques, and not the Oratory, which truly concerns you here in Montmorency. Let me assure you that whatever information you require, I shall be happy to assist you in obtaining it.'

Ferrand thought it a good idea to interrupt. 'Many things concern us, Father Bertier. But before we have lunch, I should mention to you that unforeseen circumstances have left us without accommodation here.'

Father Bertier immediately offered to make arrangements for them. 'I shall see to it that you are provided with every service you require.'

'We need no servants,' Ferrand told him. 'Only a place where we might conduct our business without hindrance.'

Bertier nodded. 'I shall see to it, rest assured.' Then he stood up and clapped his hands, as if in relief after the completion of a difficult contract. 'Now let us dine, my friends.' He began to show them out.

Ferrand said, 'Would it inconvenience you if my friend and I were to take some fresh air outside for a few minutes?'

'Of course not. Let me escort you.'

'It's not necessary,' Ferrand told Bertier, and Minard looked slightly mystified. 'Merely tell us where we are to dine, and we shall join you there very shortly.'

Father Bertier, suddenly humbled again, gave them directions, then watched Ferrand and Minard disappear downstairs.

The two friends quickly made their way back to the courtyard. 'Do you propose to go without having any lunch?' Minard hissed.

'Certainly not,' said Ferrand, 'but I want you to promise that from now on you will say absolutely nothing in company, unless it is to express agreement with me. Bertier is useful, but he is not to be trusted, and I am sure he's involved in machinations of his own, none of which I wish to be a party to. He'll find us a roof we can shelter under, and then we'll have no more need of seeing him. But carry on making your stupid remarks, Minard, and you'll put a noose round both our necks.'

Minard chose to ignore this as they walked towards the chapel. 'What about Jean-Jacques?' he asked.

'I have no intention of making myself known to him.'

'What? You would pass up an opportunity to meet such a great man? Think what he could do for us!'

Ferrand said, 'Anything which draws attention to ourselves does us no good at all. You can pay your respects to the author of *Julie* some other time, once our present difficulties have been resolved.'

They then went into the chapel, which was empty now. Ferrand wanted to check that their bundle of belongings remained undisturbed, but found it had vanished altogether. 'This is all we need,' he moaned, though such was his present state of anxiety that the disappearance of the documents contained within the parcel was almost welcome.

'Let's go and have lunch,' Minard suggested. 'We can worry about this later.' The short man was never one to lose his sense of priorities.

Returning to the main building, they were greeted at the door of the refectory by Father Bertier, who escorted them to his own table in an alcove at the far end, where they were introduced to a number of his fellow priests. Ferrand was able to relax somewhat during the meal, since his hungry friend was too busy eating to make any more foolish comments. Nevertheless Ferrand noticed that Minard, between bites of food, had a sorrowful and troubled look, and he feared his friend might burst into tears again.

'Your package was removed from the chapel by some of the boys,' one priest explained. 'Don't worry; it's in a safe place.'

'I shall have it conveyed to your accommodation,' Father Bertier told Ferrand. 'After your meal, you will be taken to the cottage of Monsieur Vernon, which is vacant for the whole of the summer, and entirely at your disposal. I shall be happy to supply you with whatever domestic assistance you require.'

'That won't be necessary,' Ferrand again insisted solemnly, remembering how important it was to remain mysterious and powerful in Bertier's eyes, and aware that any servant would only be one of Bertier's spies. Then he took a sip of wine, and felt quietly satisfied with the proposed arrangement.

Long after everyone else had finished eating and most had left, Minard was still trying to fit in another morsel. Some grapes and a piece of cheese eventually defeated him. His eyes were red and tired. Ferrand knew what troubled Minard's mind; he was thinking about the girl. The company rose to leave.

'Jacques will show you to the cottage, messieurs,' Father Bertier said with a bow, as the three men paused in the corridor in order to take leave of one another. A servant was waiting near the open door, shrouded in bright sunlight. Ferrand bowed in return, then drew Minard by the arm, but Minard suddenly turned to speak.

'One more thing,' he said to Bertier. 'There's someone I'd like to see in the village. Are you acquainted with the family of Jacqueline Cornet?'

Ferrand's dismay was made even greater when he saw the momentary reaction in Bertier's eyes; a flicker of recognition which froze Ferrand's heart.

'Cornet?' Bertier said, rubbing his brow, weighing up his response. He was looking from Ferrand to Minard, and back again; that same analytical look which had first greeted them in the chapel, and Ferrand felt that whatever power he and his friend may have acquired over the priest was in danger of evaporating now, thanks to Minard. Bertier slowly began to shake his head. 'No,' he said. 'That young woman is unknown to me. I can honestly tell you that I've never heard of her.'

And then the two friends were taken to see the little house where they were to stay as guests of this man, who still rubbed his brow in thought, even while they were being led back down the long path from the Oratory.

CHAPTER 6

A memorable passage in Brillat-Savarin's strange and delightful book of philosophy, reminiscence and gastronomy, *La Physiologie du goût*, recalls the author's encounter with a man who, as punishment for a crime committed in some African state, had suffered the misfortune of having his tongue cut out. Brillat-Savarin is interested, naturally, in the effect the victim's condition has had on his ability to discriminate between foods (the sense of taste, it would seem, is left surprisingly intact; though swallowing becomes a constant ordeal), and is outraged at the continuing existence, in the early eighteen-hundreds, of this barbarous form of judicial mutilation. Brillat-Savarin might have recalled the notorious sentence passed only a few decades earlier in his own country on the nineteen-year-old Chevalier de La Barre, who had flippantly made some unwise comments deemed blasphemous and obscene. The case was tried by one of the thirteen regional Parlements, the highest judicial bodies in eighteenth-century France. These Parlements, often fanatical and regressive, exerted enormous political power in their role as public censor and guardian of morals, and despite appeals La Barre was sentenced to be deprived of his offending organ of speech, then burnt with a copy of

Voltaire's *Dictionnaire philosophique* round his neck. Some Enlightenment values prevailed, however, for the executioner only pretended to cut out the tongue, and the lad was humanely beheaded before being thrown on to the flames.

The expression of opinion in the *ancien régime* was a risky business; and writers, not surprisingly, were kept under routine surveillance. A particularly fascinating document was described to us in a lecture I attended at a conference in Prague, during the summer following the beginning of my infatuation with Louisa.

A Paris police officer was assigned to monitor the book trade, and the records he assembled amount to a census of French literary activity in the middle years of the eighteenth century. The information came from spies and informers, from casual gossip or police interrogation, and for each writer there was a file containing a description of his appearance, an account of his activities, and even (this being the most curious and intriguing aspect of the enterprise) a critical appraisal of the author's work. Rousseau, Diderot and D'Alembert were all under surveillance; so too was every hack and dilettante who might be deemed eligible for inclusion in a dossier which, at its most innocent level, could be compared with an inventory of coal mines, or a directory of medical practitioners; for such record-keeping was a mania of the age.

Should we interpret this as evidence of the repressiveness of the *ancien régime*; a sinister police state of near-fascist complexion? This is merely to cast our own perspective, without justification, on to a world of which we have no experience. What are we to make of a police official who sets great store by the 'physiognomy' of his subjects, and is moreover a surprisingly discerning literary critic? The measurement of repression is a notoriously difficult problem. We know, for instance, that the Jansenist-dominated Parlements regularly ordered books to be burnt; but we also know that publishers would obligingly use the practice as a means of off-loading surplus stock, in an eighteenth-century version of remaindering and pulping. As long as a book was published outside France, and without the author's name, it was never likely to encounter too much trouble; and even if it did, a spell in the Bastille would do its author's reputation no harm at all. Notoriety has always provided a useful crutch for literary celebrity.

Yet in trying to envisage the life of any period, we inevitably resort to crude reductionism. Anyone of my generation knows, for example, that the 'swinging sixties' was in reality something which always seemed to be happening elsewhere, to other, more fashionable people; our own adventures were done in a spirit of imitation, and we felt like perpetual latecomers. Similarly, we regard *Les Liaisons dangereuses* as a perfect expression of the cynical morality of its own era; yet La Harpe was a contemporary of Laclos, knew the world his novel purports to describe, and called it 'the story of a couple of dozen fools and strumpets'. It had as much to do with La Harpe's reality as *Easy Rider* has to do with mine.

After the lecture, when I and my fellow delegates were invited to fill our coffee cups, I noticed someone I hadn't seen in fifteen years. Sometimes when we renew an acquaintance after a long gap, the first thing that strikes us is how much older our friend looks; we forget that what we're really being shown is how much we ourselves have aged. It was Donald Macintyre; he's a professor now, and I'd heard he was working on an important study of eighteenth-century publishing. We quickly caught up on each other's news, and then, staring at me with some concern, he asked, 'Are you feeling all right?'

Our illnesses, like our years, are in many cases delivered to us by other people. My futile obsession with Louisa was, at this stage, in its fourth or fifth month; and with each passing week I was becoming more and more convinced she must by now have found some muscly spunk-filled boy to preoccupy her, so that when the autumn term arrived she would no longer make her Thursday visits. I knew I was miserable, but it was Donald, with the eye of a stranger, who could so easily diagnose something deeper, more organic, and plainly visible on my face. I told him I felt fine.

We were drinking coffee from those thick porcelain cups, favoured on some parts of the Continent, whose curved walls make it impossible to sip without leaving drips and long brown trails down the sides. Conferences are all about standing around like this. I was observing, on my friend's moving features, the deep scores of age which initially were so shocking to me and yet, after only a minute or two of conversation, seemed always to have been there. It was as if the marks of his years were hanging veils in a theatrical production, brilliantly lit only until the commencement of the action, after which they can be allowed to melt away by a trick of illumination. He had reverted, magically, to being 'the same old Donald', and I'd swear he hadn't changed a bit.

When I first glimpsed him, standing in line to fill his coffee cup, what I saw was the truth. Now the years had lifted from him like a weathering inscription, and what I was seeing was no longer the 'real' Donald, but rather my memory of him. A similar deceit, I suspect, conceals from us our own processes of decay, while we go on regarding ourselves as being children inside, or as being whatever age it was at which we ceased to know ourselves as a stranger might.

Brillat-Savarin's analysis of the human tongue could even have led that author to the same conclusion, for modern physiologists assure us that an odour or flavour can surprise, can even be perceived, for no more than two or three seconds. The initial moment of tasting is soon replaced by one in which our enjoyment is merely a product of memory or expectation rather than experience. Truth exists only in the first bite, all else is repetition.

A similar example concerns the time when Ellen wanted new curtains for the dining room. This was a number of years ago, well before Louisa, and following a long story I have no intention of relating, in which Ellen and I had ascended several tiers of medical expertise in our quest to have a child. The damage such a process can inflict is not my present subject; I wish only to consider the curtains which, in the aftermath, provided a distraction of the kind by means of which we seek to remind and convince ourselves that 'life goes on'. Ellen had suddenly become maniacally evangelistic with regard to interior decoration, and could sermonize on the subject of sanded floorboards with all the fire and passion of a Calvin or Knox.

I went to the shop with her to choose curtain material; 'swatches' she called the little ragged samples we took home and pinned on the wall next to the window. Then we sat together in the dining room, staring at the six limp strips, comparing them with the wallpaper behind, trying to imagine each enlarged and filling the window. This is the sort of thing people do, in the wake of something too disturbing or exhausting to discuss. If a child is finally declared an impossibility, then people find something else to occupy their time and worries, and the choice of the right curtain material became a minor obsession for us. We would decide on the one with the broad stripes; then, in the middle of the night, Ellen might suddenly say, 'I've been thinking. Perhaps the stripes will look too bold when it's full size.' Yes, I'd agree, as we lay together in the darkness; it's so hard to get the complete picture when all you can see is a thin band, like the view through a letter-box. How about the flowers?

For a day or two we were so convinced by the cheerful pattern in pale blue and yellow that we almost fell in love with it. Then it too became problematic, a source of nocturnal doubt and discussion; it too was subjected to that severest test, as the swatch was held first by Ellen, then by myself, in various positions in front of the curtains, in front of the uncurtained window, and at other points around the room. Even though no curtain would ever hang from the middle of the wall, or across the armchair, its influence, we agreed, would be felt nevertheless in every colour, every ornament, every detail of the dining room, like the tiniest piece of earthly matter drawn inexorably by the gravitation of a distant star. And while one of us positioned the swatch at its various stations, the bearer remaining as inconspicuous as a shadow puppeteer in a black theatre, the other would sit and watch the performance, judge the candidate material on a hypothetical mental scale, and our life without children, our full, rewarding and happy life, could continue unexamined for another hour.

This was the phenomenon I was reminded of while talking to Donald Macintyre. Standing in the shop, Ellen and I had already known which material we'd eventually choose; but we couldn't allow ourselves to acknowledge that the first impression is the truth, and all that follows is merely the excuse of memory.

'Do you have any children?' Donald now asked with casual brutality. I thought of saying three or four, but lying doesn't come easily to me; it takes too much imagination. Some people might carry a false photograph to back up such a claim, or excuse themselves in order to make a non-existent phone call. I've never dared cross the threshold into such a shameless world of invention. My deceits have always been directed only towards myself.

After a week of agony, Ellen and I alighted on the one with the big flowers, the very first pattern we'd considered; and once the new curtains were hung we sat together in the room, side by side, upright in our dining chairs with a few inches of space between, staring at the window as if at a profound foreign film whose meaning can become clear only through long and uncomfortable exposure. There would be moments of doubt, but we convinced one another we'd done the right thing, and when we went to bed we put our arms round one another, and fell silently asleep.

A few weeks later, I didn't even notice the curtains. They'd become the unregistered backdrop they were always meant to be, and only the process of choice and decision had brought them briefly into importance. Once that process was over, we could forget about them. Sometimes, in a quiet moment over dinner, I'd nod my fork towards the window and say, 'Do you remember how much trouble we took picking those?', and we'd laugh our short, familiar laugh, and wonder how it could possibly have taken so long to make a judgement which was eminently right. All along, we'd known the truth in our hearts; it had been obvious from the start, when we first saw the material we were destined to buy. We simply needed to let our minds, and the illusion of rational choice, catch up. Now we need no longer look at the curtains; they had moved from the problematic realm of Recognition into the comfortable domain of Memory.

Donald was telling me about his glorious book. He and I were students together; I originally met Ellen through him, but we'd hardly seen each other since. Only the occasional conference, the last one a decade and a half ago, we calculated. I was describing an article I'd seen recently which he might find interesting, but what held my greater attention was the looseness of skin beneath his jaw as he turned to glance at the clock on the wall. I was sure by now that he'd always looked like this, even when he was young. History itself can be reinvented just as easily, such is the eagerness with which we cast later experience on to the supposed past. The French Revolution then arises from a society combining Nazi repression with Roman decadence, the whole thing somehow triggered by Rousseau's *Contrat social*. Or else, just as fatuously, an obsession with a girl young enough to be my daughter is explained somehow by my own failure to become a father.

Ellen's other concern was the redecoration of the spare bedroom. It was always to have been the baby room; and still, she assured me, might even serve that purpose eventually, our faith in medicine having been shattered by the unequivocal verdict which that inexact science had delivered. The room bore the wallpaper we'd inherited from the elderly lady who sold us the house, and when we first moved in, every room had been a similar eyesore. Over the months, we had worked systematically through the house; but with each piece we conquered, we lost a little of our energy. The spare room, we had decided, could be postponed until Ellen became pregnant; and as time and habit took hold of us, the room's offensiveness to the eye gradually lessened until I could no longer see anything at all wrong with it. Now Ellen proposed to decorate it solely with a view to its functioning as guest room. We could always remodel it, she suggested gently, if the situation changed.

Living within the domain of Memory, where every experience is second-hand, one becomes blind to the truth of one's own house. I saw a hideous room so often that it no longer looked hideous to me. Perhaps this was also the reason why I failed to perceive the true character of the supposedly 'swinging' decade of my adolescence, just as La Harpe misjudged his own era. I saw it all too closely, too continuously, and hence saw nothing. Historians might after all be able to understand the past, by virtue of its sheer unfamiliarity, better than those who experienced it; and the moment in which we live, like the self we inhabit, is the one we are least equipped to understand. Recognition is a faculty we are forever denied with regard to our own selves; unless perhaps one can become, at least temporarily, a person called 'I' who is not necessarily oneself.

Donald and I were talking about Rousseau. I had been telling him about an article Louisa had photocopied for me which I thought might be of relevance to his book; and I realize that I should now explain, as I believe I was about to earlier when I ran out of paper, how it was that Louisa and I had found a way of continuing our meetings which had seemed threatened with extinction when she arrived alone at my office after the last of my lectures on Proust, wearing the pink V-neck sweater which somehow (I believe I wrote) denoted sexual possibility.

In the absence of the other two members of the little band, the meeting had begun with an awkward silence. But then eventually Louisa had been able to form, slowly, like an oyster moulding a pearl inside its flesh, the question concerning Proust's contemporary André Gide which she had brought as her pretext. What exactly did I mean, she asked, when I said in my lecture that Gide (who, as reader for the publishing house NRF, turned down Proust's manuscript), was essentially another Sainte-Beuve; and as she reached the end of her sentence and raised her face and her eyes to look at me, her tongue flashed briefly between her teeth like the bright, licentious opening of a flower; and all I could imagine at this dreadful moment, easily recalled while speaking with Donald Macintyre, was what it might be like to put my cock inside her mouth.

My lecture had dealt with Proust's lifelong insistence on the division between the everyday self – revealed in conversation, friendship and other superficialities of life – and the deeper self, discoverable, perhaps, in art. I had stood before my tired audience (the other two members of the little band gazing at me like the boring women they were certain to become; organizers of offices, tennis matches, marriages), and told them how Proust dramatized this theory by way of his ferocious opposition to the writings of the great nineteenth-century critic Sainte-Beuve (Proust's novel was at one stage to be called *Contre Sainte-Beuve*), whose 'method' was to know the author as a person in order to understand his work; to learn his biography and then apply this information to writing which, Proust reminds us, has been produced by someone else entirely; a 'deep' self as distinct from the 'social' as Hyde is from Jekyll, in Proust's analogy. Readers feel they can 'know' an author through his writing; Sainte-Beuve, just as fallaciously, felt he could truly 'know' an author by first asking about his family background, his education, and the course of his career.

None of what I meant to say came across particularly clearly (in this respect I'm a fairly typical specimen of my profession), but perhaps that was my real purpose; to bewilder the little band, out of malice for two and attraction towards one; and it had worked, since Louisa had come, lured like a fish towards a lantern hung above a turbid pond, alone, to a meeting which would not be our last, and she asked what exactly I meant, when I said that Gide was another Sainte-Beuve, while her knee remained no more than a couple of inches from my own, drawn to hers yet immobilized as if held within an invisible magnetic field. The answer to her question, I thought, was obvious; in which case why had she really come?

Gide knew Proust personally, and was therefore in the poorest possible position to judge Proust's work. Gide, we might now say, could never read Proust as a stranger; he could read only his memory of a young man he'd known many years earlier; and in the reductive process we apply to those we know well enough not to have to think too deeply about them, Gide could judge Proust to be worldly, idle, precious and sycophantic; a failed social climber, a professional invalid, an incurably verbose conversationalist; certainly not a writer. This was precisely the method by which Sainte-Beuve was able to dismiss Stendahl and Baudelaire; a formula as simplistic as that which predicts the Terror from the *Contrat social*; and also the reason why, when I first saw Donald Macintyre queuing to fill his coffee cup, I did not at first recognize him, since I wasn't yet able to apply to him the face I knew he ought to have. How fortunate we are, I now reflect while writing these words before the consultant's next benevolent visit to my bed, that we can read the works of others and come to know them more honestly than we can ever understand even ourselves, precisely because we will never meet them, and their works will forever seem to us as foreign, as detached from our own fate, as the shadowy world of an X-ray.

While I spoke with Louisa, however, I hardly even listened to myself, but instead observed the responses, religiously solemn, of her attending face, while I tried to discern the reactions of that deeper, sexual self among her own numerous beings, which I hoped I was addressing, even if the message were as faint as the coded distress, tapped out by a desperate telegrapher, of a sinking ship. And she said at last, lightly, irrelevantly, that there ought to be a way for students and staff to meet like this regularly and discuss things in general. Things, she said, in general. This was her only response; and yes, I immediately agreed, why don't we put a notice up, start some kind of group; so that thanks to some swiftly made plans we were suddenly able to share a degree of enthusiasm in the public space we had allowed ourselves to inhabit together; that patch of floor where two small children now talked and played while their parents, our unexpressed desires, continued their own more significant conversation in the unchanging narrow gap between our chairs.

Jill Brandon quizzed me on the announcement I put up. There was already a FrenchSoc, and a Staff–Student Association; why, then, was I inviting students to come and chat about literature and 'things in general'; and were staff invited? Of course, I said, with the nonchalance of the truly guilty, as I drove the last drawing pin into place.

Next Thursday, four people came to my office. There was a girl called Paula who was one of my tutees and possibly had a crush on me of that tedious and ubiquitous kind well known to pedagogues at any level; there was a pale and mournful youth whose name I didn't know, though I had often seen him wandering around town on his own, his hair in permanent need of washing; there was Bob Cormack, a jovial, pipe-smoking colleague whose devotion to Rabelais amounts almost to a form of social deviancy, and who'd probably come simply in order to confirm that the event would be a disaster; and there was Louisa, for whose benefit, and with whose subtle connivance, the gathering had been convened, but who sat silently during the first ten minutes, while Bob expounded on the remark 'every liar needs a good memory', which had somehow come within his tweedy reach from my own initial ice-breaker, and which he seemed proud to have unearthed recently in Quintilian.

Paula nodded, and crossed and uncrossed her legs a great deal. It occurred to me that if I gave a sufficient degree of attention to her performance, then it might make Louisa jealous; or at least, it would demonstrate to Louisa that she wasn't the only woman I found fascinating. But as we reached the punchline of Bob's speech (the use, somewhat predictably, made by Rabelais of Quintilian's observation), I looked towards Louisa, and saw that she was giving no attention either to me, or to Paula, or even to the pale silent youth who had never introduced himself and would slip out of the door at the end of this meeting as noiselessly and with as little friction against the world as a loose chipping across a frozen pond.

I decided to move things away from Rabelais; the easiest stepping-stone was the admiration of him expressed by Montaigne, which formed some common ground between pipe-smoking Bob and myself, and at least enabled me to bring the conversation into an area where Louisa might, I hoped, become more at ease. Literature at this moment served me only as a means of winning sex; all my years of scholarship felt themselves focused into the sharp pointed finger, like those decorative aids to rabbinical study, which now traversed the hallowed names of Rousseau, Chateaubriand, Balzac, and alighted for a while (though I was listening to none of it, aware only of Louisa's continuing refusal to inhabit the nest I was so elaborately trying to prepare for her) on Flaubert. Like a child invited to sing at a party of adults, I found myself reciting the well-known story of *La Tentation de Saint Antoine*.

Having completed this early work, the young Flaubert invited his friends Maxime Du Camp and Louis Bouilhet to Croisset to hear his masterpiece. The reading took four days, with two four-hour sessions on each of them, and when it was finished, Flaubert put down the last pages of the manuscript and proudly asked for his friends' opinion. After an awkward silence, Bouilhet said the work should be thrown on to the fire and never mentioned again. Flaubert's hallucinatory fantasy, in which Saint Anthony experiences monstrous visions, encounters the devil and converses with a pig, had left its admirably patient audience merely embarrassed. Flaubert pleaded, tried to defend his work, suggested changes, but to no avail. Later, the friends took a painful, silent walk together, and Bouilhet suggested, 'Gustave, why don't you try doing something with that story that's been in the papers recently, about a doctor's wife who poisoned herself?'

Gide was famously wrong about Proust; Flaubert was famously wrong about himself. While he had been reading to Bouilhet and Du Camp, Flaubert could see his work only from within, its magnificence accessible to no one but himself. His friends had to persuade him, gradually, that he had made the mistake of falling in love with his own creation, so that all its faults became objects of further love, of 'individuality' too precious to alter. We might even say Flaubert had become as blind to his monstrosity as I was to a ghastly spare room I saw no need to redecorate. And while I was telling the group this story, wondering how my words must sound to Louisa to whom they were truly addressed, I suddenly began to wonder if we are all, in effect, the writers of private dramas, our own, which we are simply too much in love with, or take too much for granted, but which, if we were to read them aloud to our friends, would be found fit only for the fire. We see our lives only from within, and perhaps, too often, we are like those insignificant sign-painters of old Hollywood films, who patiently inscribe, in reversed lettering, the name of the private detective who employs them, on the glass panel of an office door. Our scripts are read by us from the wrong side, while a world passes by outside, unnoticed.

'What happened, then?' Louisa asked at last. 'What did Flaubert do?'

He took Bouilhet's advice, and wrote about a woman who meant nothing to him, but of whom he could eventually say, '*Madame Bovary, c'est moi.*' Paula rewarded this with the smile which publicly announces recognition; the pale silent youth gave a sneer, Bob Cormack a weary laugh, as if an old joke had just toppled to the floor. Louisa fell silent again.

Nevertheless, the 'literary meetings' went exactly according to plan. Next week, it was only Louisa and the silent youth (still unnamed) who showed up. She and I knew that the removal of this single remaining obstacle would be no more than a natural process of expulsion. On the other hand, the group had been reduced to its least forthcoming members, and without Bob Cormack to assist, or Paula to interject with nods and smiles and leg-crossings, I had to do most of the work, hoping all the while that Louisa understood what I was really trying to communicate to her.

Since Louisa had already asked on a previous occasion about my research, I chose this time to speak of Rousseau, and of Ferrand and Minard; two strange characters (*les Commères* – 'the Gossips' – was Thérèse's nickname for them) whom Rousseau met in Montmorency, and with whom he would often play chess. 'You'll find them in Book Ten of the *Confessions*,' I told her; and I also brought from a shelf, with the pride of a schoolboy, my own book on the subject. I wanted to lend it to Louisa; the presence of the silent youth prevented this. He watched her take the book from me, open it and turn aside the pages like the covers of a common bed, her head bowed over words I'd written long before I'd ever known her, though at this moment it was as if the book had always existed for no one else.

'And how are the *Commères* these days?' Donald asked me; for we are almost ready to rejoin that conversation, now that my encounters with Donald and Louisa have reached a single focus in those two shadowy figures, linked so inextricably to Rousseau's flight from Montmorency, and his madness.

But first, I shall put down my pen, and prepare to answer the consultant's 'How are we today?', for I see him coming. Later I shall have more to say about Jean-Jacques; a man who, like any of us, was blind to so much within himself that is all too obvious to anyone looking with a stranger's eyes; a vantage point from which we would all perhaps yearn to be able to see ourselves, with the honest impartiality, the callousness, the sublime and merciful indifference, of the surgeon who would propose to reduce our most precious ailments to a commonplace of textbook anatomy, and solve or abandon them with a gesture of his hands, before he goes for lunch.

CHAPTER 7

Now that Catriona's out posting the wee note you'll have read several days ago, I'll tell you what happened next.

You'll remember that I'd found a 'web page' which seemed once more to confirm the existence of our friend Jean-Bernard Rosier. Such was the excitement this caused me that I went to lie down for a minute or two, but fell asleep for an hour, and woke with my mouth all claggy and horrible and my head feeling utterly hellish. I decided it must be the 'search engine' part of my brain that was now throbbing through overstimulation, rather than the 'live video link' area lying slightly to its left. If I were now to re-energize this latter zone it might, I hoped, provide a kind of distractive therapy. I therefore tottered back to my study and 'pointed my browser' at the site where I had previously found the unclothed reader of *Ferrand and Minard*.

But now someone else was there; a girl no older, who held a large object of pink plastic between her legs. I had no real idea what was going on, and decided I ought to 'save' the picture, in the way that Catriona had shown me, so that I could let her view it when she came to clean next day. She was a life scientist, after all, so she was bound to know what sort of ritual was being performed here. I suspected that the girl in the picture might be shaving, and speculated that all women do this every day, just as men maintain the smoothness of their chins; for I had only recently discovered, after all, that women likewise have a beard of their own to tend. You see how foolish and ignorant I was! And how quickly my new window on the world has been educating me! Let us give thanks once more to the good people of Dixons.

Concerning those people (Ali in particular), I now have more to say. Contemplating the frozen image of the girl shaving (or cleaning herself, or whatever she was up to with that large pink object), I began, by analogy with the maintenance she was performing on her own body, to wonder what daily ritual of cleaning or tidying I ought to apply to my own new companion, the computer. Catriona would come back tomorrow; but did I really want the girl to visit four times a week (or even five), upsetting everything until I could train her in the details and customs of the house? Surely I could do everything for myself; even the soup would not have been beyond me, if I'd simply been bolder, though I admit I would probably have made the mistake of incorporating the ginger and avocado in my first attempt. I therefore decided that I would clean the computer. I went and fetched a bucket of soapy water and a cloth, and began the job as best I could.

This was when I learned the importance of a rule soon to be repeated to me by Ali, and by the voice at customer support. 'Always switch off the computer before undertaking any maintenance.' And indeed, another lesson: 'Never use cleaning fluids of any kind.' The screen suddenly went blank, and the folly of my efforts became correspondingly apparent. I immediately telephoned my customarily supportive friend Dave, but it was a woman's voice who answered, claiming herself to be Sandra Speaking, and I received a form of 'support' which amounted to uncontrolled laughter, once I explained the situation. 'Hang on, let me write this down,' said Sandra Speaking, then suggested I try Dixons again, where they might take pity on me if I played my cards right. Well, I said to myself, after we cordially terminated our conversation, who ever would have thought that my search for the encyclopaedia of an alternative universe, prompted by a flat tyre and a shower of rain, should have educated me in the importance of keeping fluids away from computers, and of playing one's cards right at Dixons?

I therefore went straight to the shop, determined that whatever 'cards' were in my possession would indeed be well played. Ali, characteristically, showed no understanding of the problem whatsoever, nor did he even recognize me. I didn't know the correct jargon for: 'A picture of a young lady with a pink plastic object disappeared suddenly, while I was applying soap and water to the machine', so it was necessary to enlist the help once more of Mrs J. Campbell, who was able to inform me that I had voided the terms of the warranty, and was 'on my own with this one'. If ever you want a simple answer to your enquiry, be sure to go to Dixons! I bade them a cordial farewell, and decided to stop off at the library on my way home.

Margaret asked if I was well; she'd interpreted my absence as being due to the cold I must have caught in the rain the other day. I briefly told her about my first steps in computing, Mrs B's departure, and my computer's demise. I didn't give her the whole story; she's a busy woman, and a queue was forming. 'But don't worry,' I told her; 'I can do

the "web search" all on my own now.' I then took myself to
one of the PCs, as we know to call them, entered the words
'Ferrand and Minard', and was pleasantly surprised to be
returned a 'match' enabling me to identify the book which
our unclothed reader was studying. The full title is *Ferrand
and Minard: Jean-Jacques Rousseau and the Search for Lost
Time*, and the author is Dr A.B. Petrie, who, I was able to
establish, is to be found in the Department of French at our
very own university. Now this really is very interesting, I
said to myself; for who would have thought that a 'search
engine' can be so clever as to find, when prompted on the
subject of eighteenth-century literature by the word 'Rosier',
a 'live video link' showing a woman reading a book on such
a closely related subject! Modern technology really is quite
remarkable, don't you think?

'Getting on all right?' asked Margaret, leaning pearls and
perfume across my shoulder.

'Yes, splendidly,' I told her; and was about to repeat
everything I've just written for you in the last few lines, but
desisted; for Margaret is a very busy and magnificently
efficient woman; a credit to her noble profession, in fact. So
instead I merely gave her the details of Petrie's book, and
after establishing that it was not in stock she helped me fill
in a card requesting it on inter-library loan, warmly promising that I would get it within three weeks. My quest for
Rosier was nearing its end! I left the library in a mood of
elation, but then came home, and remembered that my
computer was dead.

Truly I regretted ever having lifted the bucket, filled it
with soapy water, and applied the fatal fluid to a friend
as lost to me now as the good Mrs B, who would have
done it all so much better (with a dry duster, I reasoned). I

contemplated the darkened screen for several hours, and went to bed filled with hopelessness and despair.

Catriona arrived punctually next morning. It's good to know that some young people these days are still taught the importance of always being on time.

'You see,' I was explaining to her as I showed her in, 'I thought that a bit of a scrub would do it good . . .' And Catriona said she'd have a look at my computer.

If ever you have a faulty appliance that needs mending, don't waste your time with Dixons or support engineers – no, get yourself a life scientist! Who would have thought that this slight young girl with her ponytail, her earphones and her little unsupported breasts could walk straight into my study, assess one or two damp stains on the machine and on the wall, and immediately diagnose that I'd done nothing worse than 'blow a fuse', a condition which she rectified for me there and then, simply by taking a plug from a table lamp we discovered in the bedroom, and putting it on the end of the computer chord, which she cut for the purpose as if it were no more complicated than a piece of old rope. What astonishing inventiveness, to divert electricity meant for a table lamp I never use anyway, into the computer which suddenly whirred and glowed with resurrected life, while Catriona calmly folded the penknife she'd employed as her only instrument during the entire surgical operation! She'd even managed to mend the 'search engine', which worked exactly as before; but the admirable child answered with nothing except a laugh when I reminded her our contract stipulated she receive the 'going rate', which for the equivalent services of a support engineer would have been a sum greater than Mrs B's earnings for an entire week.

Catriona's only concern now, it seemed, was to make us both a pot of tea. I'd already had my morning glass of water, the hour for tea was a long way off; but I was too much indebted to her to refuse, and so my bladder could only complain silently in advance as we went back downstairs together to the kitchen.

I mentioned that there was a question I wished to address to a life scientist, though perhaps only a fully qualified one could answer it, and it concerned the use which some women might make of a certain pink object applied between their legs. The kettle hovered in Catriona's grip. She blushed.

'Oh dear,' I said. 'This is some kind of "women's thing", isn't it?' Well, that ought to have been obvious to me already, I suppose.

She changed the subject. 'You do take milk, don't you?'

I said to her, 'Should I perhaps consult the World Wide Web for more information on these plastic devices? It's none of my business, I suppose, but I do realize that a large realm of human experience has rather passed me by, until now. I'm not sure which keyword to use, though.'

She filled the pot, to an extent that made my bladder even more fearful than it had already been. 'Maybe we should try and find that book you're looking for, *Ferrand and Minard*.'

I should have thought that even a life scientist would know that such a wish is easily satisfied by a visit to any library, where people such as dear Margaret spend their lives endlessly gratifying desires of precisely this kind. 'I've already put it on order,' I told her triumphantly. 'It'll arrive within the next three weeks.' Catriona frowned, said that three weeks is a long time (I suppose it is, at her age), and suggested I go to Waterstone's. Now I, for once, was able to put her right straight away.

'Oh no, Catriona,' I said, refusing a biscuit (it was nearly time for lunch), 'Waterstone's is a newsagent; I made the same mistake as you once, when I went there looking for a volume of Carlyle, but I quickly understood my error.'

Catriona, on the other hand, insisted that such a shop would be the very best place to look; better even than the acres of shelves of which Margaret's realm consists. Young people these days really do have some very strange notions about the world. And such was the extent to which she persisted in her strange delusion that a paper shop such as Waterstone's would stock a hardback about people in eighteenth-century France, that she even proposed some kind of wager, saying that she'd take me there herself, and we would find it together.

Clearly, it would be some time before Catriona could perfect the ways of Mrs B. Even as we spoke, I should have been seated in my study, while Catriona should be doing whatever it was which in Mrs B's case invariably left a film of moistness on every flat surface the kitchen possessed, and whose mechanics needn't trouble me; but Catriona, to the contrary, was still sipping tea, and whenever was she going to start peeling the vegetables? It was in order to instil the concept of food in her mind, however subtly, that I agreed we would both go to Waterstone's after lunch; and then I asked if I might be excused, since all that tea had gone straight through me.

Once I was back in my study I picked up the telephone in order to call the university, having decided that a conversation with Dr Petrie might spare me the need for a futile visit to Waterstone's, if I could establish there and then the connection which his book must have with Rosier's elusive Encyclopaedia.

Unfortunately, the telephone didn't appear to be working. I wondered if I'd splashed water on its 'fuse' as well as on the computer's; or else if perhaps some law of nature states that whenever one electrical appliance is repaired, another must die in the interests of cosmic balance. Whatever the cause, the damned thing simply wasn't going.

'Catriona,' I called downstairs. I could hear some noises in the kitchen, encouragingly suggestive of cleaning or cooking. 'I think we might need to make use of your penknife again.'

Catriona came up to see what I was shouting about, held the telephone to her ear, looked at the computer with the bright young eye of an expert, and said, 'Your modem's still connected.'

Only the light of subsequent experience enables me to transcribe her statement which, at the time, meant nothing to me. 'In other words, all these "web pages" come down my telephone line?' I said, once she had explained two or three times why it was that the support engineer had supplied me with something known to people of Catriona's generation as a 'socket doubler', and why it was that I hadn't received a single phone call during the last three days. 'And will it all go on my bill?' I then asked, contemplating the many hours of possible conversations, and potential reconciliations with Mrs B, which had been replaced by a stream of 'online texts' and naked women. Catriona nodded solemnly. 'Well,' I said, 'I don't think they mentioned anything about this at Dixons,' to which Catriona only smiled, while I reminded her how fine and trustworthy I still considered that institution to be, despite its lapse of judgement in employing the unhelpful Ali.

Catriona went back to work (lunch would follow shortly, she assured me), and I phoned the university, arriving via several switchboards at the Department of French, where a woman informed me rather curtly that Dr Petrie unfortunately was on sick leave. I suggested that I might try again next week, and the secretary said he wouldn't be back by then; so I tried two weeks, and she said it was still unlikely that he'd have returned. I raised my offer to the end of the month, and when this was similarly declined, put in a final bid at eight weeks, before eventually asking the secretary, who probably learned her art of exasperating uncooperativeness at the same school as Sandra Speaking, when it was that Dr Petrie was expected to be fit to return to the world of eighteenth-century studies, which must, I suggested, be sorely wounded by his protracted absence.

The secretary gave a pause so long that I almost thought I might have 'reconnected the modem' by mistake, and had found myself inadvertently listening to the downloading of a web page. Then at last she said, 'I'm afraid Dr Petrie is seriously ill. As a matter of fact, the way it's looking now, he might not be coming back.'

'How very sad,' I offered. 'May I ask what's wrong with him?'

Again, another of those long pauses, in the handling and stretching of which the secretary appeared to be an expert, perhaps through dealing with a large number of enquiries of this kind (for I know that scholars of eighteenth-century French literature are heavily in demand in certain quarters). 'I'd better not say any more about it,' she said, in a way which Catriona would diagnose, when we discussed the matter afterwards while I was washing her back with a soapy sponge (more of this later), as being indicative of the fact that the secretary would dearly have loved to have said a great deal more about it, but wasn't allowed.

'Give Dr Petrie my best wishes for a swift recovery,' I said; and then, just before hanging up, added, 'If you see him, do be so good as to ask him whether he knows anything about *L'Encyclopédie de Jean-Bernard Rosier.*'

How strange and wonderful it is, I thought to myself, guided downstairs by the attractive smell of the lunch which was ready some time later, that such contingencies as a flat tyre and a shower of rain, and of course a technological revolution analogous, I'm told, to the invention of the wheel (a device the neglect of which had precipitated the whole story in the first place) should have brought me into a new life, in which a young girl could mend my every domestic appliance with a penknife, and I could offer some comfort to a sick man who hitherto knew nothing of my existence, of the similarity of our interests, or even, perhaps, of a woman whose pleasure it is to read his book while lying naked upon a bed.

When I entered the kitchen, I received something of a shock.

'Is that spaghetti?' I exclaimed, seeing the red writhing creature which lay crouched and coiled in a saucepan. In nearly three decades, Mrs B never served me anything but soups or stews identifiable from the pages of *Noctes Ambrosianae* or the *Annals of the Cleikum Club*. Catriona merely smiled her bright smile and excused the apparition by a name which didn't belong to any part of the Italian language I've ever been acquainted with.

'How splendid,' I politely congratulated her, taking my place at the table, and feeling my stomach cry out for the beef skink or rumbledethumps it had so confidently anticipated. Catriona was distributing the meal – a fine and admirable one in its proper place, make no mistake – onto crockery, and using utensils, none of which I recognized, having known only certain bowls and a favourite spoon during all the years of Mrs B's regime. And now, before me, a steaming, savoury, and by no means unpleasant, if unexpected, mass waited, when all I wanted was a wee slurp and a slice of crusty bread to keep me on my wheels until tomorrow.

'Well?' she said, as a strand rose, snaked, and disappeared into my pursed and anguished lips. 'Is it okay?'

'Simply wonderful,' I told her. Nothing, I reminded myself, is more free than the imagination of man, and though it cannot exceed that original stock of ideas furnished by the internal and external senses, it has unlimited power of mixing, compounding, separating, and dividing these ideas, in all the varieties of fiction and vision; and it was with this wise observation of David Hume that I consoled myself, as I attempted to recast the appearance and texture of the meal, the wormlike geometry of the pasta, the macerated clots of tomato, the wee lumpy bits (these, the easiest of all), into a mental ideal, a permutation and transformation of the sense data of 'spaghetti trovatore' (for I'm sure this was what she called it) into the thick and bubbling broth of concepts which my mind and body knew, expected, and involuntarily conjured up like an amputee's phantom limb; so that in the end I could almost convince myself the concoction really did taste the same as Mrs B's usual.

In this way, lunchtime passed.

'Do you want some more?' she asked, as soon as I managed to remove the last of a portion she had considered small. I reminded her that old farts like me can get by on a lot less pasta than is required even by the slimmest and sprightliest life scientist, and my stomach gave a final cry of complaint, before Catriona declared we should get ready for our trip to Waterstone's.

I'd already mentioned to her, and you already know, that I hadn't visited the place for years, since the time I went in by mistake. When we got off the bus and arrived at the shop, I found it to be bigger than I expected, with many more books in evidence than the newspapers, magazines and sweeties I remembered, but still hardly more helpful.

Catriona, holding my arm, said, 'Do you mind if I have a quick look for something first?' She seemed to know where she was going; up some stairs, then past a few tables on which a great many books had been left lying around in a very careless and disagreeable manner, until we were confronted by a case of shelves labelled 'General Science'.

'My, these sciences come in so many varieties,' I murmured. 'First it's life science, then general science. Whatever will they think of next?'

Catriona, however, now appeared less certain of what she was after. Her head tilted as her eye moved from one book to another. Of course, the idea that you can ever find what you want simply by glancing at shelves is one which dear Margaret could quickly have told the poor Catriona to be utterly absurd, directing her instead to the trinity of 'Index by Title', 'Index by Author' and 'Index by Subject' whose small typed cards, in their deep sewing-box drawers, I've happily thumbed this many a year, whenever I've happened to be in doubt about an item I required. I decided to leave Catriona to her fruitless search, while I went to see if Waterstone's – no longer, it would seem, the newsagent I remembered it to be – now contained an index of a similar kind, where I might look up *Ferrand and Minard*.

'Good Lord, another one,' I mentioned to a young lady walking past me, as my eyes lighted on a section called 'Computer Science'. 'These sciences are proliferating quite remarkably,' was the supplementary comment I bestowed on a boy of ten or twelve (or so he appeared) who turned out to be a member of staff, and seemed about as comprehending of the words 'card index' as was Ali (his near contemporary, and in many respects perfect equivalent) when I told him, in Dixons, about my most recent problem with my computer. The boy said something about a 'user access terminal', which only shows that he should get himself a job carrying bags at the station, which is probably all he's fit for.

'And now what's this?' I enquired of the back of a strangely scented woman who obstructed my view of the next section to come to my attention, labelled 'Personal Growth'. Something to do with child-rearing, I guessed, and therefore of no possible interest to you or me; but I noticed among the titles such curiosities as *The Life Planner: A Guide to Getting in Touch With Yourself*. Now, of all the problems I have had, particularly recently, in locating a lost book, or tracking down an elusive individual (Rosier, for instance), it has never once occurred to me that I might ever have any trouble whatsoever in 'getting in touch with myself'. Am I to suppose that I might one day lose my own address or telephone number, or perhaps my memory? It would be nice to get in touch with Mrs B again, but I already spend quite enough time with myself as it is, without my having to worry about whether I might somehow break off contact. And what about this? (the extension of my arm somehow interlocking me with my strangely scented fellow browser, who reacted awkwardly) – *Lifesong: Listen to Your Inner Self.* I happily grant that my inner self is as unknown to me as the patient action (still, after all these years, and may God be thanked for it, stoically regular) of my bowels; but I have no desire or intention ever to listen to my bowels, and similarly, I can see no possible purpose in the analysis of an 'inner self' whose only role is to serve as the engine room for this tranquil and productive life of mine (I received a very complimentary letter about that article on local monuments for *The Scots Magazine*, you know), of which I hope I can expect a year or two yet before it's run its course.

'Are you trying to intimidate me?' said the strangely scented woman, retrieving something about 'Spiritual Healing' from a niche my own arm had been unwittingly sheltering, and which limb I now withdrew, deciding to continue my search for an index elsewhere.

I went downstairs, and was pleased to notice a very large section proclaiming itself 'Scottish'. 'How pleasant it will be,' I told a passing child who was probably another employee, 'to remind myself of a passage in *Human Understanding* which came back to me earlier, in connection with some spaghetti.' And yet, for all the many shelves devoted to it, I was disappointed to find that this so-called 'Scottish' collection consisted of little but a pile of novels of a sentimental or sensational kind, even Scott and Stevenson being overwhelmed by the duplicated works of people I'd never heard of. Where was Carlyle? Where, in fact, was Hume?

Yes, this place was still a newsagent after all; they'd just got rid of the sweeties on the counter. No Boswell, Barbour, Urquhart; no Hogg except the obvious. Burns was here, but of Campbell not a trace; nor yet of Thomson, as if he never lived, or else was never Scottish. 'Perhaps they've banned him on account of "Rule Britannia",' I suggested to a man in a tie.

Clearly, I would have to have a word with the proprietor, because it was becoming obvious to me that through maliciousness, or else through the simple incompetence of children who might know how to stack boxes but couldn't be trusted to put a book on the right shelf, this 'section' had been put together all wrong. What about *Sartor Resartus* or the *Annals of the Parish*? Or even *The Hound of the Baskervilles*, *The Wind in the Willows*, *Peter Pan*? Where were all their fine Scottish authors lurking, if they were not to be found here? Let me tell you, I was almost beginning to feel a wee bit cross, and you know that's something which doesn't happen to me very often.

Then I felt a tugging at my elbow. 'Found it!' Catriona was at my side, showing me a glossy object which I immediately recognized. She had located Petrie's *Ferrand and Minard*, though how she'd achieved this feat with her skewheaded mode of searching, and in the 'General Science' section moreover, I had no idea.

'But I really must have a word with these people,' I was still telling her, as she went to queue at the desk. Not feeling able to contain my protest until the moment when our turn would come to be served, I went instead on patrol, in search now not of the card index whose existence here seemed as likely as the chances of finding anything at all by Adam

Ferguson or Dugald Stewart, which would at least have passed the time more pleasantly than listening to my inner self and experiencing the hostility of a woman who smelled like a Turkish bazaar, but rather, in search of one of those teenagers whose plastic badges alone qualify them to decide the fate of Lang or Lockhart. I was upstairs by now, and puffing a bit. 'And the most ridiculous part of it is that they don't even sell newspapers any more!' I informed a gentleman who seemed somewhat startled, though contented with the biography of some celebrity or other, which remained open beneath his nose. Then before I knew it I was back in all the sciences: 'Physical Science', 'Environmental Science' and more, which, like proliferating central-European principalities, bordered on an even greater empire of 'Studies': 'Business Studies', 'Cultural Studies', 'Women's Studies'. I suspected that these obscure little kingdoms, on closer inspection, would prove to be just as disordered, useless, and anarchic as great Caledonia downstairs; and that the shelvers' ignorance must have spread itself throughout the entire shop, so that the only way to put it right would be to knock it down and start the whole thing all over again.

Perhaps I'd better just calm down.

I'd found myself on the frontier between 'Computer Science' and 'Mathematics'. The latter is about as appealing to me as dentistry, and evokes similar recollections of childhood agony; my eye was caught by the titles which lay on the more colourful side of the border. *The Internet Guide, PC Workout, CGI Scripting for Web Developers.* Now, here was something I could understand. I began to take a few books which looked as though they might help bring me nearer to Rosier, the Xanthics, and all those other wonders which only the World Wide Web could offer in a searchable database whose chaos seemed as nought compared with the mess they'd made of this shop.

I got downstairs just in time to join Catriona at the head of the queue. That she proposed to pay for *Ferrand and Minard* was little short of an outrage, I told her (I still hadn't entirely calmed down). The other book she held, something about enzymes, was my gift to her, I said, and I put both titles on the same bill as my seven computer books, which were very reasonably priced, and came to less than two hundred pounds.

'If ever you're looking for a book about the Internet,' I said to a lady as we emerged from the shop, 'then be sure to shop at Waterstone's. The shelving is impeccable.'

We went home.

Catriona had already started reading about enzymes on the bus, while I perused the introduction to *HTML for Idiots*, whose style bore little relation to any book I'd ever read before, but was strikingly similar to that of many of the web pages I had visited. I understood absolutely none of it, and comforted myself with the thought that I was not, therefore, one of the 'idiots' to whom the book was truly addressed.

When we got off near my house, I said to Catriona that I expected she had to come in and pick up her bag before going, and she looked quizzically at me, then explained that she hadn't left anything in the house. In that case, I suggested, we can say goodbye now until tomorrow (for it was already past the hour when Mrs B would have left me).

'I'm going this way too,' Catriona informed me, accompanying me as far as my door, where, still apparently unwilling to return to her own studies (what on earth do life scientists do all day, I wonder?), she proposed a cup of tea (yes, yet another), and my bladder, tired by now of complaining, merely gave a kind of shrug, as I unlocked the door and followed my thirsty young companion inside. Oh what a thing it is, still to possess the firm yet unappreciated sphincter of youth!

'I'll just sit myself down here to read,' I informed her, choosing *Dr Cool's Web Magic* as my next distraction, while I flopped heavily into my armchair, and Catriona went to busy herself in the kitchen. This second book was as impenetrable as the first, and hardly related, it seemed, to anything anyone ever told me in Dixons; to the extent that I began to wonder whether the 'Computer Science' section of the bookshop had, after all, been as much the victim of mis-shelving as the sadly degenerate muddle which went there by the name of 'Scottish'.

'But it really is a curious and extraordinary fact,' I told Catriona, when she came back some minutes later, bearing a tray heavily laden with what included, I noted to my satisfaction, some biscuits I'd never seen before, which perhaps she'd brought with her this morning, 'that all those web pages really consist of little more than a few coded instructions in angled brackets.' For by now I had been able to assimilate something, at least, from Dr Cool's somewhat breathless transatlantic prose; and such HTML tags, I then told her (for this was what I'd just learned to call them), could even account for the correctly positioned presence on my computer screen of that strange photograph of a young woman reading precisely the book which, thanks to Catriona's quick searching, I now possessed, by another of those remarkable progressions of fact and event we like to call coincidence or chance, but which, who knows, might really be determined by some other 'source code', hidden yet unalterable.

Catriona wasn't really listening. She poured the tea (the mere sound of the trickling fluid brought forth another protest from my insides, and I silently promised myself to sip little, and slowly), then she deposited herself on the other armchair with the ease of a cat. After a while, she said, 'Could I ask you a favour?' She said it between large gulps of tea (I had been playing for time, hoping that evaporation would account for at least some of the quantity I'd been presented with).

'Of course,' I said. Her request suggested something vast, costly, and difficult, and I really wondered what was on her mind.

'It's just that we've had some problems in the flat, with the boiler . . .' Another gulp, a munch of biscuit. 'We've had no hot water for two days.'

If Catriona needed someone to mend a boiler, she was asking the wrong man (as Mrs B could so quickly have made clear). Surely Catriona could deal with such things herself, with her versatile penknife?

'I was wondering,' she said, still dragging it out, but nearly there now, 'if I could have a bath. Here.' Her face was like that of a child asking to be excused from lessons.

'By all means,' I said, and before another two minutes had passed, Catriona's tea was finished, she was already asking me about towels, and I was thinking only about whether it was worth going to the kitchen myself, in order to pour the rest of my delicious but over-abundant tea down the sink. Naturally, I had no idea where towels are kept in this house, apart from the ones which Mrs B would leave hanging on the rail for my use, and I told Catriona that if she looked in a few cupboards she was sure to come up with something. After all, she could make biscuits appear from thin air, so a towel ought not to tax her ingenuity too much. Soon, I heard her footsteps lightly tripping up the stairs.

What a thing it is, to be able to run upstairs, open three cupboards and close each again with a bump while the taps begin to roar, and to fill the bath completely, having no doubt removed every item of clothing, all in the time it takes me to rise from my chair, carry my cup to the kitchen, and watch the brown fluid escape down the plug with a swirl! I'd only managed a quarter of it, but already the effects were beginning to make themselves felt.

I considered returning to the living room in order to savour more of Dr Cool's tender wisdom, but reasoned that the urinary intimations I was now receiving would only worsen, that every movement would accelerate them, and that a better strategy would be to go upstairs to my study, near to the place of which I would have urgent need just as soon as Catriona was finished. Given the speed with which she'd started the exercise, I had little doubt that by time I got upstairs she'd be nearly finished. I therefore began my ascent.

It was on the fourth or fifth step that the urgency of the situation became apparent. Perhaps it was the splashing sounds from the bathroom that gave my waterworks the wrong idea, fooling them into the belief that I was already there and proceedings could begin. You know that my condition is one which habit alone has enabled me to deal with, but the day had been an unusual one, and it was hardly surprising if all this irregular activity should have left my bladder a little confused.

I reached the top and steered myself, with slow and

dangerous steps, each made in fear of disaster, to the bathroom door, where the stillness of the water suggested that Catriona might not actually have started yet; or else, such was the speed with which she could drink tea, find books in a shop, et cetera, that she might already have finished washing herself, and now was having a lazy soak (though even if this were the case I dreaded the possible implications of that gush and tumble which would accompany her movements as she rose from the bath, leaving me, no doubt, standing in a puddle as big as hers).

We had arrived, you see, at a delicate and somewhat crucial moment. I knocked on the door.

'Catriona?'

'Yes?'

'Are you in the bath?'

'Yes.' An unwelcome trickle and splash from her direction proved it. Then, from me:

'Can I ask you a favour too?'

I was in no mood to extend negotiations in the same way she had; necessity pressed more heavily on my loins than tact. I explained the simple facts of the matter, apologized, and said that if I didn't open the door immediately then we would be left with a problem which would challenge even the resourceful Mrs B.

'All right then,' said Catriona, amidst some greater splashing.

That there is no lock on the bathroom door is a contingency which had never before seemed relevant; but I now could understand the predetermined role which this little detail was always meant to play in the 'source code' of my life. I entered, and though my gaze was fixed firmly on the toilet bowl that was my destination (its seat frustratingly lowered), I noticed that Catriona had curled and cowered herself in the bath, her arms clinging round her raised knees, her head lowered on to them, while I went about my business, whistling loudly in the manner which I believe is the socially accepted practice on such occasions; though since a similar situation never once arose, during all my regular and continent years with Mrs B, I have no way of knowing exactly.

I finished, flushed, washed my hands with customary thoroughness, and informed Catriona that she could take as long as she wanted now. But before I could leave, she said (having remained completely silent during my flutey and imperfect rendition of 'O Star of Eve'):

'Since you're here, can you do me a favour now?'

I thought our accounts were balanced, but could hardly refuse her this next round of solicitations. She asked me to sponge her back.

'Can't you just lie down in the water?' I asked. 'That's what I always do.'

'All right,' she said, still crouched in the attitude of a prehistoric burial. 'If you'd rather not.'

I told her, 'It's not that I have any objection. I can easily roll up my sleeves if you prefer not to lie down.' Do all women need their backs scrubbed, I wondered. I never found out from my conversations with Mrs B, but I could always search the World Wide Web for an answer. Pulling my cuffs clear of my wrists, I took the sponge and rubbed Catriona's back, feeling the bony ridges of vertebrae and ribs pass beneath my touch, as warm water squeezed out and dripped between my fingers.

'It's a very nice back,' I said.

'Thank you.'

I went up and down a few times; it was no harder than washing the car (which I used to do, you'll recall), and the smaller area made the job even easier, so that I soon got into a kind of rhythm.

'That's really good,' she said; and when I was about to stop: 'Do my neck. If you don't mind.' She lowered her face more firmly on to her knees, and I resoaked the sponge in order to comply. The details of her neck, slightly inconvenient as a surface for cleaning, reminded me of the awkward curves and corners of my old Morris – how fondly I remember that trusty vehicle! – and the bony bits behind Catriona's ears put me in mind of those singular trafficators which could pop up like little railway signals whenever you wanted to turn a corner.

Catriona seemed to enjoy being washed in this way. She turned her head, and I could see that her eyes were closed, no doubt to avoid any soapy water which might get in them. Yes, it was foolish of me to think that a delicate young girl such as this should want to lie down and submerge herself under dirty water which would only go up her nose and pollute her ears, one of which I was now looking at, seeing it to be like a pink seashell amongst her wet hair; and as I drew the sponge along her shoulder, she moved an arm in order to pull aside some of this hair, which looked darker now that it was wet, and had strands of many shades. Relaxing, it would seem, she loosened the grip which the other arm still kept on her knees, lowering them, and allowing my sponge to reach the front part of her chassis, or body, I ought to say. Catriona's small breasts were still undamaged, I was relieved to discover, by all her 'jogging', and significantly different in a number of respects from those belonging to the reader of *Ferrand and Minard*.

What a strange thing it is, I said to myself, that a flat tyre and a shower of rain, the poor shelving arrangements made by child labourers in Waterstone's, and the weakness of my ageing bladder, along with countless other bits and pieces of a hidden code whose manual is no doubt to be found, misplaced, somewhere in that infinitely confusing retail outlet which calls itself a bookshop, should have brought together in this abrupt yet inevitable fashion an old man much relieved by his recent experience, and a young woman (equally pleased, it would seem), who now put her hands down beside her so as to support herself, arching slightly, while I wondered how much more of this I'd have to do before I could go and sit down.

'Do you mind if I ask something?' I said; but she didn't even open her eyes, so I assumed she didn't mind, and I then enquired, 'Do all women choose to wear a beard down there?' For I had had some opportunity to compare the light goatee between Catriona's legs with the bushier styles favoured by the two women similarly exposed to me during my visits to the 'live video link'. 'Or do most prefer to be clean shaven, or even adopt some kind of moustache?'

Now Catriona opened her eyes, as if waking from a dream, and raised her knees again. 'Have you really never seen a naked woman?' she asked, using precisely the same construction and tone with which she had framed her incredulity the previous day, regarding soup, aeroplanes, and countless other mundane items about which I happen not to know very much.

My silence made the answer obvious to her. 'It's funny,' she said, 'but I really don't mind this. It's almost as if you aren't a man. Don't get me wrong,' she added quickly, using that poor grammar which I have learned to transcribe faithfully, and to forgive (well, she is a life scientist after all, and very handy with a penknife). 'Maybe it's because you're old . . . No, I can't make it sound right. But I don't mind, that's all.' Then she slid herself back and lay down in the bath, momentarily submerging everything except her face, and I wondered why she'd put me to all the trouble of sponging her if she was simply going to do what I originally suggested anyway.

Bath-time was clearly finished, and I took my leave, hearing her rise dripping behind me as I went out the bathroom door and headed for my study. There, I suppose, the matter should have ended, and I would not even have troubled you with an account of it, were it not for the conversation which took place when she came to my study, dressed again, and with her hair wrapped in another un-familiar towel (how many had she been able to find, I wondered; and how many did I possess?).

I was trying to locate the computer file she had created for me. I was having some difficulty in this, and asked Catriona for help; though I had no idea why she had intruded yet again, unless it was to say goodbye. I was even beginning to wonder if she intended to charge overtime, or else if she felt that only an entire day's service would justify the amount I proposed to give her. When she found the item for me, and opened it to reveal the naked reader once again, she said, 'It's weird, isn't it, that someone would want to be seen like this by complete strangers.'

I willingly conceded the 'weirdness' of the situation, not wishing to detain Catriona long enough for her mind to return to the idea of tea for the umpteenth time.

'I mean,' she continued, 'she must get off on it, being

seen naked. Though maybe it's because she's in control, somehow.'

Catriona embarked on a discussion with herself which I report as accurately as I can, though you realize the effort is much like trying to copy down an inscription in Japanese, where a meaningless splodge, incorrectly made, could have serious consequences.

She continued, 'When you came into the bathroom, didn't you feel embarrassed?'

I could offer no useful comment at this point, and carried on clicking the mouse.

'It's like, when I was in the bath, I might as well have been a pile of laundry, and I respect you for that. You weren't just being polite. But maybe, for some women, like this one, I mean, reading her book, it's some kind of turn-on to imagine being watched by someone who doesn't find it arousing, isn't interested; that way you're completely in charge. It's like being looked at by, I don't know, a surgeon, or someone.'

All this, I need hardly add, meant about as much to me as *Dr Cool's Web Magic*, and was of slightly less interest, though Catriona seemed to find the subject worthy of yet further comment.

'So when this woman decided to pose in front of a camera, maybe she wasn't thinking of all the guys who'd get off on it, but was only doing it for herself, because the camera wasn't getting turned on, and it was like those men she could imagine, who'd watch her without getting off, and that can be a turn-on in itself.'

By now she'd switched 'off' and 'on' so many times that I was completely confused, and I'm sure that my transcription must be full of crucial errors, which will have completely changed her intended sense. But through sheer exposure to this jargon, in much the same way that Dr Cool's had already begun seeping into my consciousness, I felt bold enough to try using it myself.

I said to her, 'When you were in the bath then, were you "turned on"?' I hoped that by immersing myself in some kind of linguistic game, in which I pretended to know what I was talking about, I might come to understand the 'live video link' a bit better, and hence be drawn a step closer to Rosier, Ferrand and Minard, et cetera. A similar approach had worked, to some extent at least, with Ali and Mrs Campbell, so it seemed worth a try.

Catriona, meanwhile, was twiddling a fallen strand of wet hair, as if the question were difficult, subtle and profound. She'd shown a similar prevarication when I'd asked her if she was in love with that lad called Ewan or Gary or whatever it was; and once again she said, 'I don't know,' but then, after another pause, during which I'd more or less forgotten the question: 'Maybe. Somehow.' And after a still longer pause, when I'd hoped we'd got it all out of the way (I was, after all, learning nothing that would help me interpret the naked reader), she added, still with that anacoluthon which is difficult to render properly on the page, 'When you were sponging me . . . It was . . . You've got very good hands.'

'Thank you,' I said.

'I mean, I can't believe you've never done anything like that before.'

We were going to get back into the 'Have you honestly never . . . ?' routine, and in order to forestall it I asked her whether she'd thought yet about reading Hume, and when she said no, I suggested that in the meantime she might like to take a look at *Ferrand and Minard: Jean-Jacques Rousseau and the Search for Lost Time,* and let me know if it bore any relevance whatsoever to Jean-Bernard Rosier or his mysterious encyclopaedia, which is, after all, the only justification for a recent series of letters which have already gone on far too long, and require no distraction in the form of naked girls in baths, this being the kind of detail fit only for those sentimental or sensational novels which I'd found polluting the shelves of Waterstone's.

She left me, and her omission of any reference to tea was an enormous relief. I heard her footsteps go downstairs and into the living room, while I busied myself with a web search which began with Rousseau, and soon took me, by way of a series of 'hyperlinks', as Dr Cool would call them, to the National Museum of Antiquities, the Online Movie Guide, and the homepage of a young man in Texas who's studying computer science and is very interested in Tolkien. Forty-five minutes passed swiftly in this pleasant manner, without my discovering any new information of substance.

It really must be time, I decided, for Catriona to go back to her boiler-less flat and do her homework. I wasn't going to be the one responsible for sending her to the bottom of her life science classes! So I went downstairs, where I found her lying on my sofa, *Ferrand and Minard* open on her chest, and she fast asleep like a babe. I lifted the book as delicately as I could, then went back to my study and wrote a letter which, I decided, she could post for me whenever she woke up and left for home. Of that letter, I need say no more, since you've already read it; and since you've now read this one too in its entirety, I suppose I really ought to shut up until the next one.

CHAPTER 8

Ferrand and Minard were inspecting their new accommodation. Father Bertier's servant had brought them to a cottage which was small, tidy, and perfectly suited, Ferrand decided, to their needs. The servant looked as though he was expecting a tip; they managed to make him leave empty-handed.

'It's so charming!' said Minard, closing the door, then he began to pull back the window shutters while Ferrand contented himself with running his fingertips along surfaces which he found to have been recently cleaned. 'And to think that Jean-Jacques was inspired by this very countryside,' Minard enthused, admiring the view now offered to him through the open window, and allowing bright sunlight into the room.

'I've told you already,' said Ferrand; 'we will not be making Monsieur Rousseau's acquaintance.' He walked to the window, his shoes creaking on the floorboards, and pulled one half of the shutters closed again. Minard, undeterred, went about examining the furniture and exploring the cupboards and drawers so gaily that it seemed he had perhaps forgotten, at least temporarily, all the many reasons they had for feeling anything but cheerful. Then Ferrand sat down at the simple table, and said: 'This is the beginning of our new life. We shall find honest work here, and spend our days quietly together.'

Minard sat down opposite him. 'Yes,' he said, 'our new life.' He clasped Ferrand's hands, they renewed their vow of eternal friendship, and Minard must now have been reminded of all their woes, since he began to weep. 'But my poor Jacqueline!' he sobbed.

'And that's another thing,' Ferrand said wearily, patting his friend's head which was bowed in tears upon a dampening sleeve. 'You must promise me once and for all that you will never mention that girl's name again. The very trees have ears, Minard, remember that. You saw how Father Bertier reacted when you asked him about her; he knew that there was some story he could find out about us, and then our influence over him would be lost, we would have to flee to some other village, we might find ourselves fugitives for the rest of our days.'

Minard looked up, and nodded in agreement with Ferrand's wise words.

'I intend to rest now,' said Ferrand. 'Our early start this morning, and our ample meal with Father Bertier, have left me feeling rather sleepy. Do you propose to help me test the bed?'

Minard, though he had eaten far more heavily than Ferrand, and was still short of sleep despite having got more of it last night than his companion, decided he would prefer not to join him yet; and so Ferrand, looking slightly peeved, went to lie down alone on the mattress at the other side of the room. Minard remained at the table, and soon heard the light wheezing of his unconscious friend.

Some time later, there was a knock at the door. Minard

went to answer, and saw the servant again, who had brought the friends' bundle of belongings on his back, depositing it heavily at Minard's feet with a sigh of exhaustion and relief. 'Many thanks,' said Minard, wondering how he could get away without tipping the man this time. Minard pulled the bundle inside, while Ferrand's reedy breathing continued unaltered, and then Minard went out to join the servant, closing the door behind him.

'You have done well,' said Minard, 'and I shall reward you . . . though only once I am satisfied that everything in the parcel is in order, of course. But tell me, do you know where I can find a woodturner?' He meant Jacqueline's father, but intended to remain true to his promise to Ferrand by not mentioning the name of Cornet.

The servant looked puzzled. 'Is there something needs doing in the house, sir?'

Minard shook his head, but then after a pause decided it best to nod. 'Yes, but only a trifling matter.'

'Is it a table leg you need? Broken baluster?'

Minard quickly nodded again, 'Yes, that's it, a baluster's broken.' But then he shook his head just as vigorously, since the cottage had no stairs, and the servant still gazed at him, patiently waiting for an answer. Minard wasn't as good at making things up as Ferrand. 'No, I meant a table leg all along. Funny how easy it is to get them mixed up. Just poles of wood, really.'

'Table leg? And you're sure it's the turned kind? When I said table leg, I was thinking of the kind that's turned, but it might be square sectioned, perhaps I ought to have a look.'

Minard might have known the servant would turn out to

be some sort of carpenter's apprentice. 'Actually it isn't the table.'

Now the servant looked more confused than ever.

'It's a bit awkward, really,' said Minard, and he drew the servant close so that he could whisper in his ear. 'You see, we're here on official business of great importance.'

'I know that, sir.'

Minard stood back. 'You do?'

'Of course, sir. Whole village knows. That's why you aren't using your real names.'

Minard was crestfallen, but consoled himself by thinking how successful his story had been in fooling these simple country people. 'Forget the table leg. Just tell me where I can find Cornet the woodturner, there's a good man.'

'He already knows about your grandmother, sir, if that's what this is about. Very sorry, he is, and says he can well remember the feet he made for that lovely bed of hers. Gorgeous bit of walnut, that was.'

Minard, resigned to the absurdity which seemed determined to follow his every step, decided the best thing to do was to agree. 'Gorgeous indeed. And we do miss her so.'

The servant said, 'Do you want me to take you to him, sir?'

'I think you better had,' Minard replied, and the two went in search of Cornet the woodturner. Ferrand woke to see them already on their way.

Cursing Minard's stupidity – for he knew that whatever Minard was up to was sure to bring further trouble – Ferrand kneeled down beside the parcel on the floor and carefully inspected the binding. It was he who had tied the knots, though he felt sure as he began to unfasten them that these weren't his. Inside the canvas wrapper, however, he found what he was looking for: the great bundle of manuscript pages which had brought their whole sequence of misfortunes into being.

He pulled them out by the handful, unable to tell whether they had been examined by Bertier and his associates, or whether any had been removed. How could such strange documents be connected with the death of a girl; why should they be so precious? Ferrand heaped the pages, all he had, on to the table, and then seated himself, intending now to try and put everything into proper order, hoping to understand what it was that he had been asked to transcribe, and at such a terrible cost. He began to read:

The experiment was performed on 31 March 1759 at the home of my assistant Monsieur Louis Tissot. A ring belonging to his wife was hidden, without my looking, beneath one of three cups. I then placed my hand upon a cup, Tissot lifted another beneath which the ring was not to be found, and he invited me, if I wished, to alter my choice. We did the experiment more than a hundred times, and I soon discovered that changing my selection was indeed the best strategy. I was elated by this, and would have gone on even longer if Madame Tissot hadn't asked for her ring back.

Next day, inspired by my wonderful discovery, I returned to Tissot's house and proposed a new experiment. A small velvet bag containing an equal number of black and white beads was held open by Madame Tissot, while I and my assistant, blindfolded, each selected a bead. Having noted our choice, Madame Tissot would announce either, 'at least one bead is black', or 'at least one bead is white'.

The two of us, still blindfolded, would then go to opposite ends of the room, from where I would consider the probability that Tissot held black.

So contrary were the results we obtained to what one might have expected, that Tissot was led to doubt the accuracy of his wife's record-keeping; and our first run of experiments ended in an acrimonious argument between the couple, which spilled over into a debate about Madame Tissot's mother, about the burning of some cakes, and about various domestic arrangements which I found frankly distasteful. The three of us took a break, and afterwards I proposed that as soon as each of us had chosen a bead, we would hide it in our hand and remove the blindfold before walking to our respective corners, where we would then see what we held and write down its colour, so that Madame Tissot's own records could have independent verification. Madame Tissot wasn't very happy about this, but her husband said it would be a good idea, since he found it very difficult to walk without seeing where he was going, and he was sure he'd set off that injury he'd sustained two months earlier, when he was moving a wardrobe for his mother-in-law and tripped on a step, twisting his ankle in the process. Madame Tissot said he could hardly blame her mother for his sore foot, and I said we'd better just get on with it before another argument broke out between the two of them. When the three of us compared notes after many repetitions of the new procedure, we found that Madame Tissot's data had after all been impeccable.

'You see!' she said. 'I told you so!' Tissot wanted to talk about the burnt cakes again, and I left them to it while I began to study the results more closely. Whenever

Madame Tissot, for instance, had announced one bead to be black, the probability that either of us held that colour, curiously but indubitably, was not a half, but rather two thirds. Yet if I were then to look at my own bead and found it to be black, Tissot's chances of doing likewise suddenly fell to a half.

'Eureka!' I murmured, my voice betraying none of the joy and fear I felt; and looking up, I saw that the Tissots were about to swing fists at each other.

'Stop!' I cried, and ordered the next experiment to begin.

Now, Madame Tissot's reputation having been vindicated, the blindfolds would remain. Madame Tissot folded her arms in triumph; her husband complained.

'But what if I trip and set off my bad ankle?'

'Tread carefully,' I told him calmly, 'for you walk in the name of Science.'

Tissot still protested: 'Why should I wear a blindfold if I am to look at the bead as soon as I reach my corner of the room?'

On the contrary, I informed him; Tissot was never once to look at what he held. For I believed that what this experiment showed was that as soon as I saw my own bead, a wave of pure probability flew, instantaneously, from one end of the room to the other. This accounted for the sudden change from two thirds to a half, as a finite *quantum* of probability (of weight one sixth) passed miraculously between the beads, launched by my own act of observation.

Neither Tissot nor his wife had a clue what I was talking about, but they could do nothing except obey my wishes as, with an excitement bordering almost on obsession, I ordered the experiment to be repeated several hundred times in the course of that momentous spring afternoon. My two colleagues grew exhausted, ultimately somewhat careless, and Tissot stumbled, yelping about his mother-in-law's wardrobe, and about the cakes, while his wife, huffing angrily, gathered up the bag of beads which she said belonged in her sewing chest, and marched briskly out of the room. Still doubting her probity, Tissot would later suggest repeating the experiment, this time with a priest making the announcements which Madame Tissot seemed unable or unwilling to perform correctly, so strange had been the outcome; I, however, knew already how to explain it.

The theory of the Universe which I was to construct, inspired by this experiment and by other observations, is based solely on information and its transmission; reality consists of whatever can be measured. 'All is in constant flux,' I told Tissot on another occasion. 'The world is an endless sea, whose undulations are the chance and necessity which steer us all.' Tissot, who by now had moved out from the family home in order to devote himself fully to his duties as my assistant (and also so as to avoid his mother-in-law), listened attentively while I described to him what I call 'the measurement problem'.

When a man uses a ruler, I explained, he can only achieve whatever degree of accuracy the instrument's mark-ings allow. By introducing finer divisions he can obtain a better value, though still not an exact one. If he were to continue his attempts, making the scale on his ruler twice as fine each time, would he ever reach a final definite answer? I claim not; and since the 'actual' length could only be arrived at after an infinite process, it can have no physical meaning. The length of any line *does not exist*, except as a particular measurement to within some limit of accuracy. This is 'Rosier's Uncertainty Principle', named after the genius, myself, who discovered it.

I propose that what exists is only the *probability* of the line having a particular length. From a thousand measurements, one obtains a distribution of values clustered around some mean; plotting these on a chart as Tissot did, grumbling about his wife and her mother the whole time, one finds a distribution having a bell-shaped appearance, which I call a 'probability wave'; and whenever a measurement is made, this wave 'collapses' to the single value obtained. In the ball experiment, similar waves had been shown to propagate with infinite speed; their collapse was due to the crucial intervention of human consciousness. As a corollary, I was led to conclude that before I had looked at the ball in my hand, it was neither white nor black; a discovery which led me to a perplexing conjecture.

Imagine, I said to the startled Tissot, a condemned prisoner trapped in a windowless cell. He must choose between two identical potions, one of which is harmless and will enable him to go free, while the other is a deadly poison.

'Does this have anything to do with the story of the cups?' asked Tissot, who obviously hadn't been following my explanations very closely.

'One might call that case an influence, nothing more,' I told him. Now the prisoner is locked out of sight of the world while he makes his choice. Until the cell door is opened, according to my theory, we can call him neither live nor dead; he exists instead in a state which is a superposition of both, a ghostly half-life belonging neither to this world nor the next.

As the days passed, and Tissot became ever more preoccupied with his domestic problems, I perfected a philosophy in which pure information serves as the fundamental ingredient of all things. What is the swiftest way for knowledge to be conveyed, I asked Tissot while he sat writing a letter, but I received no answer. I decided that horses must provide the most rapid means for news to be disseminated over a large distance; and prompted by the sight of my sullen disciple, I began to analyse the way in which time might pass at apparently different rates for two people communicating only by way of written messages. Tissot and his wife were by this stage exchanging several angry notes in the course of a single morning; I recalled instead a story concerning a man banished for seducing a princess, whose tender letters to her, though written by him every day, became ever more protracted in their arrival owing to his continually increasing distance from her as he rode from the country. Ultimately, from the point of view of the princess who waited longer and longer for his next greeting, it was as if his days were extending themselves indefinitely. His life was slowing down beneath the weight and torment of his exile, and his final letter promised a sequel which never came. The passage of time for him, as perceived by his lover, came to a halt when he reached the remote northern border of their land, from which letters take for ever to arrive. I tried to explain to Tissot my theory that simultaneity and time itself must be regarded as relative concepts, governed by the motion of horses; but we were interrupted by a knock on the door, given by a lad who brought yet another of Madame Tissot's tirades, penned by her only a moment earlier, in which she re-affirmed her willingness to forget their differences as long as Tissot would stop associating with me and give up all this nonsense of his about a bad foot and her mother's cooking. I am pleased that Tissot chose to remain under my roof a little longer; it saddens me that he profited so little from it.

His poor grasp of my theories emerged some days later when, his sister being about to give birth, Tissot payed for a baby girl to be sent into the room, believing it would make the new child twice as likely to be born male. My pupil however gained a niece; and I found no difficulty in explaining the fallacy of his reasoning. Tissot had merely misunderstood my remarkable 'Paradox of the Twins', which states that if a boy tells you he has a sibling, then the probability of it being a sister is not a half, but two thirds. Tissot showed a similar misunderstanding of my teaching when, exasperated by his continuing moroseness and his near-permanent occupancy of my writing desk, I said to him, 'Next week I am going to bring your wife here so that you can speak to her in person and sort out your difficulties. I know you don't want to see her, and so I shall not tell you which day she will arrive; but you can be sure that you'll meet her before the week is out.'

Tissot knew his wife would not be brought to confront him next Friday, because in that case he could be certain by Thursday evening that she must be coming, and he could make himself absent. But equally, I would also have to avoid Thursday, since otherwise he would be forewarned when Wednesday passed without a scene. Dismissing every other day in a similar manner, Tissot concluded that his wife could never show up unexpectedly to harangue him; but on Thursday he answered the door to be greeted not only by her, but also by her mother, both of whom boxed him soundly about the ears while I made myself scarce, quietly judging that so poor a logician deserved everything he got.

I continued my investigations unaided while Tissot began to use my desk as his centre of operations for a proposed legal action against his mother-in-law. By now I was fully convinced my new theory would provoke an upheaval among learned men as profound as that caused by Copernicus. I prepared to communicate my ideas to Monsieur D'Alembert, regarding him as one fit to recognize their true worth; but of the shameful treatment I received from him I shall say nothing here, except to indicate it as the reason why I have been so assiduous in finding authority for my philosophy among the numerous writers whose work is assembled here in this Encyclopaedia.

As for Tissot, though I was eventually sorry to lose my assistant, I was pleased he never had recourse to the law. He reached a compromise with his wife, and as he prepared to leave I told him that if there was one thing I hoped he had learned from me, it was that no problem is insurmountable, as long as we can recognize its true nature. I reminded him of a story concerning the Emperor Nero, who is said to have objected to the way in which a certain mountain obstructed his view of the sunset, and who therefore ordered it to be removed, a stone at a time. Ten thousand men laboured for ten years to complete this task; but at what point could the mountain be said to have finally disappeared, when was its final stone taken? Philo of Argos, a Xanthic philosopher, bravely informed Nero that since a mountain cannot have a final stone, it must be either infinite or non-existent, and the emperor's men had toiled to shift an obstacle which dwelt nowhere but in their vain ruler's imagination.

Ferrand understood none of this; but he was at least able to deduce that Rosier was the name of the man behind this pile of papers; he it was, or one of his emissaries, who had met Ferrand in the Régence, and his documents amounted to the foundations of a new philosophy.

Minard, meanwhile, had arrived at Cornet's house. The servant led him to the yard at the back, where Cornet was treadling a turning-frame whose chord was slowly shaving a spinning pole of wood. Cornet looked up, noticed his visitors, and stopped work in order to greet them.

'This is Monsieur Minard,' the servant explained.

'Ah yes,' said Cornet. 'Though that's not your real name, I understand.'

'Quite. Good day to you,' Minard coughed.

'Very sorry to hear about your grandmother.' Cornet looked genuinely sympathetic, and Minard wondered how he could possibly break the news to this man, of Jacqueline's tragic death.

'You have a daughter in Paris, I believe,' Minard said, unable to think of any more subtle way to raise the subject.

Cornet nodded. 'A fine and lovely girl.' Then the burly woodturner looked at the servant, in a way which the latter took as a hint that he should leave.

Minard saw that the servant was waiting for something; he was gazing at Minard like a dog expecting a biscuit. 'I shall reward you, of course . . . later.' The servant indignantly left them.

Cornet drew closer to Minard. 'Is Jacqueline all right?'

Minard backed away from the hefty fellow. 'Of course
. . . why shouldn't she be? What I mean is that I don't know
anything about her.'

Cornet frowned suspiciously. 'Did they mention her at
the Oratory?' Minard had no idea what Cornet could be
getting at. 'Father Bertier worked very hard to get Jacqueline
that job.'

'As a seamstress, you mean?'

Cornet still hadn't taken his fearsome, searching eyes
from Minard's face. 'She's no seamstress. Whatever gave
you that idea? She's in the service of a very fine family –
writes to us about it every other day, if she gets the chance.'

'Really?' said Minard, then tried to hide his surprise. The
poor girl had clearly been lying to her family about her
occupation. 'I'm pleased to hear that she has found good
employment.'

Cornet softened. 'It was all Father Bertier's doing, really.
He's been very generous to her over the years, and to all of
us. I'll never let a bad word be spoken against him in this
household, you can be sure.'

'Is there any reason why anyone should want to speak ill
of him?' Minard asked, but Cornet only shrugged. The sad
truth of the matter was plain, though. Bertier had seduced
Jacqueline – perhaps, who knows, had even made her
pregnant – and he had sent her to Paris, either as a way of
removing her, or else so as to have easier access. Whether
Jacqueline's letters to her family were genuinely written by
her, as part of the arrangement, or else produced by another
of Bertier's lackeys, was a matter in which Minard had no
interest. It was not for him to bring the truth crashing down
on the head of this poor woodturner; not for him to pry

further into a squalid tale. 'I wish you and your family all the happiness you deserve,' he said. 'And now good day to you.'

Cornet was puzzled. 'Good day to you too, monsieur. Will that be all, then? Has Jacqueline done anything wrong? Is she in some kind of trouble?'

Minard shook his head, unable to say anything else to the unfortunate man. He turned to walk away, and soon heard Cornet treadling again, and the scraping of his blade. Once Minard was out of the man's sight, he wept again for poor, wretched Jacqueline, vowing that these tears would be his last.

Now Ferrand was lifting another item from the papers which lay scattered on the table before him:

A story is told in which a letter, written in Chinese, is sent to the keepers of a great library. The librarians do not understand the letter; however they possess a dictionary and grammar of Chinese written in that language, as well as many other oriental books, some of them printed and bound quite beautifully (a rare copy of *The Conversation in the Jade Pavilion*, exquisitely illustrated, is singled out for special praise in one account). The librarians undertake to compose a response; labouring, with the aid of their sources, to find alternatives for the characters used in the letter; studying the frequency and context of pictograms arising in every text available to them; and constructing a workable theory of a language about which, eventually, they know everything except its meaning.

Using their theory, the librarians create a reply which to them is no more than an attractive sequence of pictograms, meticulously bound by logic, but which the Chinese recipient reads and is able to understand perfectly, finding it to have come from a young woman named Xiou-Lin, with whom (in the manner of stories) he immediately falls in love. There follows an exchange of letters, eventually resulting in an arrangement of marriage, its unfortunate annulment, and the suicide of the man (an historian who had originally written to the library only so as to try and obtain information on the missionary Martin Gottfried). The story usually ends with a delegation of librarians travelling to China – where of course they are unable to make themselves understood – and they visit the historian's grave, shed tears, etc.

The librarians of this touching story acted together in the manner of a woman's mind, though each had merely followed the rules of a language none of them could comprehend. Consciousness is a property as much distinct from the unthinking components which give rise to it, as the roar of a falling bushel is from the silent dropping of a single grain of millet; and if thought, like everything else in Rosierist theory, may be reduced to the processing of information, then only the details of finding an appropriate architecture stand in the way of creating an artificial mind.

Rosier's theory of Mechanical Intelligence imagines a machine in which the individual elements of the human brain are replaced one by one, their presumed action as exchangers of information being emulated, let us say, by a system of pulleys; or by a hydraulic mechanism which, in the same way that an adequately designed mechanical heart would pump blood just as efficiently as one of natural muscle, must by imitating perfectly the operation of the organ we carry within our skulls, likewise imitate its function. The seat of consciousness within this device would be as invisible, as non-existent, as a beautiful Chinese woman arising from a collective act of symbolic manipulation, performed by a group of unconscious translators. Somewhere, within a proposed machine roughly planetary in size, among its ropes and pulleys, its polished pipes and pumps, thoughts would reside; ideas and sensations; a creature unaware of how it was made, curious perhaps to learn, and with a mind capable of responding intelligently to our questions, if only it had some means of communicating with us, and we with it.

Or else we could imagine a vast game, played out not by the staff of a library, but by the entire population of the world. Each person receives messages from other players which are simply cards bearing the sender's name; and depending on how many messages are received, the recipient sends out his own calling-cards to players included in his list of acquaintances. This social network, if the initial lists were appropriately arranged, might, we believe, imitate the actions of a mind, in which learning would correspond to the collection of new addresses, but in which thought would exist only by virtue of the countless interactions of individuals, distracted by concerns of their own, who proceed according to rules the significance of which they cannot guess.

Rosier therefore proposes the creation of a worldwide web of information which, if sufficiently large, and if its architecture can be correctly chosen, will eventually be capable of thinking for itself, though we may have no means of knowing what ideas will exist within its mind. It will be a brain whose elements are individual people, and its speed of thought will be governed by the efficiency of the postal system, which, we note with considerable excitement, improves by the day.

'Our initial experiments in Mechanical Intelligence have been based on the work of Raymond Lull, whose *Ars generalis ultima* presents tables from which logical propositions may be derived by means of the selection and combination of given phrases, according to strict rules. More advanced and versatile are the beautiful devices of concentric metal discs, finely engraved, which have been produced in many places according to Lull's principles, and which may be rotated by the user in such a way as to generate, quite involuntarily, whole phrases and sentences, conveying ideas which have arisen from nothing more than the fortuitous juxtaposition of one group of markings against another upon the discs' polished surfaces. An entire body of written text could be manufactured by one of these devices if it were sufficiently large, and the Rosierist theory of Mechanical Literature holds that such a method will one day supplant the inefficient labour of human authors that presently constitutes the only means by which a book may be written. Our own experiments in Artificial Literature have produced results which are fragmentary and provisional in nature, but provide an indication of the progress we hope to make, once the full implications of Nicolas Clairy's Mechanical Poetry have been sufficiently worked out; though as an indication of the obstacles remaining, we might mention that the important 'Three Adjectives' problem is still unsolved, and may even be unsolvable.

Clairy believed all utterances to be equivalent, by way of their numerous forces of balance, to a system of solid bodies. Conversely, any collection of objects can be translated into words, so that the very motion of the planets must amount to a hidden cosmic script. Yet we know that the planets and stars are governed by gravitation, mediated by probability waves which hold the celestial spheres in their courses through the perpetual exchange of information; and we might therefore wonder whether the universe itself can be regarded as a thinking entity, with planets and stars as its thoughtlessly interacting components, compelled in their actions, yet serving as the repository of a being in whose mind an orbit would be the precursor of a thought; one for whom a comet becomes, by an accumulation of celestial outcomes, a flash of inspiration; and for whom the precession of the equinoxes is a subtle problem of psychology, removed to the peaceful realms of mathematics. Slow, steady and magnificent would be the great turning of this cosmic imagination, pure and noble its cogitations; for surely this must be the mind of God himself, whose solitary play, and the amused observation of whose own benevolent workings, ensure the existence of each one of us. The whole of creation now lies encoded in a text which our theory calls the universal wave function, and which contains, as if within a limitless library, God's every thought. We ourselves are the cells of cells, the characters of a dream, the smallest leaves upon a tree of possibility, nourished by divine light, from whose boughs we are each of us destined soon to fall, watched only by he who makes us and is made by us, whose centre is everywhere, and whose circumference is beyond measure.

Minard was walking despondently back along the lane. He would never mention Jacqueline again; but more than that, he would never even think of her, for her fate must be connected with the sordid adventures of Father Bertier, not with the documents which Ferrand thought so valuable. Somehow, he would have to forget about her, and forget too the dreadful sight of her lifeless body, only yesterday, which no doubt Blanchot would have discovered soon after Minard fled, so that today half of Paris was already searching for him.

Might Bertier have killed her?

The thought came to Minard as he rounded a bend in the lane, and found himself ascending a gentle slope. A plump woman, some way ahead, was having difficulty with a heavy sack. Minard had been so much in awe of Father Bertier, during their meeting with him, that he had felt none of the suspicions which Ferrand had tried to share; but now, after talking to poor Cornet, Minard saw the smiling Father in a different light. As Jacqueline's seducer, he had every reason to want rid of her. He also had every opportunity. He had mentioned to them, with his characteristic taste for self-glory, his frequent visits to the capital, at whose finest salons he would spread himself like rancid butter among the *philosophes* whom he praised to their faces, then maligned behind their backs. Whenever Minard had found Jacqueline to be out, perhaps she was making an assignation with her influential protector. Bertier told them he was in Paris yesterday.

Ferrand, though, had reached a different conclusion. Jean-Bernard Rosier must be behind everything; he was the man who brought together the papers which Ferrand had been reading, this whole disordered book, this strange Encyclopaedia of Nothing. Rosier was either mad, or a genius, or more probably a bit of each. If his 'theory of the universe' was valid, then it must surely be far more important than the life of any individual; and if on the other hand the whole thing was a deranged fabrication, then surely there was no atrocity of which its crazed instigator was not capable. Ferrand's reading had therefore merely confirmed what he already knew; an innocent woman had died because of some unfathomably obscure philosophy, some paradoxes concerning probabilities. She had died because of this, and both Ferrand and Minard remained in danger, as long as they could be connected in any way with Rosier's Encyclopaedia.

Yet they couldn't dispose of the documents, Ferrand reasoned. Bertier, who had searched their bundle of belongings, knew what it contained; and if Rosier or his agents arrived in Montmorency, Bertier would be only too pleased to lead them to the door of this little cottage.

Minard drew level with the plump woman, still struggling with her sack, which he saw to contain a large quantity of vegetables. 'Would you like some help?' he said.

She turned and showed a face which was tired but cheerful, youthful in expression, though she was probably only slightly younger than Minard himself. 'You're very kind,' she said, and Minard almost wished he hadn't offered when he picked up the sack and realized how heavy it was. He was surprised she could have made it this far alone, and Minard gave a puff as he swung the sack over his shoulder, wondering whether his new life in Montmorency was destined always to be characterized by the bearing of heavy weights.

'Where are you going?' he asked her.

'I live at Montlouis,' she said, as if Minard was supposed to know where this was. He thought it best to pretend that he did, and made sure his companion was always a step in front, whenever some choice of path presented itself.

She hummed a tune to herself while she walked. He took

her to be some kind of servant, and expected that they would eventually arrive at the fine house where she must be employed.

'Haven't seen you round these parts before,' she said, interrupting her own song.

'We're visiting,' said Minard, trying to hide the difficulty he was having in carrying her vegetables.

She plucked a long blade of grass from a clump she passed at the side of the path, and began to chew on it. 'You and your family, is it?'

'I'm here with a friend.'

'Oh,' she said, 'I see,' as though Minard had told her something profound; then added, 'Friend, eh? Never trust 'em. The national state of man is solitude, you know.'

Whatever was that supposed to mean? Minard, hoping to make her pause so that he could get his breath back, said, 'I think you perhaps mean "natural".'

She didn't slow down. 'Natural, national, what's the difference? If two words sound much alike, they ought to mean the same thing, that's what I say. Don't know why they ever had to invent so many words.'

'Ouch, my foot!' cried Minard, suddenly putting down the sack and going to lean on a tree while he pulled off his shoe. 'Nail's pushing through.' It wasn't; Minard only wanted a way of stopping for a rest which would avoid a confession of fatigue.

'Them nails is nasty buggers,' the woman offered. She was a simple soul, good natured but completely stupid, and Minard was trying to decide whether to leave the sack to her and be off. 'A man's born free, but ends with his legs in irons.'

Minard had no idea where she could have come up with

these strange sayings of hers, but she clearly couldn't have got them from a book.

'You're not much of a reader, I take it,' he said, as they began walking again.

She frowned. 'Books is nasty things.'

'A bit like shoenails, in fact.'

She ignored this. 'My man says the world'd be a much happier place without 'em.'

This would make an excellent topic for a café conversation, but Minard reckoned his companion wasn't up to it. 'What does your husband do?' Probably a valet or footman.

'He's a copyist.'

Hearing of this rival worker, Minard suddenly became more interested in the woman. 'You aren't in service, then? You're not a kitchen maid or a laundrywoman?'

She seemed surprised. 'How ever did you guess my former station? No, these days I serve my own good man, who'll be eating some of those vegetables tonight, if he chooses to come home.'

A local copyist would be a very useful person to know; perhaps a way for Minard and Ferrand to obtain work. If nothing else, Minard reasoned, he ought to gauge the competition. 'I should very much like to meet your husband.'

'If you don't mind waiting, then you might get the chance,' she said.

It seemed very odd that a copyist should think the world would be a happier place without books. Minard pondered this during the last and steepest part of their journey, while he silently bore the sack which by now had made a painful trough in each of his shoulders, and the woman walked ahead, humming again.

A large house was before them, near the top of the hill,

whose high garden wall marked out an enclosure of considerable size. Reaching the crest of the hill, they arrived at the garden's wooden door, which the woman opened to reveal a much smaller building standing alone in the grounds; a workman's cottage, narrow and of two storeys, with small windows and roughly plastered walls left unpainted. Minard followed her to this little house, and when they went inside he found himself standing in a simple kitchen. Minard dropped his burden on to the stone floor, while his companion bawled out, 'Anyone at home?', several times, until the silence satisfied her that no one was upstairs.

'I'm going to make a nice soup with these carrots,' she said proudly, pulling some from the sack. 'And if my man's as late as he usually is, you might have a chance to try it for yourself.'

This seemed like quite a reasonable offer. Already, the effects of his ample lunch at the Oratory were beginning to wear off, and for Minard, the possibility of hunger was equivalent to the experiencing of it.

Then she said, 'I suppose I ought to check and see if he's working outside.'

'In the garden, you mean? I didn't notice anyone digging when we came in.'

She shook her head. 'I don't mean that. Come with me and I'll show you.' She led Minard back outside (just as he was beginning to think about food), round to the back of the cottage, and along a narrow path which followed the curved wall towards a far corner of the garden, where a small pavilion came into view, walled on three sides only, and with a steeply pitched red-tiled roof giving it the appearance of a little pagoda. The front of the structure, which would once have been open to the elements, was glazed in the manner behind which plants might be expected to be cultivated. The two of them went up the small flight of steps and could see through the glass that the room inside was unoccupied. There was a rough table burdened with papers, the inkwell had been left open with a quill beside it, and other documents were piled on the floor round about. It looked as though the place had been left in the very midst of some long and difficult work which would later be returned to, and it seemed to belong to a world very different from that of the woman who now opened the glass-panelled door.

'Want to see what he's been up to?' she said, inviting Minard to follow her inside. 'Don't half get stuffy in here when the sun shines.'

Minard entered and sat down at the copyist's desk, and the first thing he noticed was the fine view his position gave, looking back through the window and across the garden, to the valley and then, in the distance, to Paris itself, marked by tiny spires and the rising threads of black smoke, and for a moment it was as if all Minard's cares were wrapped up and banished in that far-off city, whose harsh justice could never touch him here.

Minard looked down at the papers which lay neatly gathered at the centre of the table, tied together with ribbon. On the front was written: 'Selected letters from Julie to Saint-Preux, specially chosen for Madame la Duchesse by Jean-Jacques Rousseau.'

The absent copyist had clearly found himself a magnificent task, transcribing the master's work for aristocratic patrons. And this must be the author's original copy! Turning to the woman, who was tidying some items on a shelf, Minard said, 'Have you ever seen him round here?'

'Who?'

'Monsieur Rousseau.'

She looked at him quizzically, then laughed. 'That's a good joke. Have I seen him? Well, only once or twice. Mostly he's away.'

'And has he spoken to you?'

She was still smiling. 'Yes, to ask for his pipe, or when he wants his neck rubbed. My man's usually got other things than me on his mind.'

'I'm not talking about your man, I'm talking about Rousseau . . .' But then at last the incredible truth became apparent. 'You mean, this house is his; this is the room in which he works, these papers are all his? And you're his wife . . . You?'

Her lips pursed in a curve of quiet pride. 'I'm his servant and companion, sir.'

Minard still couldn't believe it.

'And yet you said he's a copyist.'

'Oh, he is,' she said. 'That's how he makes a good and honest living. It's music that he copies – look.' She pointed to a pile of papers heaped against the wall, and Minard saw them to bear musical notation.

He was bewildered. 'Rousseau is no humble copyist; he's a writer, surely. The most famous writer in the world!'

She shrugged. 'He don't much like books. But every man needs an interest to keep him out of mischief.'

Minard laughed with joy. 'I would so dearly love to meet him. Only today, Father Bertier promised to introduce me . . .'

'You're a friend of his? Funny, he was here too this morning. If Jean-Jacques gets back before the cock crows I'm sure he'll be glad to hear the Father's news from you.

But we'd better not stand around; monsieur doesn't approve of me bringing visitors here to his room, though whenever anybody comes, this is the only place they want to see. Can't think why.'

Minard by now had grown accustomed to the woman's naivety, though it hadn't completely lost the power to amaze him. 'They come because of Julie, of course, who was born here on this very table!'

She frowned. 'There's many a tale I could tell about that young trollop if I had a mind to, but I'll spare your earholes for another day. I'm going to go and make a start on that meal. Don't be much longer, will you, and make sure you leave everything exactly as you found it.'

Then she went out and left him sitting at the great man's desk. According it the reverence of a holy relic, he delicately lifted the excerpt from *Julie*, turned a few pages, and saw that beneath it lay another work, similarly tied with ribbon, bearing the obscure title *The Social Contract*, and the signature 'J.-J. Rousseau, citizen of Geneva'. And to think that he, Minard, must be the first person in the world, apart from Rousseau himself, to see this new work!

Minard got up from the chair, aware of the tremendous power this tiny room contained, as if its walls vibrated with genius. He was almost afraid to touch anything, yet could not resist, and he crouched to inspect the music Rousseau had copied, piled on the floor, lifting several pages in awed wonder as he tried to feel the inspiration encoded within each tiny mark of the absent writer's pen.

But then he noticed something odd.

Among the music lay something else; sheets written by another hand, somewhat crumpled, which had subsequently been smoothed out and now were buried, irrelevantly and as if concealed, among the parts of a cantata. Minard drew them out, and it took him little time to recognize the text; an obscure demonstration of the non-existence of the universe. What Minard held were the very pages he had taken with him two days earlier when he went to wait at the market; the very pages he had left in Jacqueline's room. This was what had been stolen, by whoever it was who strangled the poor girl; hidden now in the workroom of Jean-Jacques Rousseau!

Minard heard the woman's voice calling some way off: 'Jean-Jacques! There you are!' Hardly aware of what he was doing, Minard stuffed the incriminating pages inside his shirt, hurrying out and closing the glass door behind him before leaping down the steps and back along the path, hoping he had not been seen. Approaching the cottage from behind, he could hear a conversation beginning at the other side.

'There's a man wants to see you. I showed him the garden.'

'You didn't let him into my room did you, Thérèse?'

'Of course not, husband. You know I'd never do a thing like that. He's a friend of Father Bertier, says the Father sent him to you with his news.'

'In that case I'd better see him. What's he called?'

'Minard, I reckon, though they say in the village that it's not his real name.'

Then Minard came round the corner, and Jean-Jacques, standing at his own front door with his walking stick held under his arm, turned to look at him, but said nothing, only studied him closely and waited for Minard, whose mouth had become completely dry, to explain himself.

CHAPTER 9

A very distinguished poet once remarked that the world would be a happier place if we were to choose our political leaders not for their promises, but on the basis of their experience as readers. Literature, we are to believe, is necessarily a civilizing influence; if delinquents could only be made to sit down with *Middlemarch*, then all our social problems would be at an end. It's the fond credo of countless school-teachers whose careers have ended in nervous breakdown beneath a hail of flying pencil-sharpeners. The many anecdotes of concentration camp commandants quoting Goethe ought to have refuted the notion by now, once and for all. Eichmann invoked Kant at his trial; but the naively optimistic view that a work of art can change the world, and for the better – a view put forward by none more passionately than by artists themselves – is one which finds itself renewed, like a persistent weed, with each generation. Well, I suppose writers have to feel they're of some use to society.

Rousseau took a very different line. For him, books are corrupting influences, and those who write them are to be despised. He didn't always feel this way; as a child he loved to read Plutarch with his father, and in the *Confessions* he describes his youthful habit of taking a book into the woods where he might mislay it, rediscovering the item weeks or months later, overgrown and rotted. His dislike of books was gradual, eventually becoming (following his madness) complete; but as it grew, and as he began to indulge more and more heavily in the very habit he loathed, Rousseau could at least claim to be gaining an honest living as a copyist, always remaining quick to point out in his writing the extent to which literary activity was, paradoxically, distasteful to him. In the preface to *Julie* he tells us, 'Big cities need plays and corrupt people need novels'; in *Émile*, his novel-treatise about a boy's education, he declares the author's profession to be as unnecessary, as much a function of luxury and idleness, as that of goldsmith.

Why then did he write at all? For the same reason as anyone; he desired to be read. Who the intended reader might be, what the expected benefits, and why the urge should be so great, are the factors which distinguish one writer from another.

Kafka's famous instruction that his work be destroyed after his death is often held up as a bitter counter-example; one which Auden explained by noting Kafka's remark that 'writing is a form of prayer'. Kafka's intended reader, it seems, was God; and I thought of this when I saw Kafka's grave in Prague, during a break in the conference I was attending. My trip to the cemetry was one of those pointless, irresistible pilgrimages which are as irrational, perhaps, as the act of writing itself; or else as easily reducible to the familiar motives which drive all our actions.

Contrary to Auden's theory, Kafka published a number of stories during his life, and was carefully preparing another collection even on his deathbed. Anything he could not subject to final correction he regarded as being unfit to be seen by God, the public, or anyone else. His request could therefore be considered a supreme act of artistic conscientiousness, which is another name for vanity.

Kafka regarded himself as a humorist, and would sometimes be helpless with laughter while reading his work to friends. But we know, of course, that his were very serious jests. In a letter to his fiancée Félice Bauer, refusing her request to be with him while he worked, Kafka explained that writing means opening yourself to the utmost; you can never be sufficiently alone when you write, there can never be enough silence, 'never enough night'. Kafka dreamed of a room in a cellar where he would work endlessly; a cell at whose door his meals would be placed at fixed hours, and from out of whose dark and solitary depths he could bring forth terrible wonders.

Proust found the same thing in his own apartment; the walls of the cell he made for himself on the Boulevard Hausmann were lined with cork in the summer of 1910, while he took a holiday in Cabourg and worked on his novel. Flaubert retreated, bear-like, to Croisset; Montaigne retired to his library, in a tower of the ancestral château near Bordeaux which I visited once with Ellen, finding the precious room to be emptied of books, and full of fellow tourists. And Jean-Jacques had his little *donjon*, as he called it, at the bottom of the garden at Montlouis; an edifice strangely resembling, to my eyes, a 1930s concrete bus shelter, on whose steps I stood once with Ellen as we gazed through the glass doors at the room where *Julie*, *Émile* and the *Contrat social* were penned, as well as other works in which Rousseau restated his belief that all scientific and cultural progress amounts to a descent from the purity of natural man, a fall from the nobility of the savage whose true condition is not to live in society, but to be alone, just as Rousseau had famously chosen to be, in his self-imposed rural exile.

Why did he write? On one occasion, Rousseau suggests his purpose is merely to assist his own memory; for his was very poor, he tells us, particularly with regard to words and quotations. He even says of one scene that since he has already written about it elsewhere, he can now no longer remember the details, as if the recording of his past amounts only to a way of ridding himself of it. A form of personal therapy, then. Yet there can be no question that Rousseau, throughout his life, craved nothing more than the favourable judgement of an attentive audience, even while ostensibly talking to himself.

Gertrude Stein said she wrote for 'myself, and strangers'; a comment which is wise and profound. Certainly, Rousseau in his later years could not have been writing for the benefit of his friends, since by then he'd managed to lose most of them, having spent much of his time denouncing those he believed to have taken part in the great conspiracy he first unearthed at Montmorency. Perhaps, when he embarked on his autobiography, Rousseau had even begun to live only for himself and the strangers who would know him through his writing. He had installed himself permanently in the *arrière boutique* which Montaigne says all of us should occasionally visit; a room at the back of the shop, a turret in a corner of our lives where there are no bonds of relationship, no ties or possessions, so that when the time comes for us to lose all those things it should not be a new experience to do without them.

Montaigne was extolling the benefits of solitude; he had followed the advice of Seneca and withdrawn himself from the world to write the essays which Sainte-Beuve exquisitely called a labyrinth whose only guiding thread is the accidental course of a man's life. Proust chose his own over-heated apartment in which to recreate Saint-Simon and Chateaubriand as his precursors; but Rousseau considered himself to be without precedent, as I mentioned to Louisa during the second meeting of our proposed 'literature group'.

The silent youth had come back too, and when I brought down from the shelf my book, *Ferrand and Minard: Jean-Jacques Rousseau and the Search for Lost Time*, it was only so as to pass it round, before it was returned to me, barely opened, as if it were an obscure artefact from an ancient culture; a carved phallus, impressive yet mildly embarrassing, placed upon a suburban coffee table for admiration.

Did Rousseau write for fame? He had no need; he was already famous before he went to Montmorency, though celebrity, like everything else, may have a different meaning when we speak of the past. His overnight success supposedly came with a prize-winning essay, thirty pages long, which made him a star of the salon circuit at the age of thirty-nine. By then he had been in Paris for nearly a decade, having arrived there from his native Geneva by way of various parts of Switzerland, Italy and France. He had started work at the age of thirteen as an engraver's apprentice; then he was a servant, and once betrayed a fellow employee over a stolen ribbon. Rousseau suggests, at the end of Book Two, that the *Confessions* were inspired by guilt over this incident, though his continued need to write the next ten Books casts doubt on this.

He had earned a living as a music teacher, as a diplomat's secretary, and as what might be called a 'toy boy', gobbling the food and kissing the chair of his '*maman*', Madame de

Warens. He received propositions from both sexes, and tells us that he had indulged since the late age of sixteen in the most natural of all pleasures, so that commentators vary in bestowing upon Rousseau or upon Proust the honour of having been the first author to bring masturbation within the scope of imaginative literature.

He arrived in Paris in 1742, hoping to make his fortune with a new system of musical notation, a scheme which should have immediately singled him out as the crank he was ultimately to become. He composed operas and ballets, contributed to the *Encyclopédie*; all this before writing the short essay which was his response to the rubric, 'Has the revival of the arts and sciences done more to corrupt or to purify morals?', proposed by the Dijon Academy, read by Rousseau in the *Mercure de France*, and given by him the answer that art and science can only corrupt. When Eichmann invoked Kant, therefore, it was a gesture which Rousseau would easily have understood as an inevitable consequence of reading, of literature, and of the advancement of human culture.

In the light of his new theory, Rousseau decided to 'reform' himself, dressing simply and renouncing all worldly ambitions. The salons loved it. Louisa suggested to me that he was the father of 'anti-fashion', and perhaps she's right; though here again we are reminded of the different meaning which fame had in those days, when the only mass medium was the newspaper, and the weekly *Mercure*, by far the biggest seller, had a Europe-wide circulation of around seven thousand. Rousseau was essentially a famous party guest, one holding opinions intriguingly at odds with those of the self-styled *philosophes* who extolled intellectual progress and enlightenment.

But still it wasn't enough for him. If Rousseau was to lead the simple life, then he would have to get away from Paris; and Madame d'Épinay, at whose salon Rousseau was the jewel, duly obliged, offering him the use of the Hermitage, her country cottage near Montmorency. Here Rousseau could begin to live out the rural fantasy which so many others would imitate, and which would bring him fame in a new, much greater, and much more modern sense. Marie-Antoinette, whose peasant games at the Petit Trianon were to be inspired by the cult of Rousseauism soon to emerge, would be among those who would make the pilgrimage to his grave, on an island at the estate of Ermenonville where he died in 1778, and to which visitors were charged admission by the entrepreneurial Marquis de Girardin, who also offered a display of the dead writer's relics and an accompanying guide book.

Such was the mythical status of the Isle of Poplars where Rousseau was laid to rest that some disciples would show their devotion by swimming there rather than taking the boat. Others contemplated the spiritual voyage for many days before finally making it, and one or two committed suicide on the island so that they could be buried beside the idol they venerated. And it was Rousseau, not Voltaire or the Encyclopaedists, whom Robespierre would anoint as the Revolution's patron saint, reinterring him with massive pomp in the Panthéon. Rousseau's bust, carved out of a huge block from the fallen Bastille, crowned with laurels and attended by six hundred white-gowned maidens and troops of guardsmen wreathed with flowers, was carried through the streets of Paris while Thérèse, who wasn't allowed to join the procession, watched it all from a window. This was to be the final dizzying triumph for the apostle of the simple life, whose rural experiment, as we shall see, had such chaotic consequences for himself and for all who really knew him.

Montaigne retired to his château, and quickly fell victim to depression; Proust's incarceration on the Boulevard Haus-mann served to exacerbate his own bizarre sleeping habits, so that he would escape in the middle of the night to the Ritz to have his 'lunch', before creeping back like a ghost to spend the daylight hours asleep. The dangers of solitude are well known, but among Rousseau's circle only one voice expressed concern at his proposal to leave Paris for Mont-morency, and it belonged to Melchior Grimm.

He was a German by birth, ten years younger than Rousseau, and a literary critic noted for his analytical style and astute judgement. Grimm had first met Madame d'Épinay thanks to Rousseau; the three played music together at her house, including some pieces composed by the hostess herself (this talented, bored woman was also to write an extraordinary *roman-à-clef*), and Grimm soon became her lover. He it was who prophetically warned no good would come of Rousseau's isolation in the countryside north of Paris. And he it also was whom Rousseau would blame for the strange sequence of events which brought an end to his stay at Montmorency, forcing him to flee under threat of arrest, and in fear of his life; for Rousseau, having sought his own dark and solitary cell from which wonders could be brought forth, unleashed demons which drove him to the very edge of sanity.

Why did he write? Perhaps the best theory is one sug-gested to me by a comment which Jill Brandon made one morning in the coffee room. All men, she said, write for sex; and after some reflection, I almost felt tempted to agree with her. Ask any man to imagine he's won a million pounds, and among his first fantasies will be the beautiful women (or men, or sheep) who now find him attractive. Money is simply one way to win sex; fame, literary or otherwise, is another; and all writing, perhaps, is a dream of glory, a futile dream of being loved. We are used to hearing rock stars describe how they learned to play the guitar simply as a way of meeting girls; why should we be surprised by someone who becomes a novelist, a philosopher, an astronaut, or a dictator, for the same banal reason? Rousseau describes, at the beginning of Book Eleven, the sensational effect which *Julie* created when it appeared in 1761. Critical opinion was divided; Grimm found the novel unstructured, bombastic, and absurd. But the women, Rousseau warmly reports, went wild; and the greatest reward of his book was that now, at the age of forty-eight, he could have any he chose, no matter how high her rank. What won their hearts, he continues, was that they imagined the novel to be his own true story; visitors begged him to show them Julie's portrait, convinced she must exist.

Julie did exist; her name was Sophie d'Houdetot and she was Madame d'Épinay's twenty-six-year-old sister-in-law. Rousseau was already halfway through his novel when Sophie appeared on the scene, but he recognized her at once as his 'first and only love', the woman he had been writing about, suddenly made real. She was a blank sheet on to which Rousseau's libidinous fantasies could be projected; he even describes in the *Confessions* the exhaustion he suffered through excessive masturbation prior to their meetings. Proust, similarly, created his Albertine long before the hapless Alfred Agostinelli stepped into the role which had been scripted and prepared for him with the patience of a nesting bird; but at least Agostinelli was not bad looking, if a little overweight. Sophie, on the other hand, was scarred by smallpox, and so shortsighted that contemporaries described her as cross-eyed. Nevertheless Rousseau was besotted by her, and Thérèse was enlisted to deliver passionate love letters written by him in a style hardly different from those he continued to add to his book. Already his tendency to confuse fact and fantasy was becoming evident; and Madame d'Épinay was none too pleased. She told him to leave the Hermitage, and it was in the *donjon* at Montlouis that an embittered Rousseau finished his novel.

All men write for sex, Jill Brandon suggested; and then, as if the subjects were somehow linked, she suddenly asked me how my 'group' was coming along, saying the word in a way which suggested not only inverted commas, but also some kind of alternative meaning, as if she were alluding by way of euphemism to a shared secret. It's coming along very well, I told her; for by now there had been five or six meetings which Louisa alone had attended.

'Do many come?' Jill asked, and I shrugged, saying that although it hadn't really got off the ground yet, I was reluctant to abandon the idea too quickly. Then, continuing to unwind her effortless chain of logic, she said, 'I still owe you one. For doing Proust, I mean.'

Bob Cormack came in and found a chair in which to smoke his pipe. By stationing himself some distance away from us, from the door, and from the window, in a gesture of apparent consideration, we found that he had managed to choose the single critical point in the room from which his smoke would be carried, by the mischievous turbulence of the air, to its every corner.

Rousseau's romance soon cooled, but *Julie* proved to be

the most successful novel of the eighteenth century. It was the *Gone With the Wind* of its day; and its author, whose simple life at Montlouis now became legendary, received appreciative letters from readers all over Europe. Rousseau's laying aside of worldly concerns had not prevented him from negotiating favourable terms with his publisher in Amsterdam; nor did it debar him from preserving his fan-mail in its entirety, which now sprawls across volumes VIII to X of his *Correspondence*. Here we find him already being treated like the secular saint he would officially become, by disciples – men and women in equal number – whose sighs and tears are much in evidence as they explain how their lives have been touched and transformed by Jean-Jacques's sensitivity. For many he was the perfect role model, the ideal man.

What those readers didn't know, of course, was that his faithful deliverer of letters, Thérèse Levasseur, had herself been delivered by now of the five children who Rousseau says were sent to orphanages as soon as they were born. Of this semi-literate former laundry servant who would remain Rousseau's mistress (latterly wife) until his death, only to watch his canonization from a window, and whom he describes as the best of all companions, he also says bluntly in the *Confessions* that at no time in his life did he ever feel any real love for her. During his visits to the Duchesse de Luxembourg at nearby Enghien, where he read his novel aloud, Rousseau tells us he would amuse his aristocratic admirer by describing Thérèse's frequent verbal gaffes, even making a list of them for circulation. He felt no qualms about any of this. In all Rousseau's hobnobbing with the elite there was only one factor that bothered him, one problem which irked the sensitive prophet of the simple life.

This was the amount of tipping that the servants always expected, which left him permanently impoverished.

He was a hypocrite, living a fantasy which thousands came to share, and when his bust was carried through the streets it was not a man who was worshipped, but an image he himself had carved for posterity, in his own writing. From this we learn that no human quality can ever be said necessarily to imply some other; a person can be both a delicately perceptive writer and a thoroughly unpleasant individual. When Eichmann invoked Kant, this was not some wicked joke; there is nothing which prohibits a man like Eichmann from appreciating the finest literature; and here we see the terrible folly of believing that art can lift humanity to a higher moral plane. If Hitler could show a devotion to the music of Wagner, Bruckner and Lehár (he was also irritatingly fond of whistling 'Who's Afraid of the Big Bad Wolf?'), we may conclude that his taste was indiscriminate, but not that the tears he shed at Bayreuth were false. A man, no matter how many good works he performs, is capable of evil; the evil man is not incapable of good. And when we hear the sad and futile insistence, by disappointed friends and relatives, that their loved one in the dock acted 'completely out of character', we know this to be meaningless; he merely acted unexpectedly. Not only should we disregard our leaders' reading habits, but we should take their entire past life as being no more than an imperfect indicator of future actions. Above all, we must beware of worshipping effigies, be they in stone or print.

Jill Brandon said to me, 'Louisa; she goes to your group, doesn't she?' It was as if a glance now passed from Jill into the knot of smoke which had Bob Cormack as its grinning centre. I nodded, stood up to leave as if I had suddenly remembered an appointment, then immediately complained about my back, which may have been hurting. I began to bend myself backwards and forwards, flexing my spine while waiting for the most recently introduced subject of conversation to be forgotten.

'*Je plie, et ne romps pas,*' Bob Cormack gaily suggested, to which Jill Brandon retorted with a comment I had heard from her before, that quotation is the most authoritarian form of discourse. This, I can only assume, is itself another quotation; though unlike her maxim concerning writing and sex (one which becomes more attractive, the more I consider it), her second motto seems worthy of nothing better than a Christmas cracker. Montaigne, for example, is the least authoritarian writer I can imagine, while Rousseau (who incidentally found Montaigne 'disingenuous') is one from whom literary allusion or quotation is astonishingly absent, perhaps simply because he had such a poor stock in his head, but more probably because Rousseau hated books, he hated writers, and the only author who interested him was himself. In the *Confessions*, as I now pointed out to Bob Cormack, I could recall only a single reference to Rabelais, and this is in Book Ten, when Rousseau describes the people he knew at Montmorency. In the sardonic smile of his friend Father Bertier, Rousseau says he observed a look which reminded him of the face of Panurge, tricking Dindenaut out of his sheep. Rousseau suspected Bertier was part of the plot.

'Ah, we're back to Ferrand and Minard again, are we?' said Jill Brandon. 'I expect you've been telling Louisa all about your theory.' Then I took my leave, convinced, as I turned my back on the two of them, that Jill and Bob were each suppressing a laugh.

I had by now persuaded Louisa to accept a signed copy of my book. Our weekly meetings continued, every one as chaste and delightful as the first, and leaving me wishing only for the days to disappear which held me back from the next. I came to know her wardrobe; on warm days, certain blouses and T-shirts; a choice of two pullovers when it was cooler. The seasons turned about an axis defined by the visibility of her bra; the months were circumscribed by her periodic odours. She said nothing about any man, any boyfriend, and I asked her nothing; her life was a perfumed void I adored but dared not fill. I knew that one day she would leave me, and my only hope was to enjoy her for a single night, like an insect, emerging from a dark aquatic larval existence, which completes the task ordained for it by nature within a few brief hours of freedom.

Ellen was going away on business. The week was a very long way off, marked in red on the washable 'Forever Friends' perpetual planner which tastelessly adorns our kitchen wall. I had already calculated the week's position in relation to Louisa's cycle, and found the heavenly wheels to be favourably aligned. Such details were of course familiar to me; Ellen's uninterrupted periods had been plotted by us over many years with the monotonous regularity of motor-way distance markers; our lives had slipped away to leave a residual future about as exciting as a forthcoming Little Chef.

I had to find a way of bringing about the required conjunction during the five days prescribed by fate, and prescribed more particularly by the plastics company which

Ellen was due to go and audit. At some point during that week, I would be unfaithful to my wife. I had no idea whether I would be able to keep up a bluff of innocence afterwards (I'm a terrible liar); but I wasn't really thinking that far ahead. I consoled myself with the thought that faithlessness to another amounted, in this case, to being faithful to myself; I was putting into practice the philosophy of Diderot, who said that one should always follow the dictates of one's heart.

Rousseau found Diderot's precept highly objectionable, though this doesn't seem to have prevented him from leading his own life according to much the same principle, conducting his liaisons without scruple. Thérèse not only knew about Sophie, but even delivered the letters; and whenever Jean-Jacques decided to spend the night with the Luxembourgs, at their Paris home or at Enghien, Thérèse asked no questions. But then, Rousseau was a genius, and a complete bastard, and the world seems strangely content to allow the two qualities to go together, as if, in the same way that art can supposedly raise us on to a higher moral plane, those who show artistic creativity can also be held exempt from moral judgement. If Eichmann had not only quoted Kant, but actually *was* Kant, I wondered, what then? Would we see countless respectable apologists, eager to show how an unhappy childhood, the slights of youth, had resulted, yes, in crimes against humanity; but also in a philosophical system which might even, they dare to claim, partly mitigate those crimes? The man in the dock defends himself as having acted 'completely out of character'; in the case of the artist, the same lapses are regarded as the essential contradictions from which creativity flows. I found myself strangely resentful of a scheme of values which makes the antics of the great the subject of admiration, while the private anguish of suburban lives is considered a sordid joke. Was it only by writing another *Julie* that I could justify sleeping with Louisa?

Although it was still months off, I started to make plans for the week when Ellen would be away. The ideas that came most quickly to me – following the general rule by which imagination proceeds – were those that were most trite, and would occur to anybody. I could for instance invite Louisa out to dinner, citing a spurious wish to discuss Montaigne or Flaubert in surroundings more pleasant than my office. That she would accept such an invitation seemed obvious, though this made it no easier for me to bring myself to propose it.

Alternatively I could invite her to my house using the lie that my wife would cook us all a wonderful meal. The insincerity of such a plan would, however, ensure the tawdriness of whatever might result from it. Better to be honest. After all, being unfaithful to Ellen only meant the breaking of a vow made according to a religion which neither she nor I believed in, the transgressing of an outmoded social custom. The single obstacle to me was my fear of hurting her; or, equivalently but perhaps more importantly, my fear of being found out. If I was never found out, she could never be hurt, and by spending a secret night with Louisa I would be increasing the sum total of human happiness. It all seemed very simple, just as long as I could find a way of arranging it.

It was while in the midst of such calculations that Louisa brought to our meeting one week an article, several pages long, which she thought might be of some interest to me. It contained a letter written to D'Alembert by someone called

Jean-Bernard Rosier, a name I had never heard of. There
was a puzzle about a man captured in Asia and subjected to
an ordeal resembling the familiar 'three cups' game, about
which the only thing I know is that it's a trick you can never
win.

Louisa said she'd found the article on the Internet and
had printed it out for me. This friendly gesture seemed the
very embodiment of love, and we sat close together while I
read it, afterwards confessing to her that I understood none
of the mathematical argument. Nor did she; we both
laughed, and in this moment of shared and acknowledged
ignorance I suddenly felt the deepest form of understanding
between us. I said to her, I've been trying to work out how
to use the Internet; why don't you show me some time? I
had suddenly and serendipitously found a way of inviting
her to my house, thanks to a collision of circumstance of a
kind which love and patience always eventually ensure. She
agreed with a smile.

I read the article several times, but its meaning became
no clearer to me. Its infernal conundrums of fractions and
probabilities reminded me of the torture of school days,
when the maths teacher's only response to the plea, 'I don't
understand', would be to repeat exactly the same explanation for the tenth time, like a sacred verse in a foreign
language. The story made me think of the famous wager of
Pascal; I thought too about the terrifying beauty of a man's
fate hanging on something as insignificant as the selection of
a cup. I thought of all the choices we make, ignorantly and
without consideration, upon which similar immensities may
depend, and I imagined those indefinitely replicated lives in
which we suppose our histories to be repeated and altered,
for better or worse, wondering if we would emerge from

such alternatives as still 'the same person', or whether we are in fact shaped only by the events which surround and transform us, so that a life may amount to something like a child's game with clay, in which certain objects idly pressed upon a receptive surface leave behind the pattern of a button or a coin, preserved in mirror-image.

The summer was approaching, our meetings were suspended because of the exams, and soon I was longing for the weeks to pass until autumn, when I would see Louisa again, and my wife would make her eagerly awaited business trip. Some distraction was provided by my trip to Prague. Academic conferences, like the jamborees of political parties, are primarily social gatherings, characterized by titles whose effort to be both general and exciting often leads only to crassness. 'Enlightenment Redefined' was the motto beneath which thirty of us gathered to hear a few lectures and catch up with old friends such as Donald Macintyre.

'And how are the *Commères* these days?' he asked me over coffee.

Rousseau first mentions them in Book Ten, just after he has described the smile of their friend Father Bertier. I have my copy of the *Confessions* to hand; one of the nurses here, displaying the well-meaning familiarity which is the emblem of her profession, nudged me yesterday, pointed to the title and laughingly suggested it sounded 'saucy', the French text inside merely adding to her mildly fascinated conviction that my bedside locker might be crammed with works of literary pornography. Rousseau writes of them:

> They were like the children of Melchisedec; no one knew
> their place of origin or their family, nor probably did they
> use their real names. They were Jansenists, and were

believed to be priests in disguise, perhaps because of their ridiculous habit of carrying rapiers from which they remained inseparable. The prodigious mystery with which they covered all their affairs gave them a managerial air, and I have always believed that they edited the *Ecclesiastical Gazette*. One of them, tall, benevolent and unctuous, called himself Monsieur Ferrand; the other, short, stocky, sniggering, pernickety, was called Monsieur Minard. They addressed one another as cousins. They lodged in Paris with D'Alembert, at the home of his foster-mother, Madame Rousseau [no relation], and at Montmorency they had taken a little apartment in which to spend their summers. They did their own housework, without a servant or runner. They took turns to buy their weekly provisions, to cook and to clean. And they lived quite well; we dined together sometimes. I do not know why they cared about me; for my part, I cared about them only because they played chess; and, in order to obtain a single brief match, I would sometimes endure four hours of boredom. Because they poked their noses everywhere and wanted to be involved in everything, Thérèse called them The Gossips (*les Commères*), and this name stuck with them at Montmorency.

The passage appears in a section covering 1759, but Rousseau's chronology is slightly dubious at this point (a common phenomenon in the *Confessions*). In the course of my research I became convinced that he could not have met Ferrand and Minard before the summer of 1761. But who exactly were they, these strange and secretive men? In French as in English, Thérèse's nickname for them is a word that originally meant 'godmother' ('god sibs' were the female friends who attended women in labour); and Rousseau's 'children of Melchisedec' refers ironically to the childless figure in Genesis, whose lack of ancestors or descendants made him, in effect, immortal. My interest in Ferrand and Minard was itself to become both paternal and almost mystical, as what had begun as a simple matter of curiosity turned into a test of historical faith, and the major concern of my PhD thesis.

That I ever went into eighteenth-century scholarship at all was largely a matter of chance. Proust was my first love; but I was plunged, by the contingencies of an educational system which gave me as supervisor the biographer of Madame Geoffrin, into the world of the salons and the *philosophes*. Donald Macintyre, enslaved to the same adviser, explored some implications of Laclos, and watched my parallel progress with a morbid fascination he now fondly recalled over his diminishing cup of coffee. We hadn't seen one another for fifteen years.

'And how are the *Commères* these days?' was his predictable, mildly condescending gambit.

Rousseau, at the time when he met them, was already slipping into the state of paranoia which is the most striking feature of his later works; and this derangement was a state of mind with which I could almost sympathize, when I began to go through the sources in search of Ferrand and Minard, hoping to be able to consign them at last to a neat footnote, yet each time finding nothing, so that before long it seemed as if it was the elusive Gossips who would form the subject of my thesis, rather than Rousseau himself. Donald, meanwhile, was unravelling the concept of melancholy in its applications to the erotic, while our supervisor, perhaps out of nothing more than sublime negligence,

ANDREW CRUMEY

allowed each of us to continue doing whatever we chose, just as long as our eventual findings would be well presented, would include citations of all his published works, and could be produced without the need for us to enter his office too often.

It was at Donald's birthday party one year that I met Ellen for the first time, and I could talk of little else apart from the frustrations of my research. She told me about her accountancy exams, I explained to her the procedure for inspecting historical manuscripts in the Bibliothèque Nationale, and some process took place between us, almost inadvertently, which would connect me with Ellen as irretrievably, as ambivalently, as chance has tied me to Rousseau. I think she found it all rather comic, knew it to be temporary, this obsessional fixation which would pass once my thesis was completed, and I could glide like a coffin into the securely tenured entombment of academic life, from which Donald had risen again today, over a cup of coffee we now went to replenish.

Melchior Grimm saw it all coming, the eventual madness into which Rousseau would descend; but this, when Jean-Jacques fled Montlouis in 1762 and escaped to Switzerland, was still just beginning to emerge. Rousseau was taken in by an exiled Scottish Jacobite in Neuchâtel; and here he started dressing, bizarrely, in Armenian costume, the long robes hiding catheters with which his urinary disorders were to some extent relieved. This was how the young James Boswell found him when he visited in 1764, not long after embarking on his own remarkable career as literary self-analyst. Rousseau complained to him about the shameful edict of the Paris Parlement which triggered his flight, Boswell asked for his thoughts on libertinism, and the two

220

parted on sufficiently good terms for Boswell later to have the opportunity of putting into practice his own thoughts on the matter with Thérèse.

Rousseau had by now declared himself to have given up literature for ever, and he continued to puzzle the good people of Neuchâtel until the following year, when – not unreasonably, in view of the disparaging opinions he freely expressed about them – they stoned the madman out of his house. Next, in keeping with his view that the natural state of man is solitude (and having shown enthusiasm for no book more than *Robinson Crusoe*), he moved to the little island of Saint-Pierre on the Lake of Bienne. Ellen and I saw it on our honeymoon; we argued about a plastic plate. He was almost happy here, with his books locked away, and without a writing desk to taunt and persecute him, in a room filled only with grasses and flowers since he now regarded himself as a botanist. But the idyll ended (Ellen and I had another argument on the way to Geneva); Rousseau's next stop on the road to mental collapse was a year in Britain, where he was offered refuge by the genial David Hume. Thérèse came separately with Boswell, who scored with her no less than thirteen times en route, by his own reckoning, before handing her over in Chiswick and going to find Johnson. Rousseau's stay ended predictably, with accusations of infamy against a bewildered Hume who was glad to be rid of him. The remaining twenty years were a continuing decline: a return to France under a false name; then a raving sequel to the *Confessions* called *Rousseau juge de Jean-Jacques* ('Rousseau, Judge of Jean-Jacques'), whose manuscript Rousseau tried to deposit on the high altar of Notre-Dame. A metal screen barred the way; he took this to be a sign from God, with whom, by now, Rousseau was on familiar terms. Still convinced he was the victim of a terrible plot, Rousseau pathetically resorted to distributing a hand-written leaflet to passers-by in the street, in which he pleaded to the people of France for their support.

Calm returns in his last book, *Les Rêveries du promeneur solitaire* ('Reveries of the Solitary Walker'), but even here Rousseau mentions quite routinely the spies who continued to follow him; and of those supposed spies, we can say that Ferrand and Minard were among the first. They make only one more appearance in the *Confessions* before vanishing for ever into the obscurity from which I hoped, more and more desperately, to raise them. Now it is the summer of 1762, about a year after Rousseau first met them, and they have moved house. Their new abode is right next to Rousseau's own; from their garden, they can easily climb into his. And things start to go missing from Rousseau's *donjon*.

Ellen thought it was all rather quaint, this obsession with people who'd been past auditing for two hundred years, and whom I would talk about as if I knew them personally. Even she would learn to bring up the Gossips at dinner parties, mockingly, as if they were members of the local tennis club. But then she must have grown used to it, and the charm wore off.

Donald and I refilled our coffee cups. I believe I have mentioned the way in which my meeting with him made me realize how moments of recognition can so quickly be replaced by the habits of memory, so that we live in a state of blindness, not even aware, for instance, that a man we know well might have shaved off his beard, or that a woman has completely altered her hairstyle (on several occasions I have been chastised for this gravest offence, second only to adultery, in the marital code of conduct). Nowhere is such blindness more acute than with regard to ourselves, and Donald had allowed me to see my own illness, to which idleness and indifference had made me vulnerable. But I could also understand now why it was that Louisa held such fascination for me. With her, no dullness of habit was possible; every moment was the first. With each of our brief meetings I received the merest taste, like the physiological impression which will cease to surprise after only a few seconds; and yet these seconds were all I ever had, in the manner of those experts who put a dozen wines into their mouths, and, by never swallowing any, are able to extend the sensation of novelty indefinitely. Louisa would always be a stranger to me, and this was why I loved her so intensely.

Nothing fuels obsession so much as ignorance. I saw this in the case of my *Commères*; it was precisely because I couldn't find them that they exerted such power over my imagination. They existed only in two brief passages of the *Confessions*, coming at a crucial point in the story of Rousseau's madness of which his book, though he did not realize it, forms the chronicle. For it was following the success of *Julie* that a series of strange events began to trouble him. He received anonymous letters, mysterious requests which seemed designed to compromise him. These letters would all, Rousseau assures us, be found among his papers after his death. Rumours were being spread about him in Paris; there were inexplicable objections to *Émile* and the *Contrat social* whose parts he was sending to Amsterdam in readiness for publication. It seemed that the packages were being intercepted, his books were being circulated in manuscript; and while the objections were suspicious, even more so was their abrupt end, when suddenly it appeared

ANDREW CRUMEY

that whatever Rousseau sent was considered fit for immediate publication, and politically harmless. He was being set up, but didn't yet know who might be behind it all.

And this was when Ferrand and Minard moved house, right next to Montlouis, to which they now had easy access. On some mornings, when Rousseau went to his *donjon* to resume his labours, he would find that his papers had been disturbed; if he locked his door, this would only make the disarray even worse next day. At one point, a book disappeared altogether, mysteriously returning, like a tomcat with a promiscuous nocturnal life of its own, two days later to the place from which it had evaporated.

The architect of the conspiracy, the vindictive poisoner of friendships who was slowly plotting Rousseau's downfall, and who would be exposed and denounced in the most vitriolic terms in the *Confessions*, was Melchior Grimm, assisted by D'Alembert and others. It was Grimm, according to Rousseau, who engineered the warrant for his arrest following the denunciation of *Émile* and the *Contrat social* by the Paris Parlement. The exile in Switzerland, in Britain; the return to France under a false name; the years of being hounded and pursued and spied upon; all this, Rousseau assures us, was because of Grimm.

In Rousseau, however, as I explained to Ellen when I first met her at Donald's party, one can never be sure where fact ends, and fantasy begins.

The anonymous messages he mentions were not, after all, discovered among his effects. And the insults which Rousseau suffered from his friends were often oblique to say the least. The rift with Diderot, for example, we can ascribe to the philosopher's delay in answering Rousseau's letters; it was compounded when Rousseau received from Diderot a copy of one of his plays and discovered in it the line: 'Only the wicked man is alone', which Rousseau paranoically took to be a reference to himself. D'Alembert's sin was equally insignificant; he obtained his information on Geneva (for an encyclopaedia entry) from Voltaire, rather than from Rousseau himself. As for Grimm, when we compare the letters which Rousseau reproduces with the same letters given differently by Madame d'Épinay, and when we consider the evidence of her memoirs, of Grimm's correspondence, of the testimony of Saint-Lambert, Diderot and others, and when we read more closely the crucial portions of the *Confessions* themselves, we discover that the crime for which Grimm paid so heavily, the offence which caused him to be portrayed by Rousseau as grand conspirator and virtual anti-Christ, was that once, while they were all staying at Madame d'Épinay's, Grimm pointed out an error which Rousseau had made in some music he was copying. Solitude was the nutrient which fed such trivial insults, until they grew into the monsters which ate Rousseau's mind.

And what about *les Commères*? D'Alembert, with whom they supposedly lodged in Paris, makes no mention of Ferrand and Minard. Rousseau must have been right, I decided, when he said their names were false; and yet D'Alembert, who admittedly had far better things to write about, says nothing about a pair of fellow lodgers by any name, one tall and pompously benevolent, the other short, thickset, and irritatingly exact; two men who breathed, walked, dined in my imagination, just as obstinately and inexplicably as they had for Rousseau. They were not connected with the *Ecclesiastical Gazette*; nor is there any police file or administrative record that can be linked to them. From each new source I checked they remained frustratingly absent, their secretive lives amounting to an invisibility which, it seemed, extended throughout the entirety of documentary, pictorial and anecdotal evidence for the period in question.

I found an answer to all this; and it came as a great relief to Ellen, who hoped that once I'd published my thesis we could perhaps forget about the matter, and even begin to take holidays in places wholly lacking in literary connections. Benidorm, say. But it is to my theory of Ferrand and Minard that I owe whatever academic status I can claim to possess; a minor notoriety, a whiff of controversy which brings me invitations from second-rank conferences like the one in Prague, where I told Donald that the *Commères* were just fine, and I was excited by the prospects computerization might provide for opening up new and more rapid ways of finding information.

'Actually,' I said, 'one of my students has been doing some research for me on the Internet.' I told him about the article which Louisa had found; perhaps it would be of relevance to the book he was writing on the French publishing industry? I didn't have it with me; I said I'd send him a copy when I got back to Britain. Then it was time for us to go to the next lecture, and during it I could think only of Louisa, and the steady approach, with each passing minute celebrated by the slowly moving hand of the clock on the wall, of the week when Ellen would be away. Sex, you see, is the sort of thing people think about, while they're supposed to be listening to a lecture on eighteenth-century literature.

CHAPTER 10

Well, I said to myself, as I began to write this letter; who would have thought that a flat tyre, a shower of rain, and a hundred and one other coincidences known or unknown, all existing somewhere within the hypertext source code of the universe (you see how much I've been brushing up, thanks to *Dr Cool's Web Magic*) should have brought about the opportunity for me to experience for the first time, at an age when most men are already dead, the various and not wholly unpleasant sensations of sexual intercourse. Yes, indeed! This is the strange turn of events which now has come to pass, and I expect you'll want to know all about it.

Last time you saw Catriona, she was fast asleep on my sofa after her bath, with *Ferrand and Minard* lying open on her chest. I gently lifted the book from her, then went back upstairs to write a letter, which I had just finished when I heard her begin to move.

'Ah, you're awake,' I called, going down to meet her in the kitchen, where I saw her reach ominously for the teapot. 'Please, none for me,' I implored. She remembered the way I'd been caught short a little earlier, and said she'd just make one for herself, if that was all right. By now it was already past five o'clock; Catriona's reluctance to leave, and her

227

enthusiasm for my PG Tips, made me wonder if her flat lacked electric lighting and a packet of teabags in addition to suffering from a defective boiler. Such are the privations which students have to endure.

I asked if she'd managed to get very far with Dr Petrie's book before she fell asleep, and she shook her head somewhat apologetically. It was a bit different from reading about enzymes, it would seem; Petrie's style was laboured and dense. 'Dead boring' was how Catriona neatly summed it up.

'What will you be doing tonight?' I then asked, for by now I was beginning to wonder if I was ever going to be rid of my helpful friend, and thought it best to suggest topics related to the concept of imminent departure. 'Do you have much homework?'

She looked at me with the same expression I'd seen recently on the face of a plooky boy in a supermarket. Then she said, 'I've got work to do, but not at home.'

I considered this very wise; a flat with no heating and a deficiency of tea was no place for a life scientist to do her essays. 'I take it you use the facilities in the university library?'

'No, I work somewhere else. I get paid for it.' I'd never heard of this kind of arrangement in higher education, so now it was my turn to stare blankly. She said, 'The Oasis. Ever heard of it?'

I knew of no such place of study; but then I suspected she meant it was her habit to go to a public house, where the heating was free, but other customers might be apt to spill alcohol on her notes while she huddled in a corner, trying to write amidst the noise. 'I went to a pub once,' I informed her. 'I found it a disgusting, smelly place. You surely don't need to go there to keep warm.'

'The Oasis isn't a pub,' she said, with a hint of sorrow. 'Actually, it's a massage parlour, though I'm only telling you about it because you don't know what that means, do you?'

She wasn't going to catch me out yet again with her 'have you honestly never' routine. 'On the contrary, I know all about such places,' I replied confidently. 'And I also know that the large amounts of steam are sure to have a detrimental effect on your lecture notes. Why, the ink must be smudged beyond recognition by the time you come out. These places may be warm, but you really shouldn't contemplate doing any kind of work there if you want a good degree.'

To be honest, I don't think she was really listening to me, but she smiled at my concern. 'I have to live,' she said. 'I don't like it, but what else can I do?'

I told her she would be better working here, where the only steam was from the kettle she insisted on boiling so frequently; and if students were now paid their grants on an hourly basis, as seemed to be the case from what Catriona had said, then I'd be perfectly happy to give her the 'going rate', the same as with the cleaning. She said she'd think about it, then glanced at her watch and saw that it was time to leave. 'Be careful of all that steam,' I reminded her as she put on her coat. 'Breathe lightly,' I advised. 'And don't swallow.'

'Oh, I never do that,' she said, greatly to my relief.

I went back to my computer, and retrieved the image which had made such an impression on poor Mrs B. Inspired by the wisdom of *Dr Cool's Web Magic*, I now decided to scrutinize its code in some detail. Of course you are completely unaware of what this could possibly mean, and of the manner in which Internet search engines prioritize their 'hits' by referring to keywords hidden as HTML meta-tags in file headers (*Dr Cool*, page 58); so let me simply explain that after an exercise hardly more lengthy or difficult than, let us say, parsing a page or two of the Latin of Buchanan, I was able to establish that the naked reader's photograph conceals an important message: a line of programming language unseen by the user, and included solely for the benefit of the search engine which had so promptly and fatefully delivered the young lady to me:

<meta name='keywords' content='Ferrand, Minard, Rosier'>

The strange photograph, which cost me one fine housekeeper and delivered another, was therefore designed specifically so that it would be brought to the attention of anyone looking for the words Ferrand, Minard or Rosier on the Internet. This was the real reason why I had come across the unknown girl, rather than the book she happened to be reading.

It was all more than enough for one day, and I went to bed a few hours later with my head fairly buzzing. My eyes still aren't used to the new demands of computer technology, and it was a revival of my headache which woke me with a thump next morning.

Catriona arrived punctually, and soon set about her work. She even promised to make soup for lunch, though I assured her that the 'Pasta Fan Tutti', or whatever she called it, had been magnificent, if somewhat abundant. I spent the morning examining the HTML code of every 'Rosier' page I had found to date, also checking the URLs and hyperlinks. If only Mrs B could see me now, I said to myself. Lunch passed, and most of the afternoon, until we entered the familiar 'sitting around drinking tea' part of the day, which I still had not quite talked Catriona out of.

'Will you be working again tonight?' I asked her, having decided that I should begin my suggestions of departure as early as possible, since I knew how long it might be before they took effect.

Catriona said no, she was going to a party; and I told her I thought this a grand idea, since young people can so easily become bored when left on their own for too long. 'I was always particularly fond of musical chairs,' I added, recalling the social gatherings of my early years. 'And will there be dancing?'

Catriona nodded. 'I expect there'll be quite a lot.'

'Dancing's a fine thing, though I could never manage a waltz, or anything else in threes.'

She told me they do a different sort of dancing these days, and I asked her for a demonstration.

'What, here? Now?' she laughed, looking at the empty floorspace in the middle of the living room. 'But we've no music.' I was about to suggest that I could whistle something, when Catriona got up from her chair to inspect the record player, which has lain silent in the corner for many a year. She examined the half-dozen neglected LPs occupying the space underneath, smiling as she drew one out. 'Kenneth McKellar? I'm not sure I can get into that.'

'Oh, you simply slide the plastic disc from the opening at the side,' I explained. 'There's some Moira Anderson, too. Jimmy Shand, all the popular acts. Mrs B left them there a long time ago.'

'I'll put something on if you like,' Catriona said, 'though we'd maybe better just sit and listen.'

I gave her a free choice, and a moment later, after a bump and hiss, there was a resounding parp from the accordion as Jimmy Shand And His Band began to play. 'You can't beat it,' I observed, recalling the wise judgement of Mrs B.

Catriona went to the kitchen, perhaps to make yet more of the tea she lives on. I called to her, raising my voice over the jaunty music, 'Is it best if I pay you daily?'

'Don't worry about it,' she called back.

'But with all the books you have to buy, and the candles I expect you need for your flat, and the odd packet of sweeties – things must be very hard for you.'

'I told you, I manage,' was the reply.

I knew that no 'going rate' could compensate for the amount of help which Catriona provided. Why, already her penknife had restored my computer to life; a job which the support engineer would have done for heaven knows how much! I still hadn't even given her the wee treat for helping me with my messages, which she'd refused after our first meeting. Not wishing to embarrass her, I decided to deposit one or two pound notes in the bag she'd left on the floor beside her chair. I don't know whether you'd call it a purse or a handbag; in our day handbags were bigger, and purses didn't have leather shoulder-straps.

To the accompaniment of 'The Dashing White Sergeant', I raised myself from my chair and brought some money from my pocket as I made my way across the room. Then I picked up Catriona's little purse-bag and opened it. There was a lipstick inside, a ballpoint pen, a bus-pass and some things wrapped in foil; then I noticed a small blue pill, with a picture of a dove on it. I'd never seen that sort of medicine, and wondered what condition Catriona might be suffering from. A 'woman's thing', I expected, and was still pondering the issue when Catriona walked back into the room.

There was an embarrassed silence. Even 'The Dashing White Sergeant' came to a halt, and the record scraped through a pause between tunes while I stood with the open purse in one hand, and the little pill held aloft in the fingers of the other. She must have seen me put the money in. 'Please don't be cross,' I said. I hoped we weren't going to have another scene with her refusing my wee treat.

'No,' she said. 'No problem.'

Well, that was fine then. But what about the pill; was Catriona unwell? Did this explain all the tea? I extended my hand in her direction, offering the medicine. 'Do you need to take this soon? After a bath, perhaps?'

Catriona took the pill from me, put it back into the purse I still held, then retrieved that as well. 'It's for tonight, actually.'

'The medicine's for the party? Well, I know that too much socializing can be apt to give one a headache.'

She laughed inexplicably and sat down on the sofa.

'I only take capsules which are blue and orange,' I said, sitting down beside her. 'And Mrs B's supply never included ones with pictures of birds.'

Catriona said, 'It isn't medicine. It's recreational.'

'How curious. So there's nothing wring with you?'

'No.'

'Then it's really just a kind of sweetie?'

She nodded.

'And do you have another which I could try? I'm rather fond of Smarties.'

She said, 'I don't think that'd be a good idea.'

'Well,' I told her, 'I expect it's time for you to go and

take your bath now.' Already we were settling into a kind
of routine; but her next comment, after a thoughtful pause,
was:

'Do you really want to try it?'

I couldn't see why a wee Smartie should be the cause of
such debate. 'If you've just got the one, then why not give
me half?'

'They're quite expensive,' she said.

I insisted I'd settle our accounts in full before the day's
end, and she went back to the kitchen, soon returning with
two pieces and some powder on a saucer, having cut the
sweet with a knife. From the record player, the accordion
gave another wheezy chord; Catriona lifted the larger piece
and said with a grin, 'Let's do it.' I followed, putting the
other half in my mouth.

'I can only say that it's the most disappointing Smartie
I've ever tasted,' I informed her. 'And if this is the state of
confectionery these days then I feel truly sorry for the
young.'

Not long afterwards, we began to dance. Catriona started
first; it sounded like 'The Bonnie Bonnie Banks', and she
looked to me as though she was going far too fast. I got up
and tried swaying a bit, and soon we were both singing,
'You take the high road', et cetera, and it nearly brought a
tear to my eye. In fact it was a relief to find my body's
waterworks concentrating their activity on a different region
from usual, and I've found that these pills, which Catriona
now buys regularly for me, have a very beneficial effect on
my bladder.

We'd hardly got going when Jimmy Shand reached the
end of side one. 'Let's have something else,' Catriona suggested, then twirled around while Kenneth McKellar sang

'The De'il's Awa' Wi' Th'Exciseman'. She subsequently did exactly the same steps to 'Ae Fond Kiss', and I wondered if this random gyrating was the only dance that still exists these days; but in that case, I decided, young people are really in a very fortunate position, never having to worry about the awkward tunes with three to a bar, and it all made me feel quite happy.

She stopped spinning for a moment, and said, 'I've been thinking about yesterday.'

Since yesterday had consisted of so many fascinating items, including a trip to a bookshop and a good deal of 'net surfing', not to mention her bath, I could quite understand why the day was worthy of contemplation.

'I mean, about me doing some work here,' she said.

By now I'd decided to sit down on the sofa. My head, I realized, was in an unusual state; not at all painful, but decidedly not its usual self. This, I reasoned, must be the consequence of all that source code I'd been studying earlier; a mental exercise whose effects now struck me as being slightly less wholesome than those of Latin grammar. 'You can do as much homework as you like,' I said. She was already drawing the curtains; I'd no idea why. 'Just add up the time at standard grant authority rates, on top of the cleaning and the pill, when we sort out your bill later.' I was a bit flushed and began to loosen my tie.

'You've really never done it before, have you?' she said. 'With a woman, I mean.'

'I can't quite remember,' I replied. 'Perhaps once or twice with Mrs B, about twenty years ago.' But when I thought harder about it I decided that dancing around in the living room was something I'd never done with any woman, not even Mrs B.

'All right then, what do you want me to do?' she asked with sudden earnestness, coming and sitting down next to me. I had no idea how I was supposed to answer this question, since I knew absolutely nothing about her course or the kind of homework she had been set.

'Just do whatever you have to,' I said. 'Don't mind me; I'll sit here and get my breath back, and I won't say a word.'

The music hadn't stopped. I removed my tie to the accompaniment of 'Charlie is My Darling', then closed my eyes, which had been sorely overstimulated by the computer, and were now rather sensitive. I thought Catriona must have gone to fetch her books, but I was surprised soon afterwards to feel her tugging at my shirt buttons, unfastening them one by one. It was a moment of some embarrassment to me, but also of relief, since my excessive proximity to the computer had, it seemed, caused a degree of physical over-heating which they'd said nothing at all about at Dixons. Then gradually, as the operation continued, I began to understand exactly what it was that the poor girl must spend her time doing at that massage parlour of hers. While my eyes remained closed and I did my best to pretend I wasn't noticing any of it, and I felt her hands start to stroke and knead my chest, I realized that this must be the sort of practical homework a life scientist is set nowadays. She was inspecting my musculature as part of her course, and I was happy to serve as model, though I wasn't sure I'd be able to remain perfectly still throughout.

Her cursory survey of my torso was carried out with the fingers of an expert. I guessed that at this stage she was merely revising a topic she already knew quite well, and I was gratified by her thoroughness in retreading old and familiar ground. Then, somewhat to my disquiet, though I still did my best to act as if I wasn't really there, she made me lie down and began to ease off my trousers; ready, it would seem, to begin a detailed analysis of the most current part of the syllabus.

Now I was naked, trying not to shiver in case it put her off, and listening with desperate attentiveness to 'My Love is Like a Red, Red Rose', while Catriona began to experiment with an item I'm surprised is even mentioned in her course, especially in front of female students. Strangely, I had no urge to resist; I reminded myself that really Catriona was a kind of nurse, and I freely allowed her academic attentions to fix themselves, with an objectivity I myself could share, on the *membrum virile* which formed the latest chapter of her education. She was stroking it, pummelling it, letting it rise and plop like a troutlet in a stream, and it was all a far cry from the rote learning that invariably constituted homework in our day, I can tell you. She didn't even seem to be taking notes, judging by the extent to which both her hands were involved in her scientific task.

I'm afraid this went on for an extremely long time. I was too polite to say anything, but eventually understood the reason she was taking such pains over her work to be not only a commendable attention to detail, but also that she required the organ to be in a very particular state; one which I gladly would have hastened if only I knew how, so that we could be finished and I could be going on with other things.

At last the apparatus was ready, however, and Catriona began to perform upon it a rhythmical and somewhat vigorous procedure, reminiscent of the way in which Mrs B used to grate lumps of cheddar. I imagined Catriona to be counting strokes as part of some general survey which her lecturer required before the end of term. Unfortunately, however, I was by now too strongly aware of the computer's deleterious effects, which had spread themselves far beyond my tingling eyes, beyond my throbbing neural centres still crying out for search engines and video links, and beyond a general yet modest warming of my body. Something far more drastic was taking place, and I appeared to be on the verge of a seizure or perhaps even death, though I still felt no urge to resist it. Then at last, for a bright and terrible second, I wondered if I'd done the right thing after all, when I abandoned my dirty dusty rubbish in favour of a machine which had so transformed my life.

She'd stopped now. I cautiously opened one eye, and saw her doing something with a paper tissue. Of textbook or lecture notes there was not a trace to be seen; the remarkable girl had done everything from memory. She stood up and left the room, and I decided it was safe for me to put on my clothes again. All that remained of my symptoms was a pain in my arm and chest, which subsided soon afterwards.

Her homework completed, Catriona now went upstairs to take her customary bath. How ever is her end of term assessment carried out, I asked myself, reknotting my tie. And in view of the strange attack I had suffered, I wondered if I ought to limit the hours I spend 'browsing' on my computer.

When Catriona returned and I raised the matter of payment, she proposed I give her only half the standard rate, whereas I insisted on double. We eventually settled on fifty pounds. She promised me more pills for my bladder problem, and I reminded her that she need no longer endure the unhealthy atmosphere of the massage parlour, now that she could do all her work here.

'Enjoy the party,' I said as she was leaving. In a sudden

outbreak of frivolity, I even suggested she bring me back a balloon, though the request had slipped both our minds when she returned next day.

By now, a pattern had been set; one as strict in its observance as had been the sacred timetable of Mrs B. Catriona would spend the morning doing chores while I downloaded web pages, being careful not to overstimulate myself with all that abundance of information. Then after lunch we would go upstairs to my bedroom and Catriona would set about her homework; though after a few days of it I began to wonder how long she intended to spend on the same topic, which should have merited hardly more than a footnote, but seemed instead to be the major item of her study. So this is what's meant by 'life sciences', I said to myself, as Catriona trundled some kind of wheel across my member, no doubt measuring it as part of yet another survey. No wonder they still haven't found out why there are no green cats or dogs, I decided, if this is how they spend all their time. And these long periods of lying still and naked, pretending that nothing was happening while another pill kept my waterworks at bay, invariably brought on a seizure again, no matter how meagre my previous exposure had been to the World Wide Web. Gradually, however, once I knew I wasn't dying, I actually came to find the experience quite pleasant, and looked forward to Catriona's study hour almost as much as she. Afterwards she would take a bath, I would scrub her back, and while she talked wistfully about that boy Gary or Ewan or whatever his name was, I would reflect that she was far better off without such a hindrance to her education.

As we made our preparations on the fourth day, still without any lecture notes in sight, she said, 'Do you want me to go all the way?' I told her yes, she should do whatever was necessary, and when she said the rate was double I readily consented, since this was what in any case I had proposed to pay her for her intellectual labours.

Her homework in this instance, when I dared open one eye to see what was going on, consisted first of putting a rubber sheath over the apparatus whose literature must fill an entire shelf in her departmental library, and then of lowering her body on to it. I began to suspect this wasn't part of the normal curriculum. My seizure was greater than ever, and difficult to conceal; she immediately followed with one of her own. My scientific education is limited only to what I have learned from Dr Cool and the World Wide Web; nevertheless I could tell that Catriona and I had engaged in sexual intercourse. The experience was not unpleasant, but it really did make me wonder what all the fuss was about, since I found it infinitely less satisfying than an equal length of time spent over *A Child's Garden of Verses*, or one of Mrs B's broths.

Really, I said to myself, students these days are required to do some extraordinary things in order to get a degree. Truly I'm glad that my own time is long past, and that I was spared such exertions by a system which in an earlier era regarded memory as being the only faculty worthy of strenuous cultivation.

Now you know how I came to have an experience that supposedly explains all those photographs which clutter the web, as well as countless novels of a sentimental or sensational kind which can be of no interest to you or me, but can be found in abundance in any bookshop. I am therefore approaching the end of what must be my last letter to you, since Catriona has made me promise to stop writing, as I shall explain.

Yesterday I heard her gathering the mail from the mat downstairs. Only a few decades ago, this was a chore to be carried out several times between dawn and dusk; but modern progress has reduced the arrival of the post to a single ritual somewhere in the middle of the morning which may well, I hear, be capable of further improvement, so that soon the flapping of the letterbox will be a bother to busy people only every second or third day, if at all. In my study, where the computer's cooling fan gently hummed and the flickering screen bewitched my vision, I could sense Catriona down below, hovering at the front door as if the letters she had gathered were a cause for deep reflection.

The morning, measured in its progress by that flutter of bills and by the subsequent birth of a familiar odour whose notes of frying onions and boiling tinned tomatoes were soon being reinforced by more subtle herbal mysteries as the pasta hour approached, ended with me gratefully terminating my Internet session and then beginning, in contrast to the effortless journey which I had made like an airborne Faust between distant continents (finding much the same thing in each), with my slow descent, one difficult step at a time, in the direction which my grateful nose now dictated. In the kitchen, I found Catriona devoting herself to her accustomed task.

She turned. 'Your mail's on the table.'

She really meant the 'work surface'; this gradual blurring of the distinction between different forms of furniture is part, I believe, of the unstoppable course of progress which will, if it continues, ultimately render all things nameable by

ANDREW CRUMEY

a single word. I saw the small collection of letters to which
she referred, and found half of them to be returned items
originating from myself. I sorted these from the rest while
Catriona watched, stirred, watched again, so that I felt
myself to be another dish whose boiling was awaited with
some apprehension.

I said, 'Mrs B always took care of these, I believe,'
pushing the returned letters in Catriona's direction, hoping
that she'd know exactly what to do with them, but aware
that there was still another part of my routine in which I
needed to instruct her, or else abandon the habit for ever.

'These are the letters I posted to your friend,' she said,
as if I didn't already know the fact. Catriona sometimes
likes to state the obvious, as if trying to remove some last
remaining doubt that what she thinks she sees is what's
really there. 'And they're all marked "GONE". Your friend
must have moved; don't you have a new address?'

I said, 'My friend has been gone for quite some time, and
to a place where even the postal service cannot, as yet,
forward deliveries.'

Catriona stared at me with such a blank, despairing look
of 'do you really mean . . . ?' that she momentarily forgot to
stir the pot, and it gave a viscous bubbling pop of complaint.
Then, 'Your friend . . . passed away?'

'Eight years and four months ago,' I explained. 'An
ending which comes to us all.'

'Then why do you keep writing?' she asked, and this was
slightly difficult to answer, because I realized I'd never
thought about it very deeply. What I mean is that you can
think you understand the reason for something, but as
soon as you try to put it into words you discover, like

St Augustine with respect to time, that you never really understood it after all.

'Some habits are very difficult to change,' I suggested. 'And without anyone to write to, what was I supposed to do? How was I to fill the two hours of every day which would suddenly find themselves empty and unoccupied? Yes, my oldest and truest friend is gone, but why should that be the end of it? How many writers, I wonder, compose works whose intended reader will never see them; and yet they write nevertheless, imagining that every word, even as it leaves their pen, is touching the eye, the ear, the thoughts and the heart of the one person to whom they wish to speak?'

I confess that this florid speech was largely cribbed from *Ferrand and Minard: Jean-Jacques Rousseau and the Search for Lost Time*. Since I could find no reason of my own, I thought it best to resort to the advice of Dr Petrie.

'Even so,' said Catriona; 'To write every day to someone who's dead. It's, well . . . it's so . . .'

I knew that 'sad' was the word she was approaching yet avoiding, and I dare say it truly is a sad turn of events that it should have been you, the patient recipient of all my ramblings, who should have departed first between the two of us. Had it rather been I who went, then no doubt your letters to me would have been infinitely more enjoyable than my own offerings. 'Friends pass away, but friendship lives forever,' I now proposed, having abandoned Petrie in favour of a line from a poem I saw in *The Scots Magazine*.

Catriona nodded solemnly. 'That's beautiful.' At least I'd steered her away from 'sad', which I've heard coming from her a little too often. Then I explained how Mrs B would dutifully post my letters, only for each one to be returned some days afterwards from the sorting office where they're used to dealing with such situations, and Mrs B would file them away. Catriona, for some reason, found this all hard to take. 'You've got to let go,' she said, though I was not even touching the letters by now, which lay resolutely upon the recently wiped work surface. 'You can't live in a fantasy. Your friend's gone; why pretend otherwise?'

Thus we see the clear vision of this admirable young girl; and who was I to argue or protest? It was not only enzymes and electric plugs she understood, or computers and little pills with birds on them; no, Catriona was a scientist of Life, and her philosophy could not accommodate the antics of a pathetic old fool like me. She made me promise that I would no longer trouble the postal service with letters which merely slow up the system for everyone else; I would no longer write tales which can be of interest and amusement only to myself, and are read by no one; I would no longer go on behaving as if my closest friend from childhood, whose warm hand I always held while we marched short-trousered together to our forms, still breathed just as I must go on doing for some years or months yet. No, I would stop all this nonsense and, as she put it technically, 'get a life'. For here you see the way in which my new education was proceeding; not only had the dirty rubbish been exorcised from my world, but now the ghosts of the past would also be banished for ever. I know it all must come as something of a shock, but I shall no doubt be joining you again permanently before too long, and then we can resume our exchanges properly.

'You're so right,' I told Catriona later, as we finished our pasta. 'My friend is no more; today he has truly died, and I can get on with my new existence.' Then I went upstairs to my computer, and resumed my search for Ferrand and Minard, wondering how many other sites might be haunted by those keywords. And there's so much I could tell you, if only you were still alive! For what I now found lurking on the Internet was an account of the two men's escape from Paris following a woman's murder, and of their subsequent fate. Now, at last, Rosier's Encyclopaedia was almost within my grasp. But I shall say no more about the matter, for I must instead bid you a final and most tender farewell.

CHAPTER 11

Minard was standing outside Rousseau's house, while the author gazed intently at him.

'This is Father Bertier's friend, Thérèse?' Rousseau said to his wife, and she nodded. 'Well, you'd better come inside, monsieur, and give me the Father's news.' And so, for the second time, Minard entered the house. Not long before, he'd been anticipating Thérèse's promised meal; now his appetite was suddenly gone.

Why, Minard wanted to know, were the papers which had disappeared from Jacqueline's room lying amongst Rousseau's manuscripts? Minard could feel those papers inside his clothes, against his chest, while Jean-Jacques ordered him to come upstairs. They passed from the small kitchen, past a partitioned section which obviously served as Thérèse's bedroom, to the twisting staircase at the far end, and as Minard watched his host ascend he tried to work out how it could possibly be, that the most famous author in the world should be mixed up in all this. Logic had never been Minard's strong point (though he had failed numerous exams in it), and the matter taxed him so gravely that he barely noticed the rooms into which they emerged at the top of the stairs. Really it was a single room, divided in much the same way as Thérèse's domain downstairs, and with a large bed built into an alcove. Rousseau invited Minard to sit down.

Jacqueline was from these parts, Minard reasoned, which was of course why he and Ferrand came here in the first place. And she knew Father Bertier, who also knew Rousseau, and so this was how the most famous author in the world had become involved in Minard's little problem of a dead woman and a pile of papers belonging to a lunatic. Yes, he'd almost got it worked out, when Rousseau thumped his stick on the floor, apparently as some kind of instruction to his female companion down below.

'Well?' said Rousseau. 'How fares the good Father?'

And Bertier was the one who killed Jacqueline, Minard almost said, which means that he must have taken the papers from her room, brought them back with him to Montmorency last night, then seen the similar documents in the bundle which Minard and Ferrand left at the Oratory this morning. But then Bertier would know that he knew that ... and it wouldn't be a very good situation for Ferrand who was still in the cottage Bertier had provided for them.

'He's the one!' Minard cried.

'I beg your pardon?'

'Who sent me,' Minard explained. 'Father Bertier is the one who sent me.'

Jean-Jacques gave an impatient shrug. 'I know that already. But what of his news?'

Minard tried to calm down. Thérèse brought in a pitcher of wine for them to drink, and Rousseau silently directed his eye to the small table where he expected it to be placed. Then, as Thérèse withdrew, the gaze fell on Minard again. 'You seem uneasy,' he suggested.

'Uneasy? Me?' Minard gave a shrill laugh, and felt the papers inside his shirt rub and tickle against his skin. He saw Jacqueline's dead face, and Bertier's smile, and wondered what Ferrand was doing now. Minard said, 'Please, tell me about *Julie*.'

'No,' Rousseau said simply. 'Tell me about Father Bertier.'

It was like a judicial investigation, and yet Minard had committed no crime. 'He's very well, and sends his regards.'

'How exactly do you know him?' Rousseau then asked. 'You see him in Paris, I take it?' Minard nodded, mentally witnessing Jacqueline's head being brutally shaken as Bertier's hands closed around her white neck, draining the life from her. 'And Diderot?' Rousseau asked. 'Do you know any of his party?'

Minard hadn't been aware that there were sides to be taken. If there were, he'd better make sure he chose the right one. 'Diderot's a very fine man,' he suggested, not wishing to commit himself.

'And D'Alembert?' Rousseau added, to which Minard gave a nod; then Rousseau said, 'I heard in the village about some friends of D'Alembert's — I believe they may even be fellow lodgers — who come here for the summer. This is you, I take it?'

'Yes, that's us,' Minard readily agreed, happy to let Jean-Jacques make up the story himself. 'Ferrand and Minard, at your service.'

Rousseau raised one eyebrow. 'Ferrand? He's the other one?'

Minard gave a nod, then added, 'Though those aren't our real names of course.'

248

For some reason, the most famous author in the world seemed to be losing patience with his visitor, who, remembering that he should be talking about Father Bertier rather than about Ferrand, decided to describe the lunch they'd all had together at the Oratory. But he'd only got as far as the terrine when Rousseau, apparently no longer listening and desirous of changing the subject, said wearily, 'Are you fond of chess?'

To which Minard replied, 'Why, the Régence is virtually my second home.' This wasn't true, of course, and when Minard remembered that the Régence was where Ferrand had met the man whose manuscripts were the start of all their misfortunes, he said, 'Though actually I prefer the Magris.'

'In that case,' Rousseau said, barely suppressing a sigh, 'why don't you choose the Magris as your second home, instead of the Régence?'

Logic, as has already been said, was never Minard's strongest point. And he was still too preoccupied with visions of Father Bertier killing Jacqueline for him to be able to think clearly about the issue. 'When I say that the Régence is my second home, what I mean is that the Magris is my first.'

'And what about your lodgings with D'Alembert?'

It wasn't getting any easier. 'Oh, I'm hardly ever there, which is why it doesn't really count as my first home.'

'Or even your third?' suggested Thérèse, who had come to check on the pitcher of wine, but whose contribution Jean-Jacques greeted with a disapproving stare.

'No,' said Minard, 'not even my third. I suppose our cottage here in Montmorency counts as our third home, and our lodgings with D'Alembert hardly figure at all.'

'And yet that is where you actually live,' Rousseau reminded him, by now slightly exasperated.

'Oh, if you can call it living,' Minard declared airily.

'What on earth do you mean by that?' Rousseau asked, dismissing Thérèse with another nod.

Having launched himself into some kind of improvisation, Minard could do nothing but continue in the same vein. 'Well, you know what D'Alembert's like. Not the sort of person I'd recommend anyone to lodge with. And as for his wife . . .'

Rousseau was scratching his head in bewilderment. 'D'Alembert has no wife! Don't tell me that you've mistaken the foster mother he lives with for his spouse . . . or else, do you mean that such an ugly, deformed, and shrill little man has finally found himself a lover?'

Clearly, Rousseau wasn't very fond of D'Alembert, and Minard regretted having associated himself with him. Just as well he'd relegated their supposed joint lodgings to third or fourth place, or wherever it was that he'd ranked it. 'I prefer Diderot's company, actually.'

Rousseau's eyes narrowed. He rubbed his chin. 'Forgive me for speaking plainly, but there's something decidedly odd about you. Is your friend Ferrand just as bad?'

'Even worse,' Minard replied with a smile, then believed he caught Rousseau's meaning. 'But there's nothing at all unhealthy about our relationship or domestic arrangements. We like our privacy, but we're just good friends. Brothers, in fact.'

'With different names?'

'Cousins, I mean.'

'Well you shall have to excuse me,' said Rousseau, rising to his feet. 'I have much work to do, and I have enjoyed our conversation immensely. I wish you and your cousin a pleasant summer in Montmorency, and now Thérèse will show you out.'

Minard descended the stairs, pleased that the interview had gone so well. Not once had he mentioned the fact that Rousseau's good friend Father Bertier was a murderer! Minard's ability to speak on one subject while thinking about something else entirely was such as to impress even himself, though he'd been doing it all his life. But why had Jean-Jacques mentioned chess? Minard called back upstairs: 'Fancy a game some time?' There was a grunt in reply. 'I'll bring Ferrand – he beats me hollow!'

As soon as Minard had wished Thérèse goodbye, regretting that he would not after all be tasting her carrot soup today, and had walked back up the garden path to the wooden door which opened on to the steet, he burst into tears. 'Poor Jacqueline,' he murmured to himself, wiping his face on his sleeve as he began to go back down the hill, and feeling the crucial papers still tickling against his chest.

He returned home to find Ferrand slumped across the table.

'My God, he's killed you too!' Minard ran to embrace his friend, who sat up from the pile of manuscripts over which he'd fallen asleep.

'Minard, sometimes I think you're the stupidest man on earth,' Ferrand decided, after Minard had explained his theory. But then Minard took the pages from beneath his shirt. They were slightly stained from perspiration, which made Ferrand hold them at arm's length while he tried to recognize them, but he had to agree that these documents belonged with the rest, a collection which Ferrand now identified as 'Rosier's Encyclopaedia'.

'Then there is only one more mystery to solve,' said Minard. 'Why was it that Bertier, having taken these papers from the scene of the crime, should have given them to Rousseau?'

Ferrand was slowly shaking his head. 'Forget those mysteries,' he solemnly instructed. 'Our only task now is to copy Rosier's Encyclopaedia. We must not allow ourselves to think of anything else.'

Ferrand then sharpened a new quill before resuming his transcription of a treatise on the Rosierist theory of agriculture, while Minard despondently lifted another item from the collection to read. Ferrand's eyes rose from his own work so as to follow Minard's hand disapprovingly while it removed the papers, and Minard sat himself down on the bundle beside the door while Ferrand wrote.

Given Minard's weakness in logic, it was perhaps both appropriate and fortunate that the document he now perused should be concerned with the manufacture of an 'inference machine'. The description suggested an exquisite contraption similar, Minard imagined, to an astrolabe or clock, though different from either, and inscribed with words and phrases rather than numbers. How the machine was to operate, he couldn't tell from what he read, nor did he fully understand the ultimate purpose of such a device, but he found pleasure in combining and rearranging in his mind the various phrase-fragments out of which deductions were to be made. Some examples were given, of the proposed machine's capacity to make logical conclusions:

All men crave glory. No man is a dog. Therefore no dog craves glory.

The glorious man is happy. No dog is glorious. There-fore none who is happy is a dog.

No man is a dog. Some men are not cowards. Therefore some dogs are not cowards.

All men are animals. Some animals have four legs. Therefore some men have four legs.

Minard decided it would be a fine contraption, if anyone ever made it; which was unlikely, unless he and Ferrand copied out the instructions according to their commission. But Minard also knew that Rosier, their mysterious patron, could never find them here in Montmorency. The Encyclopaedia was theirs now, and Ferrand's patient work, the scratching of his pen as he sat at the table, was for his benefit alone. Likewise, Minard's reading served only as a means of self-instruction, and together here in the country-side he and his friend could at last find time to learn all those subjects and disciplines of which they had formerly been so frustratingly, tantalizingly ignorant.

He had now begun with logic, therefore. Minard read very carefully, and soon felt he understood everything there was to know about syllogisms in any of their four figures and two hundred and fifty-six moods. Such purity and rigour was what Minard needed if he was ever to forget his troubles, and poor Jacqueline.

An hour passed. Ferrand wrote, Minard read, and by now he felt like a true expert. He had found little difficulty with *modus ponens* or *modus tollens*, while *modus tollendo ponens* and *modus ponendo tollens* had caused him only slightly greater difficulty, until he realized that they were really the same thing, but expressed less succinctly. Logic was no more than common sense, and he'd been practising it all his life.

Minard wondered if Jacqueline's murderer would ever be brought to account. Either the criminal would be hanged, or else he wouldn't, Minard reasoned, applying a rule he now knew to be called the principle of excluded middle. One or other must be true; but if the criminal was to be hanged then there was really no need for Minard to concern himself any more about the inevitable triumph of justice; and if not, then no amount of effort or worry on Minard's part could rectify the matter. So Minard should forget about it and devote himself to his studies.

Another hour passed, during which Minard's deductive skills increased four- or five-fold, by his own reckoning, so that at this rate it wouldn't be long before he could unravel the deepest mysteries known to man. At one point he suddenly said, 'Ferrand, do you think it true that all men are potential murderers?'

Ferrand paused just long enough to decide the question to be wholly irrelevant. 'I do not,' he said, resuming his work.

'And what would be the opposite assertion?' Minard asked, to which Ferrand, this time not even raising his head to reply, said it would be that no man is a potential murderer. 'Ha,' said Minard. 'But someone killed poor Jacqueline, and therefore every man must be a potential murderer after all.' Then he added, 'Even you or I,' but Ferrand didn't hear, or else pretended not to.

Logical deduction was merely the common sense which Minard had been flawlessly applying to everyday problems throughout his life. And yet how pleasant it was, to have a few fancy names which he could now attach to his various modes of reasoning! After ten more minutes of deep thought he suddenly cried out, 'Of course!', uttering this with such force, and with so little warning, that Ferrand's hand jumped and transformed the dot of an *i* into an unsightly blot, which he tried to remove while Minard announced: 'If I am right, then the murderer of Jacqueline Cornet is Jean-Jacques Rousseau himself!'

Ferrand crossly blew the region of paper he had scratched clean, then stared at Minard. 'What the devil are you on about?'

But it was all really quite simple, Minard explained. 'Don't you see?' he said. 'If I'm right in what I just said – that if I am right then Rousseau is a murderer – then since I *am* right, Rousseau *is* the murderer!'

Ferrand listened slowly, patiently, as he put down the corrected sheet of paper. 'Very well,' he said. 'But let's suppose – purely for the sake of argument, and as a mere hypothesis of the logic which seems, in the last two hours or more, to have stolen your wits completely from you – that you are not right.'

Minard was nodding vigorously, and smiling, as if Ferrand had walked into just the trap he had been preparing for him. 'Let me rephrase myself. If my statement is true, then Rousseau is the murderer.' He waited proudly for Ferrand's response, as if he had just said something terribly important.

'Yes,' said Ferrand eventually. 'And what if your statement is false?'

'Then its opposite must be true. Now, what is the opposite of: "If this statement is true, then Rousseau is the murderer"?'

Ferrand really had better things to do than help Minard

with his exercises in logic. 'I suppose it would be: "If this statement is false, then Rousseau is the murderer."'

'Aha!' cried Minard. 'But the statement *is* false and hence Rousseau *is* the murderer!'

'You idiot,' Ferrand muttered, but Minard was not to be silenced so easily.

'Very well then,' Minard pursued. 'If Rousseau is not the murderer, then are you the King of France?'

It seemed to Ferrand that his friend had allowed himself to become a little too enthusiastic over his studies. 'Will you be teaching me tomorrow how to square the circle and turn lead into gold?' he asked him.

'Most probably,' Minard replied, 'for I can see that Rosier's Encyclopaedia is the means by which I can at last make up for all those many examinations I failed in the past; though I only failed them because I was always ill on the day, or had allowed myself to drink a little too much wine the night before, or because the lectures were badly delivered . . .' Ferrand had heard these excuses during their very first conversation on a bench, and he had heard them on many occasions since. 'Just tell me this,' Minard eventually said, returning to his point; 'Are you the King of France?'

Ferrand did not even answer.

'But do you agree that if Rousseau were not the murderer, then you would be the King of France?'

This was an argument which Ferrand found rather hard to follow. 'If ever you become a lawyer, Minard, it will not be thanks to Rosier's Encyclopaedia. Why on earth should Rousseau's innocence make me a king?'

His friend was on his feet by now, strutting like those followers of Aristotle who were known, Minard believed he had read, for their habit of walking around. 'It follows because, as the Encyclopaedia explains, a false premise may be used to draw any conclusion. If it is false that Rousseau is not a murderer, then you are the King of France. You are not the King of France, and therefore Rousseau is the murderer. How many more ways must I find to prove to you the logical fact, as unshakeable as a mathematical theorem, that Jacqueline Cornet's white and innocent young neck was squeezed and broken by the cruel hands of the most famous author in the world!' And Minard wept, though whether it was for his poor Jacqueline, or for Ferrand's inability to follow his great chain of reason, or for Jean-Jacques Rousseau whom Minard had formerly admired, was not apparent.

'My friend, I am sorry, but you are a complete buffoon,' was Ferrand's only comment, as he went back to copying the manuscript before him on the table.

But Minard would not let the matter rest. While Ferrand worked, Minard hastily, urgently flicked the pages of Rosier's logic. If the inference machine could ever be built, then this would certainly vindicate Minard's analysis; failing this, he could at least attempt to modify the simple 'syllogistic abacus', hardly more than an educational toy, which was illustrated by a number of sketches and tables. Minard began tearing up scraps of paper.

'We've little enough to spare!' Ferrand complained, and his anger grew deeper still, when Minard sharpened a quill and thrust it into Ferrand's inkwell, nearly splashing him as he pulled out the feather in order to write upon the small strips he had prepared. The table being fully occupied, Minard had to make do with the floor, where he assembled the strips in the manner laid down by Rosier's instructions, a procedure looking to Ferrand like some form of cabbalistic ritual.

Soon, as dusk approached, Minard was kneeling at the centre of a carefully placed arrangement of some forty or fifty pieces of paper, on which were written words or phrases such as 'All murderers are cowards', or 'If man is mortal, then . . .', or 'Some dogs have four legs', the hurried inscriptions barely legible in the fading light. The strips looked as though they had fallen randomly where they lay, scattered across a large part of the floor; and yet Minard was tracing paths between them, following with his finger sequences which took him, according to rules he stopped every so often to check in the instructions, from one piece of paper to another, as if he were a mariner plotting with utmost care and skill the course of a vessel. Many paths were possible, through this labyrinth of propositions Minard had created, and yet every route led him to the same destination; a strip at the extreme edge of his arrangement, like an island remote and terrible, on which was written: 'Rousseau is the murderer!'

'I have now proved it in sixty-four ways,' he eventually said, 'and I believe there will be 1024 proofs in total.' Then there was a knock on the door, it opened, and a breeze rearranged everything. Father Bertier stood in the doorway.

'Is the cottage to your satisfaction?' the priest asked, instantly gathering all within his gaze, as Minard regrouped his little scraps of paper and Ferrand bundled his pages.

'Perfectly so,' Ferrand replied, his arm laid across his work so as to shield it from Bertier's view as he entered and looked down at Minard.

'If I can be of any assistance to you in your mission . . .' Bertier began.

Ferrand interrupted. 'You realize, Father, that the utmost discretion is essential, and it might even be best if we were to be left entirely alone, in order not to compromise the Oratory.'

'I understand,' said Father Bertier. 'But please, let us be frank for a moment.' He closed the door, and then, in a low voice, said, 'I know that the Parlement is interested in Jean-Jacques, and this is why they have sent you. You told me as much at the Oratory. I ask nothing, I make no enquiry which might embarrass you; I merely wish to let you know that I too have my friends and superiors who remain curious regarding that same man.'

Minard said, 'You know, then?' Earlier, he had for a moment believed that Bertier was Jacqueline's lover, and that she had been killed by him. What a ridiculous notion! Now it was clear that Bertier knew of Rousseau's guilt.

Once more, Ferrand chose to break in. 'It is best that we conduct our investigations quite separately.'

'Of course,' Father Bertier readily agreed. 'I only inform you of my readiness to supply whatever help I may.' To Minard, he said, 'I know that you have already made yourself personally acquainted with Rousseau, rightly presenting yourself as my friend. I shall be happy to accompany both of you to Montlouis, so as to make the introduction more formal. Jean-Jacques is a prophet of the simple life, but he still likes things done properly.' Bertier gave a laugh, nervous and ingratiating, and said, 'I speak plainly to you, messieurs. You mentioned earlier today the name of a girl from these parts, and it is apparent to me that you know a great many things which you can use in whatever way you see fit. I say only this; that we seek the same ends, that it is even quite possible we serve, you and I, the same masters. It is therefore to the advantage of each one of us that we act as allies. What we want is information on Rousseau, and we are in a position to help one another.'

Minard said, 'Will he be arrested?' and Ferrand had to resort to knocking his inkwell on to the floor in order to stop his friend saying any more.

'I would have thought that arrest might come more under your own jurisdiction,' Bertier replied. 'I have heard of the possibility; though I also believe a compromise may be reached, by means of which he will be allowed to escape from the country, and then everyone will be happy.'

Minard complained, 'But how can a man be allowed to go free in such circumstances!', and Ferrand, spattered with ink, got up from the floor where he had retrieved the rolling inkwell and grabbed his friend by the sleeve, wondering if the only way to shut the imbecile up would be to put a large ball of paper down his throat.

'Minard, patience!' said Ferrand, as calmly as he could, then added for Bertier's benefit, 'That isn't his real name, of course.'

'Of course,' said Father Bertier. 'Now, I shall be seeing Jean-Jacques at Montlouis tomorrow. If you wish to accompany me, I shall be honoured to introduce you to our author, about whom there is much that I can tell you. And naturally, during your stay in Montmorency, every comfort which the Oratory can provide will be at your disposal. You are a welcome guest at my table, and I hope you will not refuse me often.'

Minard liked the sound of this. 'We won't,' he said. 'But I really think the man should be locked up after what he's done,' and Ferrand smothered his friend's words with an inky hand.

'Goodbye until tomorrow,' said Ferrand, struggling to keep Minard's mouth covered while the shorter man wriggled and mumbled in complaint.

'And one more thing,' Bertier added, puzzled by his guests' wrestling, yet sublimely tolerant of it. 'I hear that two men, said to lodge with Monsieur D'Alembert, are now in Montmorency. I take it you are these men?'

Ferrand nodded, and screamed as Minard bit into his hand.

'Goodnight then,' said Father Bertier calmly, as he went out and closed the door behind him.

There followed an argument about a wounded hand, some spilt ink, and who should clean the floorboards. But then at last the men embraced and reaffirmed their everlasting friendship. Tears were shed, and they slept soundly in their beds.

Ferrand was right, they were just at the beginning of their new life together. During the coming months, the friends would find that the Oratory was happy to supply them with items for copying; and in this way they would be able to feed themselves, so that their visits to Father Bertier became less frequent, eventually being weekly rather than daily. This seemed to suit the priest, who paid extremely generously for the pieces they transcribed for him; and even Minard, though deprived of the pleasures of Bertier's table, grew to enjoy the art of cookery, learned by him from Rosier's Encyclopaedia, which Ferrand continued to edit and assemble. The day was long past when their patron would have expected its return, but Ferrand was sure that Rosier, if ever he found the two copyists, would kill them as casually as he must have dispatched Jacqueline Cornet; for Ferrand still

believed Rosier to be the murderer, despite Minard's prot-
estations, and a return to Paris was out of the question.

No mention, of course, was made of any of this, during
the long sessions when Ferrand and Minard would visit
Montlouis and play chess with Rousseau. During their first
formal introduction, Father Bertier had presented the two
men with a flourish, and there had been some indecision and
confusion while Rousseau sought to establish whether or
not the people calling themselves Ferrand and Minard were
priests, and whether or not they lodged with D'Alembert;
and Thérèse had brought in the wine, saying that Rousseau
ought to write another letter to D'Alembert, since the
arrangements which Father Bertier had been making in Paris
with regard to Thérèse's mother had come unstuck, and
since Rousseau seemed not to know anything at all about
this particular matter being conducted behind his back, he
flew into a rage and the visitors withdrew, Minard later
saying that this was exactly the sort of behaviour you'd
expect from a murderer, and hardly the way in which a
celebrated author should conduct himself. From now on,
said Minard to Ferrand, the two of them should not allow
themselves to be in the company of that rogue without a
sword at their sides; and this led them to adopt the wearing
of long cloaks during the visits which Minard insisted on
continuing, hoping on every occasion to secure ultimate
proof of Rousseau's guilt.

The possibilities of conversation having soon exhausted
themselves, chess remained as the only excuse for these
frequent meetings. Two would play while the third would
watch; though when Ferrand and Minard found themselves
sitting at each side of Rousseau's chessboard, Jean-Jacques
would often leave the room, and then it would be just like

the old days in the Magris, when Minard would find himself winning exactly half the games he played against Ferrand, though his victories were always the result of foolish moves which may have been deliberate mistakes, made in the name of eternal friendship.

Their life was peaceful and happy, even when winter came, the weather worsened, and Father Bertier reminded them that they had been telling everyone since June that they were only in Montmorency for the summer. Were they not expected back in Paris? Ferrand said no, but they avoided Rousseau during this period, and instead devoted themselves completely to the Encyclopaedia which grew with every day, so that by now they were experts in countless disciplines, their knowledge never overlapping, since they copied different parts of the book. This had the effect of removing any air of competition from their friendship, and also kept their conversations from growing stale.

For instance, one day Ferrand said over the dinner they shared, 'Do you recall I once mentioned a theory that fire is a form of life?'

Minard could hardly forget, since it was one of the first things Ferrand ever said to him.

'I don't know where I read it,' said Ferrand, 'but I wondered if you had seen any mention of the idea in the Encyclopaedia?'

Then Minard described the Rosierist Theory of Artificial Life, which said that life consists of the replicating of information.

'In that case,' Ferrand suggested, 'Rosier's Encyclopaedia is itself alive, and you and I are merely the organs of its generation.'

The two men agreed that this was a delightful thought,

and toasted it heartily. They had been born into this world only in order that they would meet, and together would give life to a book which would survive them. The Encyclopaedia was their child.

By Christmas, Minard considered himself adept in three forms of logic and four species of geometry. He also knew a great deal about horology and carpentry, and was experimenting in the manufacture of paper, having found that the necessary supply of rags could be augmented by saving up all the little bits of loose wool which gather in tiny balls within the less immediately accessible parts of one's body. Each night, when they undressed for bed, Minard would collect these fragments in a ritual they each came to treasure as an essential part of the day.

Their life, though, was not completely without pain or worry. Minard would still cry sometimes for his poor Jacqueline, and then he would repeat yet again his determination to bring to justice the most famous author in the world, who didn't even have the manners to stay and watch while Minard and Ferrand played chess together in his house. And Ferrand would remind his friend that nothing must be said about any of this; that Bertier spied on them as well as on Rousseau, and that Jean-Bernard Rosier would pursue his own lost Encyclopaedia until the end of time. Then Ferrand would find some wool in his navel, and offer it to Minard by way of consolation.

Spring arrived, and Ferrand knew hydrology, mineralogy and terratology with an intimacy which made Minard almost jealous. Father Bertier asked if their mission in Montmorency was nearly at an end, and reminded them that it would be consistent with their assumed identity if, like seasonal birds newly migrated, they were to begin visiting Rousseau once more. 'There's just one other thing,' Father Bertier added. It seemed that the owner of their cottage now wished it demolished, in order to use the land. Ferrand and Minard looked at one another in dismay. The house to which they had grown so accustomed, and in which for almost a year they had enjoyed the tranquillity of rural life, was soon to vanish.

'What are we to do?' Minard pleaded.

'Don't worry yourselves, sirs,' said Bertier, who had never quite lost his sense of deference toward his two fellow spies, even though their work was conducted at such a slow pace, and with so little result. 'Another property has become available, just as comfortable as this. And you will be even more pleased when you learn its location, for the house is right next to Rousseau's own!'

Father Bertier proposed that the three of them should visit Jean-Jacques that afternoon. The Duc de Luxembourg had not yet arrived from Paris, and so it was likely that Rousseau would be found working in his pavilion, rather than at the Duke's château. And the priest was right; for when the three entered the garden of Montlouis (around lunchtime, following Minard's suggestion) and saw Thérèse washing clothes in a tub, she stood up with a dripping piece in her hand, shielded her eyes to see who these visitors were, and cried out, 'My, it's the Gossips again!', loud enough for all to hear, but then checked herself and said, 'You'll find the master in his usual place.'

Ferrand and Minard followed Father Bertier round the side of the small cottage and then along the narrow path until they reached the steps of the pavilion where they could see Rousseau writing at his table. The glazed door was open; Rousseau heard them, raised his face, and his expression changed at once from that of a writer gripped by inspiration (however this may look) to that of someone who has just remembered a painful ailment.

'Jean-Jacques! How good to see you.' Bertier was ascending the few steps in order to embrace his friend; Rousseau rose to greet him, looking over Bertier's shoulder towards the others who followed.

'I think you will find,' Minard grandly announced to him, 'that my abilities in the noble game of chess have become greatly enlarged during the months of our absence.'

'And how is Monsieur D'Alembert these days?' Rousseau asked.

'D'Alembert? We haven't see him,' Minard blurted.

'He's been away a lot. And so have we.' Ferrand explained.

All four men were now standing in Rousseau's small room. During their earlier meetings with the author, Ferrand and Minard had never been invited here.

'So. What are you working on these days?' Minard asked awkwardly, fingering the wet page on the table. 'Another novel? Got a title yet?'

Bertier coughed, then said to Rousseau, 'My friends are taking new lodgings in Montmorency. And I think you will be agreeably surprised when you hear where they are to live.' Then he directed Rousseau to step just outside the door, and he pointed towards the yellow house which stood on the other side of the garden wall.

'There?' said Rousseau. 'These two are to live *there*!?'

'I knew you'd be pleased,' said Minard, slapping Rousseau so hard on the shoulder that the writer nearly lost his wig. 'Once we're neighbours, we'll be able to have our chess games every day. And I'll give you a good match, Jean-Jacques. I've been brushing up, thanks to the Encyclopaedia.'

Ferrand drew his friend aside, and the four men silently contemplated the yellow house. What their respective thoughts may have been at this moment, we can only guess; Rousseau's were indicated by touching sighs.

The wall between the two properties defined their respective gardens, long and narrow in both cases; and this wall turned at ninety degrees where it met Rousseau's raised pavilion, meaning that from their window, Ferrand and Minard would have a clear view of the place where Rousseau worked.

'We might even drop into your little hideaway for a game or two in the afternoon,' said Minard, and Ferrand thought he detected just a hint of menace in these words. The two of them had not discussed the matter for several weeks, but Ferrand knew that his friend still hoped to have Rousseau brought to account for his supposed crime, and Ferrand also knew that if Minard attempted anything of the sort, it would be the downfall of them both.

'Now, why don't we inspect your new lodgings?' Father Bertier suggested to his two companions, and he began to walk down the steps.

'No need to take the long way round, surely,' said Minard, and with that, he put his leg over the garden wall. It was greater than the height of a man, but the raised position of Rousseau's pavilion made it an easy matter to get over, then descend to the adjoining garden using the wall's rough stones as footholds. 'Come on!' Minard called up to them.

'I prefer the conventional route,' said Ferrand, following Father Bertier down the steps. 'Good day,' he said to Rousseau.

'See you later!' Minard called, walking up his new garden. Rousseau went back into his pavilion and closed the door firmly.

Ferrand and Bertier arrived at the house soon after Minard had already gone inside, finding it much larger than their former abode, and more than adequate.

'We are grateful to you,' Ferrand was drily telling the priest, as they entered the main room and saw Minard standing at the window, silently staring out on to the garden at the end of which Rousseau's workroom was plainly visible.

Bertier put his hand on Minard's shoulder. 'Perfect, isn't it?' he said to him. 'I knew you'd be pleased. Now you can study him as closely as you wish.'

'He will pay,' Minard murmured, and Ferrand intervened.

'Minard, I think perhaps you are in danger of becoming unwell. Why don't you lie down?'

It was as if this new proximity to Rousseau had finally brought to a head Minard's obsession with a theory he now had proved 4096 times, this having been the limit imposed by the availability of paper to tear up, and the size of the floor.

In a low voice, Father Bertier said, 'Once more, I offer this hospitality without asking anything in return, except that you do not forget the assistance I have given you in your mission. It will be an easy matter for you to enter Rousseau's room whenever you wish. Many people are interested in what he writes, and would pay handsomely in order to find out. If, therefore, you should ever feel that your own masters reward you insufficiently, I can assure you of a high price for anything you might bring me.'

Then Father Bertier said he would arrange for their belongings to be conveyed later that day, and he left them. When Ferrand closed the door on him, he turned to find Minard still lost in ominous contemplation.

'Minard, it is not good for us to be here. Forget Rousseau, forget Jacqueline and everything else. Why spoil our life together?'

But for the rest of the afternoon, Minard was in a dark mood.

The next days were better. Ferrand satisfied himself that his friend's suspicions had once more been reduced to the abstract combinatorial problem which he now proposed to solve by constructing, in accordance with Rosierist logic, a 'computing engine' consisting of 1,048,576 small pieces of paper arranged on a network of threads. Well, Ferrand consoled himself, everyone needs a hobby.

It was Ferrand who did most of the work which earned them a living. The papers from the Oratory were copied almost entirely by him, while Minard busied himself upstairs with his logical device. During the long evenings, Ferrand would patiently transcribe notes, and hear every now and again the bumping of the ceiling as Minard crawled around on the floor above, cursing occasionally. Sometimes, Ferrand would wonder if this new preoccupation was damaging to their relationship; if, perhaps, Minard's occasional tendency to be sullen and uncommunicative were being exacerbated by his new craze. 'If only I could find a way of increasing the memory!' Minard would say, inexplicably, of the tangle of paper and thread which sprawled across his lap and on to the floor, and whose only purpose was to prove once and for all the identity of Jacqueline's killer.

Ferrand made no objection, however, to the increasing burden of work which was placed upon his shoulders. It was his duty to support Minard through this difficult period, which would surely pass, and at least Minard was willing to go and buy their provisions, even do some cleaning and cooking before, at the end of a meal punctuated by spasmodic conversation, he would return to his computations.

Minard by now had proved Rousseau's guilt in so many ways that he was considering writing a book devoted exclusively to the subject. He imagined an entire branch of learning whose scholars would pursue no other task, and he was thinking about this while staring out of the window towards Rousseau's pavilion, in which the writer was not to be found since he was at Enghien with the Duke, when Ferrand said, 'Minard, we need to talk.'

Minard turned. 'What do we need to talk about?'

'Us.'

'What about *us*?'

Ferrand looked hurt. 'Is that all you can say; "what about *us*?"?'

Now Minard was puzzled. 'What do you mean; "Is *that* all you can say; 'what about *us*?'?"?'

This went on until it emerged that Ferrand objected to doing too much of the cooking, most of the cleaning, and nearly all of the copying. 'Sometimes you don't even get to bed until almost dawn!' he added for good measure.

Minard suggested they hire a servant.

'And are you going to do all the copying that'll be needed to pay for it?'

'What about Father Bertier? He'll give us one free.'

'Oh, yes, go running to Father Bertier for help.'

'What do you mean, "Father *Bertier*"?'

And so it continued. The argument went through recurring phases of attack and reconciliation, accusation and self-justification, until finally ending with Ferrand running upstairs in tears, and Minard declaring that he was going out for a walk.

As soon as Minard slammed the door closed, it occurred to him that he had no idea where to go, and he didn't really want to walk at all. He would have preferred to work on his computing engine, but Ferrand was in there crying now; he could hear him from the lane.

This lane ran beside their garden until it met the back of Rousseau's pavilion. Even standing here, Minard still thought he could hear Ferrand's sobs, and he thought of the tangled assembly of paper and thread in the room where Ferrand howled, which he only hoped would not now be destroyed in a fit of rage. And then Minard decided that it was time to earn some money. The lane was empty, he quickly scaled the wall, and went round to the door of the pavilion, which he found to be unlocked. Going inside, he took a bundle of pages from the middle of a pile. Even if they were missed, Minard hardly cared. He went back out, over the wall, and began to make his way to the Oratory.

Father Bertier was only too pleased to see him ('Father *Bertier*,' Minard kept saying to himself during their interview, hearing Ferrand's jealous voice in his mind).

'I am so glad that you have decided to make me your ally,' said the priest, pouring out some wine when the two of them were sitting comfortably in his private room. Bertier was inspecting the pages which Minard had brought. 'It would seem that this *Émile* of his is nearly ready. I wonder what the Parlement will make of it?' He paused, looking intently into Minard's eyes. 'But you're not with the Parlement at all, are you?' Again, another pause. 'Tell me, just who is it that you work for?'

Minard was busy re-enacting his argument with Ferrand, and was hardly listening.

'Is it D'Alembert who pays you?'

No reply.

'Or Grimm? Madame d'Épinay?'

Minard had reached the part when they argued about why it was always he who slept nearer the window, and why did this window always have to be open or closed solely according to Minard's wishes rather than Ferrand's; to which Minard had replied that if there was a problem then perhaps they should sleep in separate rooms, and Ferrand had said all right then we will, and Minard had tried to pacify him. 'If only I'd said yes, there and then,' Minard thought.

'Diderot, perhaps?' Bertier pursued. And then, 'I see. Your silence is eloquent, Monsieur Minard, and tells me everything.'

At last Minard said, 'He doesn't really do as much copying as he thinks.'

'I know,' Bertier agreed. 'I send him endless supplies of music, most of which he simply piles in that little room of his, and I pay him whether he copies it or not. With Rousseau, all that matters is that his pride is never hurt. He can pretend that he lives as a copyist, and his friends pretend they don't subsidize him. But we both know him for the hypocrite he is.'

'Yes, hypocrite,' said Minard, rejoining the conversation.

'And I don't know why it matters so much to him, whether a bedroom window is open or closed. You know, I think he might even be on the verge of some kind of crisis.'

Bertier sat up in his chair. 'Really? As a matter of fact, I've suspected this too.'

Minard explained. 'Perhaps it's all because of the Encyclopaedia. He claims to spend so much time on his copying for you, but it's the Encyclopaedia that really occupies him far more, and I don't know what he's found in the sections he's completed, but I'm sure it must have something to do with these strange moods of his.'

Bertier was completely captivated. So here it was, the real secret of Jean-Jacques's work! He was writing his own encyclopaedia, an answer to Diderot and D'Alembert whom Rousseau had rejected. 'I should dearly love to see this work,' he said. 'And I would reward you appropriately, of course.' Bertier had not yet paid Minard for this first offering. He went to his bureau and brought a purse from a locked drawer. 'A hundred livres,' he said, placing the purse on the small table next to Minard's elbow. 'Consider it an advance on the first instalment you can bring me from this encyclopaedia.' Minard put the purse in his pocket, calculating that merely the portions he himself had already copied would eventually be enough to buy a house. The Encyclopaedia had suddenly made Minard a rich man, and he realized that from this dream of wealth, Ferrand had momentarily been absent.

The men parted, and Minard returned to his home, where he embraced Ferrand warmly, but said nothing of the purse he had brought with him. In the following days, he worked out a story according to which small errands run for a local wood merchant were earning him regular amounts, thus enabling him to contribute to the keeping of the home on equal terms with Ferrand, even though Minard no longer did any copying at all. He could perfect his computing engine at leisure, and Ferrand was powerless to object. 'I don't know why you even bother,' was Minard's comment one afternoon, when he found Ferrand transcribing a new part of the Encyclopaedia. 'It'll only fill your head with stupid ideas.'

In the wake of such uneasiness between them, their visits to their next-door neighbour became still more frequent; but they now went individually. Minard preferred to spend his time at Montlouis when it was only Thérèse who was there. She was stupid, but at least she wasn't a murderer, and Minard's passion for chess was diminished by his enthusiasm for making logical inferences using his growing collection of Rosierist 'computers', those cat's cradles of paper and thread which so absorbed him. It was Ferrand who would come whenever Rousseau was at home, keeping him from his *donjon* with chess games which would extend themselves for hours, while Ferrand tried to decide if he was ready yet to face once more his morose companion next door.

And it was during these games that Minard would sometimes slip easily into Rousseau's empty workroom, still hoping to find conclusive evidence of a fact whose proofs seemed likely to extend to infinity, if only the world held enough paper and thread, and a big enough floor upon which to lay out the calculation. Scraps from his machine filled Minard's pockets; papers on which were written 'if', 'then', or 'go'; words and phrases such as 'possible guilt', 'certain desire', and 'secret life'. So careless was he with these spare components, which occasionally, after he had dug into his coat in search of something else entirely, would flutter from Minard's person like sinister snow, that once, while rooting and searching in Rousseau's pavilion, he dropped among the writer's papers a piece which Jean-Jacques subsequently discovered, bearing only the word, 'MURDERER!'

And Minard continued to visit Father Bertier, his wealth growing with each portion he delivered of the Encyclopaedia. Rumours soon spread among Rousseau's friends and acquaintances in Paris, both about the great work he was preparing, and about the extreme state into which solitude, contemplation, and the simple life had brought his mind. Now it was not only Minard and Bertier who took an interest in him, for one night when Minard scaled the wall in order to enter the pavilion, he found the door open, and a strange man inside, going through Rousseau's papers.

'Who are you?' asked Minard.

The stranger jumped with fright, peered out from the room at the new arrival, and said, 'I might ask you the same question, since clearly neither of us is meant to be here.'

'Just tell me your name,' said Minard.

'Minard,' said the stranger.

What a curious coincidence, thought Minard, whose name was obviously more common than he'd thought.

'It's not my real name, though,' said Minard.

'Nor mine,' Minard replied.

'Are you a friend of Monsieur D'Alembert's?'

'Yes,' said Minard. 'Are you?'

'Of course. But it's the Encyclopaedia that really interests me.'

'Of course. Me too.'

It was all rather confusing, and there seemed little point in continuing the conversation, so Minard (at least, that's who he thought he was), returned to his house. This puzzling episode was not repeated; indeed, Minard began to wonder if it was no more than a dream, brought about through too many late nights spent working on his computing engine, but it only made him even more subdued, and this in turn served to worsen the situation with Ferrand.

Then, one morning, the crisis came at last.

'I'm leaving you,' Ferrand announced. He was already up and dressed as Minard sleepily opened his eyes.

'What do you mean, "*leaving* me"?'

But it was too late for another of those familiar verbal battles.

'I've made up my mind, Minard. We had many happy times together, and I want to remember only those. But I'm frightened that as time goes on, these bad feelings between us will blot out everything that was good.'

Minard really hadn't the faintest idea what all this was about, or why Ferrand was talking in such strange terms. Perhaps it was due to the Encyclopaedia, or else it might have been the accursed novels of Rousseau and his imitators which Ferrand had recently taken to reading, and which, Minard guessed, were infected with precisely such meaningless sentiments, now all the rage thanks to that murderer next door.

'I'm going back to sleep,' Minard said, doing precisely that.

Some time later, another noise brought Minard from his dreams of thread and paper, in which his every belief was justified without limit. Horses, a carriage, some commotion. Minard looked out of the window, and saw Thérèse standing in the lane, shouting to the driver, 'He's gone already!'

'But we have a warrant for his arrest.'

'You can show me as many warrants as you like, but I tell you he's not here.'

They were trying to arrest Ferrand! And might there be another warrant for Minard himself? He leapt from his bed, hopping on one foot as he pulled on his stockings, put his clothes over his nightshirt, and forgot his hat entirely as he began in a panic to gather up everything he could. His computing engine was quickly reduced to an impossible knot from which torn and disengaged pieces of paper fell negligently upon the floorboards. And his money! Surely this was the most important of all! Soon they would be knocking on the door, demanding to know his whereabouts. Was it for Jacqueline's murder that Minard was about to be accused? Or for failing to return Rosier's Encyclopaedia to its rightful owner? Or for some other crime of which Minard was not even aware?

There was no chance of escape now; it sounded like twenty carriages and a hundred horses out there; perhaps a whole detachment of soldiers had been sent to surround the house. Yes! He saw from his window a well-dressed person ascend the steps of Rousseau's pavilion, looking through the glazed door. They were preparing to attack Minard's house by way of the garden!

Minard bravely hid himself under the bed, and two hours later deemed it safe to come out.

They hadn't stormed the house after all, and Minard had decided by now that Thérèse must have allowed him to avoid arrest by telling them that both he and Ferrand were already gone. She may be stupid, Minard reasoned, but she'd saved his skin this morning.

He made ready to leave. All his essentials were now

wrapped up; a few clothes, his portion of the Encyclopaedia (Ferrand having taken the rest), and the money it had earned him. But where was he to go? While he pondered this, Minard decided to pay Thérèse a last visit. He found her weeping at her kitchen table.

'What a terrible night it has been!' she moaned.

She must have heard Ferrand and Minard's last argument. They had often noticed how easily the most moderate conversation could make its way between the two houses, so that Minard would try to make his friend lower his voice, and Ferrand would say, 'Am I really such an embarrassment to you?'

'Yes, it was terrible,' Minard agreed, remembering a flying pot which nearly hit his head, just because he reminded Ferrand of his tendency to snore. 'But now he's gone.'

Thérèse moaned again, burying her face in her arms as she slumped herself across the table. 'At least he was warned,' Minard heard her say to herself.

'That's right,' said Minard. 'I told him often enough what was bound to happen.'

Thérèse sat up. 'You did? You mean you knew?'

Minard shook his head sorrowfully. 'We all saw it coming. I was only saying to Father Bertier the other day ...' Then he saw that she was looking at him in a very hostile way.

'It was you who betrayed him,' she said quietly. 'It was you who made all this happen.'

Minard thought this most unfair. After all, there's two sides to every disagreement, and he'd even allowed Ferrand to take charge of the nocturnal window-opening arrangements. But Thérèse was completely stupid, and married to a murderer, so what could you expect?

'Driven from the country he adopted and loved, all because of you,' she sobbed.

'He's left the country?' said Minard. This seemed a little extreme.

'But you and your friends won't be able to harm him once he's back in Switzerland.'

'I'd no idea he'd ever been there before,' said Minard. Somehow, travel had never come up in their conversations. 'Do you know where exactly he's gone?' Already, Minard was thinking of writing a letter to his former friend.

Thérèse said, 'Of course I know. I'll be joining him soon.'

Now Minard started to feel slightly confused. 'What do you mean, "*join* him"?'

But she was not to be drawn into a conversation of the kind which had become such a habit between Ferrand and Minard. 'I think you should go,' she said. 'I have work to do.'

No chance of some carrot soup, then. Minard went back to his house, and a shout he soon heard rising from the street meant he wouldn't need his computing engine in order to work out exactly what had happened in the early hours of the morning.

'Jean-Jacques has fled,' someone was calling. 'They say he has gone to Switzerland.' Soon, a small crowd was gathering at the gate of Montlouis.

Minard understood everything now. He checked his baggage again, making sure his money was safely hidden, and he surveyed the many items which he would leave behind;

worthless tokens of his life with Ferrand. Betrayed! He saw it all so clearly.

What was it that had been taking place, during those many long chess games which Ferrand played against Jean-Jacques? Was it Minard whom they talked about, perhaps? Did Ferrand repeat those familiar complaints, about Minard's supposed reluctance to do a fair share of the housework, about his needing to be reminded to change his undershirt, about his interest in tying together little pieces of paper with thread? Oh, they probably had a good laugh about it, Ferrand and Rousseau, while they exchanged pawns. And did Ferrand speak too of his lonely existence, left to copy pages which meant nothing to him, while Minard pursued his own interests upstairs; did Ferrand even tell Rousseau what it was that Minard thought he knew about him? He felt a chill as he imagined the scene; Rousseau and Ferrand studying the chessboard and Ferrand saying, 'He even thinks you're a murderer, Jean-Jacques! Have you ever heard anything so absurd?'

Then Jean-Jacques reaching out to touch the back of Ferrand's hand. His evil smile as he says, 'What a ridiculous idea! How could the most famous author in the world be a murderer?'

The two of them laughing, louder and louder, mocking Minard as their ridicule filled the room, the house, the garden and the whole of Montmorency, the whole of France, filling the world with their infinite laughter at him, at Minard who saw and understood these things so clearly. He was standing close to the door now, still somehow unable to leave, and clutching a small dried flower which he must have pulled from the vase on the window sill, crushing it between his fingers.

How had it all ended? Rousseau would have invited Ferrand for another chess game, then announced to him the plan. Soon he would be leaving for Switzerland, and he had heard that Ferrand was in danger; there was a warrant for his arrest.

'What about Minard?' Ferrand might have asked. Yes, Minard was sure he would have asked.

'I can only take one,' would be the answer. 'You will come with me; Thérèse will follow later.'

And this, Minard decided, was how it must have gone. He left the house, and went to arrange a carriage to Paris, from where he would begin his own journey to Switzerland. Rousseau the murderer had seduced his friend with lies, had won his trust, had taken him to a foreign country where he could do whatever he liked with him. But Minard would find them, wherever they were. He didn't know how long it would take, but one day he would be reunited with his friend, and then they would live happily together forever.

And so it was, that Minard's long quest began.

CHAPTER 12

The day was approaching when Ellen would go away on business. My meetings with Louisa had been resumed, but often she seemed anxious, her mind elsewhere. Perhaps she wanted to 'talk'; but the only thing I could talk about was literature, so each week we would sit together and she would mention an author she was reading, or force a question from her lips in the hesitant manner I would later recall in my bed before going to sleep, and the hour would quickly pass without further progress. Jill Brandon maintained a level of idle curiosity which betrayed fascination. 'Still doing your "group"?' she'd say, and each time she asked this question, the last word became more and more heavily strained, as if through overuse, until eventually it seemed no longer to bear any reference to whatever activity Louisa and I were supposed to be engaged in, behind the closed door of my office.

I needed to make plans for the forthcoming week of Ellen's absence. Once more Louisa assisted me, by bringing to the meeting another article she had found, this time concerning a literary theorist I had never heard of, named Nicolas Clairy. I reminded her of her earlier promise, which I had been tending with the care of a brooding hen until the time was right, and now proposed that she come to my house in order to show me how to explore the mysterious 'World Wide Web' from which she had obtained the information. She readily agreed, and at that moment there was a knock on the door, Louisa and I flinched, startled, as if we had been doing something wrong, and almost before I had finished saying 'Come in', the door opened to reveal Jill Brandon, who wanted nothing except to return a book she'd borrowed.

'Why, hello Louisa,' she said innocently. 'I hope you'll be getting that essay to me on time.' Louisa nodded while Jill handed me the book, and where Jill's eyes might have fallen in her examination of the room I have no idea, since mine were lowered in sudden and unaccountable embarrassment.

Jill Brandon mentioned to me later, with the pinpoint casualness of a laser-guided missile, that 'the Lawson girl' seemed 'a bit off, lately'. Had I any idea what might be wrong with her, since I clearly spent so much time in her company? Did I know why her essays were coming in late, and poorly done, and why she was apt to miss lectures? 'She still manages to attend your "group", though,' Jill said caustically, and I felt like a small grainy munitions dump being blasted on video before the indifferent gaze of the world. Then, as if the job were not already done well enough, she added, 'Perhaps you ought to talk to her.' What did she think we spent our time doing?

We like to imagine that we exist in a state of invisibility, our desires and aspirations as private as our bank accounts, and so it comes as an unpleasant surprise whenever we become aware that those faces who drift past us each day with a nod and a smile are watching us far more closely than we ever bother to observe them. Their recognition of our movements and habits is more intimate and precise even than our own; they perform inconspicuous reconnaissance operations on our lives, form theories and conjectures about us, while we read the morning paper over coffee, and glance at the clock. Was whatever was obvious to Jill Brandon just as apparent to Ellen, thanks to evidence different but no less damning?

However, the plan had been formed, and could not be altered; and so for the next ten days I followed with unusually keen interest the progress of Ellen's work, the fortunes of the plastics company she was due to visit, and the details of her itinerary, with particular reference to the times when she would be likely to phone me, and when she would return. If ever Ellen mentioned some oddness in my manner I would ascribe it, as usual, to the involuntary recollection of an abstract problem demanding further attention.

And then Ellen left, I lived on beans on toast and take-aways for a couple of days, and the evening of Louisa's visit arrived at last.

I heard the bell, and felt completely calm as I answered the door, glancing only momentarily beyond Louisa's shoulder in order to see whether anyone across the street might be watching, then asked her inside in a formal and impersonal way which any observer would take to be the same tone you might adopt with someone come to read the gas meter. She was wearing a cream-coloured blouse of a material which looked thin and light to the touch, and I directed her to the sitting room, then left her there in order to make coffee, having realized that I honestly didn't know what to say next to someone who for me, at that moment, was reduced to a piece of clothing over which she might have spared less than a minute's consideration when she put it on earlier. Hardly surprising, then, that I'd found myself rather tongue-tied, and resorted to an exchange concerning the options of milk, sugar, and biscuits, before escaping to the kitchen as quickly as I could.

When faced with an unfamiliar situation, we play the part as best we can; and our scripts can come to us from many places. These are the regions where our life, at that moment, truly exists; so that while I measured out ground coffee, spilling some of the powder and making a nervous mess, part of me was inhabiting a television commercial, another was embedded in a passage of an obscure novel, while a third belonged to a song I had found myself singing. The human willingness to resort to the comfort of cliché can act at such a deep level that it can leave us, at times, in a state which is entirely derived and inauthentic. It has been said that when we love, we perform a role learned from books, from films and gossip, and it is even said that one's whole existence may be dictated by imitation or reaction, in response to the countless gentle forces and unseen pressures by which we are all constantly directed. My whole life, I began to realize, had during many months become a form of pastiche.

Proust has much to say on this subject. He began his literary career by writing a series of newspaper articles in which he adopted the styles of a succession of authors; elsewhere, he speaks of the way in which a writer's 'melody' can infect us like a virus, lingering in the mind so that anything we subsequently think or might try to write, for some time after we have finished reading, will still bear its imprint. This echoes an identical sentiment expressed by

Montaigne, who engagingly said of Plutarch that he could never spend time in his company without coming away with a 'slice of breast or a wing'; and Pascal also understood the manner in which a book can speak to us by apparently holding a mirror to our souls. 'It is not in Montaigne but in myself that I find everything I see there,' he says of the *Essais*.

Having wandered into this digression, I break off for a few minutes in order to check Pascal's exact words in the copy I have to hand, while a passing nurse glances at me and smiles sympathetically; and having found it, I remind myself of another *pensée* of even greater bearing on the state of mind which must have prevailed while I clumsily made coffee for Louisa.

What, Pascal asks, is 'Self'? If someone is loved for their looks, or personality, is it their true Self which is loved? Of course not, says Pascal, since we can lose our looks, find our personality altered; but we would not say that our Self has been lost. But where, then, is it, this unalterable essence? And can we love anyone, except for attributes which are incidental, which may even have come from elsewhere? What we love are contingent qualities, Pascal concludes; so that not only the people we desire, but even our own Selves seem suddenly to evaporate and return to those sources from which they have been gathered, perhaps instinctively, like the bizarre dowries of leaves and fragments assembled by certain tropical birds. If I loved Louisa for a smile, an odour, a way of moving when she first entered my room with her two friends, or even for certain blouses she could change at will, then perhaps I have also loved Montaigne or Pascal just as insignificantly, my devotion amounting to the fortuitous effect of various words, observations or choices of syntax on their part; and the little piece of Self which imagines it can feel such loves is merely lifted from a television commercial, an obscure novel, a song running through my head.

I was now ready to face Louisa again, armed with a full cafetière and two mugs on a tray I've never liked. Following our usual custom, I asked her about her reading. She told me she had at last started my own book, which she had been saving until she felt 'ready' for it. Naturally, I took this readiness to be deeply symbolic, and asked if she would like me to pour the milk.

'Where's your computer?' she said.

I told her it was in the study; we could go there now if she wanted. But she said we should finish our coffee before 'getting down to business'.

She said, 'I haven't read very far into your book yet. I still don't really see what's so important about Ferrand and Minard.'

It is true that my book delays, as a kind of *dénouement*, their full significance. But surely I had already explained to Louisa on more than one occasion the theory to which my research had inescapably led; had she not been paying attention? I must have told her of the months I spent vainly hunting for them, until it began to seem as if they might never have existed. And this was the solution to my problem; this was the theory which offered itself to me, in a moment of inspiration, one afternoon while on my way to meet Ellen, not long after we became engaged. Ferrand and Minard never lived. They are creatures of fiction, invented by Rousseau.

Had I really never told Louisa about my excitement, when I finally reached Ellen standing on the corner looking

at her watch, and announced to her my great discovery? All
evening I could talk of nothing else, for suddenly everything
had become clear; the people I had been chasing were a lie,
the *Confessions* should properly be read as a work of
imaginative fantasy, no more trustworthy as history than
Proust's *Recherche*. This is the thesis which my book elab-
orates; one which gave considerable amusement to Donald
Macintyre, and was greeted by my supervisor with a look of
horror.

'You'll read all about it,' I reminded Louisa, saddened by
her apparent ignorance of the notorious insight on which
my subsequent career has in some sense depended; but since
little else offered itself as a way to pass the time while we
finished our coffee, there seemed no harm in summarizing
my argument once more.

Proust wrote a long novel which concerns a person called
'I' who is not always himself, and who is named, at only
one point in the book, as Marcel. Proust was a man who
spent his days in a cork-lined room, passed many of his
sleepless nights at a male brothel, or else found solace in the
Théâtrophone, a curious device which, for a subscription
fee, relayed live opera performances by telephone to his
bedside. Marcel, on the other hand, had holidays in Combray, fell in love with Albertine, and hoped to become a
writer. 'I' is sometimes one, sometimes the other, and sometimes, most magically of all, neither. Yet so many readers
still assume them all to be identical; they trawl through the
Recherche imagining they are simply reading someone's
memoirs.

Rousseau wrote a book about a man called Jean-Jacques,
and the book's 'I' is just as ambiguous as Proust's. Readers
of *Julie* took it to be a true story; the *Confessions* have

288

proved even more convincing, though the book contains characters as demonstrably unreal as Albertine or Bergotte. For Proust, the ubiquitous 'I' is almost a form of self-effacement; for Rousseau it was a symptom of his madness, further demonstrated in the later *Dialogues*, where the character of Jean-Jacques is discussed and analysed by speakers called 'Rousseau' and 'The Frenchman'. By then, I have no doubt, Rousseau sincerely believed that during his stay at Montmorency there really were two spies who had lived next door to him. Yet I had proved otherwise.

My supervisor shook his head sorrowfully when I told him this. You can never prove a negative, he reminded me. And what if someone were one day to search a little harder than I had; what if some previously overlooked document were to identify the real Ferrand and Minard, whose house still stands beside Montlouis, and is now, somewhat ironically, a centre for Rousseau studies? Surely somebody must have lived there.

In that case, I told my supervisor, and Donald, and Ellen, and now Louisa, those actual lodgers were merely the inspiration for the Ferrand and Minard of fiction, just as Julie can be identified with Sophie d'Houdetot, or Albertine can be traced to Alfred Agostinelli. Rousseau, it has long been known, invented the grand conspiracy which drove him from Montmorency; there was no theft of documents from his *donjon*, no spies followed him. Rousseau asks his readers to judge for themselves the plot which he himself could never fathom; that plot belongs only to the world of myth, and hence every reader's theory is equally valid.

By now, I had put down my coffee and drawn closer to Louisa. Rousseau's novel, I explained, like Proust's, is intimately concerned with the nature of writing, the penetration of reality by fantasy. In Proust, this is an explicit aim; think, for instance, of the long discussion between Albertine and Marcel about Dostoevsky; merely an essay cast unconvincingly into the mouths of the characters, serving no dramatic purpose . . .

'I disagree,' Louisa said, pulling away slightly. 'I think the episode says something about the way Marcel is smothering Albertine with his obsessive love, and she wants to escape.'

In Rousseau, I continued, the debate is of a different form; Proust can take for granted the universal significance of literature, whereas Rousseau proposes that all art is corrupting and evil, so that he immediately faces the dilemma of trying to create a book which will denounce all books. Hence his narrator must denounce himself, and this is achieved with just as much irony as is shown by Proust, in his creation of a heterosexual narrator who condemns all 'inverts'.

Louisa said she still didn't see why Ferrand and Minard were so important in all this. Indeed, for Rousseau they are merely an anecdote, peripheral to the main plot; but for me, I told her, they became almost like my own children.

She said, 'You don't have any, do you?'

'Children?' I shook my head, and there was a pause.

'I suppose, with your wife working . . . She does work, doesn't she?'

I'd never told Louisa about the world of accountancy, which has adjoined my own for so many years like a mysterious factory, known only by the busy noises it gives out from time to time.

'I suppose I'll meet her if she gets back soon enough,'

Louisa said. Then I could see her registering her error from the hesitation I made in replying. I told her Ellen was away on business.

'Oh,' she said, and we both took a large sip of coffee.

I filled the gap. 'You're right, though. It's best for Ellen. That we never had children.'

'But what about you?' She was looking into my eyes, and I could see from her earnest, searching expression that all the barriers which had ever existed between us had been put there by me; I had hidden behind the very thing we supposedly shared, our mutual love of literature.

I told her I'd have liked to have had children, but that sometimes these things turn out not to be possible, and then you face a choice either of letting your desires poison you, or else of getting on with life and forgetting about impossible dreams. She said nothing.

'Proust never had children,' I added. 'Nor did Pascal, or Flaubert. Or Rousseau.'

She looked puzzled, either by my attempt to bring us back to my favourite writers, or else by my last example.

'I thought Rousseau sent five children to an orphanage,' she said.

Had she listened to nothing at all, during all our meetings together? Had she forgotten that among Rousseau's apologists there have always been those who claim the children were not his, and that this is why they were despatched so readily? I had a different theory, of course; and though it troubled me that Louisa should still seem unaware of it, I was consoled by the interest she now showed; for in asking about Rousseau, it was as if she were enquiring about my own life.

'He invented the five children,' I told her, 'Just as he invented Ferrand and Minard. And he believed in them too, I'm sure of it.'

If none of this had been significant to Louisa during earlier conversations when I must have mentioned it, now on the other hand the subject inspired a fascination in her which I could see growing as I spoke, and to which she responded by asking, 'Why should any man make up something like that? Why should he tell the world that he'd given away his own children?'

I said, 'So as to prove to the world that he was capable of becoming a father, even though no evidence of it was to be found.'

Perhaps she would understand now the special bond, deep and painful, which has for so long attached me to this author whom I despise, as if he were a weight around my leg. For I know how he too must have loathed all men made more perfectly than himself.

'The Duchesse de Luxembourg tried to find his children, in order to adopt one,' I said. 'A search of every orphanage yielded nothing.' I had told her this before, and had also described the painful genito-urinary condition to which Rousseau often refers, and for which he needed to wear catheters. But I hadn't mentioned Rousseau's failure with a prostitute, which he says reveals more about his character than anything else, or the physician who reassured him he was so singularly made that venereal disease would in any case be an impossibility.

'I wondered what exactly this meant,' I said, while Louisa watched me intently. Ellen, too, had shown some interest while I gave myself during several weeks to the study of medical texts of the period, in order to discover why a person might be considered immune from syphilis. 'I decided that Rousseau was incapable, either through physiology or psychology, of ejaculating inside a woman.'

I was watching Louisa's mouth, and the slight quivering of her lips. There was no other response, except perhaps a mild reddening of her face, and her impassivity while I spoke only made me want to say more.

Rousseau describes an incident which took place in Turin when he was sixteen. The young Calvinist had walked all the way from Annecy – a journey longer than the six or seven days he claims for it – in order to convert to Catholicism, and he was staying at a hospice next to the church of Santo Spirito. His fellow catechumens were a strange bunch, including bandits, slave traders and 'Moors', one of whom, Rousseau says, took a fancy to him. Modern scholarship suggests this man to have been real; a Jew from Aleppo named Abraham Ruben. Not content with kisses, the Moor took out his penis one morning when he and Rousseau were alone together in the assembly hall, and he tried to make Rousseau touch it. Rousseau, who claims not to have understood what was going on, leapt away in disgust, then watched in horror as the Moor continued his fumblings until something white and sticky shot towards the fireplace and fell to the ground.

Louisa listened silently, then at last said, 'So?'

I find it interesting, I explained, suddenly with some embarrassment, that Rousseau could still profess, at sixteen, to be so naive. It was by watching the Moor that Rousseau learned how to 'cheat nature' (a deceit he would enthusiastically continue for the rest of his life), though already by then he had discovered the pleasures of being spanked by his governess (contrary to the *Confessions*, his and her respective ages at the time were not eight and thirty, but eleven and forty), which he says permanently shaped his tastes, desires and passions; and he had also by now had his encounter with the mysterious 'Mademoiselle Goton' who encouraged the fantasy they shared, of schoolmistress and naughty pupil, in which she would whip and beat him, allowing herself the 'greatest liberties', while granting Rousseau none towards her.

'He was a strange man,' Louisa conceded.

'And the most interesting thing,' I continued, reluctant to let the subject drop, though Louisa might have preferred this, 'is that after describing the Moor's ejaculation, Rousseau says that if this is how men appear to women, then women must be truly fascinated by them if they are not to find all men repulsive.'

She said, 'I suppose it depends on your point of view.'

'What do you mean?'

'Well, obviously it looks different, depending on whether you're a man or a woman. Depending on whether you can be aroused by watching someone jerking off.'

I wanted her to go on, but she fell silent. I said, 'Did I ever tell you about Proust and the rats?'

She shook her head with a doubtful air; uncertain, perhaps, of whether this was another anecdote she had merely forgotten; but I knew that like the Moor, this was one I had always held back from her, though the two incidents are of importance in my book. The story is told by Marcel Jouhandeau, a prostitute who kept a diary recording daily life at the brothel in the Rue de l'Arcade which Proust frequented. Proust would go to a room there and prepare himself, then soon afterwards Jouhandeau would follow, discovering Proust in bed with the sheet pulled up to his chin, just as visitors would find him, bed-bound, in his own apartment on the Boulevard Hausmann. Jouhandeau would be instructed to take off all his clothes, and then to masturbate, while Proust, beneath the sheet, did the same; and when it was finished, Jouhandeau would be politely asked to leave, without there being any further contact between them. But sometimes Proust would be unable to finish, perhaps as if caught by the lingering implication of some unwanted thought; and then the instruction, mechanically and without variation, was for two small cages to be brought into the room. Each of these would contain a starved rat, and the cages, resembling, one imagines, the kind in which parrots or finches are kept, would be placed upon the bed where Proust lay, pushed together like railway carriages whose meeting doors could now communicate. The doorflaps would be lifted, the rats would run to meet one another, and they would fight, tearing and biting ravenously, perhaps to the death, while Proust achieved satisfaction. The story is confirmed by Gide, who heard it from Proust himself, when their friendship was resumed after Gide made amends for his rejection of the *Recherche*.

'How horrible,' said Louisa. And I could see Proust's novel suddenly transforming itself in her imagination into the work of a monster. I could see the hawthorns, Albertine, the death of Bergotte, all contaminated for her, stained as if by the trail of a slug; and this perhaps was what I wanted. 'I don't understand men at all,' she said.

'Neither do I,' I replied. And nor did Rousseau, who, as Hume wearily declared, understood himself least of all.

Louisa said, 'But we were supposed to be talking about you. How did we get back to all these theories of yours?'

I laughed and apologized. Then there was another of

those pauses when for a moment it was as if I was about to
let out at last what was really on my mind.

She said, 'You'd have liked to be a parent, then?'

I shrugged. 'I don't give it much thought.'

This surprised her. 'No? I do. I give it a lot of thought.'

'And do you want to have children?'

Louisa said, 'For me it isn't quite so abstract. It isn't
about "children"; it's about whether I want to have a child.'

'I see.' I didn't, though.

She finished her coffee. 'I'd like to meet your wife some
time.'

I said I was sure they'd get on. I tried to imagine being
in the same room with Ellen and Louisa simultaneously, but
found this a logical problem almost as insoluble as the
legendary object which is perceived to be both green and red
at once.

She said, 'Does it bother her much?', then saw misunderstanding in my eyes. 'Children, I mean.'

I shook my head. 'Not really. In a way it came as a relief
to her.'

'Right.' Louisa was silently working it all out, and I was
thinking how strange it was that we had gone so far into a
subject I had discussed with no one; and yet this was always
Louisa's unique gift, to be able to say what was on everyone's mind, sometimes even my own. 'I knew a woman who
couldn't conceive for years, and then it just happened.'

I said, 'It isn't always the woman's fault, though.' And
quickly added, 'Like Rousseau, for example.'

'Yes. Back to Rousseau.'

No more coffee now. We had arrived at the moment
when the purpose of her visit could no longer be delayed;

yet the only desire I felt was to tell her everything, to confess.

'I suppose we ought to look at your computer,' she said. I was observing the cream-coloured blouse, the line of her breast, the imprint of a nipple, and I was imagining all the countless men who, no matter what the outcome of this meeting were to be, would certainly steal her from me.

'I can't have children,' I said.

She nodded. 'I guessed so. But from what you say, you and Ellen never really wanted that anyway. Most people spend their life either trying to have one or trying not to, so you've probably got the best deal.'

She was attempting to be sympathetic; at her age, this was all she could manage. But she was right; she didn't understand men, and there was no reason why she should. I've considered the issue from every point of view; I've learned to accept that the creation of a child would amount, for me, only to the refutation of some unfavourable percentages on a long succession of test results, regarding morphology and motility, volume and density, viscosity and agglutination; all of them attributes, as canonical and mundane as the stations of a suburban branch line, by means of which I have come to compare myself, in imagination, with every man who ever gave a lecherous look at Ellen; every student hung over and happy in his morning seminar; every careless fool who, through no more than a burst condom or a slow withdrawal, has managed effortlessly and accidentally to impregnate. No doubt if I'd gone into the subject with her, Louisa would only have said to me that if Ellen had really wanted a child so much then we could have used a donor, as if I weren't already aware that the world is full of men who would have been only too happy to do the job, and that for Ellen to have had any man's child would have been an easy matter, though highly inconvenient for her career.

I put my hand on Louisa's arm. It was the first time I'd ever dared touch her, and she looked down at my fingers as if at an insect to which she wasn't sure how to react. I said, 'If only you knew . . .' My face was moving towards hers; my head was about to light on her shoulder, where I wanted to weep. Everything, then, had been for this.

She moved her arm free, stood up and made a little speech. 'Look, I'm sorry, but I think we might have started off with different ideas of what my coming here was supposed to be about. Maybe I'd better leave.'

It was as simple as that. No more than a gesture of human contact; but she was right, of course. I wanted something impossible, and we can appreciate the impossibility of our dreams only when they meet, beyond ourselves, with the coldness of the world, in which they harden like drops of wax on water, taking forms quite unlike those we had imagined for them. To Louisa, I was like the Moor who panted hot semen on to a fireplace, or like the writer who masturbated beneath a sheet. In her universe, we were all men, all completely equivalent, and she knew exactly what we wanted.

We parted amicably, though. At the door, my farewell had every right to be the perfect replica of a conversation which would follow the ceremonial reading of the gas meter which her visit was always supposed to resemble. I looked out into the street, still an innocent man, as Louisa walked away, and it was to be the last time I would see her.

It was after her second failure to attend our Thursday

meetings that Jill Brandon asked if I knew where Louisa was, what was wrong with her, since she had been missing all her lectures. Perhaps she was ill. In fact, it transpired, she had decided to leave university altogether; though for reasons among which the unfortunate but trivial episode at my house surely had no right to figure. It was made official by a letter; I heard rumours about the contents in a conversation which passed briefly around the staff common room one afternoon, but since I was determined to maintain my usual air of indifference, I was unable to discover any further details, even if they were known. Bob Cormack said, 'Louisa? She seemed to be coping as far as I could make out, but she wasn't very bright.' To which Jill Brandon replied that her reasons for leaving were, apparently, 'personal'. And she gave me a look of quiet malice, which only those well steeped in the formaldehyde of academic life can fully understand.

I was not to be denounced; there was no complaint, no suggestion that I had ever acted improperly. Indeed, my crimes lived only in my imagination. But Louisa was gone, and I had reached the beginning of my story, because it was at this time that the illness which Donald had seen written on my face now became physical; a disturbance in my gut, a loss of appetite and weight, and after a while the passing of blood. Ellen said I should see a doctor; but I knew the cause.

Proust says we should sometimes yield to the therapeutic benefits of voluntary pastiche, in order that we do not spend the rest of our lives producing pastiche involuntarily. He was referring to the doomed imitators of Flaubert; but I came to understand his comment in terms of that person called 'I' who is not always oneself. My life had become a form of pastiche, and after failing as lover I would now surrender myself to the role of invalid; a part which is far easier to play, since one's lines, at every moment, are prompted by the kind, indifferent actors of the medical profession, whose job it is to seem to care. Sincerity is the most important thing, the old joke says; learn to fake that, and you've got it made. And this, of course, is precisely the theory proposed by Diderot in the *Paradoxe sur le comédien*. The finest performer, the finest artist, is one who conveys emotions and ideas while feeling and thinking nothing, since any such sentiments would only interfere with his ability to perform convincingly. I have never asked them to care about me, those men and women in their white coats upon whose critical judgement my fate has depended; and I in turn have sought to play my part with an attitude of detachment, to the extent that the confessions I have written here seem no longer to be about me, nor even to concern me very much.

What I have learned, is the meaning of the words spoken by the ancient, dying Fontenelle who, on being asked what he could feel, said, 'Nothing, except for a certain difficulty in living.' Life itself, we could say, is nothing, except for a stubborn difficulty in dying; one which finally passes, though it is this stubbornness which makes us demand another test, another opinion, a checking of every percentage, until the very last second. I have discovered what was meant by La Rochefoucauld when he said there are times in life when the only way out is for one to become slightly mad. I have discovered what was meant by Montaigne, who said that when reason no longer serves us, we must make use of experience. Yes, my life has been a poor, second-hand existence; but if literature has any purpose, it is in teaching us how to be ourselves.

And of course I have had time to think of how I might

have done things better, during my last meeting with Louisa. I have thought of the many beautiful speeches I could have made to her; though this is merely the phenomenon we call *esprit de l'escalier*, after Diderot, who noted in the *Paradoxe* that we are apt to become tongue-tied through emotion, and only recover our presence of mind once we reach the calmness at the bottom of the stairs.

I decided to write a novel. I felt the misguided need to express something of the unhappiness I felt in relation to Louisa; and here we see how ill equipped I was to carry out my intentions, since I should have known from Diderot's analysis of acting that you can only write well about things which mean nothing to you; that 'expression' is best left to amateur dramatics or creative writing classes. Nevertheless, I began the piece which would eventually lead me to describe myself as a 'writer', while an endoscopist's rectal probings inaugurated my career as dying man.

The novel soon taught me my limitations; just as I would soon have understood the shallow foundations of my desires for Louisa, if I had ever tried to make of them something tangible. None of our talents seem as great to us as those we leave forever untested; and we forget too easily that our supposed capacity for love amounts, in many cases, to no more than a fertility of imagination. This, however, is not to say that such dreams are negligible, and of no significance. Nothing has been more damaging to human relations than the belief that our feelings must be announced by us in order for them to become valid; that we must know a person well in order for desire to qualify as love; or even that those with whom we choose to spend the days of our lives, and those who move our hearts, should be identical people. The modern institution of marriage is based on hopeful belief in a coincidence; that we can feel friendship and passion, companionship and desire, trust and danger, peace and euphoria, all simultaneously, for a single individual; and the rarity of this coincidence, as unlikely, as startling, and as inconsequential as a celestial conjunction, is demonstrated by the corresponding frequency of marriages which believe themselves to be sick, simply because they are normal. Perhaps our greatest affairs, our greatest achievements, can take place only in our heads; but although we may therefore be denied the affection or glory we crave, we should not despise that part of our life which is seen only by ourselves, and may in some instances be its most significant portion.

My novel (it concerned D'Alembert; I shall say no more about it) was left abandoned by me before I entered hospital, where I began instead to write these pages whose purgative purpose is now served. For me to show them to anyone would be for me to resemble the person who proudly presents to visitors his own gallstones in a jar; my interior has already been made sufficiently public in this place, to the extent that my colon has become a topic of general conversation analogous to the dismal weather. When I leave I shall destroy everything I have done here, and I shall go back to my fiction. If I am to live, then it is that book which must now be finished; this page, not I myself, must surely have perished; and I will have found peace at last.

CHAPTER 13

I really was most sorry, Dr Petrie, to hear about your illness. I can only hope you're feeling better now, and that this letter finds you in a healthier state than the recipient of my other recent correspondence, an old friend of mine who has been dead for a number of years.

Your book about Ferrand and Minard has given me much pleasure, but it would seem that those gentlemen have not yet been informed of your theory concerning their non-existence, since my researches reveal them to be alive and well on 2859 Internet sites already, a number which appears to be growing by the day, as I shall explain.

Who would have thought, I was saying to Catriona as she helped me clean myself at around half-past four last Wednesday, that a flat tyre and a shower of rain . . . But perhaps I shouldn't go into all that. You don't know the story, and you don't really need to, except for the fact that some time ago a picture appeared on my computer screen of a naked girl whose name I now know to be Louisa Lawson. She's expecting a child, though you wouldn't guess it from the photograph which still slumbers somewhere in the dark fragmented sectors of my 'hard disk'. Who could this unknown girl be, I kept asking myself each night after

Catriona left me to go and stock up on the little pills which have done such wonders for my condition, and are worth every penny I've spent on them. Let me tell you, if ever you have trouble with your waterworks (and believe me, it comes to us all), then be sure to get yourself down to the nearest 'nightclub', which you'll find to be a purveyor of medication far finer than any chemist. I've never been, but Catriona has described these establishments to me in detail; they have loud music, which might not appeal (why does every shop choose to pollute the air with such stuff, when people have to go there anyway?), and sex is permitted in the toilets. This is in marked distinction to Boots, for example, which has no toilets at all; something that can be quite a problem for a man of my age, as I'm sure you must understand.

Well, who could she be, this naked girl shown reading your very own book? I decided to pay a further visit to the website where I found the photograph, and was confronted with a JPEG of another woman, performing an experiment in life science using a large plastic device. Truly, I said to myself, the Internet has proved to be a most educating medium!

Allowing the cursor to wander over the image, I noticed that each region was in fact a hyperlink. It's all very clever; a use of HTML which Dr Cool, a noted authority on the subject, singles out for special praise in his list of 'shit-hot tricks'. The photograph was more properly a map, a collection of portals and passages; so that for example the plastic object, were I to click on it, would transport me to an online shop; a breast was an invitation to visit a list of similar sites; and the woman's face served as a means for soliciting e-mail. By clicking upon her teeth, I was prompted to send a message to the creator of this curious site, and so I immediately wrote, asking for details about the girl I'd seen reading your book, as well as any other information he could supply.

I received a swift response, saying I could have everything I desired if I were to send some 'pics' in return. My invisible correspondent, who gave no name in his message, explained that he was addicted to 'pussy', and could I send him any good 'beaver shots'? Whoever would have thought that addiction could extend to such strange and irregular dimensions? I decided to tell Catriona all about it next morning, then went to bed after taking the medicine I have learned to use in order to control the headaches which prolonged browsing invariably stimulates.

Catriona arrived next day, whistling merrily as she brought a bag of messages to the kitchen and began distributing the raw components of a soon-to-be-fine lunch among the cupboards where such things belong, and I explained my need to obtain a few wildlife photographs. But how ever would I send them across the Internet, I wondered, even after I had been to the zoo in search of beavers and pussies? Catriona said I needed a digital camera, and so I immediately resolved to obtain one, leaving her to do the vacuuming while I put on my coat and set off for Dixons, a well-known high-street retailer of inexpensive gadgets. And sure enough, for less than eight hundred pounds, my friend there named Ali was able to offer me a camera which can send pictures directly on to my computer, with no need for developing. As for Boots, whose pharmaceutical purposes have already been usurped by 'nightclubs' and their alternative therapies, we now see that its photographic services must also fall by the wayside. Whatever use will soon be left for the place, and for its magnificently perfumed yet ultimately superfluous staff?

I asked Ali if the camera would be suitable for capturing beavers and pussies, and Mrs J. Campbell, overhearing our conversation, pulled a very queer face, then picked up the phone on her counter and started talking in a low but disapproving voice. Trying to account for this response, I wondered if she suspected me to be some kind of poacher.

'I won't harm the little creatures,' I told Ali, making sure that Mrs J. Campbell could hear me well. 'I only like to look. Killing isn't for me; no rods or guns or any of that stuff, oh no. Just a quick flash, and I'm done.' I also asked Ali whether the camera would be capable of dealing with the low light levels of nightclub drug dispensers, since I was curious to know what these places look like, and Ali seemed to think the camera would be fine for all my requirements, before I handed him my credit card in order to complete our most satisfactory transaction.

I returned home and proudly showed Catriona my purchase, which looked strangely shrunken once I'd removed it from the brightly coloured box and all the polystyrene packaging inside. She said, 'You really went and bought it? Just like that?' She has a habit of speaking thus at times. 'I love the way you're so easy with money,' she continued, putting her arms around my neck, and kissing me in what she has informed me to be the French manner, though I always thought that to be the stiff cheek-pecking of De Gaulle, rather than the licking, nibbling, lingering, and very wet sort of kiss which, it would seem, is the true manner by which ordinary French people greet one another in cafés and parks every day. 'And that reminds me,' she said, removing her tongue from my mouth. 'You owe me another fifty for your medicine.'

'Yes, of course,' I told her, 'but first try and explain to

me how I'm going to use this little machine in order to get a split beaver shot, whatever that means.' And I described once more, in greater detail, the request I'd received from my anonymous correspondent. Catriona then made it plain to me that the creature I was to photograph was the one that lives where women's legs meet.

'Would you mind if I took a few wee shots of yours?' I asked Catriona, and she said, 'No way'. Her use of language is something I found idiomatic and confusing at first, but it seems to be universal among her generation, and since you're involved in education I expect you must already be familiar with the dialect, which I therefore transcribe without further apology.

I said, 'There's no need for false modesty. You're as pretty down there as everywhere else, and I'm sure the camera would do you full justice. It has a very deep focal length, you know.' I recited Ali's earlier encomium in hon-our of the small device I held, and puzzled over Catriona's unwillingness to be captured by its lens; a response as irrational as that of tribespeople who supposedly fear that the taking of their image amounts to a possession of their souls. I only wanted a few beaver shots, after all.

'And what will this guy do with them? Will I end up on his website, so that total strangers can see me starkers?' I told her I only wanted to send what was required in order to further my pursuit of Rosier's Encyclopaedia. I would pay her standard modelling rates, of course.

'Tell you what,' she said. 'You can take me as long as my face isn't visible. I mean, what if my friends or lecturers saw me posing naked on the Internet?' The possibility that those people would likewise be involved in a search for the eighteenth-century arcana that would enable them to make such an encounter was an idea which would never have occurred to me; but Catriona is a scientist, and so has a very clear and methodical way of thinking about things, as well as being very handy with a penknife.

'Why don't we go upstairs, where you can take your clothes off and I'll photograph your beaver, pussy, or whatever it's supposed to be called nowadays?'

She suggested we have a cup of tea first, and I agreed on condition that I take my medicine beforehand. Catriona therefore brought a pill from her bag, which cost me less than thirty pounds. She used to bring a type with little birds on them, but the one she gave me now was white and circular, scored with a line, and bearing an inscription in capital letters which I've also seen on paracetamols. In fact, the tablets I take now are identical to paracetamols in every respect apart from their price, and the miraculous effect they have on my waterworks.

I washed it down with a swig of tea, and Catriona read the camera's instruction leaflet while drinking her own cup. Thanks to you, I told her cheerfully as my medicine began to take effect, we shall have no need of support engineers today. Then, once Catriona had experimented with the camera a couple of times, we went upstairs. She was already in the bedroom, with the curtains closed and the last of her clothing removed, when I eventually caught up with her. She lay down on the bed, and I took aim with the camera.

She cried out, 'Make sure my face isn't in it,' and then, to make doubly sure, pulled a pillow across her head. She settled down a bit, and I asked her exactly what is meant by a 'split beaver shot'. I'm sure Mrs B would never have been able to explain such wonders to me!

Catriona raised her legs, and began to tug at the not

inconsiderable flaps of skin which live folded like an air-craft's undercarriage in between. On the camera's small viewing screen I watched this moving image of pink flesh, pulled and tightened, and reminiscent of a few lean scraps of bacon, which put me in mind of that lovely wee place, the Dolphin, where you used to get a grand fry-up for not very much at all, considering. But I couldn't for the life of me see why anyone should find interesting or addictive an image such as the one I now looked at. I imagined that just as dentists no doubt find the interiors of mouths endlessly fascinating, so must there be corresponding explorers of every other orifice and cavity which the human body exhibits; and in other circumstances I could just as easily have found myself photographing Catriona's ear or nostril in my quest for Rosier's Encyclopaedia, rather than the vent she now happened to be opening. Then Catriona suddenly let go of herself in order to remove the ring from her finger. 'Somebody might recognize it,' she said from beneath the pillow, so that her voice was very muffled and I had to ask her to repeat herself. She lifted the pillow in order to do this, and her idea that you could identify a person solely from the ring they wear is but one among many observations which never would have entered my old and feeble mind, were it not for the breath of enlightenment which my dear young friend has blown into my life.

I pressed the button, and there was a flash.

'No! I wasn't ready!' Catriona sat up. 'If my face is in we've got to scrub it!' She looked at the frozen image on the viewing screen, and we were pleased to find that I had inadvertently guillotined her in just the manner she desired. She lay back in order that we could continue, and in time we both became more relaxed. The odd angle I needed to assume so as to obtain a good view of her genitals was having an adverse effect on my back; a chair cured this. And Catriona decided that the pillow over her head was an excessive precaution. She instead held it on her bosom in a manner which was sure to exclude her face from any photograph.

'How many frames are there on the film?' I asked her, having by now preserved her little rashers sufficiently many times to have become completely bored by them.

'There isn't a film in there; the images are stored in memory. I think you can get about a hundred.' Then she tugged and pulled at herself again, and slipped a finger into her wet aperture. I thought about the first time I saw this curious area of her body, when I was sponging her in the bath, and this in turn made me think about my old Morris, which was a fine wee car and very reliable. In fact, I only had one problem with it in eighteen years – a broken crankshaft – and if it had been the Morris I was driving one day when rain fell upon a town and a large potato crisp factory I have no need of naming, then there probably would have been no flat tyre, no visit to the garage, no Xanthics and Rosier, and no Catriona dribbling on my bed. So it's just as well, I thought to myself, while two of her fingers moved in and out of their rosy socket like clammy pistons, that the Morris had already left me, and it was only the trusty but inferior Nova I was driving; otherwise I wouldn't be here now, photographing this fascinating spectacle of life science with a device which cost me less than eight hundred pounds; no, I would be sitting in my study over Hume or Carlyle, and Mrs B would already have gone for the afternoon, and I would perhaps be thinking of an article I might write for *The Scots Magazine*, or a trip to see Margaret in the library; and suddenly I felt as if a little tear were almost installing itself in the corner of my left eye. I still clicked and flashed while Catriona began to bounce her bottom upon the bed, gasping from the other side of her pillow, and the little tear confirmed itself, swelled, trickled and rolled down my cheek, as I thought of Mrs B who was gone for ever, and my other friend to whom I used to write, who has gone even more certainly. But thanks to Catriona and all the wonders I'd discovered, there was no more need of reading or writing, and all the world was replaced by machines, the sale of which will keep Ali and Mrs J. Campbell in business for ever.

I'd got to eighty-four when Catriona finished, and this must surely be more than enough, I decided, to satisfy even the most dedicated enthusiast. Catriona's face and breast were flushed; she asked me if I wanted to do anything else, and I told her I wanted to go to the toilet since the medicine was wearing off, then send these pictures immediately afterwards. I did the latter while Catriona took a bath which was quick even by her usual swift standards.

The reply came after Catriona had gone, telling me that the girl I had seen, the reader of your book, is called Louisa. You know this already, of course, since I mentioned it earlier. She studied French (hence her interest in your book), and lives with the man who photographed her. He thanked me most kindly for the excellent pictures I had sent, and described them as highly 'wankable', a word I have not found in any dictionary, or even in *Dr Cool's Web Magic*. He said he'd like to trade some more, and perhaps we should get together, all four of us. This, I decided, would surely be an excellent way of discovering at last the true meaning of Rosier's Encyclopaedia, and so I made an appointment with him for the following week.

I was somewhat surprised, next day, by Catriona's disapproving reaction to the proposed meeting. I only wanted to discuss certain matters of eighteenth-century philosophy, after all.

'I can't travel there with you,' she said. 'I'd have to go separately on the train, and it's too far.'

It sounded as if she was just trying to find an excuse, but then I realized she must be worried about the fare. 'I'll cover your expenses, of course. How much do you want?'

She thought about it in her usual way, then after some further negotiation she at last said, 'All right. A hundred.'

This seemed an awful lot for a train fare to the suburbs. 'A hundred pounds? Don't you get a student reduction? I've got a pensioner's railcard; perhaps you can get away with using it . . .'

'Give me a hundred and I'll do whatever you guys want. Take it or leave it. Sorry, but you know how we do things, and I've got to eat.'

Naturally I agreed. After all, our relationship was based on a firm adherence to the 'going rate', and clearly this was the sum required if one expects a young lady to take a train to the other side of town. In my day it was all different, of course, but customs quickly change.

Later that day, while she was doing her homework on me, the phone rang. I arrived in my study at the eighth or tenth ring, naked from the waist down, and heard, when I lifted the receiver, the voice of Margaret at the library. My books were long overdue, she said; she was worried about me, and thought I might have been unwell.

Once more, I felt a strange sorrow for pleasures past, but quickly reminded myself that I was far better spending an afternoon helping Catriona get a good degree, rather than waste the hours on dirty dusty rubbish. 'I'll bring them, don't worry Margaret,' I said, then hung up and went back, regretting that Catriona's experiment, which had been interrupted just as my apparatus was at last becoming ready for it, would have to begin all over from zero. At least with a book you can put a marker between the pages, so that you can always pick up from the precise point where you left off; but my poor member was now as limp as the leather strap I saw protruding from the depths of *The Three Perils of Man*, edged in gilt and horizontally stacked in a corner, among a pile of similarly untouched volumes of which I could have no further need. But since this letter, unlike Catriona's experiment, can be hurried towards its conclusion through will alone, I should perhaps say no more about this, and instead move us on to the day of the meeting.

Catriona decided to accompany me in the car after all, though for some reason she wore a headscarf and dark glasses on a day whose weather far from warranted it. She looked like a Russian ballerina with defective vision, rather than a young life scientist who's extremely handy with a penknife. The address turned out to be a pleasant house with a recently mowed lawn before it. I always like a house with a well-kept lawn, which is why I live in a house which has no lawn at all. Well, do you think Mrs B or Catriona would have done the gardening as well?

It was Louisa who answered the door, strangely alarmed by the rate at which I was coming up the path behind Catriona who had rung the bell, as if Louisa should have some objection to being visited by an old man with a walking stick; and while I didn't notice it at the time, Catriona subsequently told me that Louisa's pregnant state, though early, was immediately apparent. Catriona said it had made her want to call everything off there and then, and this was the reason why, when she and I were left alone on the living room sofa and Louisa went to the kitchen, Catriona raised her expenses by another fifty. I was just handing her this amount in tens when Louisa came back carrying two glasses of whisky we must have asked for, or consented to when offered. Already, you see, I felt that things were moving according to a plan of their own, and I was merely a passenger of events.

'Me, I don't drink,' Louisa said. 'Because of . . .' She indicated what I took at the time to be a weight problem, and I agreed that alcohol has a deceptively high calorific value; a fact I had recently learned from a fascinating homepage belonging to the 'Society For Serious Beer Drinkers'.

Then the man appeared, shook our hands, and said, 'Just call me John. Not my real name of course.'

'I'm Sandi,' said Catriona.

'And I'm Louisa,' said Louisa, somewhat to my relief, for she proposed nothing in contradiction to what we knew already.

Looking at me, John said, 'To be honest, I'm surprised. I don't think we've ever met a like-minded soul who was so . . . mature. Have we, Louisa?'

Louisa shook her head, and I was trying to work out why there should be anything strange about a man of my years showing enthusiasm for eighteenth-century philosophy, when John said, 'I loved those pictures, Sandi. So did Louisa.'

In fact Louisa, I suspected, wasn't really so keen. She was sitting in an armchair now, looking down at her weight problem, and I could tell she thought I'd made a poor job of the photos, maybe got the lighting wrong.

Then John, picking up a whisky glass which couldn't have been for me after all, and kneeling on the carpet close to where Catriona sat, put his hand on her knee and said, 'You're a very beautiful woman, Sandi. Tell me a bit about yourself.'

Catriona/Sandi (I was a wee bit confused myself by now) was taking her time answering, so I helped her out. 'She's a life scientist at the university, you know. Very good with a vacuum cleaner, and does a magnificent cock-a-leekie. She's even better than Mrs B.'

'Mrs B?' John said with some interest, taking a sip of whisky. 'Is this someone else we ought to meet?'

'Oh, I'm afraid there's little chance of that,' I told him. 'As a matter of fact, she left me because of you, Louisa.' I regretted saying this, because Louisa already disapproved of my photographic efforts and my reference to calories, and her continued contemplation of the protuberant tummy I now could notice merely furthered my conviction that she didn't want any of us to be here.

'Well,' said John. 'Why don't we get to know each other a little better?' His hand, which had not removed itself from Catriona's knee, began to slide along her thigh.

Catriona caught hold of it, with a firmness John appeared to find entertaining, and said to him, 'Tell us a bit about yourself, "John".'

'Me? I'm a freelance software consultant.'

After an appropriately awed and respectful silence, I said, 'I was particularly interested by the HTML meta-tags in your web page. Rosier, Ferrand, Minard . . .'

John shrugged. 'Just a little joke.' Then he looked at Catriona again, his hand still in hers. 'I'm very fond of games and make-believe. Do you like that too, Sandi?'

'Sometimes,' she said. 'It depends.'

This was all very well, but I was beginning to feel a little impatient. 'What I really want to know is how you found out about Rosier's Encyclopaedia.' Even as I spoke, I saw that Catriona had lowered her face to meet John's where he knelt before her, their lips engaging in a slow exchange of saliva. John continued to hold a whisky glass in his free hand, and I sincerely hoped he didn't spill anything, because it was a very nice carpet, of a kind which Mrs B would have been only too happy to keep in pristine condition. But at last he put down his drink, and his attentions moved themselves beneath Catriona's skirt, or Sandi's, or whatever we should call her.

I turned to Louisa. 'I've been reading it too, you know.'

'What?' she said vacantly, her eyes directed towards the other couple.

'*Ferrand and Minard*. The book you were holding in the picture. I take it you're interested in Rousseau and Proust, and the theory Dr Petrie has about the role of fantasy in literature.'

Louisa made no reply, almost as if she didn't understand. John turned to her and made a nodding gesture beckoning her to come and attend to me.

'No, it's all right,' I said, 'I didn't want whisky anyway.' I nearly mentioned calories again, but fortunately checked myself. John turned to her once more, momentarily breaking away from Catriona's fingers in his hair, and repeated his gesture, somewhat crossly. I was still reaffirming my distaste for whisky while Louisa stood up and came towards me, kneeling on the floor in a mirror image of John's position. She reached for my flies, and I tried to get us back on to Rousseau, Ferrand and Minard, your book, anything. 'How exactly did you come by it?' I asked nervously as she began to unbutton me. I hadn't realized that French students do the same sort of homework as life scientists these days. I said, 'I really ought to warn you the experiment will take a very long time, so I hope you've got nothing else planned for the afternoon, and haven't left the oven on.'

Again John released his face from kissing, and said to Louisa, 'Leave it.' Then to me, 'If you just want to watch, that's fine. Why don't we all go upstairs and get more comfortable?'

As a means of finding out about certain topics in eighteenth-century literature this was all a lot slower and more complicated than a visit to dear Margaret and her well-ordered library. Here there was no system, no card index, but only John's sequential instructions, unfolding like successive lines of computer code which the rest of us merely followed. I need hardly tell you I was last to the bedroom by a long way, finding there a place I immediately recognized from a photograph I'd so often gazed at. Yet the living screen now before me still offered no answer; only a scene in which John helped the other two undress, and I quickly decided I had no interest in watching the rest of whatever tutorial was to follow. In any case I was in need of a visit to the bathroom, after which I made my sorrowful way back downstairs.

Louisa was the first to rejoin me some time later; John and Catriona were still making noises upstairs. I at once asked the only question that concerned me. 'Tell me why you were reading Petrie's book.'

She looked at me wearily. 'Why's it so important to you?' I was about to tell her a very long story which begins with a flat tyre and a shower of rain when she explained. 'Petrie was one of my lecturers. I used to meet him every week.'

'I see,' I said. 'And why did you do that?' She must have a particularly deep interest in the period, I suspected.

'I suppose it was a way of getting away from . . . this.' She waved an arm, possibly indicating a small framed picture on the wall depicting a harbour somewhere; tasteless, admittedly, but a piece of decor from which a close and thorough study of Rousseau would seem a somewhat excessive and inappropriate form of escape. She said, 'Don't think I dislike what we do here. But we went through a bad time when I wasn't sure, wasn't ready to let go, and I suppose it was comforting to have a little corner of my life that wasn't about sex. A place every Thursday filled only with books and writers. While Dr Petrie would go on about Proust, I'd be thinking about what I was getting into with John, and if it was right for me, and whether I really wanted it. My work was going downhill because of all my worries, but that's what happens when you resist your own desires and give in to internal conflicts. That's how John put it. He got a bit jealous when I kept mentioning Dr Petrie, but I never fancied him. Typical ivory-tower type and not much to look at. John read Petrie's book too; he was working at the time on a game program about an eighteenth-century virtual city full of imaginary people. Ferrand and Minard gave him the idea for a tie-in: a whispering campaign he wanted to start on the Internet. So John gave me a few spoof articles he'd written to pass on to Dr Petrie. It seemed like harmless fun.

'I was supposed to do a web search with Petrie that would lead us to John's sites. Just as well it never came off, because I found out later that the first one he wanted us to hit was full of sex shots. His idea of a joke. Things had already been getting bad between us and I just blew up, he threw me out of the house, and I had a crazy couple of weeks. I did a stupid thing with some pills and quit university altogether, hoping I could sort my head out, I was so depressed. But that's all over. Now I'm back here, and we're happy.'

She didn't look it; nor did she seem aware of her own live appearance on the Internet, but the matter was scarcely worth mentioning now. The banal truth of John's hoax had unravelled itself before me. I was relieved when he and a sullen Catriona reappeared soon afterwards, and we made ready to leave this unfortunate place.

Catriona remained quiet until we were in the car. Then she began to cry, and talked about Ewan or Gary or whatever his name was, while all I could think about was a supposed philosophy of the universe which had proved as insubstantial as a soap bubble, and now was gone. It put me in a very downcast mood; but then I remembered *Epistemology and Unreason*, whose yellowed pages had been the start of everything. Surely that book must have predated John's antics; there remained some hope of finding truth. I realized that my pursuit of Rosier, far from being over, had hardly begun. I had merely been distracted by irrelevant web pages, search engines, and bedroom tutorials; while libraries and antiquarian bookshops still had their uses after all.

We returned home, where Catriona sat in my front room sipping the tea she finds so essential in times of immobility, and told me she'd decided she should stop coming to see me. I was horrified.

'But how will I manage without you?'

She smiled gently; the first time I had seen such an expression on her face that day. 'I'll find you another housekeeper, I promise. I'll look in every newsagent's window, check every advert, and get you someone far better than I could ever be.'

I told her this would be a hard task, and naturally I would cover her expenses at the standard agency rate.

'No,' she said, 'I don't want your money.' She then reached into her pocket and drew out the hundred and fifty pounds I'd given her earlier, which she handed me back.

'You never did take the train, right enough,' I reasoned, folding the notes. 'But you really should get yourself one of those rail passes which I'm sure a young life scientist such as yourself must be entitled to.'

Catriona said, 'You're a strange man, Mr Mee. It amazes me that you've managed to live so many years yet still be so naive about the world. Didn't your parents teach you anything?'

'Oh, I never knew them,' I said, explaining to Catriona that I was raised in a place whose smell would sometimes come back to me whenever Mrs B cleaned the bathroom; a building of blackened sandstone, so crammed with children that you were never alone. The dear departed recipient of all my earlier letters was a companion from those first days, and therefore required no explanation of them, so that it is not until this very moment that I have ever found the need of committing to paper these biographical irrelevancies.

'You really never knew your parents?' Catriona asked in that charmingly tautological way of hers. 'That's so sad,' she added, somewhat predictably. 'Why were you put in a home?'

But there was no more to be said about it, unless I was

to begin telling the poor girl the entire story of my life, and if I'd done that then this letter would have required an awful lot of paper and more stamps than I could fit on the envelope. So I told her to be a good child and run along back to her flat, then call Gary or Ewan or whatever his name was, and try to sort things out sensibly. She kissed me on the cheek, said 'Thank you' in an inordinately solemn way, and I wished her goodbye and good luck as I saw her out the door. I haven't heard from her since.

Well, I said to myself, it seems I'm right back to 'first base' as Dr Cool would call it, but less than an hour later the doorbell rang, and I decided that either Catriona had forgotten something, or else she'd fulfilled her promise of finding a replacement housekeeper with astonishing speed. I opened the door, and saw two men in black uniforms, who confirmed with me that they had come to the right address, showed me a document in a plastic wallet, then walked inside, saying that they had come for my computer.

'Are you from Dixons?' I asked. I had always taken the uniformed staff in that fine retail outlet to be security personnel, but it now seemed they might be service engineers, two of whom had come to fulfil the terms of that strange and mystical contract called an 'extended warranty' which Ali had insisted on me signing at a cost of less than a hundred pounds.

'We have reason to believe your computer may contain material in contravention of the Obscene Publications Act, and we have a warrant for its seizure. I must caution you that you are not obliged to say anything, and anything you do say may be taken down and used in evidence . . .' While one of the service engineers explained these terms and conditions, none of which had been made plain to me by that damned Ali, or even by Mrs J. Campbell, his companion went upstairs to the room I indicated to him, from where I soon heard the clatter of my machine being disconnected.

'I do hope when it comes back from the shop that I'll remember how to insert the keyboard connector C into the serial port B, being careful not to force or bend the connecting pins,' I said, recalling a crucial stage of the installation which had defeated me in several languages.

The non-dismantling engineer who stood with me was shaking his head slowly. He said, 'Don't you understand? We reckon you've got child pornography on your computer.'

'Oh, I don't think so,' I told him with confidence. '*Childe Harold* perhaps, part of which I downloaded from a site about famous Aberdonians, but *Child Pornography* is one I've never even heard of. No, all you'll find are some old works long out of copyright and of interest to none but an ageing fool such as myself.'

'We'll see about that,' the engineer said with a degree of menace which is a feature, I have found, occasionally to be observed in the staff of Dixons when you treat them the wrong way. I was asked to sign a piece of paper, and then they went outside to a police car parked in the street, which formed an object of inexplicable curiosity to a group of small children, and to several neighbours who observed it from behind their curtains, or from the steps of an open door.

'Hello there Mrs MacDougall,' I waved to one such onlooker, who closed her door without reply before I closed mine.

Now I really was alone. Catriona had left me, and so too had my computer. Even my supply of medicine had dried up, and none of the nightclubs I rang had ever heard of home deliveries. Once more I was a solitary old soul with a weak bladder. But whatever hardships befall us, whichever transient companions desert us, no matter what pain and anguish we find ourselves suffering, these are all only temporary, and at such moments we know always that our first and truest friends, ones the neglect of whom has perhaps precipitated our misfortunes, will still be there for us, awaiting our return. Slowly I ascended the stairs for the last time that day, gripping the bannister with a firm hand and saying to myself 'Whoever would have thought,' et cetera, until I reached my study, unlocked the neglected cabinets, and began to draw them out one by one; my precious jewels, my true and final solace. Yes, I said to my books, you may be dirty, dusty and very old, but so too am I, and we are ideally suited one to the other. And so upon the empty desk I began to reposition them; Hogg and Stevenson and my beloved Hume, opened all of them at the marked pages where last I visited them, as if they had merely been holding their breaths during the many strange days when, having forgotten them, I imagined it was I who more truly existed, while they lived quietly, patiently on. I had been, I now knew, in a kind of dream from which at last I was rising, as if bubbling upwards from the dark green depths of a bookless, treacherous void. Once more I could smell their must, feel the crisp weight of a turning page, touch the substance of their binding.

'And tomorrow,' I said to myself, 'I shall even learn to operate the vacuum cleaner.'

This, however, proved to be quite unneccessary, and it's probably just as well. For at the appointed hour, when Catriona would be expected to arrive, the doorbell rang, and it was not my young friend who stood waiting, nor the rude engineers from Dixons; no, even as I was bringing myself down the stairs I could hear a key in the lock, sticking and rattling in a way I've known and loved these twenty-eight years, and I could hear a voice outside saying, 'Will he never get a locksmith to this tamned thing?' And there she was in the open doorway, Mrs B come back again!

'I see you're still alive, you old rogue,' she said, stepping inside.

But why ever had she come back? It seemed that Catriona, who must have found Mrs B's number from my address book, had last night pleaded with her to return to her former employment, explaining the whole story of Rosier, Louisa and the rest in an attempt to dispel Mrs B's conviction that I was a wicked and evil man who ought to be locked up.

'And it's not just me who needs to hear your excuses,' she said, alluding to certain legends which already by now, I learned, had become part of the domestic folklore of every house on the street.

'But I only ever got the computer so as to make your job a bit easier,' I pleaded, telling her it was gone now anyway, and she would find everything exactly as before.

Mrs B, taking off her coat and hat and carrying to the kitchen a highly promising-looking bag of vegetables, said, 'There's some men'll have their wee affairs with fancy women and get it all out of their system before they reach the age of forty, and there's others'll wait more than twice as long before they find what a load of nonsense it all is. And you know which kind is you, Mr Mee.'

With this reprimand, so richly deserved, our life could at last return to normal. Already I am far advanced in a study

I'm preparing for *The People's Friend*, tracing the Scottish ancestry of Jorge Luis Borges, whose fondness for West Highland Terriers qualifies him for inclusion in that fine journal. I'll send you a copy when it comes out; but for now, having reached the end of my adventures, there is nothing else for me to say except goodbye.

EPILOGUE

Now I can reveal everything at last. You must have been wondering what I was playing at: where was I hiding all this time, why did I disappear so quickly, without giving you any indication of where I was going? No, I expect you guessed it three years ago, the very day I left. All those debts piling up – you know I can't resist the roulette table, or a hand of cards – and then there was that trouble with Marie's father. Paris was no longer a sensible place to be, and a telephone engineer like myself can always find a job in any moderate-sized town, even in a foreign country. The postmark of this letter will already have told you everything. I live in Scotland, and the exchanges here are simply fascinating!

The Théâtrophone isn't quite as big here yet as it is in France, but ordinary domestic telephones are, if anything, even more popular. I know I bored you with the subject often enough when we used to meet in Paris, but I still maintain that the Théâtrophone, more than the motor car or the aeroplane, is the shape of the future itself. A system which can broadcast a theatrical production, an opera, a lecture, a concert directly into the subscriber's home, across existing telephone wires – surely you must agree that society is on the verge of a transformation, a revolution, thanks to such technology!

Many people are surprised how long it's been around. Here in Britain they call it the Electrophone, and I install three or four consoles a week to the sort of people who can afford it. Oh, costs will soon come down, I tell them, and they generally look a little disappointed. Sales were better while I was living in Sussex for a year, but since coming 'north of the border' as they say here, I've found that the Scots are just as much experts in snobbery as the English, or even the Parisians, and there's nothing they like more than to have something which other people can't afford. But at least the Scots are more sympathetic to our nation than their southern neighbours. The 'Auld Alliance' they call it. Yes, I'll say – wiring up a posh Electrophone console, the four-trumpet variety for example, with its oak stand, in some fancy drawing room where there's oil paintings and deers' heads on the walls – within ten or twenty years you'll find that every home in the land has an Electrophone, not to mention the telephone, of course.

This will be greeted by a laugh from the butler who's watching me, and then I'll say, You've got a Frenchman to thank for all this, of course. Monsieur Auder, way back in 1885. That's right, nearly thirty years ago. He set up twelve microphones in the Paris Opera and relayed the signals by telephone to receivers which reproduced the entire picture of sound, so that not only could you hear all the music, but you could even identify the positions of the singers as they moved around. Stereophony, it's called, and it's the future, believe me (though some problems with phase-difference still need sorting out). All this gramophone stuff is a waste of time; it won't last. And people go on about the new 'wireless radio', but how can such a medium possibly catch on, when there's no way to charge the listeners? Do you think that companies will be set up which give everything away for free, simply casting their wares into the atmosphere? Forget it. Copper wire is the answer, the telephone exchange is the invisible city of the future, and the great Monsieur Auder saw it all. Some people here, ones who've never been to France, are surprised when I tell them that already by the turn of the century there were Théâtrophone kiosks in hotels and restaurants all over the country, where you could get as many minutes of entertainment as you wished, as long as you kept putting in your coins; and you'll remember those cafés, at the height of the craze, which advertised themselves solely on the basis of the Théâtrophones which lovers of progress and followers of fashion would go there to use, hardly worrying about a cup of coffee or a conversation with their friends. Every Frenchman knows this, of course, but over here it's still news to some people.

Imagine the situation in a few years' time, I'll say to them, once everyone has a telephone connection, and there's an Electrophone in every respectable household, in every public library, in every school. Will people even need to leave their own armchair? Perhaps they'll use such machines to conduct their financial transactions, advertise their businesses, have discussions with people they've never even met, entertain themselves. Will people still bother to read? Will they go out to eat, or will they simply order their meal by telephone, which will then be brought to their home?

'That would be a terribly dull kind of society,' many have said to me. People will become lazy, isolated, they will no longer seek friendship, they will forget how to conduct a conversation. On the contrary, I tell them, the telephone will enlarge and enrich the field of human relationships! 'And what of the art of letter writing?' they ask me. I grant you, there'll be no need for five or six postal deliveries every day once the system is sufficiently established, but just think of all the extra time which people will have, when they can say everything directly to the person they wish to address, instead of writing it all down. What will we do with so much leisure, except enjoy ourselves? And consider the amorous possibilities which the telephone has already brought into our lives . . .

The Scots, I'll grant you, are slightly more amenable to this talk of scientific progress than either the English or the French, at least in my experience. They even claim to have invented the telephone in the first place, but so does every other advanced country in the world, as you know. The Théâtrophone, though, is truly French; and only a Frenchman, surely, could have had the vision to see telephony as a branch of artistic culture, a medium of human creativity and emotional enrichment.

But none of these dreams were of much help to me while I was running up my gambling debts. The Théâtrophone Company paid good money, there was no shortage of Parisians wanting to get hold of a machine, but that was precisely the problem; because as you know, the more I earned, the more I risked at the gaming table.

I remember the very last Théâtrophone I installed before leaving France. It was an address on the Boulevard Haus-mann, not far from Printemps (department stores, by the way, will soon be obsolete too, of course), and nearly opposite the little park with that ugly old memorial to Louis XVI (when will they ever get round to pulling it down?). 102 was the number on my schedule; a big apartment

ANDREW CRUMEY

building of three or four floors, and I went upstairs carrying the receiver in its box in one hand, and my tool kit in the other. I came round the bend in the stairs, and beside the apartment door there was a round window looking on to the stairwell, through which I saw the face of a young maid standing guard, glowering at me. She opened the door before I'd even rung the bell, and I introduced myself while she inspected me from head to toe, scrutinizing the wooden box and the tool bag, sniffing slightly as if she suspected an animal to be hidden among my luggage. Then she stood aside to let me in, not a word from her, and once she'd closed the door she led the way.

To the left of the entrance lobby I saw the open door of a dining room so cluttered with furniture that you wouldn't have been able to move in it if you tried. Not a lot of dinners go on in there, I said to myself, and I walked behind her, through another door at the far end of the lobby and then past a reception room which looked equally unused, until we reached the master's door, which she knocked. Ah, I thought, the study. Not a bit of it, though. This was his bedroom, as I saw when the maid opened the door.

The heavy curtains were drawn shut and the lamp was lit, even though it was broad daylight outside, and by God, that room was heated so stiflingly you could've roasted a chicken in it. Gloomy too, with a cloth over the lamp so that all was in shadow, yellow and sickly, and there on the bed in the far corner was the master himself, lying with a sheet pulled right up to his nose and looking, from the little I could see of him, like a frightened rabbit. An invalid, I realized, and one who hadn't visited the other rooms of his apartment for quite some time. Just the sort of housebound customer the Théâtrophone is ideally suited to, though this

330

was all a very queer scene, I can tell you, and not one I'll forget in a hurry. Strangest of all were the walls, for they were crudely covered, from top to bottom, with square panels of cheap cork, though don't ask me why. It was like walking into the nest of an insect, him lying on the bed wrapped up in his white cocoon. Probably not much past forty and still with a thick head of black hair and a moustache to match, but he wouldn't have long to go if he kept his bedroom so damned hot and airless.

'Good day, monsieur,' I said to him, but this hardly put him at ease. I could see that he was shivering despite the temperature, and I only hoped I didn't catch whatever it was he was dying of. The maid left us.

'Where's it to go?' I asked. He looked puzzled, pulled a funny face. 'The Théâtrophone,' I explained, pointing to the box. What else did he think I'd come here for?

'Ah,' he said, 'of course.' Then he nodded towards the table at the side of his bed, still without letting the sheet go below his chin.

'We'd better move some of this stuff first,' I suggested, because as well as the telephone which already sat there, the table was crammed with medicine bottles and an enormous number of bound exercise books. I lifted some of them.

'I should be very careful with those,' he said. Then he explained that they were part of a novel, and I can only tell you that it promises to be the longest novel ever written, judging by the heap of exercise books it already fills.

'Well,' I said, 'If you don't mind, I'll just move your novel somewhere else.' He pointed to the place where he wanted his books taken, and I did it in three trips, leaving the telephone and medicine bottles on the table, pushed within his easy reach so as to make a space where I put the box. 'You're a writer, then?' I said. He gave his timid nod again. 'So, what sort of books do you write?'

He frowned, as if this was a really hard one. Then, 'I believe that I am only writing a single book,' he began to say, 'which concerns . . .' but he interrupted himself with a very loud sneeze that shook him so seriously I thought I might need to call for the maid. Once he'd recovered he looked at me earnestly and asked, 'Do you have any flowers on you?' He could see perfectly well that my buttonhole was empty. 'Or have you been close to any? Did you perhaps visit a florist before coming here?'

Strangely enough, I had been to one the previous day, and I wondered if this writer fellow was some kind of mystic. Saw right through me, he did. 'That's quite amazing,' I said.

He raised his hand to his nose, but didn't sneeze this time, only turned his head away slightly, like he was avoiding something he didn't want to inhale, though I'd had a very thorough wash in the morning. 'Trousselier?' he asked.

'The florist?' He meant the posh place just down the road. 'No,' I said, 'I went into a little one on the Boulevard des Capucines, not far from the Café de la Paix.'

'Ah.' It was as if this was all very important to him. 'I don't believe I know it. Is it new?'

I had no idea, but he couldn't stop asking me about it.

'Which flowers did you see?' he enquired.

I remembered some lilies, hyacinths, orchids, a few big red ones. I was only looking for something for Marie by way of apology for staying at the casino when I was meant to be with her.

'And cattleyas? Were there any cattleyas?' he asked urgently.

'I suppose so.' And when he didn't seem to like this answer, I said, 'Yes, there were quite a few cattleyas, but they were too expensive for me.'

'How much were they?'

'Oh . . . I really can't remember.' I couldn't be bothered making up any more. I had a job to do, after all.

'You can't remember, I see. And yet you were there only yesterday.'

I conceded to the writer that my memory perhaps isn't what it should be. Then he looked at me with an expression which was genuinely kind. 'If we do not cultivate and nourish the faculty of memory, in all its forms, then what else, ultimately, will be left to us?' I admit he'd got me on that one. Clever buggers, these writers.

But he still hadn't given up on the florist's. 'Was it a marble floor?' he asked. 'And how many assistants were there?' Goodness knows why, but he wanted the whole story, most of which I made up, of course, in the hope that I could get on with my work before the month was out. What were the sounds like in the street outside, he asked me; was there one of those little bowls of perfumed water on the counter for the cleaning of one's fingers; were there vases of the oriental kind, and what about shelves? I could see why his book was so bloody long, if this is his way of going about things. If I'd been doing it, I'd have said: bloke goes into shop to get flowers for Marie, but finds he can't afford any. But how did the writer know that I'd been to a florist, that's what I'd like to know.

'I suppose you don't go out very often,' I said. Well, he was obviously on his last legs, and anyone who cares so much about a florist's can't have seen one for a very long time. Anyway, the writer said nothing by way of contradicting me. 'So, where do you get all your ideas?' I asked him. 'Must be hard, if you don't get out; stuck in here, looking at the curtains and a lot of cork panels. Don't tell me your whole book is about lying in bed!'

He didn't seem to find this joke amusing. He told me that memory was his only material, and since we seemed in danger of getting on to florists again, I quickly changed tack. 'Well, I'm sure you'll want to put this in your book,' I said, pointing to the box I still hadn't opened. 'The Théâtrophone, I mean.'

He looked at me rather blankly, then said something like, 'I have noticed how the telephone confers on the human voice a form of alteration, a change of proportion from the time when it is whole, so that it reaches us completely alone, without the accompaniment of face and features, and only then can we discover how sweet and tender it really is.'

I expect I haven't got the words anywhere near exact, but you could tell this bloke was a writer; they do have such a neat turn of phrase. Anyway, I was a shade disappointed that he didn't seem keen on putting the Théâtrophone in his book, and so I decided to impress him. 'My great-great-grandfather knew Jean-Jacques Rousseau.' The writer raised an eyebrow. 'Oh yes. Have you read the *Confessions*? My ancestor's in there. Him and a friend of his were mates of Jean-Jacques in Montmorency; and quite an adventure they had, I can tell you.'

Now I'd got him hooked. There's nothing that catches a writer's attention so much as a story about another author who's more famous. This fellow in bed with his unpublished heap of papers on the floor thought that he was so much better than a telephone engineer, but I was the one with

Rousseau in my family, sort of, and I could see the instant respect it earned me.

'And I'll bet you never knew that Rousseau was a murderer, either.'

Now the writer's deep-set eyes nearly popped out from the dark rings which surrounded them. 'A murderer?'

I told him a story which you know well, and needs no repeating here.

'Are you absolutely sure of all this?' he asked me.

Well, of course I was. How could I be at all unsure of a story I must have told a thousand times? 'But then Ferrand disappeared, and Minard assumed his friend must have gone to Switzerland with Jean-Jacques, so he went after him. After a month or so he tracked Rousseau down to Neuchâtel, where the French and the Genevans couldn't touch him, and Rousseau was protected by the Scottish governor.'

The writer seemed to remember all this from the *Confessions*, but he said he didn't recall anything about Ferrand going there with him.

'That's right,' I said. 'Perhaps Minard was mistaken and Ferrand was safely back in Paris with his half of Rosier's Encyclopaedia, but that didn't stop my ancestor pursuing Jean-Jacques in search of his lost friend. Minard went around in disguise, asking local people for information and trying to get as close to Rousseau as he could, and then he began to suspect that Rousseau must have killed Ferrand as well as Jacqueline.'

The writer said, 'I find it slightly difficult to believe that the author of the *Confessions* could have harboured such a terrible secret, yet never once so much as alluded to it in his autobiography.'

You know that I've had to deal with this argument many times. I said, 'Is it really beyond all possibility that a great writer can have some terrible sin on his conscience, which makes him write all manner of things in such a way as to disguise it?'

And the writer said, 'You speak more truly than you can ever know.'

I added, 'Rousseau felt so guilty over his crimes that he made up countless lesser ones as a way of easing his conscience. He never had children, for example; all that stuff about sending them to an orphanage was a lie. So was a story about a ribbon he stole – as if this were the worse thing he ever did!'

'Such, I take it, was the theory of your ancestor?'

Well, this writer really was quick on the uptake. 'Yes, him,' I said, 'and his computing engine.' Then I explained how my great-great-grandfather continued to devise networks of thread and paper which he believed would one day be able to perform any logical calculation you can imagine. 'You see,' I said, 'I take after him in a way. With him it was inference machines, with me it's telephone exchanges. Must be in the blood, this interest in technology.'

You know the rest. My ancestor proved that Ferrand died by Rousseau's hand, and when he failed to convince the authorities, he started spreading word around the inns and taverns, until he got together a mob who stoned Rousseau out of his home. And quite right too, if you ask me. 'But my great-great-grandfather never gave up,' I said. 'He followed Rousseau wherever he went; first to Britain, then back to France, shadowing him under the many disguises he learned from the Rosierist Theory of Facial Types. Even tried running him over once with a cart, but a dog got in the way. In the end Rousseau escaped earthly justice, but my ancestor had made sure he'd had as hard a time of it in this life as he'd surely find in the next; and the success of the plan is clear from the terrible effect it had on Rousseau's mind.'

'What was your ancestor's first name?'

'Funnily enough, no one knew it; not even his wife, who was more than forty years his junior when they married, but still bore the old devil the son who was to be my great-grandfather. Even to his own family he was always just plain "Minard", maintaining to the end that it wasn't his real name anyway, and occasionally weeping in the night for his poor Jacqueline, or his poor lost Ferrand.'

Well, you know what writers are like, and this one was determined to find fault with my story. 'Surely Minard could not have been able to afford his itinerant, clandestine existence, over very many years, simply on the basis of what he earned from Father Bertier?'

'That's where the Rosierist Theory of False Coin came in,' I explained. My great-great-grandfather didn't make them personally, but to one of the more enterprising among the good citizens of Neuchâtel he sold the instructions for making coins of glass, coated with a thin layer of metal, for which he subsequently received a healthy commission, until the crime was discovered, a few glass-blowers were hanged, and my ancestor resorted instead to Rosier's Theory of Tetrahedral Merchandising. You know the details; the writer didn't seem particularly interested when I explained. Suffice to say, I told him, that thanks to Rosier's Encyclopaedia my forebear had more than enough tricks up his sleeve, or perhaps I should say in his bag, to last him a lifetime, and although he never became rich, neither did he go hungry, even though he was a man with a considerable

ANDREW CRUMEY

appetite, and a particular fondness for roast duck, which I haven't really inherited, being quite content for my part with a consommé or bouillabaisse and a good hunk of bread.

'That is all very interesting,' said the writer. 'But forgive me for saying that family legends are in many cases tainted by distortion or exaggeration. Can you even be sure that you are descended from the Minard you describe, whose story is so incredible?'

I said, 'I can see why you find it hard to believe. But look at this.' Then I took from my pocket a coin, and handed it to the writer, who briefly released the bedsheet he had been clutching throughout the whole of my tale, in order to study the object.

'It looks very old,' he said, observantly. 'And the scratches upon its gold surface are of a strangely dark appearance, whereas such impressions ought to scatter and reflect light instead of absorbing it.'

'Look more closely,' I said. 'The scratches reveal the green bottle glass underneath. You see, it's one of the false coins of which I spoke; a lucky token and a most precious heirloom, as I'm sure you can understand.'

The writer let me take it back. He said, 'Do not allow yourself to be the prisoner of an inheritance. My apartment is still overfilled, even though I gave away much of the furniture which passed to me after the death of my *maman.* That's her over there.' He nodded in the direction of a picture on the wall. 'What do you think of her?'

I told him she was a very fine-looking woman, and may she rest in peace; but here I was giving him the most marvellous ideas for his novel, and all he could do was talk about his dear departed mother! 'Don't you think a fine book could be written about my ancestor's adventures?'

The writer nodded, but without much enthusiasm.

'You have my full permission to use their story, though you wouldn't be the first,' I told him proudly. 'It's said that the tale of the copyists became quite well known, and several scribblers tried their hand. One of them was very famous; I think you would certainly have heard of him, and I'll mention no names. It was about forty or fifty years ago; he was having trouble with a novel he just couldn't get right. He'd been rehashing it again and again for decades; the first time he'd been told to throw the whole thing on the fire, which he certainly ought to have done, but he'd written other books instead, while he kept this first one on the go. At last a friend said to him, "Sort it out and publish it once and for all, and then for heaven's sake do something else, since really you've been wasting your whole life on stuff that simply isn't you. All you've achieved is some celebrity, thanks to scandal more than anything else; but now you're fat and tired, and might not even have long to go." You see, he was a good friend, who spoke truthfully when he had to. "Now Gustave, why don't you write about these two copyists I've heard about, who go off to the countryside together . . ." Of course, when the novelist wrote the book he got it all completely wrong, but I believe that's how writers like to work; they start with a few facts, then mangle them beyond recognition.'

My sickly customer said to me, 'If you are looking for someone who will lend yet more literary fame to your ancestor, then I'm afraid I am probably too weak, and insufficiently talented, to satisfy you; though I do have a promising young poet friend named Cocteau whose enthusiasm for the esoteric might make Rosierism attractive to him.'

'Oh, don't worry,' I said. 'There's already been Jean-

Jacques and this more recent plagiarist; it'd be a lot for you or any of your friends to live up to. But good luck with your book, and I'm sure you'll manage to get it published if you try hard enough. Thought about who you'll send it to?'

It seemed he hadn't. I was tossing the glass coin on my flicking thumb, watching it land heads or tails in my palm, then spinning it again. Everything comes down to chance, you see. 'And you aren't even impressed by the false coin? It'd make a great metaphor; I know that's the sort of thing you artists like best. You can be sure that somebody'll use it, if they haven't already; and my family story has done the rounds, I can tell you. In fact, I reckon that if you search hard enough you can probably find my ancestor in all sorts of fancy books, and I'm sure he'll be turning up again for a good many years to come. Grandfather thought about writing to the papers to complain when that last book got the story so completely wrong, but since it had been published posthumously there seemed little point pursuing the issue. To tell you the truth, though it's a matter of family honour and all that, I don't really let myself get worked up about it. My cousin Pierre is the one who guards the tradition now; he's the literary one, and a chess fanatic too, though he's taken lately to playing a new version in which one of the rook's pawns is left out. He's a bit of an eccentric; likes to spell his surname with an *e*, just to be different.'

By now I could see that my writer friend was getting tired, and perhaps it was time for me to install the Théâtrophone before I outstayed my welcome; though I was only trying to help him with his novel, giving him a few hints which have become part of the unacknowledged stock-in-trade of our national literature, thanks to my glorious ancestor and his legacy. 'Now let's see what we have in here,' I said, opening the box to reveal his brand new Théâtrophone; the single-trumpet Solitaire model. 'All Paris will be brought to your ear by way of this beauty,' I proudly told him, while I unfurled its black cable. It goes on to the existing telephone connection; just a matter of wiring it to the spare terminals in the junction box on the window frame.

'As long as it can bring me *Pelléas* from the Opéra Comique,' the writer said wistfully, 'and perhaps some scenes from Wagner whose scores Céline once spoiled with the furniture polish, then I shall be perfectly happy.' I brought the pliers from my pocket and got to work.

The whole job takes only a couple of minutes; I'm sure that in a few years' time it'll be a simple case of pushing a jack plug into a socket built into a corner of every room, no more complicated than hanging your coat.

'And have you got a title for this book of yours?' I asked, preparing to test the machine.

He said that originally it was called *Against Sainte-Beuve*, but the plot had changed a great deal since then, and the title didn't fit any more. I decided not to tell him I thought this was probably a good thing, since I couldn't imagine anyone buying a book with a name like that on it. 'I have also contemplated *Irregularities of the Heart*,' he went on; and although such a title would certainly fit the man's state of health, I couldn't really see it flying off the shelves.

'You know one I always liked?' I said. '*Lost Illusions*.'

'Ah, Balzac,' he murmured.

I've never read it, but I really think it's a great title, and to be honest, I feel like I know the book better than a lot I've read, just because the name has stuck. 'And *Paradise Lost*,' I added; '*Paradise Regained*. Can't beat Shakespeare for a good masthead, eh? Secret to success: get the name right first. Look at the Théâtrophone.' To be honest, I'd really grown to like this poor writer by now, genuinely wanted to help him out, and felt sorry that he was so ill he'd probably never live to finish his book.

Now I picked up the telephone and dialled the company. '29205, Hausmann 102, engineer speaking. Want to do a test on the Théâtrophone; give us whatever you've got.'

We waited for a few moments while I began to explain to the writer how telephone exchanges work, until I was interrupted by the new machine coming alive with crackling voices we began to discern. *'Would you like to study the natural sciences?'* says one; *'Natural sciences? What are they all about?'* asks the other.

'I do believe it's Molière at the Comédie,' said the writer. 'The machine appears to be working perfectly; but you may switch it off now so that I can rest.'

I did as he asked, and hoped he'd be very happy with his new entertainment, though I won't say it'll give him any ideas for his book, since everything else I'd said clearly hadn't.

'Yes, Milton,' he was saying to himself as I packed up. Must be a character in that play we'd heard. 'And yet it is not Paradise which may be lost and found by us, but only Time, which is transmitted, as if by the electrical impulses of numerous hidden threads, existing everywhere, through the conductive medium of memory.'

I left him babbling on like that, as I said good day and the maid came to show me out. He told her to fetch him a fresh exercise book, then fry him a sole, and I left them to it, went down the stairs thinking about that poor fellow, wasting his life away in a sweltering room, worrying about books and ideas; and outside in the street I saw the motor cars and vans going past, and a couple of very fetching young women wrapped up in coats, and the barrow boys and all the rest, going about their existences and enjoying it while it lasts, and as I breathed the fresh air again I said to myself, who ever would have thought that the story of my ancestor could keep so many people busy; who would have thought that if he'd died too soon then I'd never even have been born and there'd be one less telephone engineer in the world; and who would guess, apart from one or two like me, that in just a few years' time everything will be different, the whole world will have been transformed so that there'll be aeroplanes instead of motor cars or wagons, you'll never hear a hoof or wheel in the street, only a whirring overhead; everyone will be in their homes listening to the voice of the Théâtrophone, and nobody'll have any more use at all for books, or for writers like that crazy invalid upstairs.

I thought all this, and then I remembered my debts, and Marie, and her father. I remembered all my worries, and the plan I'd made. You see, even though the company expected me to deliver two more Théâtrophones that day, I had already decided that Boulevard Hausmann was to be the last I'd ever do for them. My passage was booked, and the train was due from the Gare du Nord in less than an hour.

I was making the same journey as my ancestor, when he pursued Rousseau across the channel and made the acquaintance of those men Boswell and Hume, to both of whom he gave some useful advice, as I think I've told you before. I too would go to Britain; and like my ancestor, I would start a new life, I would even take a new name, though my pursuers were not the likes of Bertier and Rosier, but only a few casino managers and money lenders, and the father of a girl who'd hardly been what you'd call unwilling, as you and everyone know well.

So here I am, safe and alive in Scotland. I can't say I've completely changed my ways; the Electrophone Company treats me well, and there are all the tips, and there are race courses here almost as fine as Chantilly, where my lucky coin sometimes brings me a winner, sometimes not. But other things have cropped up along the way; women for example, one of whom was even more careless than I thought and, well, she's in a difficult condition. I'm not asking for money, but you know people, a doctor perhaps. She wants me to marry her, but I can't see how I can possibly support a child, and sometimes I wonder if I did the right thing leaving Paris, where everyone has a much better attitude concerning these matters. I don't quite know what is to become of us, but this is the reason why I've broken my silence, come out of hiding, and revealed myself to you again. Alas! If it wasn't for a baby which nobody wants, what a fortunate ending my story could surely have! If it wasn't for a child I don't know what to do with, I could be happy like everyone else, sharing in the sunshine and the feeling I believe to be general, that we are all of us, in this young century, on the verge of limitless peace and prosperity, thanks to the miracles of science, and to methods of communication which can bring an entire planet within the palm of a person's hand.

And so it is that I close, with warmest embraces from your friend who once was known as Minard, but now calls himself,

Mr Mee.

Glasgow, 27 June 1914